~ Acclaim for Shehanne Moore ~

Praise for *The Unraveling of Lady Fury*

"Have you ever read a book where the start leaves you panting? Every page you turn there's nothing to bog the feeling down? With every chapter you grow shorter and shorter of breath until three-quarters of the way through? Then your eyes sting, breathing becomes impossible and a looming sense of dread keeps you reading faster and faster? And the end comes and that sting in your eyes turns to proper tears, streaming down your face, barely pausing and you can take a full breath again? But your heart warms, and you have a fuzzy feeling inside, and you want to tell the world because this book was such an emotional ride that you will never, ever forget a thing about it? *The Unraveling of Lady Fury* is such a book. A keeper, and one I'll read over and over."

— Author Aimee Duffy, *Monster of Fame* and *Isle of Sensuality*

"Smart. Sexy. Raw. Real. A staggeringly good read… A powerful love story that exhales turmoil, emotional and physical. Written with grit and blood, the imagery is poignantly beautiful and the humour rich… Strap yourself in before immersing yourself in Ms Moore's world…"

— Author Incy Black, *Sins of the Father*

"I loved the attitude and the games in this story."

— Author Anne Lange, *Worth the Risk*

"I couldn't put this down. It never sagged, or drifted for one second and I loved the two main characters."

—Author Antonia Van Zandt, *Vienna Valentine, Seducing Amanda*

"This stormy romance is more than a love story—it's a well-drawn literary adventure."

—*Hot and Spicy Tales*

"The chemistry–and sparks–between her and Flint had me ducking for cover."

—Author Noelle Clark, *Let Angels Fly, Rosamanti*

Praise for *His Judas Bride*

"A rich, red, full bodied Burgundy of a novel. Bring Callm and Kara together and the result is explosive."

—Author Antonia Van Zandt, *Seducing Amanda* and *Vienna Valentine*

"The sex is raw, the sex is scorching, it is never gratuitous, it is always real."

—Author Incy Black, *Sins of the Father*

"Characters who were scarred by deep wounds and fighters to the bitter end, made this a compelling and page-turning read. A book I couldn't put down."

—Author Sharon Struth, *The Hourglass*

~ Look for these titles from Shehanne Moore ~

Now Available from Etopia Press

The Unraveling of Lady Fury

His Judas Bride

Loving Lady Lazuli

The Unraveling of Lady Fury

Shehanne Moore

etopia
press

Etopia Press
1643 Warwick Ave., #124
Warwick, RI 02889
http://www.etopia-press.net

THE UNRAVELING OF LADY FURY

Print ISBN: 978-1-940223-86-5
Digital ISBN: 978-1-939194-76-3

First Etopia Press electronic publication: March 2013

First Etopia Press print publication: February 2014

~ Dedication ~

To John, for all his love and support. And to Mum and Dad, who didn't always believe but who always hoped.

With extra special thanks to Lorraine, who did both; Irene and Joan, who listened; Coreen and Eilis for being there; Incy for being a great writing buddy; Annie Melton for making it possible; Amber Shah Designs for bringing Fury to life; my wonderful editor Lauren Triola for knocking all the rough edges off.

Chapter One

Genoa 1820

Malmesbury would father the heir to the Beaumont dukedom. Count Vellaggio wasn't a contender. What she had logged in her book about him this afternoon said it would be a huge mistake anyway. The same for the Duke of Southey — Byronesque handsome, but a drunk with disconcertingly filthy fingernails and ring-laden hands. No, Malmesbury was the best. The only. Intelligent without being painful, fashionable yet not a dandy, and retaining enough of his looks at the age of fifty not to be outright repulsive.

Of course it would have helped if Thomas could have fathered the Beaumont heir himself. But as he lay dead in a box in the cellar, that wasn't likely.

"Gentlemen, you know as well as I do, this is an unusual evening." Delicate shivers chased up and down Lady Fury Shelton's spine as she stood in the center of her darkened bedchamber.

With its festooned corners and gold scrolled furniture, the red-painted room was the best place for such an assignment, although the tiled floor and the cool clang of evening bells snaking in through the parted shutters made it chillier than usual. As did the candlelight glinting on the pale oval of Messalina's face on the hanging above the bed. Earlier the air had felt so stifling she changed twice in the space of an hour.

"Here, here." Southey raised his crystal glass. Where else, but to his lips. A toast to her or the transaction would be too much to expect of him. Or for him to sit facing her too, as the other men were, their drinks untouched on the tiny tables beside them.

"My interviews are complete. Shortly I will make my choice. Then, having done so, I will invite the said gentleman to this bedroom, where he will perform his duty as often as necessary."

"All in one night. That's a tall order for a man, I must say."

For Southey, yes, it would be. The state he'd arrived at her door this afternoon and what he'd sunk of her amaretto and limoncello in the meantime, it was a miracle he could still stand there against the marble fireplace. Never mind anything else. But she wasn't about to debate the subject. She kept her face a studied mask and her voice calm, but her hands clenched to snap the spine of the tooled leather book she clutched for support.

"I say, Fury, how the blazes are you going to tell right away?" Southey hiccupped. "Don't them things take weeks and weeks to find out?"

"The one chosen will be here for weeks. Those not chosen will leave within the hour. I think we may be clear that at any time in the future, should any of you breathe a word to anyone about this, I will find out. I have sufficient information in this book here to ruin each and every one of you. Make no mistake, I will use it."

Malmesbury, who had so far watched the proceedings with an amused smile, swore. "By God, Fury, you don't need to talk like that about any of us, I'm sure. You want to get one over on Thomas; I, for one, don't blame you. We all saw him sneaking about with that Porto Antican tart when you first arrived."

"Yes." Who hadn't?

"And do you think we're unaware what his illness has done to him? The rages? The drinking? The way he keeps you here like a poodle?"

That too. Thomas was not who she was getting one over on, but she daren't say it here. She held in her hands every dirty little secret concerning these men. All documented there in the yellow, dog-eared pages. The leaves also contained letters, bills, testimonies, transactions. She kept it all beneath lock and key. Therefore they obeyed her, and she was safe for another hour, another day. She couldn't countenance losing that necessary balance of control for a second by admitting that.

She could have paid a Porto Antican organ grinder to father her child and walk away, no questions asked. The one at the end of the harbor looked handsome enough. But Lady Margaret would smell an organ grinder's bastard at twenty paces. Hadn't the woman scented Fury?

Malmesbury shifted in his chair. "Where is he, by the way?"

"Who? Thomas? Thomas is visiting his father."

No lie. Had any of these men facing her in the flickering candlelight known whether Thomas's father lived or died, she would not have chosen them.

"Even were he not, Thomas wants you to know me well. That is why he has gone." She hesitated. Thomas would have spared her this next lie, although she supposed there was more than one grain of truth in it now. "Sadly it is more than he can do himself these days. Now, I must ask you all to return to your chambers and wait. My mind is almost made up. Susan, here, will call in due course for the chosen one to return."

"Dash it, that's good to know." Southey clanked his glass down on the marble mantelpiece.

In addition to his drinking, his casual mistreatment of the

Murano goblet, while not worth an entry in Fury's book, made
him all the more unsuitable. What careless traits might a child
inherit? Besides, his odor as he staggered past her made her
stomach heave. It took every ounce of her self-control to remain
where she was, inhaling of the citrus-scented candle Susan had
lit to disperse the gloom.

He paused and turned toward her. "All this cloak and
dagger stuff is killing, you know."

Malmesbury got to his feet. "I shall wait then." His murmur
was to himself more than anyone else in the room.

There was no doubt his palms itched to touch her, but she
shrank from letting him brush his lips across the back of her
hand. It did not bode well for later, but at least he didn't smell.
His silver frock coat was immaculate, possessing not a single
crease. And his shoe buckles not only shone, they sparkled. His
valet must be remarkable, whoever he was.

Only Count Vellaggio said nothing. Speaking limited
English — and Italian — he never did, unless it was absolutely
necessary.

Thank God. It was one mercy at least.

* * *

"Will I now fetch the chosen one, madam?" Susan issued her
demand the instant the door closed.

Fury walked three paces forward and sank down at her
dressing table. "Just cover the bruises, will you?" She tossed the
book into the open drawer. "I can't have them on show. It might
affect the conception. At least it might affect their ability to
perform. They see that and God knows what they'll think."

"Madam—"

"I know. I know. But you know I believe in looking my best,
regardless of the situation."

"For a bunch of drunken old coots. Sadistic old coots. Do

you know what I heard about Vellaggio today?"

"You shouldn't have been listening."

"It was at the market. He uses boys. Young boys. Whether they want to or not. He whips them too."

For a moment Fury rested her forehead on the marbled surface of the table, as if she could draw strength from its veins to hers. Of course, she had expected this. Susan didn't approve. To feel so strongly was good of her, but all very well. Susan wasn't in the mess Fury was in. It was difficult to think of anyone who was.

"Really? Well I heard he used girls. But whichever it is, we both know it's this or nothing. I can't...I won't be cast off without a penny. Not again. And anyway, it's no more than Lady Margaret deserves." Wincing, she swept the dark fall of hair back from her neck. "Now, please, a little powder—"

"A little powder?" Susan made no move to accede to her wishes. "It will take more than a little powder to cover that mess."

"Just think like Lady Macbeth, will you? And stop arguing." Fury raised her head; a gust of wind blew in through the open shutters. "You've done it before. Anyway, they're not all of them old. Or coots."

"Oh, very well."

Fury almost ceased breathing as Susan secured the shutters and bustled across the room to help her. She just wished everything else that was going to happen tonight would be over as *gently*. She tilted her head further as Susan swept Fury's hair over her shoulder. The scent of beeswax polish that permeated Susan's plump fingers reassured her somehow.

"Have it your own way, madam. You always do. But I'm not thinking of Lady Margaret. I'm thinking of you."

"Then don't. You know I don't require it."

"I'm thinking you should just tell that old toad where to

stuff her money. You could find a protector here in Genoa. A woman like you."

A woman like her? Fury met her reflection in the not yet paid for glass. And what was that exactly? Long ago she'd stopped wondering, buffeted by fortune's changing winds. Forced to snatch what she could to survive. Always knowing one false foot would bring her down. However, she was certain of one thing.

"I don't want a protector." Thomas had been that at the start. Now look at her, without a penny to her name. Again. "I've had my fill of them. I want to guarantee my future. The future of…" her voice trailed off, eyes dulling in the glass. "Anyway, things that are dear."

Susan knew the dire nature of her predicament. When Thomas had first taken Fury to meet his mother, the dislike had been instantaneous. It had flourished down the years, until now, it consumed her.

Fury imagined that at night Lady Margaret lay awake thinking of new ways to torture and humiliate her. But poisoning Thomas's father against her? Cajoling him on his deathbed into insisting Thomas must provide an heir before succeeding to the dukedom? It was one blessing at least that Lady Margaret lived in England and Fury here.

"You know what I must guarantee and why."

Susan sprinkled a dusting of powder onto the dressing table as if she were measuring the ingredients for a cake and then wiped her hands down her apron. "Indeed I do, madam, I just—"

Despite herself, Fury touched what glittered around her neck. The single midnight blue pendant Thomas had given her two Christmases ago. The copy of it, rather. Because that, like this, was also burning necessity. Her Hatton Garden jewel-maker had served her well, though. Thomas had never once suspected a thing of her need for that kind of money and how it ran to more than blackmail.

"Before you say another word, Susan, even this jewel here wouldn't pay for that. It's like me. Fake."

"Undervalued is what I'd say. What about blackmail then? That book—"

Fury shook her head. "Blackmail is messy, which is why I'm locking the book away again."

"It's not my business, but when I think of all the years you've bribed dressmakers and housemaids and coachmen to get what's in it."

"Out of necessity. Knowing that at any time this could all tumble down. No. This is the best way. Besides, think how good it will feel outfoxing Lady Margaret. She insisted on an heir. She gets one. Do you think I care if she coos over some child that's not Thomas's? No. What I want is for you to make me irresistible, as you always do."

"Who are you considering? Southey? He's handsome in his way, I suppose."

"I was thinking… I was thinking…Malmesbury actually."

"Malmesbury?" Susan's fingers didn't falter, but Fury sensed the surprise in her voice. And not in admiration of Fury's sense of judgment either.

"Probably Southey would be less trouble. But Malmesbury's not one-legged and toothless, is he? So long as he's—not like Thomas—what does it matter?"

She felt guilty for saying it. Truth to tell, if anyone understood her predicament, Thomas would have. For her sake, he had tried ensuring an heir. But these last six months, since what had pressed on his brain swelled, well…she didn't want any man treating her like Thomas.

"That would be hard, madam, given the things His Grace did to you."

"I know. But he wasn't always like that. No. I think Malmesbury, and I…think I should just get it over with. The sooner the better, don't you?" Fury smoothed a smoky curl into place on her forehead. Anything to quell the tremor rising in her hands now the hour approached and she felt sicker than ever before. "Besides, my reckoning is he positively expects it."

"What? Malmesbury?"

"Oh, yes." She reached toward the open trinket chest. "What do you think? Sapphire earrings or plain gold?"

"I don't see either matter since they're not going to be on very long."

"Pragmatic as ever." She fastened on the sapphire drops. "But really, didn't you see the way he stared just now? I don't think he can contain himself."

"The old goat."

"Yes. Who knows? If he's a randy one, it might even be fun." She marveled at herself for laughing when a leaden weight sat in her chest. Maybe that was the way to get through this.

Susan's hand rested on her shoulder. "Then I'll get him for you, madam, if that's your choice."

"No." Fun or not—and she thought not—the notion of admitting him here, to the bed she'd shared with Thomas, seemed wrong, even if she managed to conceive the Beaumont heir. "I—I'll do it. I need to calm my nerves. What bedroom is he in again? I confess I've forgotten."

"The Blue Chamber."

"Well then, think of England, as they say. Wish me luck. And remember to lock the drawer. However I choose to use it, that book is still the world to me. We must see it doesn't fall into the wrong hands."

She rose, smoothed her dress, and took the candlestick. If she did this, she forfeited forever her claim to be a respectable woman. Although, as the deed was more than likely to remain another secret of this villa, she failed to understand quite why her indigo gown clung tightly to her shaking form, for all it was so loose. Her stays confined so, and she struggled to breathe.

If she didn't execute this task, then she faced being in the same position as she had been in seven years ago. It was fine at eighteen. But now, she needed to secure some things. Once she had, she would be free of men and all their machinations. Women too.

The Blue Chamber stood at the far end of the landing near the stairs, and she padded there noiselessly in the arc of the flickering candle, past the disapproving busts of Signor Santa-Rosa's ancestors and the draped apertures, which she sometimes imagined hid more secrets than she did.

Malmesbury would be surprised to see her. Irresistibly dressed, jeweled, and, hopefully, willing—as much as she could make herself anyway. Who would know that beneath the rustling indigo silk, the heady, intoxicating jasmine she had bathed in earlier, she was like a skittish colt, ready to bolt? This was how Marie Antoinette must have felt going to her execution. Another woman Fury admired, if not for her ideals, but her courage.

Still, surprise could sometimes be the best method of attack. A man was, after all, a man. And, as she'd said to Susan, it might even be fun, although she doubted it. The sooner, the better. Then she could retire to her own bedroom and bolt the blasted door. And lie with cool lavender scented cloths on her head, for that matter, just to remove herself from the jarring awfulness of this.

Drawing a breath to quell her hammering heart, she raised her quivering hand to tap on the door. A low, American Southern voice drawled. Not from the other side of the door where she expected to hear something, but close by in her ear.

"Hello, sweetheart. Imagine seeing you here."

Fury jerked up her chin and swung around, the candle flame sputtering.

"You." Imagine, indeed.

Flint. Not just a voice in her ear. A voice from that place she had locked it, locked him, and thrown away the key. A voice from memory's dark swamp.

But as if it were yesterday, he stepped toward her and she fought the swell of panic. She couldn't help it. She parted her lips in shock.

"No. Don't scream." He held up a warning hand.

"Give me one good reason why I shouldn't." She had had seven years of acknowledging this man did not exist. She did not want to see him now. Not when she stood on Malmesbury's doorstep, on the very trembling edge of — *this. Go away*, she nearly hissed. She must be mistaken. He couldn't be here. It wasn't possible.

He loomed over her, and her whole body stiffened. He *was* here.

"Because I doubt you want your guests out their chambers any more than I do right now, sweetheart, with what you got sitting down in your cellar." His voice was a rich baritone.

She fumbled with the candlestick, almost dropping it. "Did no one ever tell you it's rude to go poking your nose around in other people's houses? No. I think they forgot. Of course. You never had a father."

"You always did have an answer for everything, Fury." He creased his all too sensuous lips into a smile. "But after that little business you got up to in Jamaica, I'd watch my tongue."

Jamaica? She straightened, steadying herself. Wasn't he just mean enough to remember that. And the damned place she wished she'd never seen let alone been born in.

"How did you —" *Find me*, were the wrong words to use. James Flint Blackmoore was not a man to look. How well did she know that. "What do you want?"

His crystal blue gaze slid over her face. Looking at the jewels, no doubt. What else would he look at, after all? She had never truly interested him.

"A moment of your time."

That was nothing, she supposed. A great deal less than he'd demanded the last time she had asked him that question. But it would still be a huge mistake to give that moment here. Malmesbury might have been fifty, but his hearing was acute.

They could go to her bedroom. With Susan in it, it would be safe. But it wasn't just that Flint wore no cravat—he wasn't gentlemanly enough to have ever worn one. She adhered to the mantra no bedroom was safe with Flint Blackmoore in it. There was also the matter of her book of secrets. As for the cellar, she couldn't possibly take him there.

"Downstairs. And hurry up. I don't have all night."

"Isn't that an offer a man might find hard to refuse?"

She regretted speaking to him so unpleasantly. Not because he was Flint Blackmoore. No. Those feelings had long departed her heart. She would rather spit on him than butter him. But he had been in the cellar and seen Thomas. Although quite how he had seen Thomas…he must have opened the box.

"This way." Reaching the foot of the staircase, she threw open the doors to the sitting room.

She entered and smiled. Why not? Flint did not look as she remembered him now that she considered it, after the first shock had passed and she could take in the details. Tall, yes. The lean limbs, easy gait, and sloping shoulders that had so beguiled her, oh, yes. That was unchanged. But his sharp-angled face seemed different somehow, although only a little more lined than before. The corn-colored hair framing it was tidier and therefore lanker than when he had stood on the deck of the *Calypso* with a sea breeze ruffling it. Although he had never been one for elaborate garments, the starkness of the worn corded breeches, even the tricorne hat, was astonishing.

"Sit down, won't you?"

"Is it safe?"

Ignoring him, she lit the candles beneath the hanging of Salome. It seemed apt somehow for her to stand there to recollect herself. She had always understood the strength of these women better than most. The villa was only the second she and Thomas had looked at when they arrived overland from France, and it sat further from the center of the town than Susan would have liked. A place at the mercy of cicadas and church bells. But the hanging of the white-gowned, barefoot Salome had determined her. Coupled with the crimson opulence of the room, the frowning portraits of nameless contessas, she saw now she could not have chosen a better place to face this man and show him just how well she was doing.

It might even have been that the whole thing was preordained. It was not the kind of room he would blend in to. Rather the kind to highlight the poverty-stricken nature of his scruffy breeches and the worn boots that stretched to his thighs.

"So, James." Knowing how much it was always *Captain Flint* to him, she said it deliberately. "What brings you here?"

As if she could not guess. There was only one thing he could want: money.

Removing his hat, he eased down into the satin upholstered chair. Of course, he wasn't going to look anything other than ridiculously uncomfortable on that, with his long legs and tall body. Flint Blackmoore and cream satin. It was probably why his sigh came all the way from his bones.

"What do you think? I'm Malmesbury's valet." He adjusted his beige coat.

"What?" She had wondered about his valet, hadn't she?

"Yes. I—"

"But how—"

"I lost the *Calypso*."

"The *Calypso*?" His pride and joy. The thing he loved best in the whole world. The only thing, she remembered with a pang. For an instant she couldn't speak, thinking how precious that creaking hulk was to him. "That still doesn't explain why you're a valet."

He shifted uncomfortably and gritted through his teeth. "He bought me, right? Privateer's life, sweetheart. Of course, I should never have listened to De Wolfe. I know that now."

"But you said sailing under a United States flag gave you work."

"Eight years ago, sweetheart. Before I met you. I thought it was enough to tell you that much."

"And the British deserved everything they got?"

"Sure they did. It was war, wasn't it? But that was then. This is now. Now, we got hunted down. Stopped from bringing our booty into ports. I got captured for trying. Among other things."

How like him to hedge around the specifics. Even when she'd first known him, the only person he'd served was himself. In fact she was never clear whose side he was on, apart from his own.

"That's how I got wind of this little scheme of yours."

"Mine?" For a second she wondered if she could blame Susan for the whole sordid thing. Truth to tell, she was so stunned she struggled to wonder anything. James Flint…James Flint Blackmoore could not have been caught and sold *as a servant*. A valet, of all things.

"Look. The years obviously haven't been any kinder to you than they have to me."

The remark astonished her. If she removed the bruises from the equation, she felt she was doing not so badly. But how like Captain Flint to think otherwise.

"Look, I mean…you know what I mean." He gestured wearily.

"No. Not really. I can't say as I do."

She considered asking him to leave, but because he was Malmesbury's valet, she swallowed the consideration. Where would he go, after all, except back upstairs to tell Malmesbury everything?

"It's like this, James. They have and they haven't been." She assumed the armchair opposite. She even fingered her throat, largely to mask the shudder of unease that passed through her that he knew of her scheme. Although it wouldn't have surprised her in the least to find the paste sapphire absent from her neck. The chain it sat on too. Without her even noticing it had gone.

"Thomas is dead. In fact I think you may even have seen him in the cellar. Unfortunately, his mother never liked me and has made that disdain plain, for reasons I have never been able to understand."

He glanced at her. "Me neither, sweetheart, you want to know the truth."

The truth? It would be a first. Him pretending to like her too. All the same, it didn't matter. She'd do anything not to lose this now. "Look, if it's money you want, I can help you, for old time's sake. I just can't do it right now. The fact is these jewels are all I have." Naturally she wasn't about to impart the fact they were paste, although if he tried to blackmail her—something he was adept at—he could have them and be welcome.

His gleaming blue eyes stared as if he had no idea what she meant. As if he didn't have the foggiest what a jewel was. Or money either. "So? What the hell will you do, Fury?"

She tightened her mouth. One thing was for certain, she wasn't going to be touched by his *concern*. No. The jewels weren't the only fake thing around here. Did he think she didn't see through this…this novel hangdog approach? He wasn't interested in her welfare any more than he was in her. He never had been.

"What about?"

"What do you think? This mess you're in."

"What else can I do? I need to produce an heir. That's why Malmesbury's here."

"Malmesbury?"

Why did he look so astonished, as if Malmesbury were some drooling idiot and she needed her head examined? Why? Her plan was perfect.

"And the others, yes." Her voice was vaguely strangled.

"You think this will work?"

"Since Thomas's mother is in England, yes." She didn't feel it was a mistake to blurt this. Not when she'd promised him money. The one thing he understood. Even if he'd have to wait for it. "I am going to bury him. Just not yet. How can I?"

"I'm not meaning that. You think Malmesbury and the others can have children?"

"Oh, yes. I have every dirty little secret there is to be had on them. As some of these secrets include bastards, I think we can conclude they can. That's also why I know they won't talk."

"Impressive." For a second his gaze held hers in the candlelit darkness. Subtly. Acknowledging. So much like old times she thanked God he did not ask about her own ability to produce a child. Then he eased back, setting his long legs forward. "Actually I have a proposition for you."

She rose from her chair. "I don't think I am in the mood for any business proposition of yours right now. Not with so much at stake. I've said to you I have no money to hand, and I am a little busy trying to secure —"

"Let me do it."

"W-what?" Her face reddened. Never mind the intense focus

of his regard made her jittery. Was it any wonder? *Him?*

He curved his sensuous mouth upward. "You heard."

She had heard. She just hadn't wanted to.

"No." The word burst from her before she could stop it. Burst nastily, forcefully, in a way that struck her dumb. But James Flint Blackmoore? What was there to consider about this, after all? Nothing, which was why she hadn't wanted to consider it even before he asked, before he strolled in here, before she saw him in that flickering candlelight arc.

"What's so wrong with that, sweetheart?" He didn't shift his gaze, his body, anything. "That way, you at least know what you're getting. Not like with these monsters."

She did know, which was why the tiny flicker of memory of the nights spent in his bed shamed her. Nights where she had sought his touch, his embrace, and her fingers had tangled in that same hair now framing his scholarly-looking face in unrestrained passion.

She also remembered how he had abandoned her on a London quay and the words he had used to dismiss her.

When it came to monsters, she'd known the very best. She was not even going to consider this. It would give her such pleasure to refuse him now she saw he was every bit as desperate as she'd been that day and had lost everything he had.

She tilted her chin. Of course she could and would keep it civil, no matter that her hands quivered in the folds of her gown. Revenge was always best executed cold. Heat only showed passion. She had none for him.

"And why should I do that?"

"Haven't I just said? Isn't what we were before reason enough?" He looked at her, and for a second not only was the old Flint in his eyes and the tilt of his jaw, but she saw what the damned man wore didn't matter. Whatever he wore, he wore with that casual air. No woman would look at the clothes, but would instead think about what lay underneath them.

"Look, I'm not even asking you to buy my freedom, seeing as you've got no money. I'm just asking you to use that information you said you have. Then we can get to it. Just like old times. Never knew another woman like you, Fury."

How like him to pretend not to see what she really meant. Oh, yes, this would be a pleasure through and through.

"No, James. Why should I? Why should you? Never mind what you did to me. A valet? The father of my child? The Beaumont heir? I think not. You know, one must be fussy about these things."

His gaze froze, still focused on her face. She swept across the elegant floor tiles, past the eroded statues of Cupid, toward the doors.

"It's not just that I don't think so. In fact you may even say that first I would rather rot in everlasting hell." She grasped the handles and drew the doors open. Oh, she felt good about this. "Now, if you don't mind…"

She waited for him to rise and amble out. He would do so, surely? Instead his voice came from the darkness behind her, as only Flint's could. Calm. Quiet. Measured. Enough to send chills sweeping up her spine.

"You might not think that when it happens, sweetheart."

She laughed, discomfited. "I'll take my chances. Preferable to taking you."

"Not really. You see, as it happens, when it comes to putting my cards on the table, I have the ace."

"Oh, do you?"

"You want me telling these gentlemen upstairs who you really are?"

"You wouldn't dare."

His gaze met hers. "Try me."

Chapter Two

Fury gained the darkened hallway in an instant. He'd tell them who she was? Damn him. How dare he think he could hold anything over her head like this? Hadn't she spent seven years insuring herself against the moment that ever came out? Chiseling, cajoling, bribing? Extorting every piece of information she could so she would be safe?

Hearing his footsteps thundering behind her, she grasped her skirts and swept toward the curved staircase.

"No, James. It distresses me to shatter your illusions, but you try me."

In a bound he reached the bottom stair before her, his eyes blue-ice slits, his mouth set, his muscle working in his stubbled jaw. He did, at least, have the common decency to lower his voice as he stood glaring.

"Confound and damn you to hell, Fury. Obviously you're not paying enough attention to what I'm saying to you here."

A lesser woman might have quaked. Fury was not a lesser woman. Astonished perhaps. James Flint Blackmore always held his temper. Perhaps because he never felt passionate enough about anything to lose it, the *Calypso* aside. Yet he contorted his handsome face in rage. It may have been one of the first times in his life anyone had denied him anything.

Too bad.

She tilted her nose a few degrees higher and sailed past him. Not paying attention? Just because she wasn't listening to him? "Oh, I think when it comes to the dunce's cap, your head's a much better fit than mine."

"My head?" He pounded his feet up the stairs beside hers, and she had to hold her skirts higher before he stood on the hem. "How's that when your head's the one made of muffin dough?"

"Mixture. And mixture, dough or not, you're not holding any rods over it. Not anymore."

"*Over your head?* I been halfway over the Caribbean, sweetheart, and let me tell you that's one position that ain't never been heard of. You? Do something I told you? When was this exactly?"

The fury he reeked astounded her. The cheap jibe more so. Pride, a man's most tender part. Flint, the great and mighty, would naturally find it hard to believe any woman could possibly be impervious to his charms.

Grasping her skirt tighter, she hurried on. "Now, you know how very vexed you get when you start sounding like a Savannah farm boy instead of the scourge of the Caribbean. But perhaps you haven't been taking yourself them damned fine elocution lessons since you wound up top of the bill at a lil' ole slave auction."

Why she mocked him like this, bringing up things he'd sooner die than admit to, she had no idea, except perhaps because her heart beat too fast and her hands shook until she felt as if a fever lay on her skin.

"Damn you, Fury, it's 'little old,' not 'lil' ole,' and well you know it."

"Yes. The old Flint, now there's a man I might conceivably have been frightened of. But this new you? Hmm…"

"What I remember, you weren't exactly scared of the old me

either."

"First impressions can on occasion be misleading."

Before she could stop him, he lunged for her wrist and she crashed into the metal banister. Remembering last night's unfortunate debacle with Thomas at this same spot, she muffled a horrified shriek.

"Then just you tell me if I'm wrong here. About that little business with Celie." He gritted his teeth and tightened his fingers until she swore he would leave bruises — even more for Susan to deal with. "And now, your lately shuffled off this mortal coil husband lying face down in a box. In your cellar, Fury."

She made a sterling effort to stand on her heels. So, she was right about that? Just what Celia had been to him? She'd thought she was, all that time on the *Calypso*, although he'd always denied it. Now he had just given it away.

Taking a breath, she looked at him squarely. "I believe she would have been Lady Celia to you."

The choking sound that issued from the back of his throat told her all she needed to know, except for whether Lady Celia had known him as Captain Flint, scourge of the Caribbean, or the more respectable Captain Blackmoore, who could pass himself off at a governor's dinner table as a legitimate seafaring man. He could fool an enemy ship into thinking it was all he was.

"Whatever her name was, Celie or Celia, doesn't make no difference seeing as she's dead." Another grit of his teeth. "Like everyone else who comes into contact with you. You ever think that's why people don't like you?"

People didn't like her? She had known *Flint* never cared a jot for her. But to hear it confirmed…

She swallowed the burning constriction. In truth she wanted to cry at her own stupidity. But after she first eviscerated his cheekbones with her nails, if he would only free her. But it was as if he knew her intention to damage that handsome damned face of his.

"No, docile's hardly the word for you. It never was."

"Why should it be?" She steadied herself. No. She would not debase herself before him. No matter how much he hurt her. "The things you did to me."

He frowned. "What things?"

"Oh, please, allow me to spend the night telling you when I've nothing better to do. But since you're asking, why don't we start with the way you took my virginity?"

"Took it? Hell. You were giving it away."

"So it pleased you to believe."

"Never saw you refusing, sweetheart." His gaze picked over her face. Then he narrowed his eyes seductively. "Leastways…" He stepped closer in that way that had always made him very dangerous. "I'm offering now to get you out this little hole you're in."

Of course.

"I don't need any shovel of yours for that. I've got myself out of more than one these past seven years, after you left me."

"That's not how it looks to me this time, which is why I've just about had enough of this. Now." He yanked her closer, so she could feel the hard press of his body through the enveloping layers of satin and wool. "You want that heir or not?"

She almost fainted with shock. Straight to the point as ever. So straight she was appalled by what flamed in her blood, how he towered, and how his body — scent and strength — was pure, beckoning male. She had only to reach out and sweep the hair back from his face to let him take control, as he always had.

But not only did she not want her guests coming from their chambers to find him taking control against the banister or even the wall — the stairs, as she had learned last night, were not ideal — she remembered the last time he had issued a similar threat, about her wanting something or not.

Then her trunk, or rather Lady Celia's, had landed with a thud on Fishside Wharf, displaying its contents for all to see. She did not want the Beaumont heir following suit.

She cleared her throat — if nothing else, it was an action designed to remind herself his offer was outrageous. She refused to be tempted like this.

"No. Not particularly. I believe...I believe I have said all there is to say on that subject." She lowered her gaze. My God, he was handsome. Made to be admired. And so like his old self that way, brightening a woman's day with his casual sexuality, that she spoke with difficulty. Lied with difficulty too. "In fact you might even say I've changed my mind about all of it. So, if you don't mind removing your hand?" She stared at it. He'd always had nice hands.

He huffed out a breath. "Fine." His voice seemed to come from way down in his boots. "That's what you want."

For a second she stared in horror. That Flint Blackmoore, the scourge of various seas, should accept defeat was too perfect. She should gloat. But her heart beat to a tempo even faster than before. Something other than her temper swam too close to the surface. Something that... She quashed it, summoning her best smile in the hope of making herself appear serene.

"It is. Yes. Thank you. It has, of course, been a pleasure seeing you. As ever. Now, if you will release me. Thank you."

Grasping her skirt, she resumed her ascent of the stairs. The little smile framing his mouth would only be construed as alarming were this Captain Flint. He wasn't. No, he was only a pitiful excuse. A shadow of his former self.

Besides, had he wanted to raise any roofs, he'd have done it by now. Certainly he wouldn't have removed his hand. Flint Blackmore was not a man to prevaricate.

But after his shabby attempt to blackmail her, there would be no money. Why should she part with even a half farthing's worth of what she was bound to inherit when she produced the heir? To him?

A quarter's worth would be too great. Especially as there were no circumstances on the face of this earth in which she could now countenance Malmesbury as the father of the Beaumont heir. Unless he first disposed of his valet. Or she did. No. She must rethink this. Fortunately she stood near enough the top of the stairs and her bedroom to do so.

"Same here, seeing you, sweetheart." His drawl came from behind her. Naturally he desired the last word. He always did. "But the acquaintance isn't over yet."

"No?"

"Nope. Your Grace!"

She froze. How could he yell like that? In a way guaranteed to waken—maybe not the dead exactly, but—

"Duke Malmesbury! Sir! Your Grace, you anywhere there, sir?"

"What?" A muffled sound came from the Blue Chamber. A damned pity the Blue Chamber stood so close to the top of the stairs.

"Stop it, James!"

"Don't say I didn't warn you. Signor Vella-ghio! Duke Malmesbury! Damn it, what the hell's the other one's name again?"

It didn't much matter what the other one's name was. Southey's door flew open first. Malmesbury followed him onto the landing, carrying a candle and wearing a nightshirt and cap. And Vellaggio followed him, wearing nothing very much at all.

"Dalm it, Fury." Southey staggered toward her. "Amn't I—*hic*—the lucky one? *Hic*. Well, come in…come in…gel. Come in. Can't guarantee anything right now, but I'll dalm well do me best. *Hic.*"

That they should come out here and stand and look expectant when all she could think about was what Flint was going to tell them didn't make her groan. It made her consider the marble stairs as a resting place. But she couldn't very well lie there.

What she knew of these men would not outweigh the fact Thomas lay in the cellar and she was not Celia Fury Shelton. She was now, anyway, and had been since she had married Thomas. It was just before, during the time Flint knew about, when she hadn't been Celia anything but plain Fury Fontanelli, and Celia had been like Thomas—dead.

Flint smirked. "Should have just tried me the other way, sweetheart. I'm an awful lot safer."

She could barely believe the audacity with which he bounded by on his long legs. All the way up the stairs, two at a time, to the very top.

Dear God, it would mean the ruin of everything if he opened his mouth. She had only meant to secure her future. And now the only way to do that was by taking this man into her bed.

She couldn't. She wouldn't. Her pride and every other part of her rebelled. She'd sooner run. She'd sooner abandon everything.

Yet, she also did this to outfox Lady Margaret, didn't she? Should she give the woman the pleasure of denying her everything, after every agony she had suffered with Thomas, because of this man? This *stranger* from her past? Who had done everything to hurt and humiliate her?

Who did she hate more? Well?

In that instant she made up her mind. She would wait to hear what he had to say first.

"Now gentlemen, sorry to bring you out your rooms like

this, but Miss Fury here has something to tell you all. And if she can't, then I will."

The words were not encouraging. In fact, they were as damned discouraging as Flint could make them. Was it any wonder? He need only consider the way she'd rather rot in everlasting hell than help him out, when he was damned desperate enough to have begged her on bended knees. *Him*—a man who hadn't known it was possible knees could do anything so elastic twelve short months ago.

Hell. It wasn't as though he even wanted to sleep with her. The damn trouble she'd always been.

But, for the present, he needed to swallow his first urge, which was to throttle her with his bare hands. When it came to cards, she never knew when she held the ace. Now he'd gotten her potential lovers in this raving scheme of hers, exactly where he wanted them, he needed to keep the pressure on. He had no desire to wind up dangling from a yardarm in Jamaica.

He tilted his jaw. "Well, isn't that so, Miss Fury?"

"Yes."

He could tell by the way she squirmed and looked over her shoulder, she intended to bolt out the front door. Then he'd never get his boat back. He'd be dusting frock coats and spitting on shoe buckles for the rest of his life.

At least he'd be doing it till he could think of something. Nothing in his situation so far had presented an escape route. Seeing her, then seeing what she had in that box in the cellar, was his first hopeful sliver in months. He was damned glad he'd resisted the urge to stay out of that trunk. Gut instinct said she was bound to be up to her neck in trouble. She always was. Gut instinct was right.

"So then, you want to come up here and do it, or are you happy where you are?" He kept his gaze locked on her.

"I'm fine here. Thank you, *James*."

Oh, that was good. *James.* The manners were different from how he remembered them. In fact a lot was. His eyes roamed her curled, tinted coiffure. From what he recalled, she had worn her hair long and straight, with a thick fringe framing her heart-shaped face. And it had been darker then. Ebony in fact, whereas now he detected traces of tinting.

She was still the same bother though, for all her polished air, or the elegant indigo dress that set off her pale skin to perfection, and her slender figure too for all that the gown flowed loosely to the floor.

The same? She was more. Already he felt he had to raise his game high as the yardarm to deal with her. "All right, then *Miss Fury —*"

"Milss Fury?" The man who thought himself the lucky one — lucky? Easy seeing he'd no damned notion of what lay stone dead in that cellar — fumbled in his coat pocket. "What is this Milss Fury? *Hic.* Who is this damned ingrate, if you please?" He pulled out a handkerchief and held it against his mouth.

Flint just hoped it wasn't because he noticed the smell of decomposition. But Flint had been very careful to put the lid back on the box and close the cellar door behind him.

"Only my valet, sir," Malmesbury said.

"Your valet? Then he should know the correct form of address — *hic.* I, for one, have never heard such a confounded, damn affront. It's Layldy Fury. You hear, you damned peasant? Let's hear it."

"Layldy Fury then." There was little point losing this on a point of etiquette, after all.

"And a bow. *Hic.*"

"A bow?" Before her? The way she utterly failed to accommodate his wishes and said she'd rather rot in everlasting hell than sleep with him? He bent his head, seeking to ignore the way her eyes brimmed with disbelief and she tightened her mouth as if *he* were being ungracious.

"Fine."

"Valet? He don't look like no damned valet to me." A drunken cackle cut the air.

For God's sake, what was she thinking, considering buffoons like this?

"Malmsie, old boy, are you sure he hasn't just wandered in here off the streets and intends getting his feet under our table? *Hic.*"

"My valet will be beaten for his impertinence. Let me assure you of that."

"Fine, fine." Flint jerked up his head. "You beat me all you like. Just so long as you save something in the stick for our Lady Fury there. The little secrets she's hiding."

"Secrets? I say. *Hic.* Secrets? Extraordinary. You, Fury?"

"Pay no attention to him." She met Flint's eyes with admirable coolness. "He's joking."

"I think we agreed, that joke could be on you, and hell's not a nice resting place, sweetheart."

With difficulty he fought the vague frisson in his blood. He'd bedded her before because that was what he did. And he'd do it now because that was what he'd need to do. But the frisson... He didn't need the distraction of frissons when he stood on this cold, unforgiving staircase fighting for his existence. How could she live in a place like this either?

"*Sweetheart. Hic.* How confounded outrageous is that? What do you think this is — *hic* – a brothel? With yourself as keeper?"

Flint wondered if she intended to prevaricate. All right, he'd left her on that quay, but how could she have thought it was ever any more than a one-way ticket? Getting set, she was, to take over his cabin with all her damned falderals. The parasol. The fancy cream coat.

The parakeet in the gilded cage he had heard screeching

from the other end of the dock had been the last, the *final* straw. Never mind the pile of boxes she had five laborers carrying in her wake, like some Nile queen. He'd *had* to do something. He didn't want a woman in his life. He especially didn't want her.

Unless memory lied though, she had never refused him before. No matter what mood he was in. And he couldn't think of the reason for it now. Unless she was aware of her hand? He was outnumbered, after all. What did she hope for? Him to give the whole game away by behaving like Captain Flint? Holding a knife to Malmesbury's throat? Swinging from the chandelier?

"I wouldn't call it a house of pure repute. Not what's been going on here." He held up a warning hand. "Your call, Miss Fury."

"You…you mean the signora has made her mind up? Finally?" Vellaggio piped up for the first time.

"She has indeed. And depending on who it is, two of you might just get a small guided tour of this house, with all its many attractions."

"Attractions? You mean zere are more than Signora Furee?"

"Oh, there are plenty more. Isn't that so, Fury?"

Her darkening eyes were like pistols at five paces. But that was all right because his own could be just as dangerous, when he chose to make them so. He chose now.

"I know it's maybe not what you agreed with them, all that leaving within the hour stuff and that. But you want me to do that, don't you? Show the gentlemen around while you're busy? Then, while I'm about it, have a chat about old times…in Jamaica."

"Old times? In Jamaica?" The lucky one hiccupped, lowering the handkerchief from his mouth. "I say, Fury, what is he on about? *Hic*. You was never in Jamaica, was you?"

She parted her lips, as if he'd said something ghastly. "He…he means that he knows me. That is what this is about, unfortunately."

This time, because she did not look at him, he had the opportunity to study her. But then she did look at him, and he wished she hadn't. He didn't want any pang about those pretty little emerald eyes of hers or the straight way she stood, just like the day he had flung that trunk at her on the quay, nipping his — if he'd had a heart, that trunk would still be on the *Calypso*.

Which was more than he was right now. He tilted his jaw, offering his best glare.

"He knows you?" Malmesbury demanded.

"Yes. From — from Jamaica, where I...I must have lived for a while."

"Must have?"

Malmesbury cocked an eyebrow. So, Flint wasn't alone in feeling pressured?

"Fury, this is most unusual, not to mention outright ridiculous." Malmesbury crossed his arms. "Either you did or you didn't."

She tensed her hands in her flowing skirt. "I did."

"Before you met Thom — "

"Yes. Amazing, isn't it?" She didn't sound as though she thought so. In fact Flint wasn't too sure how she sounded. She narrowed her eyes. "We were friends."

Malmesbury dropped his jaw open. Dropped it so far, Flint expected to be told to retrieve it from the floor. Vellaggio's too. A miracle they thought she'd have any? Or that she did and it was Flint?

"Nothing more. Although he is, of course, most keen and eager to continue the association. And I...I...well...*I...*" She looked as if she stared down a viper on the staircase.

"*What?*"

Flint hoped he'd kept his mouth shut and that exclamation had come from Malmesbury, not him. So long as she was nice about it, he wouldn't see her stuck. Right now, he hadn't decided. Because what she'd just said about him being keen to continue the association, keen was an overstatement, given the fact her husband lay in a box in the cellar.

How could any man possibly be keen? Certainly not one in his right mind. Anyway, the damned baggage hadn't exactly said *yes*, yet, had she? And her look was not encouraging. Would she really rather swallow poison? The old Fury would have leaped into bed with him in an instant. But this one just stood like a horrified statue beneath his gaze.

"Continue? An association? With him?" Malmesbury's uneasy chuckle echoed through the hall.

Fury's eyes darkened in a way Flint had never seen before. Uneasy laughter or not, Flint seethed with a fury that was almost forlorn. Just his luck she'd chosen to call here tonight the very types to make him look ridiculous. And it was ridiculous, he supposed. What they were and what he was.

She didn't need telling. And her silence gave consent to making him feel all the things he'd felt since he was captured.

"Oh, don't be so silly. Next you'll be telling us you're picking him. My damn valet, for God's sake. Now stop it. You have *not* called us all here to do that."

"Actually…actually this man, this man you talk so freely of beating, sir, is not a valet, by nature or inclination."

And now, *now* she was going to blab he was Captain Flint, master of the *Calypso*—the very last thing he needed. So then they could laugh very loudly indeed. And send him back to Jamaica in chains, if they let him live that long. She had been on that boat too.

"Not a valet?" Malmesbury said before Flint could open his mouth to defend himself. "You two could have fooled me, when I've had him polishing my shoe buckles and fitting on my clothes, pressing them too, since I bought him in Jamaica. At a slave auction."

"A—Sir, Capt—"

"Let it go, Fury." Flint gritted his teeth.

Furious color bloomed along her cheekbones. "No. I shan't let it go." To his astonishment she turned to Malmesbury. "Indeed, you must think yourself very clever, sir. But if he has been doing these things, then it will stop."

"Stop? I beg your pardon? Stop? Why the hell should it stop?" Malmesbury strode forward. The fact he stood on the landing lent his squat, night-shirted body the power to glare down at her. "You give orders very lightly, madam, with a disdain for my position and my person I do not deserve. I have come here tonight as an obligement to you. Not for you to order me about in the matter of my servants."

"Allow me to put it another way, sir. You will release him from these duties, so I can make use of him *here*."

Malmesbury glanced about him. No one laughed now. She had emptied the hall of all humor. The cool, taut way she said the word *here* stole the breath from more than Malmesbury. Flint raised his chin, scarcely able to believe it. Although, was it so astonishing? Even someone as recalcitrant and as troublesome as this creature was bound to see Flint was preferable to a yardarm, eventually.

"I will do no such thing. Are you mad?"

"Not at all." She spoke as if the idea were inconceivable in connection with herself. But the words still carried weight in the stunned silence. "I think we can agree that with what I have on you, you will do it now or face the opening of my little book."

Flint didn't know what to think. Fury's behavior in the last few seconds was very different from several moments ago. As if there were still, after all, something between them. Something only evidenced when they were being circled there as if by sharks. He didn't understand it. Her taking his side? Not after the way she'd fought him.

All the same he wasn't going to argue when she glided up the marble stairs in a cool swish of indigo skirts. Even if his heart had begun to thud with dread at the awful prospect of what was probably coming next.

"Now, come, James."

Chapter Three

"Pen and paper, Susan." Striding into the chamber she seemed to have left so short a time, yet a whole world ago, Fury wanted to shriek and scream. She had no fears about Susan falling beneath Flint's spell. At least, she corrected herself, she had no worries about Flint going beyond that lazy grin with her. Susan was old enough to be his mother. Plump enough too. And Fury would remind her of that later. She gazed into the gilt-framed dressing table mirror.

No. She had confused this. Confused herself. The question was not whether to let him win or lose. The question was whether *she* won or lost. Certainly it had been until his tricorne thudded into the ring. Then she had reacted in a stupid and bizarre fashion. How much simpler to have said, *Yes James, let me think it over*, wasn't it?

There would be no repeat now that she was going to have to suffer him here.

"And ink." Fury added to her request after seeing Susan make no effort to obey. Yes, whether he went beyond it or not, Flint's lazy grin *was* devastating. Here Susan was straightening her cap like a moonstruck girl.

"Yes, madam."

Fury's eyes narrowed in the mirror. "When it is convenient

to you." Was there no end to the man's lazy appeal?

"Yes, ma'am." Tearing her gaze away from Flint, Susan fumbled in the bedside table drawer. "I was just…the ink's there. Here, I mean."

"James, sit down." Fury took the ink bottle before the contents spilt on the floor. "There is a chair there. Susan, this…" She hesitated over the word *gentleman*. There were other, more suitable words. Even to think them would be a further distraction in a very distracted situation. "This is James by the way. You will see a lot of him over the coming weeks. I advise you to get used to that fact."

"You mean? But—"

Give Susan her dues; her jaw might have dropped open, but she knew better than to let anything away. Later Susan would likely ask where she got him. And Fury would not tell her. There were some things that were made to be kept secret. That was certainly one.

"Oh, James and I are old friends. James, have you sat down yet?"

"Hmm?" Flint ceased his contemplation of the hanging of Messalina adorning the wall behind the bed. Of course he would have ambled there already.

"What me?" He smiled, removing his coat. "What do you want me to do that for? This is a nice bed you've got here. Don't you just want to spread out and get to it?"

"No. Susan, leave us."

"Yes, madam."

The door clicked shut. Fury could see what a mistake this was. But there was no way out. That was why, in determining the necessity of governing her hatred, she had equally determined what was going to happen would be no pleasure for her.

As for him, well, unfortunately there was going to have to be pleasure for him — whoever made that rule had made it one way for men — but she would ensure it was of the most stringent sort.

If she could not keep Captain Flint out her bed, she would certainly keep him out her heart.

The man — the man was perhaps not entirely as she had first imagined him downstairs. Indeed, the scholarly look she had noticed before had slipped from his features as he had stood, persecuting her on that landing. But a weariness was still there. She saw it in the way he'd stared at that hanging.

He had forced her into a corner. But the worst of it was the indignation that had torn her heart when Malmesbury laughed, and she could imagine the life he'd been leading. Flint, the great and mighty, wasn't made to polish shoe buckles. As for him being beaten *all Malmesbury liked*? Something in her had revolted at the thought, something she was not responsible for. Some latent form of idiocy that must run in her family, which unfortunately no one had thought to mention she might one day inherit.

Because, of course, he was made to polish shoe buckles, to do whatever he was told. Damn him. And if he had been beaten, then it hadn't been hard enough. A man like him. That weariness was something she must exploit. He would do what he was told. Exactly what he was told.

"What was that about weeks, Fury?"

She sat down and dipped the quill into the ink. She detected the faintest trace of nerves. It must have been the fact Thomas lay in the cellar. Why else would a man, so great, so stalwart, so worldly as Captain Flint be nervous of her?

"Well, yes." She listened to the pleasing scratch of the nib on the soft paper. "Babies are not always made in a night. Of course, you wouldn't know that, being you. It will take time."

"All the more reason then to just get going. After all this time, sweetheart, you don't know how eager I am."

He strode across the tiled floor. The ink trailed a long, dark path across the paper as he dragged her to her feet. Had it blobbed it might have been something to worry about. But she was very set on this. And calm. As calm as one could be having this man in her bedroom, knowing what was coming next out of dire necessity, her husband in a box in the cellar and her cast-off potential lovers on their way out the door.

"No." She held a hand up between their lips. "There will be no kissing."

"No kissing? Why in hell not?"

It displaced her calm to see him grin. She would have preferred that he was indignant. Especially as he was a man who thought he could settle all his arguments — with women anyway — with a kiss. But she kept her face cold, blank.

"Because." In some ways she was cold. Cold with rage.

"Aw, come on, Fury, didn't you like my kissing? Hmm?" His breath, hot and male, brushed her fingertips. He wrapped his arms around her, splaying his hands across her back, so her hand might as well not have been there for all the protection it was.

But she was calm. Didn't she have to get into bed with him after all? Even the impulse to squirm was one she would squash. When she thought of all he had done to her, she would give him nothing. Not even the knowledge she found his proximity so unsettling that she sought to pull away.

"Your kissing was fine, in its way, I suppose. But kissing is a sign of affection."

"How do you make that out?"

She knew exactly why he scratched his head. Their lovemaking had been torrid. It had been sensual. It had been shaming. And it had been absent of any affection. Certainly on his part. Why would a kiss be a sign of anything? To him anyway. She was the damn fool who had thought it had. Who even now was forced to concede the pleasure it would be to take her hand across his face to assist his understanding of her feelings. The impertinence of the damn man, the stinging ignorance.

"It just is." She eased the distance between them a whisper. "So there will be none. Not now. Not at all."

"All right then. Saves time. It means—"

"Rule two." She saw his eyes freeze as he readied himself to yank off his shirt. She persisted anyway. Why not? In many ways she walked a tightrope here. If she paused it might be to her detriment. "You will be fully dressed at all times."

"What? How the hell am I meant to—"

"I am sure you will manage. You managed plenty before. But I do not desire to look at your body before, during, or after. Nor in any shape or form wandering about this house in just your breeches. Is that understood?"

His dropped his hands from his shirt and glared, so he must have. "You wanted to look at it plenty before. In fact, it makes my head spin, just how often you—"

True. But that was then. "Rule three." Clasping her fingers around the cool edge of the dressing table to create another inch of distance, she continued.

"Rule three? You mean there's more?"

"I will not touch you in any place, intimate or otherwise. I will lie. You will perform."

Oh, this new Flint—this new Flint couldn't make sense of what he heard. Because of course, the old Flint had hands of velvet and a body of silk. He knew how to please and he enjoyed being pleased. He should, the lovers he'd had. That damned bed of his had already been warm when he had blackmailed her into it.

The new Flint could only stand there breathing heavily, looking as if he wanted to strike her. Something the old Flint had looked too on occasion, although he had never done it.

"I realize that, of course, you may have to touch me. But—rule four—you will do so as little as humanly possible."

"What?"

"Yes, offering no pleasure. This is a business arrangement. A simple in and out will suffice, with no talking, no exclaiming, no use of any obscene language—rule five."

"I never used any obscene language."

She raised her chin. "Endearments to you would be obscene, should you think of uttering any. Not that you ever did, mind."

"Hell, I was a pirate captain, not some fancy, dressed-up buffoon with pompoms on his shoes."

"Afterward—rule six—you will remove yourself in all respects and wait until, rule seven, you are summoned again. I trust I am making myself clear. But in case there is something in what I have said that is hard to understand, I have set the terms down here in black and white for you to read—rule eight—and sign—rule nine—so there can be no misunderstanding, resulting in a breach of this agreement—rule ten."

After his performance on the staircase when he had pushed her against the banister and the way he loomed now, she braced as she squeezed around for the paper. Although, really, the man was at a disadvantage. No matter how he had strode across the floor and tried to impose himself like before, he fooled nobody.

"This is going to be so much fun. I confess I can hardly wait." She picked up the pen. "We will start as soon as you have signed it. And it has been witnessed—rule eleven."

He shifted his lips into a sardonic twist. "So, what's rule twelve? You going to call the household in to witness this simple in and out."

Of course he'd be difficult. "What a ghastly proposition. No. I've not thought of that yet, but it will be something to mull over when we're—I think you've described it rather well. I have to say you're learning fast. I'm impressed."

His hand descended on the paper, and she thought he would crush it. Indeed she waited with unashamed longing for him to do so. She wanted to think she'd needled him, although the fuse with Flint always burnt slower than a fire in the Arctic wastes.

"Very generous." His blue gaze burned as he studied her. "You think I don't know what your little game is here, sweetheart? If it had been Malmesbury or what's his name—"

She faced him. "If you mean Vellaggio or Southey, not at all. There would be rules for anyone doing this. Some a little different, it is true. The siring of the Beaumont heir is not to be taken lightly. May I remind you, you asked."

"Hmm." His gaze dropped to the paper, and he squared his jaw. "What's this rule four, a simple in and out? How am I meant to do that if you're not—"

"I will use a cream." A faint blush crept over her cheekbones. Trust Flint to think of something so basic. It did, however, please her to see him so docile. Almost as much as it would have pleased her to see him needled. Slow to burn or not, he would accept this even if he seethed.

"After all, I wouldn't like to make it difficult for you or suffer more in your embrace than necessary." She smiled and tilted her jaw. "Why don't you just make your mark on the paper so we can—how was it you put it again—get to it?" She tossed him the pen.

He caught it and stared, for a long brittle moment. Then with an abrupt movement he tossed it on the floor, where it clattered and rolled, blobbing ink across the tiles. Wordless, he walked to the end of the dressing table and held the paper in the candle flame. A blaze came from it, and she watched as black cinders showered, like so many dead moths, onto the marble surface of the table.

"What…what do you think you're doing?"

"What you said. Making my mark. Now, that's your terms. Here's mine."

Dread held her immobile. She quaked a little. She had gone a little far with the business of the mark—she was the first to admit it. Flint was the most intelligent man she'd ever met. He could read and write perfectly. But she felt trapped and confined by this. Now she shuddered to think what terms he'd insist on. She ran her tongue around her lips to moisten them. "And what are they?"

His gaze swept the room as it had the hanging of Messalina earlier, as if she were very comfortable here, as if she had everything, when in fact none of it belonged to her and there were bills, certain bills in her possession only Susan knew about. Bills from just about everyone in Genoa it was possible to have bills from. Then his gaze swept her. Making her wait. Tweaking her nerve endings. Heightening her anticipation. The old Flint was always a master at doing that.

This was the new Fury, and she had neither nerve endings nor anything left to heighten. She was sorry, *yes*, that she had insulted him, because of course, he would wreak his revenge and he was in a strong bargaining position. But nerve endings? Oh, dear Lord, no. The thought almost made her laugh out loud. She could not afford nerve endings in this situation.

He ambled across to the fireplace. The irritating little smile, which had come and gone with alarming ease, touched his lips as he paused. "What do you think?" He surveyed her.

"I'm sure I don't know." She lied. Of course.

Silence, broken only by the ticking of the mantelshelf clock, cloaked the room.

"An imaginative woman like you? Are you joking?"

Her stomach churned. All right, perhaps she was a little edgy. There were things to be edgy about. Only a fool would have failed to see, when the inevitable was upon her, that delay was a bad thing. And the little heap of cinders on the dressing table was a glaring reminder of her folly.

"Isn't it obvious what I'd like? How can a woman have forgotten so much?"

A stutter would look too much like defeat. She braced herself. "Imagination is a luxury I am afraid I have not been able to afford in my position." More lies. But she would die before she said *because it pains me to remember.*

Her mind raced. Oh, God. What would it be? Sex, obviously. Which she shouldn't be too upset about, given the Beaumont heir couldn't be conceived without it. She wasn't the Virgin Mary after all. But sex — sex on his terms, what she remembered of those. She tried not to clench her fists. Was the Beaumont heir worth that? Would it not be better to beg on the streets? Do as Susan suggested and find a protector? One who would pay for herself, Susan, and…

"You, sweetheart? Unimaginative? With what's in your cellar? And that little plan you made over the head of it?"

He tossed his hair back from his face. Something burned very close to the surface in his eyes, in the tilt of his head. Was it slow burning enough to fizzle out? To see what was at stake for him? Or had she made him angry enough to demand anything?

"Go on. Insult me. You think I care? Or that you have terms? Just — just tell me what they are. As I said before, if it's money, if it's jewels, you'll have to wait. I can't give you what I don't have. Unless you want me to write you a debtor's note?"

"Hmm." He drummed his long fingers on the mantelshelf. "Money? Sweetheart, is that as much as you think of me?"

"I don't think of you." She straightened her spine. "You flatter yourself. But money was always something dear to your heart. Perhaps not quite so dear as the *Calypso*, which was your heart."

His expression changed at that. It *was* what he wanted. And no doubt it killed him not to be standing on the deck, the wind ruffling his hair, bossing every member of his crew senseless.

It gave her a bargaining counter. This would be worse, a hundred times worse, if he actually wanted her. If he'd pined and rotted in the same hell she had found herself in. If he had any feeling in his heart at all, if the blackguard even had a heart. She wasn't going to fool herself on that score.

Again he twisted his lips into the little sardonic smile. "Here was me thinking you liked me."

"I don't like you any more than you like me." She lifted her chin. "I would like to say I wish I'd never met you. As I said already, this arrangement isn't about like. So, why even say—"

"Because you put down an ultimatum, sweetheart."

"Me?"

"Which I burnt in that candle flame, same as I'm going to do with any debtor's note you write me."

She might have guessed, although what he did with the note was the least of her troubles standing there. "I'm sure you did, which is why I'm asking for your terms. What do you want?"

"All right then, if it's no trouble to you. That little rule you have…"

She swallowed. Her hands were beginning to sweat, but she didn't want to wipe them on her gown. "What rule?"

"The one about being fully clothed."

"What about it?"

"It could be difficult, you see, with what I'd like right now."

Her mouth dried. "And how do you make that out?"

"Because I need to take my breeches off, sweetheart."

As if he needed to, from what she remembered of him. She fought a blush. "Well, I—I—"

"And that little rule."

"I'm afraid it would be…that is…if you wish to undress, so

long as you do not expect…me…"

"Why should I expect you, unless you want to join me?"

"I will be joining you."

"You got a big enough tub?"

"A tub?"

"I'd like a bath."

She blinked. "A bath?"

The first time he'd called her to his cabin on board the *Calypso* and explained that he knew she wasn't Lady Celia, he outlaid what he was going to do about it — now, a bath was nothing. Certainly she'd misheard. "A bath?"

"I like to be clean."

"I see." She recollected herself.

If Flint was only going to ask for that — *a bath* — she could oblige. Although it was ridiculous she was at his mercy like this. Why should she? She wasn't buying his freedom for him to have a bath. But if she didn't let him, what else might he demand?

She walked to the door to call Susan to fill the copper tub. As she did, it occurred to her she had no other servants and just maybe he knew that. A bath? Odd, when he was so keen *to get to it*. He'd offered her the heir right there on the staircase, and now he procrastinated. Was that to pay her back? File her nerve endings to tiny heaps? Or was it something more?

What if he didn't mean to help her at all? What if he intended to escape? She'd have to fall back on Malmesbury or worse. A bad idea now that they knew she had a past and she would have to face them with the shaming knowledge she'd allowed Flint Blackmoore to escape. No. The tub must come in here.

"I'll call Susan and we'll bring the tub in here."

"That's very nice of you, putting yourself about like this." He walked to the chair and eased down.

"It's no trouble."

How deeply did she regret saying that? By the time the tub had been lugged up the stairs and maneuvered through the door, which she felt she daren't take her eyes off for a second, by the time her back felt broken—and her arms—the answer to that was *to the bone.* Look at him sitting there. Like a king. Not even his boots off. And the tub still needed to be filled.

It took some effort.

"Madam, are you sure about this?" Susan and Fury were on their tenth trip up the stairs with the copper kettle and the bucket. She wouldn't ask Susan to do anything she wouldn't do herself.

"I have no choice." Fury had scarcely any breath left to speak. Thank God Malmesbury and the others had gone. She would die if they saw her like this, with her hair askew and her dress falling off her shoulders. "He's all I've got. Now stand at that door. Make sure he doesn't leave the room. Do you hear me?"

Susan smiled knowingly. How dare she imagine Fury was so desperate to keep him for his sexual charms that she didn't want to let him out of her sight? Or maybe Susan was silly enough to imagine his lazy smile was for her alone? A dumpy middle-aged servant? Couldn't she see how dangerous the man was?

"I think you're doing very nicely." Flint eased his long legs out. "I never took you for the athletic type."

He didn't deign to help in any way. Why should he, now he'd made his first demand? If he met her with that lazy, insinuating stare once more, she would tip the boiling contents of the kettle over him. In his lap would be preferable. But that might affect his chances of fathering the heir. She'd have to settle for his head.

"I'm glad you think so."

It took some effort not to gasp, but she managed. When he'd

had his bath and he'd obliged her, it would be over for tonight. She could lie down and forget this horrible nightmare.

He pulled off his boots—at least he didn't expect her to do that for him—and set them to the side of the chair. Then he tore off his stockings.

"You don't have to stay." He raised his head. "Seeing as you have all these fancy rules. I wouldn't want for you to break them so soon."

As ever his unbridled impertinence knew no bounds. She bit her lip. She'd sooner not stay. But it might be another mistake to leave him alone.

"It's fine."

He stood, his long mouth carving tiny grooves in his tanned cheeks—and Fury was back on the deck of the *Calypso* again. He peeled off his shirt.

His body—he knew his body looked every bit as good as when he had stridden that same deck, stripped to the waist, for all he was seven years older. And he was, as usual, not the least embarrassed about himself. No. As the deceptively lazy grin said, if ever a man wanted a woman to look at him, if ever a man thought he should be looked at it, it was Flint.

His deft fingers dropped to the buttons of his breeches. Her glance became a stare before she could stop it. Embarrassed, she turned away.

All right, fair enough. Flint's well-sculpted body still had the power to fill her with longing. But only if she allowed it.

After a few seconds she heard him amble toward the copper tub, toward her, at an even slower pace than usual. Daring her to turn her head. Never mind rot, first she would fry in hell.

"Is—is the water fine? To your liking?" Somehow she found her voice, although it came out slightly raised, as if his naked proximity sucked all the air from her.

"I've not stepped in yet. I just want to make sure there's not a shoal of piranhas swimming about beneath these waves. A man never knows with you."

"Why would I do that? I want to ensure the conception of the Beaumont heir. Not have anything gnaw the one thing that might give me it."

"How come Thomas ended up in the cellar if you wanted to do that?"

Give Flint the chance to sneer by telling him everything that had happened? "None of your business."

She wished to God she would hear the splash of water that meant he'd stepped into the tub. He was so beautiful, lean, golden, sculpted...even the silly male pride she knew she'd see on his face affected her. It always had.

They said one man was very much like another. But Thomas had never had a body like Flint Blackmoore, which was also why he'd never have stood naked in the middle of her floor like this.

"If you don't want the bath..."

"No, it's fine. You've no idea how a simple thing can make a man feel good about himself, so long as the water's not burning."

"It's not."

Dragging a breath, she crossed to the fireplace. It was such an odd confession for him. But if he had been beaten, of course he'd feel that way.

It was another reason not to look at him. She stared at the mantelshelf. The ormolu clock said midnight. *Midnight?* Time hadn't just gone, it had been wasted. Squandered, while he splashed about in a bath.

"You think you can get my back?"

"No, I don't. I think we agreed that I will not touch you."

"Then why don't I just lie here? Water's nice and warm. I could stay all night."

Damn him. He would too. Till icicles formed. Touching him,

washing his back, was an intimacy she couldn't allow. If she touched him, she risked exposing herself to shameful thoughts, to a resurgence of things that were dead.

The aim of this was to father the heir. So far, although James Flint Blackmoore had been in this bedroom a total of two hours, she was no closer to being pregnant than a day, a week, or a month ago. Lady Margaret might be in England, but Thomas lay in the cellar.

Setting her jaw, she swept across the floor. "The sponge, if you please."

It would not do, after all, to put her hand in that tub and grasp something other than that. That would give him ideas. Although the sight of him, slippery with suds, the corn-husk hair clinging to the sides of his face, the blue eyes so dazzling it hurt her to look at them, made it hard not to have some ideas of her own. How easy it would be with his face as close as this, when their fingertips brushed, to reach into that tub. To touch him. To have all this as it once was.

"Just my shoulders, will you?"

She swallowed and took the sponge.

He sat back, flinching as his back brushed the curve of the tub. "The rest is fine."

She didn't doubt it and she refused to question the flinch. There was something too intimate about this. The sponge separated her fingers from his skin, but her detachment was starting to crumble.

He would never, ever, have let her drip water on him like this on the *Calypso*. There he'd been master of everything. Including her.

"So." She dusted the nape of his neck. "What happened to your arm?"

"My arm?"

"Yes." She applied the sponge to his shoulder. "That mark.

Were you shot?"

He turned his head, his lazy gaze colliding with hers. "Looking are you?"

She dipped the sponge back in the water. "Not especially. But it would be hard not to see when you're sitting beneath my nose."

"It's the same as you said to me." His gaze iced. "None of your damn business."

The mercurial change—now that was more like Flint.

She lowered her head. "So? Is this one of your terms?" She strove to sound forbidding. In truth it was far harder than she'd thought.

Flint had this way, this horrible, flirtatious way. She hesitated to consider him a moth to a flame, when, in fact, he was the flame. However she'd no doubt he still considered it the way to bring her to her knees. He was close enough for his breath to brush her face, so she kept it averted.

"Is what one of my terms?"

"Me servicing you."

She heard the faint huff of his breath and cursed herself for using that word.

"I'd hate to think if you were. Your touch isn't exactly soft." Without warning, he rose, water cascading from his sculpted body. "But I am ready for my next term."

She almost dropped the sponge. "Term?" Ready? She was ashamed to find herself staring at the sleek line of his buttocks. "And what—what is that going to be?" Good lord, the water was a mess on the floor. There would be the devil to pay with Susan, having to mop this. "Time…time is going on. I don't like to say, but we don't have all night."

"Then pass me that towel. So my butt nakedness doesn't offend you."

"Yes." She groped without looking and passed it above her

head. "J-just tell me w-what it is and I—" Did she stammer this
much as a rule? She began mopping in earnest.

"Something to eat, I think." He stepped out of the tub.

She jerked to her feet. "Something—something to eat?"

"Anything will do." He wrapped the towel around himself
and padded across the floor. "I'm not fussy. Just whatever you
have in your kitchen."

That would be a scrap of bread and some moldy cheese.
There were some tomatoes on the plant in the garden. Some
being the operative word. At the last count it was three. If she
gave him one that would be two.

"I'll get dressed while you fix it."

Precisely. Then what? All he had to do was slip down the
stairs while she was doing that. She considered waking Susan,
then she considered against it. Susan may have rescued her from
Fishside Wharf, but there were aspects of her life she discussed
with no one. Flint Blackmoore was one, because he hadn't just
left her on Fishside Wharf.

"There's some fruit there in the bowl. It would save me
waking the kitchen staff at this hour."

Flint sank his teeth into an apple. The crisp, clean bite cut the
air.

"You got anything to wash it down with?" His rudeness was
preferable to him discovering she'd no kitchen staff—at least it
meant he'd not poked his nose in there. "Some rum?"

"Why would I keep rum? What do you think I am? Next
you'll be expecting me to call you 'me hearty.'"

He grinned. "It's preferable to some of the things you have
called me."

She swallowed her ire as he strolled toward his clothes.
Food. Drink. She must keep him happy. No matter whether or
not it killed her. Then he'd…well, the list couldn't be endless,
could it?

"I have some brandy and some claret. Which would you prefer?"

"Either. Long as it's good."

Out of the corner of her eye she saw him wedge the apple between his teeth, then tug his shirt over his head.

"Long as you don't go putting any arsenic in it."

"No, and I won't spit in it either." She edged the top off the crystal decanter. At least the wine cellar was stocked. That would keep Flint happy enough, so long as it did not detract from his ability to perform. "Here."

"Set it down, will you?"

She wanted to set it down his throat. But he was in the process of thrusting his leg into his breeches and she feared she might spill it. Already she had a floor to mop.

"Certainly. Where would you like me to put it?"

"I'll just spread out over there."

"Where?"

"The bed. Just let me get dressed, like you said."

She tightened her throat. She hadn't made any stipulation about the bed. She suspected the beautiful silk damask bedcover would soon be ruined by the intrusion of his boots. He must keep them off. She didn't want an argument with Signor Santa-Rosa that she had left his villa in a worse state than she had found it.

"Fine." *The bed.* It wasn't just Signor Santa-Rosa was it? The thing — the awful thing was she had nothing on Flint Blackmoore he hadn't already paid for. Nothing she could use against him. Not a bill, not a jotting, not a witnessed statement. Not even the pretense of one. So all she could do was walk to the bed.

Raising her chin, she proceeded. Why wait? So far the evening had been a complete disaster. Well, maybe not quite a disaster. At least she had procured a contender. Even if it was the last man in the world she'd thought it would be.

She set the glass of claret down on the scrolled bedside cabinet. Then she walked around the bed and sat down.

Desire had played such a small role in her life for the last seven years, and perhaps that was why her heart hammered now. But she *would* control it.

"Thanks, Fury."

Bending down she eased off her shoes. "You're welcome."

Anyway, after the way Thomas had behaved, she wasn't likely…all right, never mind Thomas, after seven years, she still knew what this man was capable of. She cleared her throat. If only she could clear her mind as easily.

"You mind if I have some grapes?"

She straightened. Mind? She endeavored not to bore a mental hole in his head. It was tomorrow's breakfast after all. But she needed him so she couldn't afford to mind. She was also more than a little preoccupied, a little harried by this. It outweighed the desire to mind.

"Not at all. Just you make yourself at home."

"I will." He reached into the brass fruit bowl. Then he picked it up by the pedestal stem.

"Have the whole bowl." She gestured graciously.

"All right."

Although it infuriated her, if these were his terms, she could meet them. So long as he just did this. She huffed out a breath. After the first time, it would be all right. She reached into the drawer on her side of the bed.

"What's that you've got there?"

"The — the cream."

God, how humiliating. If he refused, if he said something about it… He surveyed her with a narrowed gaze. Was it indignant? To her shame she couldn't tell. She hoped not. She needed to get this over with quickly.

"Just let me get something to eat first. These are mighty fine grapes." He tossed one into his mouth. "Then I still got my brandy to get."

"Claret."

"Hmm?" He ambled toward the bed and took a sip. "It's nice." It must have been because then he took a gulp. He sat down on the edge of the bed and drained the glass. "You got any more?"

"The decanter is over there."

"You don't mind me helping myself?"

"Not at all, please." She held out a hand.

"That's mighty kind of you. I'll just bring it over here. Then I can get comfortable."

He did, with a deep sigh. The mattress sank as he stretched his long legs out, making himself at home as Captain Flint always did on such a piece of furniture. "Food. Drink. What more can a man want? And, like I said, this is a nice bed you've got here."

It should be. It cost a maharajah's fortune to rent.

"I forgot." His lazy gaze studied her. "You want me to put my boots back on?"

What she wanted was to get this over with. He sprawled so close, his back against the pillows, and he smelled so heady, her heart raced. But she was — she was going to do this. Every stretched nerve ending in her body said she was going to do this. Because she had no choice.

"I don't think that is necessary. Please, just give me a minute." She rose and walked to the screen. It was one preparation she couldn't bear to make before him. God knows how she even managed the lid off the jar, the way her hands shook. But it would be worse to think herself aroused or let him think she was.

Smothering the little shiver of apprehension his warmth aroused, she bent her head. She'd be in trouble if she started thinking this way. Or about how lethal he looked sprawled there in the soft candlelight. When she'd applied a smooth dollop of cream, she would walk back to the bed and lie down, showing no trace of vulnerability. The inevitable was now upon her. Why delay?

She lowered her skirt and wiped her fingers dry on a lace handkerchief. Now that was dealt with, she reminded herself of all her reasons to hate him. His indifference, his arrogance, his obstinacy, his callous abandonment of her on that wharf. She walked back to the bed. Her heart racing harder, she spread herself out on the mattress.

"*If* you have no more demands…"

He removed the apple from between his teeth and looked at her. Suddenly even the simple action of what to do with her hands was a problem. On her chest, as if in prayer? Above her head? Absolutely not. By her sides? Possibly.

She tried each in turn, while he continued to stare, as only he could, turning a chunk of apple over and over on his tongue, as if he were going to spit it out.

Except he had never stared like that in bed. On deck maybe, when presented with some situation he didn't like. Or on the quay when he wrangled over some chiseling supplier. But he never stared like this when confronted with the possibility of boarding a woman.

"I'm just…just…" She cleared her throat. "Getting comfortable." Heavens, what next? Should she raise her skirts? Or should he?

"You sure about that?"

"Sure about what?" Taking a deep breath, she tried edging her gown up a notch. It wouldn't budge because she lay on top of it.

Suddenly the mechanics of this, of keeping him at bay, did not seem so clever. But if she were to reach out and touch him in some way, that might be worse. No. She had done this now. She had made these terms, even if he hadn't exactly kept a copy.

She closed her eyes. It was easier in the dark to wriggle the skirt a notch or two. At least as far as her knees. She wasn't going further than that. Surely it wasn't beyond him to do the rest.

She heard him take another bite out of the apple. He crunched so loud that she jerked her eyes open.

"Of course I'm sure. I'm just making myself…ready…at ease."

He furrowed his brow. "You mean—"

"That was why I went behind the screen. I'm ready and waiting for you."

God, would he stop chewing the apple and *get to it?* She had meant to govern this situation. Govern him. Not allow him to govern her.

A deal was a deal. Had he not stood on that staircase and blackmailed her into it? Why should he sound surprised, as if he'd no idea what he'd been fetched here for?

"Isn't that a shame?"

"A shame? What do you mean?"

"What I said." He tossed the hair out his eyes. "You're wasting that cream. You know what I think of waste."

A faint smile edged his lips. Her heart almost stopped dead. All right, so he wanted to touch her. Preferred to, rather than have her use the cream. She didn't want him to. But she could allow it.

She had been wrong to insult him when she needed his seed. If he wanted to think she desired him, just this once, was it such a mistake? After all, her way wasn't a raging success, was it?

"Then I am sorry." The words sounded mushy in her mouth. "I won't do it again."

He took another bite of the apple and then tossed it over his shoulder. James Flint Blackmoore did not need prompting in the art of sex. He would understand what her words meant.

It was more than she did herself at this moment, the way her mind raced at the thought of what was going to happen now finally she had his undivided attention. Or at least, she would have when he finished chewing.

She waited, her heart in her throat, for him to hitch her skirt. Any minute now. God, she was so nervous, her eyes watered.

"Is that right, sweetheart?"

She nodded. Her throat was too dry to speak.

"That's good to know. You do what you like. Right now, this nice bed you've got here, what I'd most like to do is...sleep."

"Sleep?" She fought not to let her voice notch several octaves.

"I'm kind of tired. Been a long day. Surprising too."

"James." It pained her to hear what crept into her voice. The harrying edge that made her sound like a desperate woman. She *was* desperate.

"What?"

"I brought you here for a purpose." She sat up, her scrutiny traveling over his face. "We agreed, did we not...after you offered...you would help me conceive the Beaumont heir."

"You agreed. There didn't seem much fun in it for me."

She resisted the urge to strike him. Of course Flint Blackmoore would only think of himself. "So, what are you saying? That you've changed your mind? Because if you have, the door is —"

"There's no need for you to go getting yourself fiked up."

True. But she was.

"Stropping neither."

"I'm not fiked up. Stropping either."

"That's a change."

"I just thought... you offered. And as you saw for yourself,

Thomas is in the cellar."

He nodded. "He looks like he's staying in it too."

"I cannot keep him there indefinitely. If—if this is because I was lax in choosing you…"

"You think I couldn't bring you around eventually? I'm just not a performing seal. You let me get rested and I'll see what I can come up with." He sighed and settled himself down on the silk bedspread, his hands behind his head. "You can lie down beside me, if you want."

"I—"

"Maybe you'd rather sleep in one of the other rooms? Or the chair there?"

She would not be sleeping. How could she? She should just have taken the heir when he'd offered. How humiliating was this? To be refused in her own bed? She felt the blood flood and then drain from her face.

"Are you saying that in the morning…"

She should never have tried to shackle him with that contract. She should have been nice, welcoming, amenable. The things she could not be in connection with him.

He deigned to open his eyes. "Hmmm? The morning…or whenever. Just let me get some rest in. You've no idea how tiring it is polishing shoe buckles."

She fought back fire. The tightrope she walked stood suspended across a gorge so perilous, she could not afford another slip. She didn't want him pleading some *woman's excuse* next. A headache. Or worse.

"Of course. I understand."

He smothered a yawn. "That's certainly a change. You don't usually."

She bit her tongue. "And there is no problem. None at all. Just make yourself as comfortable as possible."

"Thank you."

"And we can talk in the morning."

"Suits me. Now, if you don't mind being quiet?"

She nodded. What else could she do but lie down at the far side of the bed...and pray?

Chapter Four

"Six months, Lady Margaret."

"Six months?" The dowager duchess could find no fault with the figure presented to her. Or Fury's. "So?"

"Alas, Thomas lived just long enough to know of the great joy that was going to be his. It has been a sad time for all. But, now I am home at Ravenhurst, I am sure my fortunes will improve."

Fury's eyes pinged open before she could discover whether her fortunes did in fact improve. Her gaze shrank from the sunlight filtering through the shutters, and she realized, as she closed her eyes again, she wasn't in a dream anymore. The nightmare was all still there before her. Beside her rather.

She shook her head to clear it. Even as she tried, the clatter of crockery defeated her.

"Good morning, madam." Susan set a tray down on the dressing table. "Or would you prefer it in bed?"

Fury bolted up. Coffee steamed in a silver pot. Was that fresh bread?

"Where did you get—" Her gaze skittered sideways. She didn't want Flint knowing her straits were so tight it was a wonder she could breathe through them.

At least he was still here. He hadn't run in the darkness.

"Don't worry. I pawned the salon candlesticks, madam. We can get them back before Signor Santa-Rosa finds out. But you'll need to feed *him*." Susan lifted the coffee pot. "Now…"

Fury straightened her shoulders and tossed her hair out her eyes. She could see the tanned oval of Flint's face behind the disheveled corn-hued hair. She could even hear him breathing. She felt exasperated just thinking about the fact she'd been forced to lie on top of the same bed as him all night, her nerves stretched to breaking point, while he just slept.

Susan would think the deed was accomplished. No doubt, she even brought them breakfast in bed because she thought that was where they'd be spending the day.

Susan smirked, as though she considered Fury a lucky woman with a man of Flint's easy sexuality in her bed. But he was fully dressed, as she was herself. Didn't Susan see that? Or the cinders dusting the dressing table? The markers of Fury's own stupidity?

"Just…just leave the tray there, will you?"

"Madam, is everything all right?"

"It…it will be. Thank you for pawning the candlesticks. I'm ashamed I didn't think of it myself."

"I didn't think you'd mind. But you'll need money if you're going to keep him."

Money. It was how her life revolved. The bitter need of it. What did Lady Margaret know of that, safe in Ravenhurst? Why, even in Fury's dream she'd had that horrible, bombastic expression and seemed surprised Fury was pregnant. Fury would be surprised herself, the night she'd just spent.

James Flint Blackmore, lying next to her again, after seven years. Fury had been at great pains to keep a foot free in the middle of the bed, as she lay staring at the ceiling. What had pricked her eyes had nearly betrayed her. The memories, the thoughts of the nights they had once spent together.

"You can't expect a gentleman to pay for himself in the circumstances."

Fury paced across to the dressing table, battling her annoyance. "He's not a gentleman. But let's not go into what he is."

Her hands shaking, Fury lifted the coffee cup to her lips, waiting for Susan to leave the room. It was morning, by God, and she needed to put an end to this charade. She had allowed herself, with good cause, to be drawn into making that contract. He had responded, as he always responded, by grabbing the upper hand. Her body would only be her downfall if she allowed it to be.

This was a business agreement and the sooner it was undertaken, the better. The man was a privateer. Privateers had rules. He wanted his ship. She wanted the Beaumont heir. No matter how last night had happened, he surely understood that.

"Wake up. Coffee." Fury set the cup and saucer down on the bedside cabinet. And yet, even looking at him lying there, her heart tilted.

"Hmmm?"

"Coffee."

Cursing, he dragged the pillow over his head.

"And hot rolls."

"What the hell would I be wanting hot rolls for this time in the morning? You lost your head?"

The bad temper wasn't feigned. He had been asleep. Last night she'd thought he had planned to bolt. No doubt he was furious he hadn't.

"No. But we do have work to do."

"You know what they say all work makes."

"Perhaps you'd prefer rum? I can send Susan."

He took his head out from under the pillow, his eyes

narrowed in a way she'd never seen before. For a second she wondered what had been inflicted on the man to make him look shocked that anyone would offer him anything.

"Coffee's fine. As long as you never poisoned it. How did Thomas die anyway?"

"He just did. If I said otherwise, you'd never believe me."

The puzzled grimace convinced her she'd won whatever round this was. At least she'd given him something to think about. With Flint, that was everything.

She reached for the butter knife. "Now then, some butter, some apricot preserve on your rolls?"

"What?"

"Some—"

"I heard." He grabbed a hunk of dry bread.

She looked at him without flinching. "Isn't this nice? Me seeing you again. You seeing me."

To be truthful, the way his eyes glazed and his teeth paused midway tearing off the hunk of bread, it was plain the last thing he wanted to see this morning was her. If she did not press the advantage now she'd lose it. Flint was slippery, waiting only for the moment her back was turned. He must be. Otherwise he'd have made some insinuating remark about the rolls.

He tore another mouthful. "That depends."

"Of course it depends. Here you are, eating my nice bread and—"

"On the eye of the beholder."

She forbore to tell him that was supposed to be *beauty*. And *in*. She supposed it was the same thing.

"So don't pretend we're either of us dancing with joy."

"Very well, I won't. Last night I gave you my rules, you gave me yours. Now..."

She hesitated. She could send him back to Malmesbury. All it would take was a short note. Although notes and her were not exactly a raging success.

James Flint Blackmoore and her were not a raging success either, which was why she wished her mind wouldn't niggle about the way Malmesbury treated him.

She could just let him go, but then she'd have to choose Southey or cast herself on Malmesbury's mercy with some tale of woe. Being the little woman in need of protection was not a role that came easily. It would come less so with a man who threw a whip about the way some did their money.

No. She must do this.

She refilled her coffee cup. "This morning it's time to parley. Privateer fashion. About this transaction. Because of course, if you're somehow incapable…"

He set his coffee cup down on the saucer with a clink and then passed the back of his hand over his mouth. He looked at her, his blue eyes studying her in a way she'd never seen before, his lower lip seeming much fuller than usual.

"You just tell me when you're ready."

When she was ready? Of course he meant to parley.

"Let's just do this. Just the way you told me. Since I'm not getting out of this."

She almost fell on the floor. But it would have ruined her attempt to appear stalwart, unflinching. Yet, it was what she wanted. More than anything. So why feel the need to procrastinate? That would be to show him nerves. She swallowed the knot that rose in her throat.

"Very well."

She sat down, feeling the mattress sink beneath her quivering body. Prayers were for those who hadn't come to the kind of place she had, so she emptied her mind. But she did drag a deep quiet breath. Until she had lain down, she'd no idea how much she needed to.

Just the way she'd told him. Oh God, what was that again?

"So…what…what?" God, this was worse than being a virgin again. The problem of her hands and what to do with them. At least that first time…that first time there had been no conditions like this.

Flint had waited till the *Calypso* was underway, then he'd called her to his cabin. It hadn't been quite as basic as that, in terms of what he'd then outlaid. At least he'd had the decency to let her eat supper first before offering to throw her overboard if she didn't get into his bed. Nicely, his little smile suggestive of the fact he wouldn't really do it. It was just his way of asserting himself. But there was so little telling with him, she hadn't dared refuse.

What should she look at now? The ceiling? Or darkness? Or—he rolled over—*him?*

"What…what about my skirt?"

"Hell, that's not my worry, is it? I got enough going on."

At least he didn't add *You think I want to do this?*

Without a word she dragged up her skirt as far as her thighs. This would have been so different had she not made these conditions.

She'd had to make these conditions. Already her heart kicked worse than a maddened horse. He hadn't even touched her yet. Nor was he going to, she reminded herself.

"You been busy with the cream under there?"

She wasn't about to admit to him, in her panic, she'd forgotten the necessary preparation.

"Your consideration is flattering. Last night's will suffice. After all, it's not as if it were used."

What was this? She had at least expected Flint Blackmoore to attempt to seduce her, no matter the terms of the contract, which he had burned anyway. Flint liked to prove a point. And that point was that no woman born was immune to him.

So the lazy smile, the little tease, the running of his deft hands over her body — these were the things she expected and was ready to resist. The things she was waiting for, with a certain *uncertain* abandon. But this man who simply undid the fastenings on his breeches…

"What?" He caught her staring. "You did say to touch you little as possible. I'm just doing what I'm told."

Flint? Snowballs would survive in hell.

She swallowed the thought. At least he must be erect. She could always count on him to be that if nothing else. She parted her legs. Oh, God, this was going to be basic, wasn't it? Unless, of course, he said, *Let me, sweetheart.* And then he…he…

He didn't. He didn't do anything. A pity she hadn't allowed a little contact. A kiss.

She couldn't. A kiss would have melted her. Even now.

She turned her face away. When he touched her, she must offer nothing. This was for the Beaumont heir. Money. Lady Margaret. But it wasn't all for that. The thought rose up and swamped her, and a betraying gasp escaped her. She doused the thought. She placed her palms against the silken bedspread to cool them.

"Fine. Then do it." She spoke as if she had lumps of ice in her mouth.

"Your skirt. You want to take that up? It's just, you did say."

"James…"

She bit her tongue. She was not going to lose her temper. She had not, so far as she could recall, said anything in the rules about her skirt and who would not have the right to touch it. But she did not want to display herself to him in this cold, clinical fashion.

"Of course." She forced her lips to curve. Although quite how they curved, when they seemed frozen in her face, she didn't understand.

"I won't look if that's your worry. Even if it's nothing I

haven't seen before."

"Are you enjoying this?"

"What? You want to write that in your terms, I'm not allowed to?"

"If I'd thought of it."

"You could be in trouble there if I don't. That's the fundamental difference between men and women. What you do about that is up to you. Though I'm guessing with that set of rules, enjoyment is off the menu."

Of course it was. But how like him to know so. *And* say so.

"Now. Hold steady, while I get on top."

The commentary was unnecessary. Every breath clogged her lungs.

"I think I said no talking."

"I'm just trying. You think you can move a little there?" He grunted. "Your legs, so I can get between them. You know, spread them or something?"

She bit back a shriek as he set his knee between her legs. How awful this was. But she could not make it any different. Awful or not, what flared, what betrayed her, as his knee brushed her bare leg, was enough to convince her she had done the right thing to protect herself.

He knelt between her legs, looking at her. "You all right there? You want me just to do it?"

She could not bear to turn her head. There would be no enjoyment in this for her. Enjoyment, after all he had done to her, would be the ultimate betrayal of herself. Yet, now the inevitable was upon her, the circumstances were such that she was shocked by her desire to change things. This man wasn't the Flint she knew.

"If you desire."

"I don't, sweetheart, but here goes anyway."

Exhaling sharply, he leaned forward on his elbow, and she

focused all her gaze, every particle of it, on the bedside table, hiding her alarm beneath an impressive façade. He fumbled his hand at the opening of his breeches.

"James." Her throat fluttered. "You—"

"Hush. I don't need the distraction." He skirted his fingers over her sex. "I mean, this is how you want it, right? I mean, I'm to—"

She stared harder. So much so, her eyes watered. The closeness. The feel of his breath on her cheek, her forehead. The warm scent of him. He panted as he spoke, in that way she remembered so well.

"I don't care. Just do it. With as little touching. Thank you."

He adjusted his weight, and she closed her eyes, her breath catching, as she felt him enter her.

"So, how's this?"

She felt the tension in his muscles.

"Am I touching you as little as possible?"

He reached over her and grasped the bed railing with one hand. "Hmm? You want me to go on?" His voice came from deep in his chest.

"Please."

"You're dry. Don't say I didn't warn you."

She didn't care. A little pain might be a good thing. A little pain might stop her heart pounding and her breath coming in shallow waves.

"See, I don't want you slapping me with a rule about that next."

"I won't. Please. I just want you to do it. As you promised."

How on earth was her voice so calm—a little faint perhaps—when she herself trembled from head to toe?

"Did I?"

Her insides tightened. But not because of what he said. Or the knowledge of what would be discomfort, if not pain, when he pushed inside her sensitive flesh. If only. No. It was the knowledge of being sex against sex like this. Of feeling his hardened flesh against her. Just like before.

As he grasped the bed rail tighter and thrust so she could feel every hard inch of him, she had to keep her fingers fisted on the bedcover for fear she'd raise them to his face and do something silly, like drag it down so her lips could meet his and she could immerse herself in the heat, the ecstasy, the passion she had known with this man.

The physical sensation of him inside her was too much. She had to master it. This was not old times. This was a business transaction. *Lady Margaret. Lady Margaret. Lady Margaret.*

"If you want me to do something about the fact you're dry as dust, say so. But don't say I never warned you about the cream."

"It's fine. Pray continue."

Pray? She would like to. She would like to pray to…*Lady Margaret.* England, they said, was very nice at this time of year. Full of daisies. And the thing—the awful thing was he'd no sooner thrust than her discomfort eased. How was that?

"Silently." Although he hadn't opened his mouth, she felt obliged to remind him.

She reddened at the telltale moisture between her legs, as if she wanted him. She didn't want him. She couldn't afford to want him. Mindless copulation was all she sought to father the Beaumont heir. Her body could lie all it liked. Her mind knew what was required.

But he was exactly as she remembered. Except he'd not set a rhythm yet. She fisted her hands tighter on the silken damask. She'd rather he didn't wait. She shifted on the bedspread, a tingling sensation in her blood.

"Don't worry, I'll be silent and quick as I can."

She smothered the words *No, you don't have to.*

"I just don't want to touch you more than is *humanly* possible."

"Perhaps if you used both your hands?"

"Hmm? You mean you want me to—"

She jerked her eyes open. "To grasp the bedrail, that is."

Had she said that? She ground her teeth. Of course she had. And she'd said it to protect herself. She'd never thought it would be as awful, as basic, as this. Or that what would rise would be so primitive. Flint hadn't kissed her. He hadn't, beyond that brief sensation of his cool fingers against her skin, touched her. Yet some animal part of herself stirred. She tightened her muscles against it.

"I'm doing my best."

He was. And so was she, to bite back everything that flooded her mind. She closed her eyes again in a frantic bid to remember how this had been with Thomas. At that moment Flint embedded himself so deep, her body teetered on the edge. Telltale tingles, too delicious, too pronounced to ignore, spiked her center. It might be fine now to take that warm, wanton pleasure, but how would she feel afterward?

She felt him reach fulfillment. No, she would *not* let herself. She braced, holding her breath till she feared her lungs would burst. It was over. Thank God.

For a long moment she lay, trying to collect her shattered thoughts and drag some air into her parched lungs, trying to keep her face averted. How it had been for him, copulating with a woman he didn't even like, wasn't something she wished to consider.

Loosening his hold of the bedrail, he pulled out. The movement sent warm ripples cascading through her. Pleasure bubbled, to her mortification. In a panic, she jerked upright.

"What do you think you're doing?"

"What do you think I'm doing? I'm getting up." Under no

circumstances would she consider what she quashed — *pleasure*. Under even less would she let him believe he had, in any way, pleasured her. "I want to… My leg has a cramp. I just need — *ouch* — I need to stand."

"Fine. But you do that and you'll have to do it all again."

"I'm sorry?"

She couldn't do it all again. Not without setting some very stringent conditions on it first. Were there any left? She jerked her head around to meet his gaze. She didn't want him knowing she didn't have cramp either.

"Me too, sweetheart. And you might say I'm not for it right now. Later." He cut her off as her lips parted. A bargain was a bargain after all. "Now, you want that heir, you lie down."

He reached toward her, a study in rumpled sexuality. His shirt cascaded over his breeches, which somehow adhered, just, to his narrow hips. Nothing, yet everything on display.

"I don't see what business — "

"Didn't your ma teach you anything? Or wasn't she around long enough?"

"Let's leave my mother out of this, shall we? This has nothing to do with her, or indeed, with you."

"Fine. But you want to be one yourself, you need to give things time to settle."

The fine hair stood up on the back of her neck.

"You haven't the faintest notion what I'm talking about, do you?"

A huff of breath escaped her. The faintest notion? He was the one who didn't have that.

Mastering the thought, she lowered her gaze. She had only to observe how spectacularly she had ruined this so far to know, if he had something to impart, some knowledge, the gist of which she could actually guess, she should govern her fury and pretend to listen.

It wasn't as if she wanted to sleep with him.

"My mother died when I was four." A blush crept up her cheek. God rest her, if she saw the lengths Fury had gone to, the straits she was in, it was probably as well. "You're meaning I should lie down if I want to conceive?"

"Absolutely. I couldn't put it better. You're a married woman. How come you don't know these things?"

"How come you do?"

"Because I been halfway 'round the Caribbean. But maybe that's why you and old Tommie had a problem."

Old Tommie? Governing her fury was going to take a bit of doing. Her voice lashed out as a hissing snap. "Thomas, which is what you will call him, was a year younger than you."

"Younger?"

He raised his eyebrows, and his voice rose on the word. No doubt he thought living with her must have put years on Thomas, aging him beyond recognition.

"He was twenty-nine. Why does that surprise you?"

Flint shrugged.

"Illness had, of course, wreaked havoc on him."

"Tommie was ill?"

A horrified furrow dented the bridge of his nose. Now he was going to accuse her of poisoning him, wasn't he? But he did, just possibly, have a point about the conception. She had not been able to lie down with Thomas, not since he had become ill and his physical cruelties had been things she needed to escape.

Although quite how the blazes *he* could know, a man like Flint, who didn't care where he spilled his seed, was beyond her comprehension.

"He was very ill." She swiveled her legs back onto the bed. "Especially by the time I had finished with him."

Flint shifted, uncomfortable. That was to be expected. But

the thing with Fury Fontanelli was, you never knew. The Lord couldn't have been harder on Moses. She might as well have added *Thou shalt not shag* to those stone tablets she'd hammered him with.

And what had he just gone and done? Screwed her.

It wasn't even like it was a good screw. In fact, lousy was the word for it. And he hadn't had a screw in months. Months and months. It was something else that had been denied him.

"Here." He stuck a cushion under her feet. "You should keep them raised."

He blamed the bed for the fact he'd screwed her instead of scarpering. It was the one welcoming thing in this whole damned place.

"My feet?"

"No. Your legs."

But it would have been just his luck to get caught flogging her candlesticks. Also these damned jewels of hers looked paste, even if they gleamed around her neck. He'd know for certain if he bit one. But so far, she hadn't let him near enough to sink his teeth into anything.

He'd thought this would be simple. He'd thought — all right — he'd protested a bit about the screwing. Maybe he wasn't eager. But she opened her legs, and a woman was still a woman. Once he'd gotten in the swing, he reckoned he could do worse.

So it was a great shock him to realize he couldn't. This was as bad as it got.

He should never have risen to her bait. The baggage meant every word she'd said about rotting.

What the hell was she going to do if he kissed her? Or, for that matter, yanked her skirt up and touched her in places he remembered touching? Made her give him her body the way he wanted?

When he'd done that before, she had been his though, hadn't

she? It wasn't about that. It was about his damned boat. If he got in tugs with her, well, he'd just have to suffer the various cuts to his pride.

"There. That's the way you've got to lie."

She looked at him as if he were incapable of chivalry, although his generosity was motivated by purely altruistic intentions. All these terms and conditions and the length of time it might take to make this baby. He wasn't hanging around *that* long, putting up with it. Putting up with her. He would get this over with fast. If not today, then tomorrow, provided he hung about that long. He might still see what was worth plundering and scarper.

"James, I...*I*..."

Did she think he was just low enough to attempt to maneuver her into some fancy position? Where he could screw her better? Not for all the boats in the Caribbean.

"Trust me. What do you think I'm doing here? Trying to get my way with you?"

She bit her lip. "To be truthful, I don't know."

"What do I need to do that for, when I'll be getting more of it later?" Lucky him.

"I didn't. It just seems...you know a lot."

The blush that spread across her face—even that first time, when he'd informed her how he knew she wasn't Celie (and if anyone was bound to know she wasn't, it was him) she hadn't blushed like that. He was sure he'd remember. It was almost infectious. Enough to drive the thought she probably suspected he planned on escaping from his head.

"I don't say I know it all, but I do know some stuff about this."

"W-what? James, that's—"

"You got to lie down with your legs raised. Give the seed a chance to plant. It's what you want isn't it?"

"It...it is. Yes. But I—I just don't know how you can know. I didn't think it ever bothered you whether your seeds got planted or not."

"I'm a man. Long as I didn't get the clap was as much as I worried about."

He trailed off at the indignation brimming in her eyes. All right, maybe that wasn't the thing to say right now. But it was true. So long as he didn't get it, what did anything else matter?

The thing was he'd never quite understood what it was about Fury Fontanelli. In seven years he had not thought of her, at all. Except perhaps now and again—he wouldn't say it was more than that—that little moment when he dumped her on Fishside Wharf.

Oh, and just maybe occasionally, like once, twice a year—he wouldn't say it was more than that either—the first time he'd glimpsed her, standing at the rail of the *Calypso*. In Celie's frock. At least, he hadn't known it was Celie's frock. Only that Celie had one just like it he'd given her from some French frigate he'd plundered.

Because his attention had been riveted straight off by the knowledge that it clung a hell of a lot tighter to this woman's breasts and hips than it had to Celie's.

Then he had been riveted by the fact that his first mate, Black Hawk Dawkins, said she had put it around half the crew that she *was* Celie. Celie, who was dead—information he got from Fury eventually after he'd threatened to make her walk the plank in Celie's pretty shoes, a mile out to sea.

Though quite how she died or how Fury had come by Celie's trunk, her clothes, her identity, he didn't ask. Such interest would have shown Celie meant something. The handful that Fury was though, he'd had suspicions.

He had wanted revenge for Celie. Hell, how was he meant to spend a voyage with no woman in his bed, warming his nights—and his days? And every other moment it needed warming? But even then, even now, he knew, Fury threatened him on some bone-deep level.

It had disturbed him, when it had been meant to be revenge for Celie, that he should enjoy it so much. Not the revenge. *Her.* Fury Fontanelli. Of course he had needed to keep her at arm's length. He always did with specimens he didn't understand. And he had made damn sure, though she warmed his bed, it was all she had warmed. Women and boats didn't mix. Not permanently.

There was always a port with some harlot in it. One he could kiss goodbye to. Although harlots carried risks. Like clap.

"I don't have it by the way. In case you're worried about this heir. Leastways, I reckon I'd know about it by now if I did have it."

Her green eyes glinted in the shaded light. "How refreshing to know. For a second there I thought you were going to surprise me."

"Me, sweetheart? This cushion, isn't it a surprise?"

"If you stuck it over your face, perhaps."

"*My* face?"

What the hell had he gone and said that was wrong now? Until he'd come in here he hadn't realized it was possible for him to say anything that was.

Even as he opened his mouth to say *Your face is as good a resting place as any*, he gravitated back to her troubled gaze. And his tongue froze. His eyes too. He'd never been more conscious of staring at a woman right on the edge. Maybe she hated him. But she needed him. And if he walked out that would leave her stranded.

Maybe it was as well it was a lousy screw. A halfway decent screw with her could conflict him. It wasn't all down to what she had in that cellar that made him unwilling. Gut instinct was whispering *Don't.*

"Don't you worry about what you might give me."

"Well, I'm—"

"Not? So?" She shifted in a rustle of silk. "How long am I meant to lie here?"

Listening to his insults? He could be mean, couldn't he? Suppose too, he sat her here while he rifled the house. Except the way she looked...

"I don't know. Ma always said—"

"*Ma?* What is this, old wives tales now? Next you'll be telling me that if you'd kept your boots on or I stood on my hands in the washbasin there, it would be a boy. *Ma.* Excuse me, I'm getting—"

"She was a midwife—before she was a whore." Her stillness made him wish he hadn't admitted that.

She had always thought, as had everyone else, he was just a dirt-poor farm boy from Savannah. Because that was as much as he let them think.

"You never said—"

With difficulty he bared his teeth. It wasn't that he was ashamed. It wasn't that nothing he'd done had ever been enough to outrun the humbleness of his birth and his childhood. It wasn't even that he'd somehow parted with this miserable fact. It was that her eyes studied him as if she felt his pain with a sick certainty. Her brows knitted, her lips parted...

It was vital her lips didn't, that he re-erect the barrier, close the tiny rift that had somehow opened in his chest. The one that seemed to point the way to him not running out on her.

"You could say she knew her stuff. And I just hope it's something you've thought about. But maybe you've not."

"Thought about what?"

"Married woman who doesn't know about lying down and things? Probably not."

"What are you talking about?"

He didn't know. But he didn't want her to know he didn't know. He'd only spoken to mask his discomfort. And now, now he needed to come up with something.

"Thought about if it's a girl. I mean anything's possible in this crackpot scheme you got here."

"I didn't notice you thinking so last night, when you blackmailed me into it. But for your information, Lady Margaret did not specify as such."

"What? Doesn't she care?"

"A girl could not succeed to the actual title. But, so long as I provide a child from a confirmed pregnancy, there is nothing Lady Margaret can do about the inheritance. Beggars cannot be choosers."

"You mean yourself or Lady Margaret here?"

"A boy would, of course, guarantee things." She paused. "You know about such things do you?"

The glance she slanted him from beneath her sooty lashes said as much as he needed to know about her thoughts.

He rose to his feet. "What things, sweetheart?"

"You know. How to conceive a boy."

He shrugged, helping himself to a piece of bread. "Maybe. Maybe not." He paused. His boat wasn't even a speck on the horizon. He didn't have a thread in his pocket. Never mind a lire. If he was going to stay, maybe it wasn't so bad revealing what he just had. "I'm sure Ma told me a thing or two. Provided I can remember it all."

A strange sound emanated from her throat. He considered he'd risen a notch. Now she might elevate him to the Blue Chamber. Or maybe even a renegotiation of that ball-breaking contract of hers.

As he wiped crumbs off his mouth, he swore he could even hear her mind whirring.

"Can I trust you?"

"Trust me?" What a stupid question. Of course she couldn't. He stuffed the remains of the hunk of bread in his mouth.

"Not to run away."

"Me?" He tried to sound surprised. Despite all the surprises he'd had since he pried the lid off that box in her cellar, it was actually far harder than he imagined. "And leave you?"

If he didn't know any better, he'd swear she'd made up that contract on the spot without the least thought about the realities of its execution. Simple things like where he was going to go between their sessions. His gaze skirted her face.

She had, hadn't she?

After all, he hadn't imagined the business of her staring at the nymphs frolicking on the ceiling half the night.

"Hmm. I do, of course, want to be fair to you when you are doing so much to oblige me." Her soft red lips, which he found he could not take his eyes off, parted before he could even start protesting. "But I don't want you making off with the candlesticks. Because Signor Santa-Rosa would be most displeased."

"That would make two of us." If she explained Captain Flint had stolen them, certainly. "What kind of person do you think I am?"

"A pirate."

He bit off another mouthful of bread. He'd passed himself off as the cabin boy when he had been captured. A trifle fanciful for a man of thirty, but there it was. To save his skin he'd have passed himself off as the Queen of Sheba. Or one of her fancy wall hangings there. Anything.

But now, if it came out he wasn't a cabin boy, he'd hang. And despite finding life impossible and degrading in the months since his capture, he wasn't ready to leave it yet.

"*If* I can trust you, and it is very much an *if*—" She took on that refined voice she'd somehow cultivated. "Then you may have the Blue Chamber."

"I may? The Blue Chamber?"

"It's a nice room, as you will have seen. You may use it freely."

Rules thirteen and fourteen, no doubt. Amazing what the assumption of a little knowledge did for people. He swallowed the hunk of bread in his mouth. "That's mighty nice of you."

"Yes. Susan will serve you your meals."

"I look forward to it. I'm 'specially fond of callaloo and goat."

"Goat?"

"Plenty of them running about the hillsides. You just get Susan or some of your men up there to catch them."

"Susan? Or—" She tightened her dropping jaw. "If you want a goat you must catch it and kill it yourself."

Right.

"Any steak will do. I'm not fussy. Chicken too. Oh, and rum. Heaps of it. Tell you what, why don't I give her a list?"

Why the hell had her jaw dropped like that? So far, a bread roll and a handful of grapes was a starvation diet for a man being asked to do what she expected of him. Twice a day was nothing. But to order? When she didn't even want him?

He'd thought Ma's knowledge would guarantee more than the Blue Chamber.

"It's up to you. Chicken and rum are good for a man, an awful lot better than bread and coffee when he's—well, you know—got to get with his lady twice a day, to become a daddy."

Her face turned green as though she were in the throes of morning sickness already. A daddy. His heart gave a thump. He supposed he hadn't thought about it himself. But if his seed took he would be. And she…she would be the mother. God help the Sheltons.

"Yes. Yes, of course. I will speak to Susan about that. Although rum, in Genoa, might prove a little difficult to come by."

He stared, his gaze impassive. The more he thought about this, it was a battle he would win. She was rich, right? "Seaport, isn't it?"

"Of course."

"Let me speak to her. Save you getting up."

"I —"

What? Did she think he wasn't to be trusted with *Susan*? Or was it the candlesticks, the silver, all the other articles of finery she'd got stashed around here?

"No, no, Fury. You lie here. You're going to be the mother of the heir. I can't have you running around after me."

"Fine." She clenched her fists.

Giving into him nearly killed her. But that was all right. Because she had given in. Although, for such an intelligent woman, he wondered at her believing him. Especially the stuff about the chicken and the rum.

"When do you want me back here?"

"This evening. I'll send Susan."

* * *

Fury waited till she heard what she hoped was the Blue Chamber door shut before rising from the bed. The last thing she wanted was Flint prowling the villa. The second last actually. The last was Flint handing Susan a list of all his requirements.

Maybe she was playing this all wrong. Maybe she should have chosen Signor Santa-Rosa to father the Beaumont heir. He was pushing sixty but it would take more than the pawning of a pair of his candlesticks to keep Flint in sustenance, now he'd regained his taste for the high life. And had her just where he wanted her.

She swallowed a mouthful of stone-cold coffee. A little knowledge was a dangerous thing. She wanted to believe otherwise, but would even he stoop so low as to make up that story about his mother?

No, in that second she had seen a different Flint. The boy, not the man. Vulnerable. Uncertain. And that was the most frightening thing about the encounter, when she needed to face him again and the tightrope she walked, so high, so dazzling, had just become even more precarious.

She would need to plan their next encounter very, very carefully, if she did not want to plummet to earth.

Chapter Five

Fury dabbed another blotch of perfume on her wrists as someone knocked on her chamber door. She turned her head over her shoulder. "Come in."

Susan entered, but not before Fury heard her low chuckle and the rumble of a male voice.

"Madam, it's James."

Fury could see that. Her most loyal servant. A woman of fifty. Two seconds in this man's company and look at her. Demolished. Not once, in all the years they'd known each other, had Fury ever seen Susan's eyes shine like that. Or seen her unable to take them off a man. Fury was willing to bet that cap was freshly laundered. The apron too. And since when did Susan tong her hair? Where had she even gotten the tongs?

Flint was a sexual tease, a flirt. He knew it too. A smile, a joke, a glance even, made women behave like dolts. Walking along a quayside with him was like ambling through a well-stocked brothel. How could she ever forget the looks, the suggestions from the dockside whores?

Had he ignored them? No. That would have been an ungallant thing for Flint, the great and inveterate womanizer, to do. He'd always tipped his hat and grinned. Even called them *Ladies*.

Fury had hoped to take Susan aside about Thomas. The cellar was the coolest place in the house, but in this hot weather decomposition would be rapid. To be truthful she began to think it might be better to bury him somewhere. A deserted hillside perhaps. She had already said he was visiting his father.

But now Susan had fallen victim to the Flint curse, and Fury could forget all that.

"Fury."

How could he make her name sound the same as when he had addressed those dockside whores? Why, he even had the temerity to grin. If he had a hat, she believed he'd tip it.

She tilted her chin and glared, the temperature of her voice sinking several notches. "James."

She set the bottle of perfume back on the dressing table. At least he hadn't bolted and she wasn't required to dig him out of some harbor-front drinking den. It was something, she supposed. It would be terrible to be left alone here with only Thomas in the cellar for company. Artificial insemination with a corpse was something even she had never considered.

A pity. Moreover the child would be Thomas's. It might even resemble him instead of…

"Will you be requiring anything, madam?" Susan's voice jerked Fury from her unwelcome thoughts.

Fury shook her head, not trusting herself to speak.

"All right, then."

Susan glanced sideways at Flint as she headed out of the room. Maybe Fury had this wrong. Maybe she should just have let Susan conceive the heir. Except Susan was too old.

Besides Fury intended to present herself at Ravenhurst while pregnant. Lady Margaret would of course demand confirmation. Something to prove Fury hadn't stuffed a cushion up her skirt. Otherwise Fury would have done so and borrowed a foundling.

"So, James." The sharp ache in her wrists made her aware of

how tightly she clenched her fists. "Susan fetched you all your requirements? The callaloo would prove a little difficult."

His eyes glinted as if the callaloo wasn't the only thing. Fury felt her hackles rise. In planning this second encounter she had wracked her already beaten brain. How could she make it more uninspiring than she already had, when, despite the conditions she'd set and the awfulness of the encounter itself, he had almost moved her to ecstasy?

Of course, he had taken her somewhat by surprise.

She unclenched her fists and folded her hands together. The pose looked cool, sophisticated, but she knew that most of all, when she had practiced in the mirror earlier, it had looked controlled.

"We must get you something better to wear. Your clothes are so *shabby*." This next encounter might go more smoothly, but a little denigration, when he hated to be denigrated, was no bad thing.

"Is this since I'm going to be wearing them a lot?"

He may have ambled into the room, but he'd taken up an unwilling stance between the bed and the fireplace since. Perhaps he was waiting to be told to take a chair? Only with Flint, if she said that, the chances were he'd be straight out the front door after it.

Better to let him stand there, although it was quite unlike him not to make himself at home.

She sighed. "Wearing them a lot? It has nothing to do with that, James."

"You know my name is Flint."

"Of course I do. But whether I can call you by it is another matter."

She swept across the floor and sat down on the bed. As with the business of the pose, the movement had been rehearsed several times.

Flint may have blackmailed her, he may have protested about the terms she had set, but what had he done really? The old Flint would never have stood for her tossing her head at him like this. He would have seized her and he'd have kissed her. Then he'd have *gotten to it.*

This new Flint, although not as docile as she'd have liked, at least created spaces. He knew something of distance. Why fear a man she could dominate? No. What she feared here was herself.

She reached down and removed her slippers. She had dressed for the encounter in a simple cotton nightdress and velvet robe. No jewels. No encumbrances. Not even her wedding band. No stockings. Everything plain. A little perfume to cool her wrists and forehead. No more.

Her other necessary precaution had been taken. This afternoon she had even rehearsed the removal of the robe and the arrangement of the nightdress. Never again would she be at his mercy, wondering what to do with such a simple thing as her hands. After setting her slippers to the side, she reached for the hooks of her gown.

Without looking, she sensed him shift around the room.

He cleared his throat. "Same terms apply, do they?"

She raised her chin. "I think we dealt with your half of the bargain adequately. Should you desire another bath, there is already plenty of water in the kitchen. And as you've already eaten, you can't be hungry." She peeled off her robe. "Unless, of course, you have some new conditions? Although I'm sure you know yourself, being a privateer, these should have been agreed last time around. Now…"

Swiveling, she raised her legs onto the bed. Earlier, when she had rehearsed it, this was the bit that had caused her knees to shake and her legs to falter. Now she did it without a hitch.

"Glad I taught you something, sweetheart."

"You taught me lots." She was even able to adjust the pillow height without fumbling, so often had she done it this afternoon. After punching it to make sure it was comfortable, she lay down. "Now, if you'd like to come over here."

"That's one hell of an offer. The trouble is I'm not sure I do."

She should have known he would take that as an entendre. But, unlike this morning, unlike last night, she'd had the opportunity to don her armor.

She had two ways of dealing with a threat. She could cower in fear of what it might do to her, or she could step out and face it. She had chosen the latter.

"When you are ready, that is. Your comment last night was probably entirely justified."

"What comment was this?"

"I realize, after some consideration, that no man is a performing seal. Not even one like you. If I was peremptory, forgive me. But, I was surprised and overwhelmed by your offer, to say the least. Now…"

Drawing a breath she placed her hands by her sides. Then she closed her eyes. When she thought about this morning, when she thought about how nervous she had been, this was altogether different. She would not even blanch when she felt him raise her nightdress.

"Any reason you're lying there like that?"

As if he didn't know. Fortunately she was even prepared for him to try and undermine her.

"What do you think? For you to fulfill your part of the bargain."

"Hang on."

He ambled across the floor in the direction of — the lacquered cabinet? It was hard to tell when she refused to open an eye. But what she could tell was that it was away from her.

So she did open an eye and saw him examining the contents of the fruit bowl. She resisted saying a word. Even when he dusted an apple on his shirt. Instead she closed her eyes and listened to him making an incision.

It would be a lie to say she was pleased. However, if for some strange reason, he required to eat an apple to get himself aroused, was it any concern of hers? She thought not. So long as he did not expect her to arouse him.

"You want me over there?" He spoke with his mouth full.

"When you are ready. Obviously the readier you are, the sooner the encounter can begin. The sooner it begins, the sooner it will end. I'm not a complete fool. I realize a simple in and out is not always possible."

"That depends. See, for some men that's as much as they're capable of. While some men got a lady who gets them so fired—"

"James."

"Fine. But you want me over there you're going to have to do something."

"We agreed. I have made my conditions plain. I am doing nothing."

"Maybe that's so, but you want the heir, you're going to have to get on top."

"*What?*"

Although she believed she'd misheard, she still thanked God she was lying down.

"You're going to have to get on top."

It wasn't the response she expected. Shocked disbelief juddered through her. She fought to keep her voice calm.

"Me?"

"What's the problem with it?" He stood chewing. "There was nothing in that contract of yours specifying anything about that. Not far as I remember anyway. But maybe I'm wrong. Now, shove over."

She jerked upright. "Just so you know, I am not getting on

top."

He took a step toward her and she almost leaped off the bed. It took every shred of her self-control to remain where she sat. He looked so much taller all of a sudden, and the power he exuded made her aware of her own lack. He curled his mouth into a sardonic smile.

"You want that heir, you will."

Her throat dried. She had misjudged him. "Whether it was specified or not, you cannot expect me..." She cursed, but then rallied. "I said I would not touch you."

"I'm not asking you to touch me. I'm asking you to get on top."

"But if I get on top, I will be... You know what that will be like."

His expression didn't change, but a man of his experience must know she was appealing to him. What he meant was unmistakable—for her to do all the work. And she couldn't do all the work. It was too intimate. But she hadn't specified, because she hadn't expected him to find such a vile loophole. After the afternoon she'd spent planning every single aspect of this encounter to protect her inner core from further intrusion, it didn't seem possible.

It was difficult, the horror his words engendered, to speak through her frozen lips. "Whether it was in the agreement or not—"

"Yeah, yeah. So you've said already." Ignoring her protestations, he dragged his shirt free of his breeches. "Excuse me while I just make myself comfortable."

"I am not doing it."

"That's a pity." He assessed her in that deceptively lazy fashion, as if he were really sorry about all this. "You don't have a lot of choice, you want that heir."

"I do." She gulped and cursed herself for gulping. Damn

him. "I want that heir, and I do have a lot of choices. One is that you will leave here. You will do so now."

He plunked himself down on the other side of the bed and removed his boots with a deep sigh. The kind that didn't fool her in the least into thinking the man was nothing less than dangerous.

"But I thought I was to be at your disposal? Are you telling me I'm not?"

"Exclusively. But not in this manner. If you are to be at my disposal, then you will do as I say."

She extracted the words from some deep inner part of herself, some part she had always marveled at, and now she came to think of it, he had never liked. Yet she knew, by the whole lazy way he settled himself down, he wasn't listening to a word she said.

"That's a pity. Did I tell you what a comfy bed you have here?"

Though the bed was comfortable, that wasn't the reason he now spread himself out, sticking his hands behind his head with a long, contemplative sigh, and crossed his ankles.

She should have realized he'd strike back and would go on doing so, until he was in charge of the encounter. How could she let him be in charge? It wasn't simply the thought of how he might humiliate her. The memory flashed of her on that quay. She could never go to that place again. Never.

"If it is the bed you desire, I will wait in the Blue Chamber until you are of a mind to comport yourself as we agreed."

"Door's there, sweetheart."

"I'm not going to kiss you, or touch you, or do any of the things you seem to think will make this encounter *pleasanter*." She didn't say, *like old times*. "Like taking my clothes off or letting you remove yours. No. This will be straight sex or nothing. Now, you may tell anybody what you like. About me.

Or Thomas. At the end of the day, I may hang. But you are a servant. And you will go back to being a servant—"

"Kiss me? And take your clothes off? Who said anything about that?" A slow grin spread across his face.

"Not if you paid me. Not if—"

"Paying you? Count your stars I don't have no money. You know what that would make you?"

Her fists clenched at his sheer, barefaced audacity. No matter how she kept her voice low, no matter how she didn't snarl, she started to unravel. Didn't she? Because no matter the lowness of his suggestion, it was only a suggestion. He wasn't forcing her. All she had needed to do was refuse. Instead she'd gone up like a rocket. Raking over the rules in a way guaranteed to let him see she feared breaking them.

She had to be careful in her determination not to be that girl, the one he had been able to take such a loan of, to treat like a fool. But she must ensure that determination didn't make her do just that.

It wasn't just about being that girl. It was about control. Something he enjoyed and she would rather rot in hell than give him. But there were reasons, too many to ignore, why she couldn't rot in hell.

Her gaze lowered, seeking to look anywhere but into his. As ever his gibes were cheap. She had slept with him, but it didn't make her a dockside whore.

"It doesn't make me anything. Because that's not how this is going to be."

"Glad to hear it." His lazy gaze flicked over her. "Because then you'd have to be worth it."

No, she would not rise to this. Even if the blood rose like a wave in her ears and she clenched her fists. She should know from old. It was what he wanted. Insulting her. Cutting her. It wasn't anything new.

Maybe for that matter, he hoped for it. For her to prove she was worth it. She had no need of descending to common little contests. She *knew* she was.

"May I remind you, in some ways I am paying you—"

"About that. See, you didn't specify just what you are pay—"

"*And* the clock is ticking."

"I can just get to it same as this morning, if you want. Though clock's ticking and that, and you want a boy…"

If she wanted a boy… She bit her bottom lip. Why, she'd never heard of such a thing. Did he think she was fool enough to fall for some old wives' tale? But she did want this over and she must be careful not to dismiss because she had presumed.

There was also the matter of her own reaction. It would demonstrate to him his shabby attempt to gain control by turning things on their head meant nothing. And she would, she would be in control, instead of worrying herself senseless about him trying to seduce her.

"Go on."

"I don't know. All I know is I heard it. From Ma."

"And she would know about this, would she?"

It was a stupid question to ask about a whore and a midwife. Was Fury going to let her disquiet about Flint stop her doing this?

"Where do you think she got me?"

"Very well." She endeavored not to speak through her teeth, although there was no denying she cringed. "Then we shall do it that way."

He deepened his smile. "I'm glad you see sense."

He was desperate to enjoy her humiliation. Only her pride made it possible for her to keep her expression neutral as she sat up.

"So long as you do not expect me to touch you or tell me it is necessary to look at your face to make this a boy. I will be looking at the wall."

She hardly cared how unpleasant the words sounded. This nightmare that trapped her was endless. And she still had Thomas's disposal to consider.

Assuming an air of confidence, she grasped her nightdress as if to lift it. "Well?"

"Hang on a moment, sweetheart."

His astonishment didn't fool her. She waited, with as much calmness as she could muster, while he located the buttons of his breeches. She had planned this encounter to the letter and now, in taking control, she would not allow her mask to slip for a second.

She was the wind in full sail, to use a seagoing analogy. She would do this. Even if her stomach churned with nerves and her throat had dried.

"Just you tell me when you're ready, although I'm assuming that you are."

She met his eyes with cool deliberation. Ever since she'd glimpsed him striding on board the *Calypso* — Captain Blackmoore, not Captain Flint, in his black tricorne and plain-cut coat — he'd disturbed her. This was one occasion he wasn't disturbing her.

Flint narrowed his blue eyes, staring at her. Oh, the duel had begun. Except this wasn't a duel. This was to conceive the Beaumont heir. So he could stare as he unbuttoned himself with deliberate slowness as much as he liked. So long as he unbuttoned himself.

"There we go. You want me to — "

"We agreed I would not touch you. So I think you will." Her throat was so dry she wondered she could speak at all. It was, however, amazing what one could do when the occasion demanded it. "I'll just — " She clasped her nightdress and rose on her knees. "You know…"

Edging her knee across his hips, she straddled him. "You just hold yourself still. If you don't mind, that is."

He loosened his breeches and held himself with one hand. His thumb brushed against the back of her thigh as she positioned herself with as much decorum as she could. He could have spared her this. But she was not looking for that now. Raising her chin she fixed her gaze on the pale oval of Messalina's face, visible opposite her in the flickering candlelight.

Flint shifted beneath her. "I found grasping the bedrail helpful. Since I wasn't allowed to touch you."

"Thank you, but I think I gave you the advice."

So long as she got through this with her inner self intact. "But first, if you will just give me a minute?"

She couldn't believe how cool she sounded as she braced herself up on her knees. This coupling was cold though. Why not be so herself? Yet she wondered, would another man hold himself so hard in the circumstances? Of course Flint had considerable sexual needs. And he'd no doubt been without since he was captured. Was it so miraculous?

She edged down. "Just tell me, if I'm not right."

"You said I was to touch you little as possible."

She looked at him for a second through downcast lashes. Damn him. She was going to have to use her fingers just to make sure he didn't hurt her. But the knowledge of his unhelpfulness gave her the impetus to press herself through her gown. Then she sucked a breath and edged down further.

The feel...the feel was like drowning...in a tub of icy cold water, the lack of air in her lungs. All the time she stared at Messalina, horrified, dismayed. Oh God. Why hadn't she let him kiss her?

"There." Her breath was unsteady.

"Sure it is, sweetheart. But you want to just get going." It wasn't a question. "You don't satisfy me, it's going to be a waste of time."

"Of course." Her skin tightened. That was why she hadn't let him. Damn him. Did he think she didn't see exactly the kind of bid for mastery this was? "Is that a threat?"

"It's what it is. A man needs to be satisfied."

And so far she wasn't doing very well. Were those the words he omitted? The reason he now folded his hands on his chest as if he were in church, praying?

She grasped the bedrail. Had her mind really whispered *Lady Margaret* this morning? *James Flint Blackmoore. Pig. Pig. Complete. Absolute. Pig.* That was more appropriate.

"If you need to be satisfied, I suggest you try being quiet, or that's not going to happen."

"I will if you will. There is just one thing more though."

A miracle it was only one.

"And what's that?"

"You have to go all the way."

"Are you saying I haven't?" She gritted her teeth. The man was too frank. She had never had a discussion about the actual mechanics of sex with anyone. And what was he trying to imply? That she was hopeless?

She jerked upward, an uncontrolled spasm. The preparation she'd taken in private with the cream would still help her here. Her nerves were what she must master.

Flint had set her this task. If she proved inept, he'd know he'd won. The conception of the Beaumont heir wasn't about that. But the preservation of her inner self was. He didn't even like her. Was she going to make a fool of herself by showing she couldn't do this?

She began to move up and down, moving her hips. It was like being a whore, offering pleasure, taking none. Flint enjoyed whores—although, Fury had the feeling, they enjoyed him too.

She drew another breath into her suffocating lungs. So long as she didn't start thinking of the reasons whores enjoyed him, that was fine, because she knew, she knew from before, Flint wouldn't lie there like this. He'd touch, he'd kiss. He'd clasp her thighs.

Why did she remember so much, when she was meant to be thinking of the whores?

It made desire spike, and she didn't want it spiking. In desperation she jerked faster. Surely to God, he must be near breaking. But she daren't look to see whether his eyes glittered with arousal. Or he breathed more heavily than usual. Or groaned. She daren't do anything, except keep jerking up and down, trying to ignore the indignity of this. And if she asked him — not that it should matter when she knew her sexual prowess was nonexistent — he'd probably insult her.

Was he purposely holding off? Or did he do this to show her just what the previous encounter had been like?

In a panic she jerked upward and dislodged him.

"Easy, easy. You want to damage the merchandize?"

Raising her eyes to the ceiling, she attempted to reseat herself, her lungs so starved she could barely breathe. "I'm doing my best. It would help if you would."

"I did. I told you what to do."

"What do you think I'm...that I'm attempting anyway? You're not exactly..."

Could this get any worse? Had it even been as bad as this with Thomas? All those times that he couldn't. And he had hit her because of it.

"Exactly what?"

"You know fine what. It would help if you'd just — "

He rose off the bed. In the same moment his arms enfolded her. The breath jerked from her body as he flicked her over onto her back.

"Keep still."

This wasn't allowed. Not him holding her like this. His scent swimming in her head. Masculine. Soapy. Flint never wore scent. But he'd shaved, and the essence of citrus oil enveloped her, so powerful it stopped her breath.

"I—"

"Shh."

Her face, should she allow him to touch her face, even if his fingers were only headed for the bottom of the bed rail? Except he was inside her, so she was going to obey whatever instruction he gave her. Breathless, she lay with her face upturned, aware her lips were parted but no sound came. And her palm landed somehow on his back.

"I got this."

Her eyes widened. This was not how she imagined this encounter would be. She had not thought she would be held. She had not thought she would feel his body so close. She had not realized that feeling him inside her—fully inside her—his breath coming in controlled gasps, the longing, the need to clench him and feel pleasure bubble through her, would overwhelm her. That she'd need to fight so hard to stop herself. Right as she poised on the brink. The drive toward fulfillment almost overpowered her, because she hadn't been fulfilled and she couldn't let herself be. But *he had*…and that was all that mattered.

She was stunned.

He really had helped her there, hadn't he?

For a long time she lay, not moving, the ragged huff and mingle of their breaths all she could hear. And maybe, outside, faint laughter, drifting up to her window shutters. Laughter that belonged to another world. One where her nightdress wasn't rumpled around her thighs, trying to conceive the Beaumont heir.

"You—you all right there?" His voice rumbled against her forehead.

"I—"

He'd somehow won, hadn't he? She'd almost failed to satisfy him. If she didn't satisfy him she wouldn't conceive. When she considered every sexual encounter with him—not that she remembered them all, she'd need a longer life than this— there probably wasn't one so shaming. One he'd had to finish for her.

She tightened her throat. "Don't think I was very good."

As she sucked air into her fluttering lungs, she wished she wasn't stupid enough to say so. Especially to him, because the vulnerability she felt right now, where was there to go? She felt naked and foolish. But the words came out anyway.

"That's all right."

Had his voice been smug, had it been any of the things she knew so well—but it wasn't. It was weary, weary as she felt herself.

"Flint, I…" *Flint?* She prayed he hadn't heard that—in the deepest regions of her soul. Now he'd gloat and she could not bear it. "I would like to lie here." She was aware of each breath entering her lungs, as if it were being pushed there. "As you said, or maybe your Ma for that matter, it's a good idea."

In some respects, this was worse than when he had left her on that quay. When he hadn't wanted to know what she couldn't tell him. When she had believed he'd gone forever.

"Ma said it. Hell, you should know I don't know nothing."

Anything…for as long as she could remember, he'd have died before he said *nothing*. It had been what those lessons he'd taken when the *Calypso* docked in port had been about.

She closed her eyes tighter. If she opened them she'd glimpse too much. Maybe she hadn't known the reason for the effort that went into making James Flint Blackmoore.

She didn't want to.

One day she'd have everything she wanted. One day she wouldn't be standing on the tightrope, unable to take her next step because some man or other twanged it. Or the sun came out to dazzle her.

What he did here—well, of course he had finished things, was in no danger of not finishing things; it was his way of taking control. No doubt in the hope of touching her. Or worse, having her touch him.

So, if he thought she stiffened as he pulled himself free because he disgusted her, so much the better. When it came to touching, she had been close to doing just that. And more.

"But sure you should lie here."

"Yes. And I will."

"Till tomorrow morning then."

Tomorrow morning. She didn't need to look at the ceiling or the oval of Messalina's pale, traumatized face to know there were pertinent reasons she already dreaded it.

* * *

Get on top. Ambling along the corridor, Flint wondered how even his twisted mind could have conceived such a thing. Even by his own unexacting standard of lowness, he'd plumbed a whole new depth. He pushed open the door to the Blue Chamber. This place was nice. Not quite his taste. But comfortable.

He closed the door and poured a glass of rum from the bottle that now stood on the washstand. As if the best place for it was down the sink.

The saw of crickets, dwindling now the evening air had cooled, drifted through the slats in the shutters as he poured the glassful down his throat.

To be truthful, for what he'd done in there, he despised

himself. Maybe it was just the dynamics of the situation. Sex, but not. Maybe it was his hunger for a screw, a decent one, none of this *hands off, don't touch my tits or anything else for that matter* stuff. He still hadn't the faintest idea why something so simple — her, facing him in that soft robe, the candlelight playing about the tumble of black hair on her shoulders — should remind him of so damned much. His throat clenched even as he thought about it. Those days on the *Calypso*.

But much more than that resonated deep within him.

Flint had bedded enough women in his time to know. The hunger wasn't just for the taste of her succulent lips, of her sweet flesh against his own. It was for her to look into his eyes as she had then as if he were the only man in the world. As if he pleased her so completely, and not just in bed, she didn't want anything else. It had made him feel like King Flint.

Ridiculous. But never had he felt the passage of the years so acutely. The sheer rightness of that moment, when all the gloss and all the polish slid off. Gloss and polish had its uses, like when she faced down Malmesbury. But it was still nicer without it.

Then what did she do?

Spread out on that bed like he should fall to his knees and thank Christ for the miracle he witnessed there. Fury Fontanelli letting him board her. When she needed him and he could bring her down in a second with what lay in that cellar.

So, what did he do to retaliate?

Simple.

He sloshed another glassful and ambled to the upholstered chair. Even when she had messed up, and he had to step in, she was still something though. All right, maybe he'd grinned — any man would, when he fought not to gasp his pleasure beneath her — and that had put her off. Was it any wonder? Where the hell had she learned to move like that?

He would like to take the credit. She had been a virgin when she had boarded the *Calypso*. And she had remained that way for the first twenty-four hours they had been underway. It would be kidding himself though. He was no lover of renown. He just loved sex.

Once, he'd loved it with her.

Chapter Six

Acooling, citrus-scented breeze, just enough to stir the olive trees and mute the cicadas, fluttered across the lawn. Fury frowned, wishing she could enjoy the stroll when it was boiling indoors, but Malmesbury, damn him, was as encroaching as ever. She should have been preparing for her third attempt at conceiving the Beaumont heir, but he had appeared, large as life and twice as unpleasant, on her doorstep.

All it required was Lady Margaret turning up unannounced to finish this.

"Return him to you, when I have done?" She swung on her heel. "Yes, yes, but he's not finished. How can you think so?"

"I have left you alone with this—"

"Alone?" The barefaced cheek of the man. As if it had anything to do with him.

"Indeed. But, Fury, I should remind you we didn't discuss this the other evening."

Swallowing her ire, Fury walked on. The thick carpet of grass beneath her feet was pleasant if nothing else was.

"You, of all people, should know babies aren't made in a day." She raised her cheeks to the sun. "There's certainly enough information about the ones you made in my little black book."

"And I should remind you, I paid good money for him at a

slave auction. Do you know what he is?"

A bubble of laughter almost escaped her. Uncharacteristic, although harsh, at least. The words, *an arrogant swine of a man, an insufferable pig*, hovered on her lips. *A despicable cad* — who yet had saved the situation last night.

She pushed the thought away. "Oh, let me think — "

"He's a cabin boy."

"What?"

"Yes. Of some damnable pirate."

Fury blinked. "Flint?"

"Yes, that's the fellow's name. The scourge of the Caribbean, so I was told. And that is the scourge's cabin boy, James."

Cabin boy? But was it so surprising? It was just the thing Flint would do if he were cornered and there was no other way out. But not telling her, when he had the temerity to blackmail her, was another matter.

"Small wonder he's so good at cleaning shoe buckles." Malmesbury huffed out a small laugh. "Imagine the consequences if you messed that up on board the ship of a scourge. You'd probably be marooned on some deserted island in the middle of nowhere, made to walk the plank."

Indeed. "So this Flint was never caught?"

"How the blazes would I know what the blazes Flint was? Next you'll be telling me you knew the scurvy damned blackguard — "

Intimately.

" — and you sailed the Caribbean with him — "

Sort of.

" — and then he brought you to London, where you met Thomas."

Her gaze froze. To guess so much, if not quite everything...

"Me?" She shrugged. She tried to keep her expression neutral. If Malmesbury or any of the others knew, she would be back on that wharf, working it. If she were lucky. "I've heard of him, but that's all. In Jamaica, everyone had. His name was legendary. But, as you know yourself, Jamaica is a big place."

She hoped her voice didn't sound too distant. In truth she had heard of Flint. Everyone had. She'd just never met the notorious bastard until she had stepped on board the *Calypso*.

"I imagine there would be quite a reward for him. But that's of no importance to me."

No. But it was useful information just the same. No wonder Flint hadn't wanted her to tell Malmesbury and the others who he was. Flint was slippery all right. And whatever Malmesbury said, his tone spoke differently.

He would love to hunt down Flint. It was probably why he'd bought his supposed cabin boy. Probably why he beat him too. A complete waste. As if Flint would give away himself. You would have to kill him first.

Or was there more to this little conversation? Had Malmesbury, a complete stranger to mathematics, succeeded in placing two and two together, making four? A cabin boy? Flint was thirty.

Her heart skipped the tiniest fraction of a beat. Malmesbury must want his hands on that little book of hers really badly.

"And what if I don't return him?"

"What if you what?"

She turned, taking the time to arch her eyebrows in what she hoped was a gesture of perfect disdain. "Now, Lionel, I'm sure you heard. What if I choose to pay him for his services and his silence and then set him free?"

She might as well ask. It was always preferable to know exactly where one stood.

"After all, your main desire, so far as I can see anyway, is to mistreat him."

"Because he's a dog."

To her astonishment Malmesbury slammed his fist into his palm, although she didn't, by any manner of means, think the anger was as simple as that.

"He's an infidel who doesn't know his place." He paused to recollect himself, although the noise he made at the back of his throat and the way he spat the words were no less alarming than before. "I'm astonished you don't see it."

"Me?" Allowing a laugh to escape her, she placed a languid hand on her bodice. "Well, why should I? So long as he does what I'm paying for, I don't care what he is." Telling that lie she almost stumbled onto the path. "You know, I'm astonished by your words. I thought we had an agreement about him? About this?"

"Did we?"

She lowered her gaze. She didn't want to think so, because she had enough to worry her right now, but Malmesbury's behavior was so unnerving she could only take one thing from it. He liked her. Enough to wish he was in Flint's shoes.

She shivered in the bright sunlight. As if she could ever have bedded Malmesbury, with his thin, cruel mouth and desire to treat people like so many pieces of rubbish. It was something to thank Flint for.

Malmesbury leaned closer. "As you can see, I don't know if we had an agreement or not." He fisted his pudgy hands. "But I warn you—"

"Warn me?" She jerked her gaze upward. Disquiet might have stirred, but it was very important she faced this snake down, even if the business of facing him down over Flint was ludicrous. She could barely get Flint to stay around. Did Malmesbury think Flint would do it for him? "You know, I find that astonishing."

"You find that what you like."

Although she raked her brain, she did not think she had ever heard him snarl like that. Or seen spittle bead his jaw and his eyes bulge either.

"Then I shall. But I think you should know you are in no position to warn. Thomas would tell you that too."

"Thomas?"

This snarl was even more unexpected, unless someone had talked. She tilted her chin and spoke with perfect coolness, although her heart hammered.

"Yes. In his letter to me this morning, Thomas did say he hoped that whatever my choice was, you would remember certain things."

This was Malmesbury's chance. His opportunity if he knew what lay in that box in the cellar to tell her, in prayer book terms, or forever hold his peace. And the only way he could know, the only person who could have talked, was Flint.

Malmesbury's squat chin tilted to match her own. "Me, Fury?"

"Hmmm. Yes. You, Lionel." She used his name carefully. "Thomas was very specific. I could show you the letter, if you desire. But, given this unfortunate outburst, I should prefer it if you would go now."

"Go?"

"Yes. The gate's there. You realize—" He made a move toward her and she placed a hand on his chest. "I can't ask you into the villa. Why, think of how unseemly it would be."

"Unseemly? When you are bedding that blackguard?"

"For Thomas's sake and with his blessing." How she kept the blush from spreading to the roots of her hair, how she made herself appear dignified at all, was down to one thing. The knowledge she still had her book to protect her. After all, the years spent securing her false position had not been wasted.

"Your concern is touching. It is what this is about, isn't it? And I promise, I will let you know when I'm done with James.

He is your servant, after all. But at this time, don't you think that's my affair? Conceiving an heir with a complete stranger is difficult enough. A woman trying for a baby should not be subject to hassle."

* * *

Flint had listened to every single word between Fury and Malmesbury through the shutters in the Blue Chamber, but as he reached the foot of the stairs in time to see her enter the villa, he knew one thing. No way was he going to admit it.

"Fury."

She stiffened. She wasn't in the mood, now was she? For *it* or him. That was, she was even less in the mood than previously. It was saying a hell of a lot. Flint didn't think it was possible to be less in the mood than she'd been so far. It just went to show how wrong it was possible for a man to be.

"I will be there in a moment. I was just speaking to your employer. You heard it all, I presume?"

He could be truthful of course, but in that second self-preservation kicked in. She never said the word *former* after all. "No."

"No?" Her emerald eyes appraised him. "Then why are you out here? Out of your chamber, I mean."

It was a good question. Maybe she was genuinely astonished, after the rum and stuff she'd given him, to see him here. But he doubted it. Only with the greatest difficulty did she manage not to sound as if he were the biggest nuisance not just to wander the face of the earth but out of the Blue Chamber especially.

When he knew he could look after himself, why wish she never held the ace?

Because, when it came to mercy, no matter the rot he'd talked, he didn't want to be at hers. Anyone's. But hers most of all. There was nothing like a few licks with the whip and days of eating grit to make a man feel edgy.

"Well, James?"

"I smelled Thomas."

With Fury Fontanelli, surprise was always the best method of attack. Anyway, he was sure that if he went down to the cellar it would be no lie.

"And really," Flint said, "I think it's only a matter of time before Malmesbury and his lippy cronies—hell, the whole of Genoa does the same."

Like yesterday he somehow spoke without thinking. To save his skin. The outer shell. But now he had, why not save what lay beneath? The bone and essence that was himself. Reestablish his foothold? Make himself of use in other ways. So maybe she'd respect him. Even if he didn't give a damn about her respect and, probably, she didn't either.

"Fury, I know you've been busy, but haven't you thought about that?"

For all she gave a tiny start, not by any stretch of the imagination would he call it a flinch. A pity.

"Yes. I have." She tugged at the ribbons on her cherry-patterned sunbonnet. "I think I said to you I'd deal with it when the time comes."

"I'd say that time is now. Just take a breath."

"No, thank you." She endeavored to swish past him in a swirl of dove-gray skirts.

"A deep one. Go on. That's it. See."

Her mystified air didn't deter him. Not when it was his chance.

"You mean you don't smell it?"

"No, I don't. I don't smell anything."

"You don't?"

Yet was it his chance? Even the way she had come up the steps and into the house had been crooked. As if she had clung to the balustrade for support. Maybe she had faced Malmesbury down; the man was a slimy poke. Flint conceded—and all right, he loathed to—he hadn't just run down here for himself. He'd run down here for her. Laughable, when if ever there was a woman who could take care of herself it was this one.

"Maybe you've not been downwind of him. What lies have you told about his whereabouts?"

She wrinkled her brow. She laid the bonnet on a chair. "Lies?"

"These little things you're so good at. Where did you tell them he was? Because he's not here, is he?"

"I said he was visiting his father."

He didn't know what astonished him most, the fact she answered him, the fact she didn't tell him to quit it with the nose in her business, or that he persisted.

"Well, is this in heaven or what?"

"It could be anywhere." She shrugged.

"And Susan knows?"

"Susan knows everything." She turned to face him. "How do you think I got him down to the cellar?"

"That's all very well, but now we need to get him out of there again."

Her eyes glinted. Doubtless she was weighing placing herself in his debt as opposed to keeping him in hers.

"Us?"

It was going to be the latter, wasn't it? Him being kept in her debt. Wasn't that just dandy when he did this to help himself? He did, didn't he? After all, why help her when her contempt was plain? And yet, for himself would he be quite so passionate?

"Listen to me. Malmesbury's a dangerous man. You needn't think what dirty little secrets you possess in that book of yours will save you if he gets any wind of Thomas. He doesn't enjoy being thwarted."

"Don't you seem to know a lot about him?"

"You might say. I've seen him in action plenty. Unlike you."

"I know that. I just don't have a lot of choice. And at least I do have their secrets. It's better than having nothing. Now, if you will excuse me?"

Maybe it was the weary, yet unyielding, set of her shoulders. Maybe it was the proud tilt of her head. Or her eyes, steely, yet despairing. Whatever it was, she attempted to brush past him, and he caught her arm.

Immediately, he wished he hadn't. He was doing this to help himself. Not her, right? Yet the feel of her arm through the soft gray dress was a cool, silky echo of what he remembered. Something started up in him. Something ridiculously like longing. Something that made no sense when the conceiving of the Beaumont heir allowed him at regular intervals between her legs. Only with the greatest of difficulty did he force himself not to draw even closer, with what seemed to hover there for the briefest of seconds between them.

"You'll hang. You know that, don't you?"

"I—"

She parted her lips so he saw the cool darkness within. It was like staring at a heaven, the gates of which weren't just shut to him, but barred and bolted. He couldn't remember wanting a woman more. All of her. How did she do this to him? He just wanted…he just wanted his boat. And it wasn't as though she wanted him. Just his seed.

"What do you suggest?" She stared at his hand as if it were going to bite her.

"I bury him here."

She widened her eyes. "You can't." She shook her head. "It's Signor Santa-Rosa's villa. I told you yesterday about the candlesticks. You can't bury him in the garden. What if a dog or something finds it and digs it up again, thinking it's a bone?"

He tried to think. But her closeness clouded his mind. On board the *Calypso*, now, the sweat sitting along his skin, he'd just take her down to his cabin. A bit of impassioned kissing. A quick tumble. Then his thoughts were clear. But if he tried pulling her skirts up like that here—rule fifteen—no doubt, rule sixteen was she'd probably eviscerate him. Then—rule seventeen—he'd be in that cellar sharing that box with Thomas. It was large enough for two.

"Fine, but this business of you waiting till you conceive is the plum stupidest thing going. We got to deal with this now, before that smell gets worse. What if you can't ever conceive and that corpse rots while you're trying?"

"Hardly."

"How do you know?"

She swallowed and he grinned. He couldn't help it. The blush that crept up over her cheekbones. And the stiff, horrified, denying look she cast him, as if all this were a secret. The way she tightened her succulent mouth too. When she hadn't blushed to get someone to fill old Tommie's boots. What was going on here?

"You mean you and old Tommie, down there, already did?"

"I just—I mean that I can. That's all." She dragged her arm free as if he burnt her.

"All right." He rubbed the back of his neck. Why go where he wasn't welcome? Again? Although her reaction, even the way she froze, was intriguing. "That's just something I didn't know, when we set out here. Even so, you can't go keeping him here till it happens again. We need to get somewhere else. Then you get a load of stones, to bury in the cemetery. Or you just go home to England, burying nothing."

She tilted her chin, as though it pleased her to find him so enterprising. She was kindly welcome. If he'd known just how good it was going to make him feel, doing something altruistic, he'd have acquainted himself with it a lot sooner.

"I would need a funeral to convince Lady Margaret. She isn't going to believe I didn't do something to Thomas. And I'm not sure I can just bury a heap of stones. No, I think I'd need a corpse from somewhere."

Flint's first thought — so long as it wasn't himself — was overridden by his second. This was the longest, least rancorous conversation they'd had.

"Thomas was ill. That is known around here. Maybe just not how ill. He had a tumor. In his brain. Oh, for goodness sake, I didn't poison him if that's what you're thinking. He fell."

"Right."

"On...on the stairs there. Some kind of fit."

"Inconvenient."

Flint very much suspected the slow drain of color from her pretty heart-shaped face said Thomas hadn't just fallen on the stairs there. But so long as Flint didn't follow, he was prepared to help her on this. He just needed to think how.

"James, if you're going to—"

"I'm not anything. All right?" He sighed, feeling his hackles rise in response to the sting.

Here he was prepared to accept her story — why would even she be so stupid as to deliberately push Thomas when she needed the heir, after all? — and what did she do? Ignore his magnanimity, that's what. When he could see damn fine, the way she'd stared at these stairs, she'd done something. Did she think he was blind as well as stupid?

He swallowed his ire. "I'm just thinking how to help you get him out of here. I'll need a cart and a boat."

She jerked her chin up as if now he'd said something distasteful. "A boat?"

"I'm not meaning a fully rigged ship. A rowing one will do."

"But you in a boat..."

Him in a boat? What? Shouldn't Thomas, or rather what hadn't decomposed of him, be what she was thinking of *in the boat*, here? Not Flint.

"Yes, me in a boat. With Thomas. And I'll dump him far out at sea. Look, what's wrong with it?"

Her eyes darkened. "What do you think, seeing as you're so clever? Besides, where am I going to get a boat from exactly?"

He wanted to think the recalcitrance was because she thought he might drown. But no. She had to go and think the worst—he wanted that boat to escape. He couldn't believe it.

"There must be another way." She shot him a glance. "A way that doesn't involve boats."

"I'm going to escape? That what you think?"

"Right now, I don't know what to think. The offer is tempting. But yes." Raising her chin higher, she eyed him squarely. "Since you ask, I'd need to know I can trust you. And I don't know I can."

Wasn't that great, when he offered his services altruistically. For what was conceivably the first time in his life.

She really did think he was the lowest of the low, didn't she? Because he didn't think he was that transparent. Or maybe he just was. And she just did.

He gritted his teeth. Why the hell did he even need that foothold anyway? Staying here playing her damn silly games. What he had on her, he didn't need to protect her. Give his seed for a damned boat. He sure to hell wasn't that damaged polishing shoe buckles to the tune of a whip that he couldn't leave here now and just find one.

"Like I said, I was going to take Thomas out to sea. I'm sure it's preferable to him stinking up the cellar. But hell, that's up to you. It's no skin off my nose if you get caught."

What the hell did she want to keep him for, when her contempt was plain? What she thought he knew? Rub his nose in fly shit was more like it.

"Look at it this way, I don't come back, you get yourself someone else. Someone you don't need all these fancy terms and conditions with, because you got yourself that little book. Now, how damned hard is that?"

Well, of course it wasn't. Her head canted as though someone shone a beam of light across her thoughts. She was only ashamed she hadn't thought of it that way herself. Because there wasn't any other reason for her to look at him like that.

"Or maybe, sweetheart, you just want to keep me because you like me."

She parted her lips. "Let...let me think about it."

"You do that." He wasn't going to hold his breath. "I'll be waiting upstairs for your answer."

Even as Fury stood taut and motionless, watching him stride up the stairs two at a time, her mind screamed that she had no choice. He was right about everything. How could she be so foolish as to keep Thomas in the cellar any longer? She risked disease; she risked all kinds of things. But Flint had blackmailed her into choosing him. Had she known that truth, that he had been sold as his own damned cabin boy, would she have done it?

She swung on her heel and walked into the salon.

"Madam." Susan's feather duster clattered to the floor.

Fury didn't care Susan was there. What didn't Susan know? Anyway, without her coming to her rescue that day on the quay, Fury would have been in some mess.

"Don't mind me." Fury bit her lip. "I just need a moment. You heard all that, I suppose?"

"Well, it would have—"

"Been hard not to?"

Susan stooped down and grabbed the duster, snapping back

up again like a curtsey. "Madam, it seems a reasonable offer."

"Reasonable? Give you less to dust you mean."

"We'd have to pawn more than the candlesticks of course. But what choice do we have?"

Straight to the point as ever. At least Susan didn't lie to her. She couldn't bear another lie this morning, although Flint's lie was only to be expected.

Fury walked to the window and looked out at the faint breeze rustling the olive trees. She had loved the pretty view to start with. She had never seen anything like it in Jamaica or England. But somewhere all that had disappeared, and now it left her as soulless as everything else.

There was only one thing that didn't. And it seemed even that was being taken from her, in dribs and drabs, every time Flint touched her. Was it worth it? She had begun to question if there wasn't a simpler way to live. People didn't have to have everything. It wasn't that she did. But security was meat and drink to her.

"I'll have to pawn more. Let's not pretend about that."

"Well then, madam. It's not as if you won't replace it all when you inherit the money."

She parted her lips around her dismay. Pawning Signor Santa-Rosa's belongings was the least of her worries. Putting her soul into hock was another matter.

No doubt Flint had overheard everything. The one thing about the blackmailing blackguard that could be counted on was that he'd not stoop to helping her otherwise. But there was no denying that in a crisis he could be counted on to be businesslike. She'd glimpsed the old Flint standing there. Maybe that had drawn her into listening when any woman, in her right mind, wouldn't have entertained him.

The silver goblets clinked as Susan continued to dust. "You can always leave a note for Signor Santa-Rosa. You'll have to anyway now."

She would, wouldn't she? But if she took Flint's help, it put her in his debt. It wasn't the place to be with Flint. What if he started demanding things? Other things. Things like she touch him or he touch her. What if he wanted the boat to run off?

"I just don't know. I don't know if it's worth it."

"Madam, what is it about him you don't like?"

She shrugged. "Oh, please, don't have me go into that. I've no wish to stand here all week."

"Is it—is he—"

Fury dragged up her chin. "What makes you think that?"

"He's quite a dish. I always thought—"

"Quite a—him?"

"Oh, yes, madam. I'd far rather a man like that in my bed than any of those others. I bet he's good. I bet—"

"Fortunately you're not me."

In another second the woman would drool.

"Falling for him, are you? It's the only other reason I can think you don't like him, *if* that's not—"

Susan's voice held a degree of triumph, and something in Fury snapped.

"May I remind you, I am a widow. Recent, if not respectable. He's not *him*. He's not anyone but a rogue and a blackguard. He's no one."

"Why did you choose him?"

"What has that got to do with it?"

"Why won't you let him do this if he's no one?"

"Because—"

No. She would not be trapped into saying. She would first bite off her tongue than answer any of these questions. The real reason she couldn't let him in.

"Maybe I will let him. Yes. You're right, of course. It's a good offer. One of the best I've had recently. I'm silly to refuse it.

You just have to understand James is ruthless and self-seeking. He knows no better. He will want something in return. From me."

"If it's his freedom, you could give him that, couldn't you? What's Malmesbury going to do about that with what you have on him?"

Fury hesitated. *Look at it this way, I don't come back, you get yourself someone else. Someone you don't need all these fancy terms and conditions with.* That was what he'd said, wasn't it? Standing there so vital and handsome in the white sunlight it broke her heart to look at him.

If he left — she might already be pregnant. But she could not afford to wait to find out. She would need to get somebody else. Then she would never know who had fathered the heir.

It was that, wasn't it? That stopped her from giving him the boat, that stopped her now, when freedom was something he'd take anyway. It was just a question of when. Maybe even right now, for that matter, with that proud way of his, he was upstairs putting together his things.

And that was silly, when she couldn't choose Malmesbury. What terrified her more? Giving Flint the boat? Or being in his debt?

She forced a smile. "We will pawn the dining room silver."

"Very good, madam."

Chapter Seven

In resigned silence, Fury entered the Blue Chamber. She knocked, of course, and Flint's low voice told her to enter. His eyes widened when she walked in. He must have expected Susan, not her. But he didn't alter his relaxed stance, although his lazy grin hardened.

"Welcome to my humble abode. To what do I owe this very great honor?

Humble? How like him to take a cheap poke, particularly when his *humble* was costing her a veritable fortune she didn't yet possess and reduced her to pawning the dining room silver to pay for it. At least the rent was paid for another three months. And her fare home. If nothing else, it was one blessing.

"Since it's also my abode, I take it as read I am welcome. I've decided to accept your generous offer."

He canted his chin. "You've decided?"

"Yes. Susan is making the necessary arrangements with our bank."

"She's what?"

How good he was at feigning surprise. Did he think she couldn't see the wheels whirring in that self-seeking mind of his?

"You talked a great deal of sense." Fury spoke before he could ask why. Or maybe even flatter himself into thinking it was because she liked him. "Malmesbury is dangerous. But if you are able, under cover of darkness, to remove Thomas's body and give it a decent burial, then I'm happy to provide the cart and the boat. Just don't expect me to say a few words. And you must go in disguise. I don't want anything traced back to me. Do you understand? Because what traces back to me, traces back to you."

Even as she spoke, instinct screamed that she was making a calamitous mistake. But what other choice did she have? And if he went… She pushed the thought away. She must be sure to have her money's worth first then, mustn't she? Right now, if necessary.

"A boat?" He drew his brows together, something sharp gleaming in his eyes. "You're giving me a boat?"

She stood and faced him, impassive. "Yes." She walked to the bed.

If he thought she was providing the means for her to get shot of him, so much the better, because he was too handsome standing there, sunlight streaming across his chiseled features.

She could never let Flint be more than a means to an end. Even had he never left her on that quay, she'd be wrong to believe he could ever give her the only thing that could ever make that right. Love.

He could never give her — give any woman — that. He was a plunderer to his black-hearted soul. It would never have worked, and it would probably have destroyed her.

She had been young. It was excusable to think something would be forever. Not now though. If he took the boat and never came back it was no greater loss than before. So long as he disposed of Thomas, what did it matter?

Flint scratched the back of his neck. "That's assuming I still want a boat, sweetheart. Maybe I don't. Maybe I could get myself into a lot of trouble. You thought of that?"

Near the end, Thomas had beaten her. He had torn her hair. There had been times when he had still been able to discuss her situation rationally, when he had told her she had to do whatever it took to procure an heir. Surely, though, even he had not meant her to put up with this.

With a swish of her gray skirts she walked to the other side of the room. If she didn't do this, if she walked out the room, when she sensed that towering pride of his forced these words from him... She swallowed. Well, she supposed she could get her money's worth before she cut her losses.

"No, I mean it. Why should I go risking my neck helping you? It's not like I put Thomas in that box."

"Malmesbury told me about you disguising yourself as your own cabin boy. Fanciful, don't you think? Almost as much as you pretending you didn't hear everything he said out there." She wasn't for cutting her losses generously. "It is information with which I intend doing nothing, whether or not you help me. Enough time has been wasted this morning. I think we should just proceed."

Hoping that her extravagant invitation to do so would convince him to obey, she turned. He stood with no trace of that look, the one that said he was grappling for some inner truth. She'd thought he would. She was a little ashamed to say in some deep part of herself she found it endearing.

This look of pure burning steel was a little more dangerous. Disquiet flickered. Proceeding, while he looked like that, was perhaps unwise. And yet, what could he do to her?

"Isn't that a bit unusual for you?"

"Not really. I need this heir."

"I'm meaning having that information and doing nothing with it."

She shrugged. "It's not that I'm dazzled with your charms. Let's just say for old time's sake, I'm prepared to keep quiet.

Unlike you were the other night about certain things. Of course, I realize you were desperate. Now..."

This time his inhalation was furious. Muffled, but there just the same. Of course, she realized, as she walked to the bed, walking to the door might be a better option. The morning had been fraught with trial. But enough time had ticked away.

"In some respects, you have me wrong." She sat down on the unmade bed. "You think I use everything that comes my way. You think I murdered Thomas and Celia."

"You did have her things."

She tilted her chin.

"And you said you were her."

"Had I known that you and she were lovers, I might have kept my mouth shut. But the thing is, you never said. Not once. So how was I meant to know?" She leaned down and edged off her shoes. "Anyway."

"Wait a minute, you want to do this here? Now?"

Imagine that. James Flint Blackmoore opposed to sex, the man who could work his way through a whorehouse in a morning. And be back in the afternoon for more.

She raised her chin and leveled her eyes at him. "Here and now is as good a place and time as any."

He gestured at the door. "It's just I thought..."

"You have some objection?"

Actually, she wasn't wrong. For all her heart stuttered in the confines of her bodice, for all her stomach both churned and fluttered with nerves, now was as good a time as any. At any rate, she felt in control for the first time since she'd accepted him as the father of the heir. There would be no games. No tricks. She had made her preparation in private, before coming in here, just in case.

And she was not getting on top, no matter what he said. Not that she disbelieved him. But after last time and the manner in which he had finished things, when she had failed so spectacularly, she was not laying herself open to even the faintest possibility of any enjoyment.

For all he was unable to grasp the meagerest straw of self-knowledge, Flint was clever. If he might somehow realize it was possible to move her, he'd do it. Hadn't she already overreacted to the thought of the boat?

It shouldn't have mattered. Yet, somehow it did.

It was vital, while she shrunk from the barest thought of this encounter, that she engage in it. And in a manner satisfactory to herself. Or she wouldn't; she couldn't do this again.

He knitted his brows. For whatever reason, he didn't want her here like this.

"You see, I didn't imagine you would object." She set her shoes to the side.

His gaze froze. Yes, it *was* one thing for him to waltz into her room—when asked, of course—and another for her to meet him here. She'd remember that. She needed all the help she could get.

"Of course not. You want to shove over and I'll see what I can do."

"I have been thinking about this. And I realize I may have been a trifle harsh." Her wrists ached as she gripped the mattress edge with hands frozen into claws. "I realize I may have expected impossible things of you. No?"

She shifted her shoulders. It didn't pay to have him think she insulted him. After that blasted boat of his, the one thing the great Captain Flint took the most pride in was his sexual prowess. His body like a Greek god's. His ability to do it at the drop of a hat.

"In terms of my own demands."

It didn't pay either, *not* to insult him. She thought her meaning was unmistakable, but she wanted to swipe that lazy grin from his face.

"Just so you know, I'm adopting a change of position."

Of course his eyes would gleam.

"I'm going to turn around."

She considered telling him to take the grin off his face. But she welcomed the strongly sexual Flint to whatever pleasure he could derive from this encounter. It was far more important she close any potential rifts he might open. Anyway, she wasn't done yet. Not by any manner of means.

"Yes. Having given the matter some thought, I realize it's better if I don't see your face and you don't see mine."

He tightened his jaw, but his gaze didn't freeze. He was getting better at this. "And why's that?"

"Forced intimacy is very difficult. Your face is getting in the way of the ceiling—"

"My face?"

"—which is what I wish to look at it. The ceiling, that is. I would have added it to the contract except I was uncertain it was possible physically. And as I can't ask you not to get in the way of it—"

"Not get in the way of it?"

She held up a hand. "Before you say another word, as I know you're going to do, I know how much you dislike me. How much you pretend. Since the feeling is mutual, I think it's best."

In some corner of her soul, that wasn't all that far, she knew this wasn't the way to proceed and hope she would keep him, with his mile-high pride. But it was astonishing to think he believed he could do all that to her and she would still hold a candle in her heart for him. It didn't matter he didn't know all he'd done to her, which was maybe why he thought certain flames still burned.

"What about you getting on top?"

"Oh, I've been doing some research into that."

"And?"

"And do you know — I never would have believed it — but it transpires that lying on my front is as good a way as any to conceive a boy. So long as you don't stand up."

Where she got this from she didn't know. But she thanked heaven for it anyway.

"You saying Ma was wrong?"

"I'm not saying anything. I'm sure she was right, a knowledgeable woman like her. But, as you always used to say to me aboard the *Calypso*, there's more than one way of being right."

She'd liked to say his recovery was instant. It usually was. But the bruising way his gaze held hers, she wasn't sure.

"Fine. Turn over."

She tightened her throat.

"You made your preparations, I'm sure."

She licked her dry lips. "Yes. I—"

"Then just do it."

His fingers went to the fastening of his breeches and her mouth dried. This wasn't the lazy Flint, the one who liked to coax, grin, and play — not that she had allowed him to do much of that.

This was the other Flint. The one who settled an argument with sex. The one she'd sometimes fought, to no avail, on the *Calypso*. In his bed, wasn't she? So, what was the problem? The one she shrank from now, because even then, she hadn't been immune. Just wanting him to be nice to her, instead of in some black mood about something or other that had gone wrong on deck. And worried, if she slammed him with more than her fists, he'd next throw her overboard.

She wasn't on the *Calypso*, and yet it seemed no matter how far she'd come, it wasn't far enough.

"Very well. But I trust you not to look at anything else."

"Then lift your own skirt. That way you know it will be done to your satisfaction."

"I am grateful for your help. All of it. I just think it would be better if we didn't look at each other, that's all. It…it makes the conditions I set easier."

"I know what you think. Now turn around."

Her face burning, she did so. If she drove him away over this — oh, God, she must be harsh about this.

"Sort your skirt, sweetheart, if you want this. I ain't got all day and I'm sure you don't either. Not if we're to do it all again later."

Ain't? The blood sank from her cheeks. He was angry. She angled her suddenly stiff body onto her knees and prayed he wasn't going to hurt her, the way Thomas sometimes had.

"I—" She hated herself for pleading. She didn't plead as a rule. But suddenly this didn't seem such a good idea.

"You want to kneel forward or lie down?"

Actually, him hurting her wasn't the reason she prayed. Because, even angry, Flint wouldn't do such a thing as hurt her. Not physically, anyway. The indignity of the position was suddenly apparent. Her kneeling with her backside in the air? He'd like that.

"I—I will lie down. Once you're fully inside, that is." How mortifying to have to say so.

"Whatever, sweetheart. But sort your skirt, you don't want me seeing that nice little derriere of yours."

Was this happening? Yes. And she had chosen this position to ensure there would be no enjoyment. How could there be? Even the frisson of it? Not if she lay flat down on her face.

What was mortifying for her plainly didn't disturb him in the least. She sought to adjust her skirt. His voice was so brusque. She imagined the hard-honed way he stared. Sometimes it was hard to tell which had a greater effect on a woman, that or the lazy one. The virile purpose behind both was exactly the same.

She'd be damned if she'd fumble as she hitched her skirt, though. Damned if she'd display anything to him either. This *was* the ideal position.

Well, wasn't it? But her skirt didn't budge any better than it had the other way, because she knelt on it. She hadn't thought about this. Not really. She didn't want to wriggle any more than she wanted to look at his face. Wriggling would be undignified, and already it was undignified enough.

She didn't want him to see anything either. She suspected he was waiting for it, and that for the word *nice* he really meant *tasty.* Flint always had a nose, or rather, an eye, for such matters. He wasn't the gentlemanly sort to look the other way. He would have stared at the Virgin Mary — a woman who did not grace the wall hangings — had she been unfortunate enough for the wind to catch her hem and drag up her skirt in public.

Of course, had this been done with love, for pleasure, instead of in this burning, brittle silence, for monetary gain, it wouldn't matter how she wriggled or what she showed him. But it wasn't.

In some ways the Virgin Mary had been lucky. She hadn't had to suffer any of this.

The mattress sank beneath him. "Kneel forward. Unless you want to kneel up."

Lucky? If only the lord had looked down from heaven and seen fit to grace Fury that way, with a handy passing angel. But he hadn't. Instead he had sent her James Flint Blackmoore, who sounded angry enough to kill her.

Maybe he would and it would be an end to this.

"Hardly." She hastened to obey. "Will this do?"

His fingers, cool and skilled as she remembered them, reached under her skirt, and she bit back a shriek. The ideal position? Maybe not. But it was impossible to remind him to touch her as little as possible when his cool fingers brushed over her sex. Then, in the next instant he edged the tip of one inside her and held it just there.

"You want to open your legs a bit, so I can get in there."

"I—"

She wanted to but she couldn't. The tip of his finger sitting inside her was unpleasant because of how cold it felt and how hot she must be to notice. And lush. Like some dockside hussy, with a warm, welcoming… She swallowed her gasp.

Who would have thought that would happen? Obviously not herself or she'd never have suggested this position. She wouldn't want him to edge his finger further.

She prayed he thought it was the cream. She had used a lot. And it might even be he would believe it had heat-giving qualities.

"Yes. Yes, of course." As if from a great height, she saw herself move. "There. Is that better?"

"It'll do, I suppose."

He tugged her skirt higher, and her heart nearly burst from her ribcage as he dipped his hips against her buttocks.

"Lie down."

"But I don't feel—"

"You do now." He removed his fingers, and she gasped as he jerked. "Unless you want to kneel."

She didn't. But the shock of the hardened feel of him inside her made it impossible to move. She didn't know either, she realized with a horrible shock, how she was going to lie down without dislodging him, unless she held herself—and him. She *couldn't* touch him. Not even the tiniest bit of him. Not there. Unless she did it through her dress. Or she clenched, hard.

Again, had this been done with passion, with heat—actually she didn't know about the heat, she felt she was burning—with love, these movements would all be natural. Instead it penetrated her scattered senses that to clench would be a response.

"I—I—"

Bunching her skirt she sprawled forward and strove to press her burning cheek against the pillow to cool it. Even then, though she didn't want to feel him there inside her, his heat burnt as he thrust into her flesh. His elbows came down on either side of her. What had she said about touching her as little as possible? He was so angry though, she didn't want to complain about the fact that he breathed too close to her hair.

This wasn't like those other times. This was… She forbore to think because whatever it was, he was still completely in control of himself and her. She bit the pillow to try to escape the rhythm he set, every muscle straining not to respond.

The way he thrust she had only to reach down and touch herself to be plunged into ecstasy, stronger and darker than she'd experienced in years. Ecstasy that—she grasped the pillow, clinging with every ounce of strength—she wouldn't lose a shred of her self-control to experience now.

This would be over soon. His body stiffened and a gasp almost of distaste issued from him. Then she would look herself in the eye in the mirror and that was more important. She would never look at herself in the mirror if she allowed herself to enjoy this. She had managed not to before, hadn't she?

If only he would remove himself though. But he held himself there as if he wanted to make sure of everything. For a second she sprawled, trying to savor the crisp cotton of the pillowcase, cool and somehow calming against her face, to grasp a breath into her parched lungs. In the same second, he pulled himself out. His rough exhalation sounded even more disgusted.

"Now, I don't care what Ma said, you get out of here."

He probably found it disgusting having sex with a woman

he despised, who did nothing to make him like her, but her mind still reeled.

"Yes." She would, even though this was her house. Her room, if not her actual bedroom. How could she do otherwise? She'd infuriated him, hadn't she? Not even the solace, the great lover usually found in sex, had softened him. His clothes rustled behind her. He fumbled as he fastened up his breeches.

She stood. That she did, when her legs felt like shaking leaves, and between them felt numbed, was a miracle. Bending down she edged on her shoes. As she did a hot trickle oozed down her leg. She would indeed be fortunate to have conceived the Beaumont heir this morning.

Did it matter though? Right now it was more important she left with her head high and — as she straightened, the trickle became a gush — no stains down the back of her dress.

In her chamber she would bathe, rest, and recover herself. It would be pleasant. Something to look forward to. Then she would consider her next move. Maybe after all, with what stung her eyes, it would be better to find a cushion, a foundling, and a doctor she could bribe. So long as she could first manage to the door.

She reached it when his voice, even grittier than a second ago, sanded her skin like glass paper.

"Just tell me one thing."

She almost didn't answer. She felt too broken up inside. And the door handle stood inches away. It made better sense to grip it than indulge with him in another fencing match. But this was one encounter she didn't want him to win.

Weary, she raised her chin. "What?"

"Where'd you get them?"

She strove not to let her shoulders sag. What had she said about Flint's nose? How like him to have found or spotted something left by some previous incumbent of the room. Like

Malmesbury. Or…

She tried to rake her thoughts, to remember who else had stayed here. But her mind was a frightening blank. In truth she felt very weary. But she made herself sound stalwart.

"Get what?"

"Them bruises."

She froze. "Bruises?"

She heard him leave the bed and stride toward her. She edged her hand to her shoulder. A pity she'd forgotten the gown had a low back, and her hair, which she had tied at the side with a ribbon, didn't cover it.

"I didn't. I… Dye marks."

Why give him what he didn't need? The opportunity to say that if Thomas had beaten her, it hadn't been hard enough? But Flint stepped between her and the door, and for the first time she saw how rail thin he was about the waist and hips. Attractive, as Flint was always attractive, in fact, possibly more so, because it made him seem even taller than he was. But thinner than the man she'd known.

He'd been starved. By Malmesbury? Or in prison? Was it any wonder he was so hungry she had to pawn the candlesticks and more? She swallowed the fugitive thought.

He narrowed his eyes. "Dye marks? Let me see that."

Before she could stop him he reached for her wrist. She fought the desire to squeal as he dragged her hand from her shoulder. His touch—she'd suffered his touch and the lack of it a lot in the last thirty-six hours—was second to the knowledge of her own pride. She took his seed. She took his help, because she had no choice but to. But she could not take him knowing what Thomas did and laughing about it.

He touched the shoulder of her gown before she could stop him. "Did he beat you?"

"For goodness sake, take your hands off me. Thomas

wouldn't harm a hair on my head. He loved me."

He lifted his chin and looked into her eyes for a long moment. "This is me you're talking to. So just quit lying."

She wished she could take issue. Say how dare he think Thomas didn't love her. That no one would. But then she realized that wasn't what he meant.

A tight knot formed in her stomach. This, no matter how she wished not to see it, was a man she might like. A man she might trust. And a sweat, cold and icy, yet hot and prickling, formed along her palms.

"He hit you, didn't he?"

"Yes." It was better to admit it and keep control, than let that knowledge surge further. "It was Lady Margaret's fault. Putting down that silly condition. So, he did hit me. I know you're going to say not hard enough."

"I've never hit a woman. I don't hold with it."

She supposed he hadn't. She supposed she couldn't think he had ever hurt her that way. With the cool feel of his fingers on her shoulder, expressly as she'd told him not to touch her, and the way he looked at her, she was going to start seeing him differently, and let him in. Already he stood too close for comfort, trapping her between him and the door.

She gritted her teeth. "I'm surprised about that. I thought you did and held with most things."

She felt so bad saying it, she fought the urge to wipe her palms down her dress. But what other choice did she have?

This man had turned her into gray stone. She had come back from that. But sunshine had never flickered on her until this moment. Memory and lust perhaps, the things that made the tightrope so perilous to walk.

Yet not so perilous she couldn't keep her eyes trained on the true reason her deepest self must remain unmoved.

But this might dazzle her and there were only rocks below.

"Now, you asked me to go." She met his gaze without flinching. "So, if you don't mind."

The words were not an invitation. He *would* take his hand off her. He *would* keep his blue eyes to himself.

"Fury."

He *would* keep his lips. No matter how close they hovered.

"Thomas just couldn't, you see." Her throat clogged, her body tensed. For one dizzying moment she thought she would meet his lips, but she continued. "Conceive the heir, that is. Because he was so very ill. But it didn't stop him trying. And getting frustrated. And that's all there is to it. Now…"

Never mind his lips. What about hers? She couldn't. She mustn't kiss him. Not here. Not now.

"All right, sweetheart." He released her. But while relief flooded, she didn't miss the way he still stared. "You get me the money for the boat. I'll do what I can."

"The boat? But you said —"

"Give him the send-off he deserves."

The bastard was no doubt the word he wanted to use. She swallowed. It wasn't like him. Not over her. She wished he'd never seen those marks. But with everything that had happened today, she hadn't thought to cover them.

"You mean?"

"I'll do it. No questions asked. Come and tell me when you've got it. All right?"

The Beaumont heir was her prime consideration. But she did not think she could do this again today. That might propel her toward the rocks. She must gather her mettle first. But she could not afford to make it look like retreat either.

"Of course. I'll send Susan. You — you are, of course going to help me this evening. It's enough to do, and you may be out late. We'll forgo the other, till tomorrow."

She waited for him to protest or grin.

Instead he glanced at her sidelong. "Is that how Thomas fell?"

"What?"

"On the stairs? Because he was beating you?"

The rocks drew closer. He was not going to let up, was he? And not only was she in his debt, she saw with a sickening clarity, she only had control because he had let her.

"He fell because I pushed him." She shut the door behind her.

Chapter Eight

Genoa was a seaport like any other, so far as Flint was concerned, and being accustomed to seaports he knew where to find the kind of place he sought. A simple little inn, on the simple little harbor front, catering for the needs of men like him, which forty-eight hours ago were the same as the inn and the harbor front. Simple. Little.

He entered and then sat down at one of the tables. Bustle and noise surrounded him. The contrast to the quiet dark along the bay where he'd slipped Thomas's body into the water couldn't be more complete. Or his thoughts at that moment when he'd done it either.

All he'd had to do was row the skiff further along the coast to make good on the escape. He'd considered it that morning, when the disdainful way she'd treated him, coupled with her decision to think about giving him a boat instead of just handing one over, so prickled his hackles he'd nearly left there and then.

"Rum, sweetheart, you got any?"

The barmaid was olive-skinned beautiful with the hottest blue eyes he'd seen this side of the equator. The hottest pair of something else too. But he didn't even feel a flicker.

"Rum, *per fervore*." He sighed and set his hat on the table. "You know where I can get a room 'round these parts? *Una stanza*. Per — per — " Christ, his Italian stunk.

No wonder she curved her lush lips upward. "Per *stanotte*?"

"*Ci*. Yip, that's the one. Stanotte."

He bared his teeth. *But not with you, sweetheart.*

The rum arrived at the table, and he threw a few of the coins down he'd kept from haggling down the price of the boat from the larcenous keeper. This notion that he felt protective toward Fury, because Malmesbury got bossy and she'd a few bruises on her shoulders, was absurd as seeing a bucket load of fishes dance on deck in fancy costumes and things.

He sank a glass of rum. Then he sank another.

But he did, didn't he?

It was more than a few bruises. It was the notion someone had done that to her. And she stood so tall about it. For the first time he could understand her pride.

Raising his head, he glanced around the low-roofed cavern. There was always a boy in a place like this. A wharf rat who ran errands. Took money. Carried notes. Arranged assignations with suitable whores.

"Hey." He was almost surprised to hear his own voice.

A boy in the corner looked up. "Signore?"

"You got paper? Pen?"

The boy scratched his head and Flint made a play of writing on the scored tabletop.

"Oh. Si." The boy nodded his dark head. "*Documento? Per caro?*"

"Hmm." Flint gritted his teeth. Caro wasn't it exactly. Still he nodded. "Ci. That's what I need."

He did, didn't he? In more ways than one.

The thing Flint wanted most in the world, after the long, tortuous affront to his pride and dignity this entire year had been, the thing he believed would make him feel like a man again, the thing his hunger for amounted to starvation was to stand on the deck of the *Calypso*, wind in his hair, spray in his face, deck swaying beneath his feet, breathing that cool sea air.

But Fury Fontanelli's disdain for him was like a gauntlet. The more she faced him down, the more he started to feel that the thing — the only thing — that would come anywhere close to making him feel like a man was actually for her to look into his eyes. Deep into them, as she once had and make him believe he was the only man in the world. For her to part her thighs. Not as she parted them now, with every type of damned, ball-breaking condition she could think up on her lips. To want him. Really, truly want him. In every respect. As a man. As a lover. As a person she somehow cared about. Not just his seed.

Try as he might, he could ignore it less than he could the gut-wrenching fact that he couldn't determine if this was just some stupid hole in his masculine pride, some deep-seated need in him to tick off that particular box with her, or something more.

Something far deeper. Something that had always been there.

But it felt as though he were swimming hopelessly, not just against the tide, but a tsunami.

Why not just up anchor and walk away? He could, of course, and there was nothing to stop him. Except, in a confused way, it didn't feel right. In life you did things because they felt right. Felt proper.

He'd given his word. He didn't know if he could break it to a woman who stood as she had earlier.

There was also the matter of confirming there was no lower form of animal life.

But because he couldn't seem to stop himself getting into wars with her, and these wars seemed destined to conflict him further, he needed to find somewhere else to stay.

There was no way on the face of the earth he wanted the

Calypso sailing on its way without him, leaving him shackled to a life of domesticity he dreaded.

* * *

The sharp *rat-a-tat* at her chamber door jerked Fury from her edgy contemplation of herself in the mirror. Setting the hairbrush down, she raised her chin. "Come."

It was absurd the way her heart hammered. Unless Flint could walk through walls, it couldn't be him.

The door creaked open, and she was appalled to find herself on her feet. Her heart sank. "Susan."

Was she stupid? Flint hadn't come in. She'd lain awake all night, listening. Some of the time with the pillow on her head so that she wouldn't.

"Madam."

"Has he..."

She'd been to his room, too, this morning. Twice. The bed hadn't been touched since yesterday. Of course it was to be expected of a lowdown dog like Flint that he was probably in some whorehouse sleeping off the money she'd given him. She just hoped he'd gotten rid of Thomas first and not left him in his wrappings in the street. She didn't want the authorities at the door.

She dabbed a drop of cologne behind her ears. "I mean, I know he's not here. So I was dressing."

"Who? James?"

The familiarity rankled. Well, she'd thought, hadn't she, that Flint might be better to conceive the heir with Susan. No doubt they wouldn't have surfaced for days. Setting her lips in a smile, she padded across the floor in her bare feet.

At least her hair was combed. She didn't want Susan to know anything of the knot that had formed in the pit of her stomach. The coldness that swept her skin. Older but no wiser wasn't the way to appear here. Not when Susan already suspected too much.

"Yes, James. I thought I might wear this. The purple." She dragged a gown from its hanger. "And call on Malmesbury."

"Malmesbury?"

"There's no need to sound surprised. I could have told you James was hardly reliable. I thought I'd give the poor beggar a chance. But now I see how misguided that was."

If she'd been a fraction less self-possessed, she'd have sunk beneath the weight of her own folly. Something burned behind her eyes. Not tears exactly. She wasn't going to cry. She had never imagined Flint would do anything other than abandon her — again. She was just appalled to feel anything, as if the test were one she had failed.

She held the purple satin against herself. "You can see how I am repaid. At least Malmesbury won't require us to pawn any more of Signor Santa-Rosa's candlesticks, will he? He's hardly short."

Malmesbury. She shrank from the thought. But what other choice did she have?

"But James has sent a note, madam."

Fury stared at the crisp piece of paper Susan clutched. What kinds of things would that contain? She hardened her jaw. If it came from where she thought, all kinds of awful things. But a note? How unusual.

"He brought it himself. Not half an hour ago."

And didn't bother to speak to Fury.

"Tear it up, will you?"

"Tear it—"

"Yes. Now." She stepped into the gown, the material cool against her hot palms. Her theatrical behavior didn't bother her. In some respects it offered as much refuge as cool, clinging satin. What was there to read after all? Her wish was granted. She was rid of him.

"I have more pressing matters to attend to. You see the embarrassing position he has put me in? And not for the first time."

"But madam, if you go to Malmesbury—"

"You honestly think I care I might not know who the father of the Beaumont heir is? Now, fasten my dress."

"Madam, you—'Dear Fury…'"

To her horror Susan had torn open the letter.

"Give me that!"

"'Sorry on account of you receiving this from Frau Berthe's down on the harbor—'"

The thought arrested her mid-lunge.

"Isn't she that German woman, madam?" Susan held the letter out of reach. "'But I prefer it here, to there.'"

At those words Fury's hands clenched, around nothing in particular since Flint's neck was not present. The damn cheek. If she had the letter she would tear it. Or better still, light the candle to turn it into blackened moth's wings.

"Isn't that nice? James always was a man of quite unusual tastes." She rummaged in the wardrobe. "Now. Which hat do you think—"

"He says here he wants to see you."

In a whorehouse? She would not countenance such a thing. Her face flamed. For a second it flamed so badly, she thought *she* might burn to moths' wings if she did not calm down.

"To spare you being in Malmesbury's debt. You can't go to Malmesbury, madam."

Fury swallowed the constriction, choking and flaming, in her throat. The purple bonnet was perhaps a little fussier than the cream, and the black, a far better fit, but she did not want to look like a crow.

"I can do what I damn well please. Captain Flint Blackmoore

does not own me."

"*Captain?*"

That Susan would find out who he really was, was worse. She must regain control. But she seemed momentarily to have lost it. And no matter how she looked, it wasn't even within her grasp. Like the end of a ball of wool that had spun somewhere, beneath the chair there—or worse, to Frau Berthe's whorehouse.

Susan passed her tongue over her lips. "Madam, if that is who he is, and he doesn't want you in Malmesbury's debt, won't you at least hear what he has to say?"

Fury rather thought she had. She wanted not to have to do this. If there was one thing yesterday morning had shown her, it was that she'd prefer not to go to Malmesbury. If there was one thing the afternoon had, it was that Flint could not be trusted.

Was a known devil better, though? Or worse? As the evening before that had so clearly demonstrated, she was perhaps a little guilty of leaping to quite monstrous conclusions. That he had forced her to get on top, for example. When all he had done was suggest it.

"Very well. But he will see me out of Malmesbury's debt here. If he thinks for one moment I am visiting him in some ghastly harbor-front whorehouse, belonging to some German fraulein, he is not only mistaken, but out of his mind."

* * *

Rounding the bend in the stairs, Fury did her best to keep her gauzy veil intact. Frau Berthe's was not the place a woman of any standing should be seen in. Alive or dead. But since she began to think she had none, she had gone past caring whether it mattered.

In any case not only was she veiled, she was cloaked. So long as Lady Margaret never found out Fury had set foot in a whorehouse. And how the blazes would she? Fury had been very careful coming here, turning at every corner to make sure she wasn't followed and that Susan had trailed at a discreet distance.

Flint wanted to stay here. She was here to tell him he couldn't. She could not afford the extravagance of a whorehouse. Signor Santa-Rosa's belongings couldn't be pawned further.

Besides, she'd made it clear. Flint in a whorehouse was like asking a bear to remove its paws from the honey jar and keep them out. She didn't want him — or the Beaumont heir — afflicted with some hideous disease. All caught through his association with some whore.

He would agree to return with her now. If he did not... She straightened her shoulders.

Flint reminded her of so much, for all she'd vowed to remain unmoved. The familiarity of his body made it difficult in that regard. But, having allowed what she could of herself to become reacquainted with it, God alone knew what another man would be like in bed. In all her life she'd known two men, Flint and Thomas.

A faint trembling shook her. Nerves and stress and perhaps a twinge of fear. Something no one around her seemed even remotely capable of understanding. As if playing this game were easy. And so was trying to conceive a child. It wasn't easy. But straightening her spine she knocked on the door.

The baby, when it was born, would be proud and strong. It wouldn't know a thing of its mother's unhappiness. Heavens, she didn't want it suffering from a nervous disposition because she felt flummoxed.

Of course, she had still to conceive the baby. She would. When she got Flint back home. This wasn't the time to think *please, oh please, let him do that.* This was the time to think *he will.*

A soft creak caused her to tighten her jaw. Footsteps, not exactly alacritous ones, eased across the floor behind the door.

They paused and she fought to still the desperate beat of her heart. He was playing this for what it was worth, wasn't he?

A head appeared out a door further along the open landing, and she turned the other way. Even if her face couldn't be seen, she didn't want to be spotted. Genoa was a large place. And she and Thomas were barely known. Even so.

She raised her hand and knocked again.

"That you, Fury?"

Flint's voice was gravelly. And rich. That low timbre sometimes sounded as if it came from his boots.

"Who do you think it is? Your—" she paused on the word *whore*, "mother?"

She had no qualm of morality about herself or what she did in that regard. Too much was at stake. Besides, she was paying him in a way. He had his freedom and now, if she did not prevent it, he'd have this room here, instead of with her. And whores. Whores galore.

What he did afterward when she was pregnant, well, she'd promised him something, hadn't she? She supposed she'd have to stand by her word. Take back the decision about the quarter halfpenny's worth.

"Now, open the damned door. People are watching. Maybe you want them to see me and ruin my reputation?"

The door creaked open, and he surveyed her for a moment with his shadowed eyes. "You think my mother would come to a place like this?"

She clutched her reticule. He hadn't shaved since yesterday, and the stubble darkening his jaw made her want to rub her fingers over it. Fortunately though, she both wore gloves and had a reticule to control.

"If you are casting aspersions about me, then cast." After all the remark about reputation was one she was surprised she had the temerity to utter. "Otherwise, good morning, James. If you are taking visitors, I should like to come in."

It wasn't that she desired to. But she wasn't going to discuss something so perilously dear to her heart as the conception of the Beaumont heir on one of Frau Berthe's multitude of doorsteps. People were listening. And she didn't want them listening to some unseemly row between herself and Flint if he tried digging his heels in.

He wouldn't. If she had to offer her body in fawning supplication he wouldn't.

"Be my guest."

There was no point asking what the lazy bow denoted. Not when the fathering of the Beaumont heir must be above suspicion. And the irritation that sparked in her said she might lose her temper and say things she knew she would regret. She would sweep in, she would sweep out. With him.

"Thank you."

Tilting her chin, she glided past him. A perfectly ordinary room greeted her. Very plain for a whorehouse. Although, of course Frau Berthe was German and perhaps they did things differently there. Either that, or there were hidden mirrors and things that came out the walls later at the cranking of some mechanism. But of even seedy, disgusting bedding, and grimy lower-class furnishings, there were none. Just white walls and the faint tang of ocean spray wending through the wide-open shutters. The door creaked shut behind her.

"It's a plain lodging house, by the way."

"And you would be doing what in a plain lodging house?"

He ambled, in that way that always worked such magic on her heart, to stand before her. "What you asked me to do."

She hoped the noise that emanated from her throat betrayed her doubt, not her surprise. Was she meant to be pleased with this?

Flint the-suit-himself Blackmoore was not the kind of man to do any woman's bidding. Least of all hers.

So it was unlikely he did it now, and she must be careful when he stood there, the deep ocean blue of his eyes intensified by sunlight, golden as his skin, not to believe so. She'd come to take him home. She wouldn't settle for less. Anyway, what was he really doing here?

"What I asked you to do? And why would you stay away from whores to please me, when you like them so very much?"

"Don't you like to think so?" He'd the temerity to grin.

"I don't actually. Indeed I find it sad that a man so besotted with his manhood can give so little consideration to its welfare, as to parade it through—"

"I never cheated on you, Fury."

She swallowed the gulp. There was no point losing this on a triviality. How he saw things and how she did. A suspicion grew in her mind. That was what he wanted. Her to lose this. She wasn't going to.

"Well. Certainly not once, James."

"Looking isn't the same as touching. You should know that, intelligent woman like you. No. You just liked to think I did."

Lie? He did it through his teeth. With the skill and temerity not just to believe himself but to put the onus back on her. So she was the bad one for not believing him. The poor misunderstood Captain Flint.

"I could have. I could have plenty. That time in San Domingo. In Trinidad. Hell, let's not even mention that pretty little blackamoor floozy you nearly swiped the face off in Martinique."

Her? The fine hairs rose all along the back of Fury's neck. Her breath puffed faster than usual.

"But I didn't."

She could settle this. She would have to. "Then what were you doing in all those whorehouses then, pray tell? Admiring the view?"

He slanted her a long, narrowed gaze. "I thought you killed Celie. All right?"

She had known that but for him to confess it, and that this was why he had pretended…

"I thought you killed her. But, even then, it wasn't as simple as that."

Not as simple. God, the rage she tried to master in that instant was too great to govern. It burned from the tips of her toes, all the way up her shaking legs, through her churning stomach, to her fingertips. To her very reticule. Which descended on his chest. Followed by her fists.

Her mind emptied, except of one thought. He had done it to spite her.

"Whoa. Fury — what do you — steady — "

The consolation of seeing him duck disappeared when he grabbed hold of her wrists. She struggled, making herself look stupid. Wrists flailing. Breath coming in ragged pants. Like all those other times, when he'd insulted her, then had the temerity to browbeat her into his bed.

Was that to be next? In this place? The way he'd captured her wrists and twirled her around to restrain her and — his hand was in her hair. Stroking. Somehow her veil had become dislodged.

"Shh, Fury. Whoa…hell, what'd I go and say now?"

How could he not know what he'd said, what he'd done? No tigress in defense of its young could have sunk its teeth more ferociously than she did in that second. Right into his knuckles.

"Jesus! Goddamn bitch."

If only she could clamp them on something else, but God knows what they might catch. She had to think of the heir not being infected.

Anyway, she would need to yank her teeth free. She would

need access to his breeches.

"Ouch. Hell. Quit biting, will you?"

She should have done this years ago. To him. To Thomas.

Even if Flint wanted to cheat but couldn't, how the blazes did that make it better?

What it made it was worse.

She elbowed his ribcage and sprang away.

She made a supreme effort to adjust her veil. "What you have said is probably not the point. We have an agreement."

His blue eyes said that was unlikely. Indeed, they said that only in her dreams was it likely, although possibly her ability to return the interview to businesslike terms had stunned him. With so much at stake, what else could she do though?

"No. What we've got is some stuff you made up."

"That is not so."

"Stuff that involves me not even getting to kiss you."

She clutched her reticule so it almost snapped in two. With effort, she unclenched her fists. Why on earth would he want to do that? Particularly when she had sunk her teeth into his knuckles?

"Now. I'm not asking you to stop doing that so I can kiss you. No." He eyed her. "Because I know you've got your reasons."

She swallowed a gulp. The manner in which he stared. Thank God, for the concealing veil. The blush pulsing to her hair roots would be undisguisable on her pale skin otherwise.

The things he knew and, worse, understood about a woman's femininity. Her sexuality. And wasn't remotely ashamed to discuss them either. The strange conviction rose, which she strove to quash, that it actually made him quite *safe* to be with.

She should turn on her heel and run. Not stand here listening to him. But she had sworn, hadn't she? There would be no pawning of candlesticks to keep him here.

"I'm telling you right now, you want to get to it, from now on, we do it here. Your house if you prefer. Just so long as you know, that's the deal and I'm for staying here, not there."

"What?" Of course. She expected as much.

His supercilious eyebrows rose. "Just that."

"I am not getting to it in a whorehouse."

"What did I say? This isn't a whorehouse."

"It looks like one to me."

"Clearly you ain't never been in a whorehouse."

She had lied, of course. The place looked perfectly all right. And clean. Sometimes places did. People did too. As it had yesterday, heat gathered in her hands. She stepped away. "That's where you're wrong."

"Me, sweetheart?"

She felt his gaze follow her. But that may have been because her veil still stood at half-mast and she fumbled to straighten it.

"Oh, of course, I forgot. How hellish clumsy of me, not to remember to let you take what your father ran in Jamaica out on me."

How dare he? She was not taking anything out on him. Certainly she was not taking that business of her father. "Well. Celia was in it."

"Let's leave her out of this, shall we? This isn't about her."

"Then what is it about?"

"Me, giving you my seed, so you can have that baby. It's only going to happen if I stay here."

She considered turning on her heel and leaving. Walking straight out of here and never coming back. But it wasn't an option. Because it was as inevitable as night followed day, he spoke the truth. She needed his seed.

The suspicion crept that he'd only offered to help her with Thomas, taking advantage of her when she was weak and vulnerable, to maneuver her into this present position. Indeed it did more than creep, when she recalled how close his lips had come to hers yesterday. How caressing his gaze had been. And she, weak fool, had almost responded. Had not been able to face another session because of it. And thought, when she returned to her room, it was because they had had sex and he had been moved by the fact Thomas had beaten her.

When had James Flint Blackmoore ever done anything for anyone? He had succeeded for one reason only: She'd let him. In applying business rules to this transaction, she had failed to keep it businesslike.

In the pit of her stomach she shivered. Offering her body in fawning supplication had never been an option. It was less so since he'd said that she wouldn't even let him kiss her. The absolute bastard. So what was she going to do about what he'd just said?

"But, but…of course."

"Of course, what?"

She felt his gaze on her, with that harsh appraising gleam.

"Excuse me?" he asked. "Of course it's not about Celie? Or, of course I can stay here?"

An illusion she could refuse him. If she went on with this though, she was going to have to take care to keep him at arm's length, the things she had learned here today. About Celia, about those women.

In that respect it might be easier to let him just stay here, as opposed to having him under her nose at the villa.

But it would also mean trusting him to be faithful to her. It should not matter, when her only use for him was to father her child, if he chose to give some other woman the benefit of that body? Of his caresses? His kisses?

She still hated to think that it did and that she had no control over it.

"So then, Fury? What's the answer to be?"

She smiled. It was important in acknowledging her defeat not to show she felt the bitter sting of it. It may even be…well, Flint was proud and he loathed being caged. Perhaps he felt better, throwing off the shackles of the villa. In that case she might feel she was doing a good deed for the damned bastard.

"Of course you can stay here." He took a step toward her, and she held up her hand. "Although if you do—rule twelve—the onus will be on you to ensure you are not observed calling at the villa. Do you understand?"

"I'm not stupid. I think I get that you don't want to be discovered."

"Should you be—seen, that is—although the same goes if you are stupid, you may consider the arrangement terminated. Rule thirteen. I've no desire for my reputation to be ruined."

She drew herself up. To her credit she uttered the remark without blushing. Already she'd lost restraint. And there was nothing so dreadful as trying to regain it while trying to proceed as if nothing had happened and she had greeted his confession about Celia and the whores with serenity and grace.

"Me neither, sweetheart. I've got my own to think of. Think how it would plummet being seen with some woman who just wants me for my seed."

"I doubt that. I don't think your reputation could get much lower than it already is."

His gaze didn't freeze as she hoped. Nor did he rake in deep bemusement into some subterranean depth. But it was still early in this encounter to reduce that dazzling grin to rubble.

"Takes one to know one, does it? You mind paying Frau Berthe on the way out?"

"Frau—"

"I told her last night you would. She likes her money in advance. She was prepared to waive it last night but…" He poured some water from the blue jug on the nightstand into the basin. "She doesn't look like someone you'd want to tangle with."

Frau Berthe. That dreadful woman who'd answered the door with a rolling pin. No, she didn't. In all her thoughts about keeping Flint at arm's length, Fury had forgotten Frau Berthe.

She swallowed the sick thought. It was as if Flint smelled the fact she'd no money and was determined to break her. Every day, that little bit more. Till nothing remained. She could tell him of course. It might prove advantageous in bringing him home.

The knowledge sat uneasily that he'd think it a cheap trick, or worse, laugh and tell her to stop lying. Wasn't she Lady Shelton after all? Or worse still, laugh *period.* Anyway, in some respects it was better to see him out of her sights.

She raised her chin. "By all means. I will get Susan to make the necessary arrangements with my banker."

"Thank you. Frau Berthe likes a whole month up front if you're staying that long. But I'm sure if you explain to her Susan's making the arrangements, she won't get fickle and aggravated. There's nothing worse than a woman that gets fickle and aggravated."

Did he, by any chance, mean Fury?

"And if I don't?"

She couldn't help it. A month? That might completely denude the villa.

"There's plenty boats out there. Sure some of them are going to Jamaica. Or somewhere, that is. I can just sign on."

He would too. He set his face in the basin of water in a lazy, unconcerned way and gurgled in it. A month? She knew she must do something to govern this. If she did not set conditions on this, his demands would be endless.

Not for sex. No, he was already getting that. But food. Drink. Maybe, for that matter, it might even be for whores. He was just low enough.

There must be a way out of this. A way to move even a boulder like Flint back up the hill.

"Of course." In that second it came to her. "As I've already said, you will call discreetly at the villa, following at a safe distance when I leave here. Rule twelve. That will count for the requisite once. Then, you will return late afternoon. That will count as the requisite twice. Then, since it might be advisable to speed things up, after all, the sooner I conceive, the better, you will come back late evening. That will be three. Rule fourteen."

Drops of water splashed from his face as he dragged it out the basin, but she continued anyway. If he thought she had somehow lost her senses and spoke randomly and desperately, he was mistaken.

"The villa is a full hour's walk from here. Of course last night you had a cart."

Oh, yes, six hours a day spent walking in the baking heat might factor in Flint's considerations about staying here and spare her finances.

Although, God knows, even as she spoke, she realized she placed herself in further jeopardy, even if increasing their sessions by one should not make a deal of difference.

But after today, it was preferable to end this. The sooner the better. And the only way to end it was to conceive.

"I trust you are capable?" she added.

"Capable?" Baring his teeth in a grin, Flint flung the towel over his shoulder. "Hell." Then he reached for the shaving soap. "I knew sooner or later you'd not be able to keep your pretty little hands off me." He dunked the soap in the bowl. "We can make it four or five, six even, if you—" The door reverberated on its hinges, before he could say *want*.

Counting to five, the time he reckoned it would take her to

reach the stairs, he cursed and flung soap and towel into the water. *Capable?* Him? Who no woman ever dared asked such a question of?

He closed his eyes and counted to ten. He was doing it again, wasn't he?

Well, he wouldn't do it. Why the hell should he? More pleasure was to be had screwing a statue. Least a statue didn't complain. It didn't have rules. Least with a statue, you knew straight upfront what you were getting.

Even those costly words she'd somehow leeched from him about Celie hadn't satisfied her. On the contrary he had teeth marks on his knuckles to show he should just have kept his big mouth shut.

All he wanted was her to see she needn't worry about him staying here, especially as it wasn't as though he planned to budge back to the villa.

He'd thought she'd like knowing she was woman enough for him. But no. She hadn't. Life was so much easier spitting on shoe buckles at Malmesbury's, when his next thrashing was as much as he had to worry about.

Rolling his sleeves back, he bent over the basin, dabbed the pinpricks with the wet towel.

Next boat out of here, he was taking it. He was damned to her. Damned to her rules. And damned to ever setting foot back in that damned villa.

* * *

"You found your way then, James?" Fury shut her bedroom door. Obviously he had, but she said it anyway. After this morning the need to reassert herself on the situation was paramount. But she had the loss of Santa-Rosa's silver hair combs and brushes to sustain her. What was one more bedding in these circumstances?

Financially staggering.

So she was not going to worry about stretching to three sessions a day when so far, God almighty, she had barely risen to two. He was here, wasn't he? And once he saw how much of a plod it was back and forward, he was sure to come to heel.

"Sort of. I'd say so anyway. But maybe you won't. So how about I just keep quiet and don't say?"

She didn't like the way he stood there. Or twisted his hat. As if he'd something very important to say to her. He probably did. It was just what she was waiting for.

"Look. If it's about the walk. The thought of a carriage is nice but that is all it's going to be."

"That ain't—"

"It was your idea, remember, not to come home. So, whatever it is, frankly, is your affair. Weren't you the one this morning who thought six times a day was nothing?"

That little prick caught him on the hop. His tiny smile seethed.

He'd thought he could be clever here. And it wasn't happening. Because learning what she had this morning about Celia, she was ready for this.

"That's *not* what I want to talk about."

"Your room is, of course, still here if you want it. If you don't, that's up to you."

Besides, not only might she now have to pawn Salome's hanging to pay for it, which she was unprepared to do, there was a decorum to be observed here. She didn't want it getting around the carriage drivers that she received the same man three times a day at her villa, and no husband present. Not even a dead one.

"Now." Fingering her wrap, she crossed to the bed. Then she peeled it from her shoulders. "It's been twenty-four hours. Let's do this, shall we?"

Flint stood riveted. Damn him to everlasting hell. The sight of her in her nightgown was nothing he hadn't seen before, so why did he stare like that, as if his eyes were going to pop from his head? And if he wanted the carriage, as she knew he did, why not say so?

"Well?"

She was preparing to get on her hands and knees but there was something discomfiting about the heat of his stare, as if she were being a little too inviting. Although it might seem a fabulous invitation to any man, surely he knew it wasn't.

"Well, what?" He knocked his hat against his thigh.

"Don't be coy. What do you think?"

"Far as I know you're not paying me to think. So I don't give a rat's tit what, sweetheart. Its ass neither. You want me to think, that'll be extra."

The grin wasn't as pointed as usual. In fact it was more grit than grin. And why on earth, when this was bad enough already, did he keep glancing at the door? It wasn't as if he didn't know where it stood. Maybe that was the whole idea though? Another shabby attempt to beat her down about the carriage?

"Then I don't." She wriggled her gown above her knees. "Although I don't suppose it would cost that much."

He gritted his teeth. She was sure he did. Too bad.

"Now, let me see. Just what would it cost? Hmm?" She tapped her forefinger against her lower lip, pretending to be doing her sums. "Half a lire? A quarter maybe?"

"Then that's half a lire you can keep. The quarter too."

"An eighth would be more likely. I was always prone to over calculation."

"Look—" He took an angry step toward her.

"Is there something wrong?"

There was, wasn't there? To do with that damned carriage in

all probability. Or maybe it was what she'd said earlier about him being capable? What she'd said a moment ago for that matter. Whatever tiresome thing it was, she slipped a hand under the tumble of her hair and shook it, so it spilt down her back.

"It's just...I'm waiting." She knelt forward on an elbow. The trick here was not to look too seductive but get him to drop all this nonsense about whatever bothered him. To get him to come over here and perform as agreed. "I have very little time to waste."

She edged her free hand behind her thighs and grasped the hem of the shift, waiting to adjust it.

He threw off his coat and crossed the floor. With one determined movement he grasped the hem of her gown from her. Then, before she could protest, he yanked it back, baring her flesh.

"My God, James, what do you think you're doing?" She crawled away in shock. At least she did her damnedest. But he caught her ankle and yanked her back. "You can't. I thought we agreed—"

"What do you think I'm doing?" His breath brushed her hair, as he trapped her beneath him. "I'm giving you the heir just like you want, sweetheart."

Of course she should have known better than to ask him so stupid a question. Or to ask him to do this for that matter. Instead of wasting all that money on food, Thomas, and Frau Berthe, why hadn't she just paid him to go away?

"Thing is, you've just got no damned idea, have you, when you start playing games with a man, how dangerous they can get."

She only wished.

"I told you no touching, I told you—"

"Never said anything about looking though, did you?"

Hadn't she? How in God's name had she managed to overlook something so vital? She must have swallowed a mouthful of pillow while she tried covering herself.

"And like I told you earlier, looking's not touching."

"I did. It comes under being fully clothed. And I have every knowledge." She panted, squirming for a hold on the damask bedspread. "How do you think Thomas fell? Now, get off me!"

She tried to kick free but he slipped am arm around her waist. Instead, she smothered a shriek as he flipped her over onto her back.

"I'm not talking the game. I'm talking the man. Anyway, I know how Thomas fell. You pushed him."

Another secret she'd given away. "Because he was being demanding, just like this. Now." She stuck a foot in his chest.

Not that having a foot stuck in his chest made a great deal of difference to a man like Flint Blackmoore.

"What?" He took hold of her ankle and moved it behind him. "Did you have a contract with him too? Is that what happens when you break it? You push a man down the stairs? I better be careful then. Seems I'm bedding the black widow spider."

"You are not bedding anything, just so you know." It would be a very great mistake to rise to this, especially with her defenses scattered sufficiently as to be flattened. "I did not have a contract with Thomas, but I swear I will push you off this bed if you don't proceed as agreed."

"Push me?" He tossed his hair back from his face and she saw just how alight with reckless intent it was. Amusement too. She didn't know which was more dangerous, because she knew them both of old.

"I will scream."

"What's that?" He took hold of her wrists even as she tried pushing him away. "A new clause?"

"All right. All right." She turned her head to the side. It wouldn't do to let him know how badly he shook her cool. Had she not suffered assaults from Thomas — though not in the same way — she might have shrieked. "You don't like the other position, we can…we can do it this way if you prefer. But I'm not quite ready. I still have a preparation to make."

"Either's fine. You should know that." He leaned over her, so close the ends of his hair brushed her cheek. And his scent. Warm, clean skin surrounded her. "And the way you were posing earlier, don't tell me you don't know that. Don't tell me you never made that preparation either." His voice slid over her like warm honey. "Hmmm, Jasmine. Very pretty."

She gulped. Was he breathing her? Something she didn't know she could quite smother oozed along her veins. A desperate yearning to feel his lips, which hovered so close, on her skin. Mouth, neck, breast.

"You must adhere to the rules." She tried. But it was impossible. "These do not include—"

"I am."

Lower. Stomach. Thighs. Sex.

"No, you're not."

"I think if you had that bit of paper still you'd see. There was nothing about smelling you."

Smelling her? Dear God. Why not? Why hadn't she put that in?

"James." She hated that her voice trembled. And that his mouth hovered so close to her skin, it sent delicious shivers up her spine. Physically she felt overpowered. The room wavered and spun. "I drew that contract up for a reason."

He lifted his head and looked at her with his lazy gaze. "I know you did. And I know why too. You don't want to enjoy this, because it's business and it might remind you of old times. But, sweetheart…"

He bent his head and she tried to jerk away, in awful anticipation of what he might do. Where were the rules governing this encounter? She melted with desire. All she could feel was the heat from his body. How was that when she couldn't let herself? When he behaved in this animalistic fashion, trying to take what she didn't want to give.

"That is not so. I did it to protect you."

"Me?"

"And myself from getting—from viewing this as anything more than business."

"That's just what I said. I'm glad we're finally in agreement here."

"Sex…sex in these circumstances was always going to be very difficult. Very difficult. Are you listening to me?"

"Oh, sex was going to be damned nigh impossible." He leaned in close to her ear, letting the words excite. "Which is why I've not been able to stop thinking about how different it could be if you were just to want me a little."

"Could, but *can't* is the word I think we will use here. Now I must insist—I must insist that you honor your end of it."

"Hmmm. What do you think I'm doing?"

She stifled a gasp as his lips brushed her forehead. A light, sensual caress that raised prickles of desire on her skin.

"I said no kissing."

"That's right. If I remember, you said it was a sign of affection. Have you thought that just maybe I love your forehead."

"You don't."

"Your cheeks too. As for your neck, your neck, I could send valentines to."

He couldn't. He wouldn't. But the trail of fire blazed by his lips, all the way down her neck, left her swallowing a groan. His fragrant, soapy smell and the brush of his hair against her skin made her gulp. If he could do this with a kiss, a look… As if she were the only one in the world and he would die to have her.

If? There was no if. What they'd had this far was nothing. A travesty. A joke. She knew what he could and would do to her. She could not let him.

"Stop it. Thomas is dead. That is another reason I made that contract, so you would behave with decorum and kindness toward his memory. And pity the fact I had to leave his bed for yours, when he was not yet cold."

"He looked pretty cold to me. Anyway, the things you said, you hadn't been having any for a while."

"A new widow."

"See, I assume by kissing what you really mean is on the lips."

He raised his head. For all there was no question of her believing it, for all she'd seen it before, she tingled beneath his regard. She had to fight to turn her head away.

"But the thing is, you didn't specify. So I'm guessing that means everywhere else is good."

"Good?"

"All right then." He sounded so pleased with himself she wished she'd kept her mouth shut. "Remember you're the one who said so."

"James…"

She moaned in protest as his mouth found her shoulder. This was what he was born to do. Unfortunately. Reduce even the most stalwart, the most protesting, the most indifferent woman to rubble. But this mood wouldn't just be his mood for now — it would be his mood from now on if she did not reinforce the boundaries. And that would be impossible to fight. Because the truth of the matter, when it came to being indifferent, she was lying to think she was.

"I meant no kissing. No kissing, period." She reached up

and batted his hand away as the pad of his thumb brushed her lower lip. "Rule four. And no touching either."

"Rule four? I must touch you as little as humanly possible. Well, I am. For me, anyway. This is sex. I don't know where you get this notion you can touch as little as humanly possible when part of me is inside part of you. Unless, of course, you're a virgin, which we both know you're not, seeing as that was something you gave to me. You remember?"

She would rather not, especially with the way he smiled down at her. But she did. "Not exactly. I don't remember horrible things as a rule."

He nuzzled her neck. "That's funny, it was so horrible you wanted me to do it again."

"I was making sure."

"And again."

Her throat dried. Yes. The memories existed beneath the frost. But why did he, out of everything and all the women he had ever known, remember that? Why had he smiled at her, as if the remembrance was fond?

"Had I known you were doing all of it to get revenge for Celia I'd have walked the plank." She hauled in a determined breath. "Because let's face it, it would have spoilt everything if you couldn't make me your slave. So, when you're done touching me and you're done kissing me, you might just like to do it."

"Making you hungry, am I?"

"For my lunch, yes. Do you know what time it is? Nearly afternoon. And Susan's making roast lamb. It's her specialty."

He raised his head and narrowed his eyes. She wished she could say it was in that hot, glazed way she remembered. Because that she would have been comfortable with. But something undercut it. The tiniest trace of longing. It was ridiculous. He'd had her several times. But perhaps, the thought flickered, not entirely to his satisfaction.

"Then how about you adhere to that other rule?"

"Which one?"

"The three-minute rule."

"Now you're making this up. There is no three-minute rule." She was not having this.

"Yes, there is. It comes under the heading of no talking."

Three minutes? Of this? She would never last three minutes.

"James."

He tilted his chin and she turned her head away.

"Very well."

There were ways for a woman to feign boredom. She could stare at the ceiling. Or immerse her nose in the tooled jacket of that book there. She could recount the list of things she'd pawned from the villa.

But somehow, she did not feel able to do any of it.

So long as she did not moan. So long as she lay like a doll. No matter what he did. So long as, if there was pleasure, she didn't sink into it.

"Three minutes. Very well. Believe me, I'm going to count every second."

Flint's throat dried. Him too. Three minutes — she'd be moaning in ecstasy.

Three minutes. It was tight but he could do this. He hadn't walked in the opposite direction from the door not to, especially after the words about not bothering to send the money to Frau Berthe had sunk into his teeth.

He edged his hand down her slender body. The sensation of the soft linen against his palm sent a bolt of heat through him. For all he didn't touch her skin, he could imagine the lissome, living silk of it. Soft, like she'd just bathed in warm, scented water. Supple, like it existed solely for his touch.

Imagine easing the linen off. Imagine pressing his mouth to her skin. Her body. Imagine burying his face in that sweet-scented hair tumbled all over the pillow in smoky colored waves. He inhaled a deep lungful. Jasmine. He'd been trying since this morning to work out that scent.

"Is this what you want? Me to moan? Because I'll do it. Otherwise you just lost yourself ten seconds."

He swallowed. The way she spoke was unexpected. But ten seconds was nothing. Out of three minutes, it still left—nothing he was going to waste time counting.

He could do this. Best part of three minutes. What was the problem? His body was rock hard, breathing its desire as it leaned over hers. Every pore. Every muscle. Every inch of skin trembled, sweated with intoxicating longing for her. For her body, and all the sweet things it could give him. And he could give her.

She stiffened. "I'll writhe too."

"What I want here is for you to shut up. You open your god-damned mouth again..."

She sighed. She sighed in a long, low, imitation of ecstasy. "And you'll what?" She turned her head to look right into his eyes.

He didn't know if he'd ever seen such a look on the face of any woman. Heard a sound like that either, like a pained walrus. He grabbed the sides of her face and bent his head abruptly.

She might have her lips clamped tighter than a clamshell, top on bottom. But he was a plunderer. He wanted her. All of her. He couldn't stop kissing her, even if he wanted to. Anyway, her lips weren't exactly shut, seeing as she'd parted them to moan. Soon she'd be opening them some more. Moan for real. Why not?

Never had he encountered desire for a woman who didn't want him. But then, never had he encountered a woman who didn't want him. The sensation was new and not the least bit thrilling.

Because the desire, as he'd observed more than once, wasn't for her body as such, for all that the feel of her lips was so much lusher than he remembered that he wanted to tell her to open them fully. He wanted — shock held him still. The tiniest parting of her lips, sweeter than ever he remembered, even that first time, froze his breath. Next, his heart.

Her lips parted further, enough to give his tongue access. Even in this charged state, Flint acknowledged the awful risk he took here. She might bite his tongue. But at this minute, how many into the three minutes he'd lost track of, it was a risk he was prepared to take.

He captured her indrawn breath in his mouth and slid in his tongue. Slowly. He might be desperate with longing, he might be drowning in the honey-nectar of her sweet, cool lips, but he still wanted to savor this moment. To make time stagger to a halt. So that the three minutes became an eternity. So that she forgot that she'd said three minutes.

The merest, faintest touch of her soft fingers, not even on him, but below his waist on the hem of his shirt, froze his lips and his gaze. But not his heart, which broke into a pounding race. At last. All he wanted. To feel like a man again. A proper man. Not some stud whose balls she broke three times a day for his seed. She was going to touch him.

"That's one minute." The words came from the very back of her throat.

What the hell did she sound like a speaking clock for?

"One minute and one second. Two seconds." She spoke again. A little shuddery, a little uncertain, but even so.

How the hell was he meant to continue with her doing it at all, even if her fingers still clutched his shirt?

"Three seconds. Four seconds."

He stilled his mouth. So help him God, if she had done this with Thomas, he could understand him striking her.

"I told you—"

"And I told you, this is a business arrangement. Five seconds."

Christ give him the strength and forbearance to control his rocketing temper, when his balls felt like shot rock, and his heart hammered like a fist in his chest. Because to lose it, when his gut had told him to walk away instead of letting himself think he could make her want him—and five seconds, five seconds was still only five seconds less—was something he could not prevent.

"Then what the hell are you touching me for?"

"I—I—"

Oh, she needn't gulp as if she didn't know. As though it were a surprise to her.

"Trying to drag me out my shirt?"

"I'm not. I—I—"

"What's this?" Reaching down between their bodies he clamped her hand. "Scotch mist?"

She widened her eyes in horror. "It—it's—"

"Hell. Don't tell me you don't damn well know what you're doing." He thrust her hand away.

"I—"

"Your hand just somehow wound up there? Just plum damn well wandered of its own—"

Black, blinding frustration filled him, so why the hell did he want to say *come here*? Where did the rust of tenderness come from, engendered by the sight of her lying there, taut and trembling?

He set his teeth. He could—he could just take her, because if there was one thing he didn't like, it was a woman who teased. That was the whole thing of this though, wasn't it? He got to *anyway*. But it was how he got to that damn well counted.

Forgetting something important, wasn't he? This wasn't just about him. It was a business arrangement. Nothing more. His seed for his freedom. Maybe she did want him, underneath the stony front. He'd felt she had there. Was it fair to make her lose a control she strove to keep?

Three minutes would be a torture, if that was the case. Wouldn't it?

He swallowed. He almost didn't want to do this now. *Him,* just imagine that. But if he didn't, he didn't want to look stupid. Not when she lay there at his mercy.

Cursing beneath his breath, he undid the fastenings on his breeches. "Fine." He tried not to look at her. "So how much time is left? Two minutes? One and a half?"

"Please, I didn't—"

"Fury…"

"Two minutes."

"Then let's just get this over with quickly, shall we? Rather than lose this golden opportunity. I got to be getting home."

Her throat fluttered into life. "Thank you."

Grunting his response, he tugged himself free of his breeches.

"If you're tired, from the walk, that is, you can always stay in the Blue Chamber. You know that." Again her throat moved. "For tonight anyway."

"I'm not tired from the walk. Let's just get on with this."

"I am sure Susan will give you something to eat, just the same, before you go on your way. I'm sure you must be hungry. And six miles a day is a lot."

"Shh, will you? We agreed no talking. You ready?"

Her thigh was soft. But he refused to take advantage of it. Not even to play pretend she wanted him.

He'd betrayed enough of his need. It would be a mistake to let her know this was in danger of becoming more than a business arrangement.

* * *

The door had no sooner clicked shut than Fury flicked her eyes open. She rolled over onto her side, hugging her arms around her knees, as if for protection, although he was gone now. She had come within a hair's breadth of making the mistake of her life there, hadn't she? She had very nearly given him her mouth. Very nearly removed his shirt. Very nearly parted her legs in more than the necessary businesslike fashion. The tightrope had never seemed narrower. When he had finally entered her, she had very nearly given in and clasped her arms around him.

But she hadn't. Although now, in a few hours, she had it all to face again.

She edged a breath. Flint broke through her barricades and he could have forced her pleasure. But he hadn't. Indeed, he had become almost businesslike. Which, for Flint, was a first.

Perhaps, after all, he understood her need not to respond to him, without her having to spell it out to him. And if he did, there would be no need for further games. They could share the brisk businesslike nature of the transaction.

Fury prayed so.

Now she'd finally got it to this stage she didn't understand why she felt so awful and so wrong about an encounter that was finally right.

Chapter Nine

"Thank you, Frau Berthe, but I know the way from here. I have been before, you know."

As she stormed up the metal staircase that led from Frau Berthe's bougainvillea-scented courtyard to the rooms upstairs, Fury felt the same rage as her name spark all along her veins.

Flint knew he was expected at ten o'clock. For the second day running he wasn't just late, he was absent. Yesterday he had called once. As for the day before that... She didn't want to think about the day before that. But she had smelled drink on his breath. Rum. Quite a lot of it. What a surprise. Give the man an inch and he was sure to take ten miles.

Of course, she had known it would take less than a week to let her down. She was only surprised he had managed the seven days. He was unreliable. He was untrustworthy. He was everything she did not want in the father of her child. And he had placed her in the unenviable position of having to fish him out. Of *this* place.

She was here to tell him if he could not start behaving like a gentleman she would cut the rent. He could live on the streets, in the gutter, on the quay, for all she cared. She could only pray her labors had borne fruit. Pray God, she was pregnant. In all honesty, she could not take another month of this, any of it. From his failure to appear, to the brittle, burning silence of the exchanges when he did.

Malmesbury would make a better choice. A dog would make a better choice.

Reaching the top of the steps, she grasped a breath into her choked lungs. The day was hot and the striped muslin of her dress clung to her drenched form. She would have liked the luxury of a carriage to ride in. It wasn't an option. This morning she'd had to pay creditors. Madame Angelina, her gown-maker, Signor Rossi, Thomas's wine-merchant. She'd had to pawn one of the statues of Cupid to do it.

"Madam?"

Damn it. Must Frau Berthe pant along behind her on the staircase like this? A woman of her age and bulk, it was undignified, not to mention intrusive.

"Madam, I do not think the Signor would wish you to go in there right now."

Who? Flint? She would give him *the Signor* when she got her hands on him. That nip of his knuckles was nothing compared to what she would do.

Just look at Frau Berthe. Built like a battleship, with a face like lumpy dough, yet clearly under Flint's spell. Barging past as if her feet were propelled. Calling him the Signor, for God's sake.

"Thank you, Frau Berthe. But since I'm paying for the Signor's room, the Signor doesn't have a say in it. Now, if you will excuse me." She tried ducking round, but the woman planted herself in her path.

"He is not at home." Frau Berthe folded her arms.

Fury raised her eyebrows. How undignified was it to get in a scrap over Flint. She was done with such things, surely?

"Then I'll wait. Thank you." She pushed past Frau Berthe toward the door.

"Madam—"

"I'll wait in here."

Fury grasped the handle. Really, anyone would think Flint was up to something the way Frau Berthe tried so hard to keep her out. Fury flung the door open.

Oh God, he was up to something. It was all Fury's jaw could do not to hit the floor. Mother of God, he had a roomful of whores. Vilely insinuating. Buxomly pretty. Garishly dressed— *at least they were dressed.* How could Frau Berthe allow this?

Never mind Frau Berthe.

She thought she was going to collapse. This was like that moment on the quay, as God awful as it was unexpected. She couldn't breathe or see or think, as if she'd run right into a wall.

She fought for the strength to turn on her heel and head straight back down the staircase, to lose her swimming senses in the bustle of the crowded street. But her paper legs betrayed her.

She'd asked him to refrain from whoring while the heir was conceived. It wasn't as if he wasn't getting any sex. She swallowed a gasp. Was this why he'd become *ineffectual* of late? Because he was getting too damned much?

Frau Berthe clapped her hands, a sharp *tap tap.* Fury turned to glare. Good God, what kind of place was this? His antics weren't worthy of applause. Had or had she not pawned Signor Santa-Rosa's silver combs for this?

"*Verlassen!*" Frau Berthe barked.

The women—*two,* though whether there were two or twenty was not the point—peeled themselves out of their poses and gathered their shawls and bags. Each with the slow, studied temerity to plant a kiss on Flint's cheeks.

Fury felt the breath tightening in her lungs, as if she'd labored to the very top of the city's bell tower. Whores didn't kiss. No wonder he curved his lips upward.

"Ciao, Flintee."

Flintee? Fury thought she was going to vomit with what curdled in her stomach. And the looks they gave her, as they brushed past, saying wasn't she the lucky one, getting to bed *Flintee?*

She could only pray this nausea meant she was pregnant. And it was all of it, Lady Margaret, the money, Signor Santa-Rosa, going to be all right.

But for a second she stood. Not because she wanted to. Because she did not know what to do.

Never had she been so aware of that little word, *if,* beating at her senses like a bat. *If* Lady Margaret had liked her. *If* Flint hadn't come back into her life. *If* she continued with this. She felt too old, too worn out for *if.* All this just to get the Beaumont heir didn't seem worth it somehow.

"Excuse me." Frau Berthe nodded. Her heels clinked all the way to the bottom of the metal staircase.

Fury swallowed. The pain in her throat was so acute. To add to her distress, in her haste to rush here, she had flung the veil over her straw hat. Only now did she realize that she looked like a beekeeper.

She could deal with that at least. Even as she reached to snatch the veil off, the thought occurred it would mean showing her face. And then he would see what glistened in her eyes.

She hesitated. *If* she didn't, though, he might think she was upset at finding him with not just one woman, but two.

But Frau Berthe hadn't been mortified, had she? No, because no doubt she'd been run off her feet all week, showing women up the stairs and down. No doubt her only astonishment was that Fury here made it three.

No. Whatever else Fury did or didn't do here, she would sooner die on the floor there than give him the slightest inkling she was, in any way, upset.

Her pride would not allow it. She must remove the veil or

she must leave. And that, too, would only signal to him how deeply he had betrayed her. Over a business transaction. She raised her chin.

"It's...it's not what it looks like." His voice, rich and low, washed over her. "All right?"

No. It wasn't. But how typical of him to think it might be. Raising her hands to her head she grasped the veil.

"Not what it looks like? Do pray tell me what it is. Even if what it is, in all honesty, neither surprises nor bothers me."

She marveled at her fingers not only for undoing the pins, but folding, with perfect symmetry, the veil into a neat rectangular bundle, which she could place over her arm. And at her voice, for sounding so cool, so amused, as if she cared not a jot.

"You know I believed we had a deal. But perhaps not."

Flint closed his eyes for a second. "Fury." He huffed out a breath. "Look. About that...that deal."

She walked to the bed. It was an awful lot better than standing in the doorway after all, entertaining Frau Berthe's other residents with the salacious details of his God-awful inability to keep his breeches secured.

Although when she considered the entertainment Frau Berthe's other residents had had all week, this was probably poor fare. But her knees shook. It would be better to place herself near something she could sit down on should the need arise, rather than let him see she was anything less than contained.

"About what? The fact you appear to have broken your end of it, and, never mind me, my child may now be riddled with God alone knows what disease, because not even you yourself would know at this moment in time. How much sex does one man need in the day?"

"Hell, I never did anything, all right?"

What did that exasperated grit in his voice mean? And the

way his hands clenched?

She hesitated. The whores had been fully clothed. And so was he. His breeches weren't even undone. She glanced away after noticing. He wasn't the only one with the unfortunate ability to look where one shouldn't.

Or was he just sorry he'd been caught?

"Goodness. Next you'll be telling me you wouldn't."

"Couldn't is more like it."

Him? Did he want her to laugh?

He went to close the door, and her gaze fell on the tiny bedside table. What sat on it affronted her vision. Or at least it hit it. She didn't know if it affronted it. Surely she would not feel the need to look closer if it had?

"I didn't mean you to see that."

Before she could examine things further, he strode across the room. But even as he snapped up what sat on the table, a book, the images displayed were enough to fill her with thoughts and feelings she could not quantify.

Mother of God, how could Frau Berthe allow such a thing in her house? And yet, imagine if Flint did to her the things she saw displayed in those etchings.

Imagine? What did she need to imagine for? He had.

What was going on here? Flint didn't look at things like this, not that she knew of anyway. He didn't need to.

"Look…"

She would have liked to, but he held the book under his arm. Her gaze was riveted, and not just by the book, which absurdly she suddenly wanted to be, tucked beneath his arm. He looked so uncomfortable standing there. No less a man. He could never be that. No matter what she made him.

"Were…were you going to touch those whores?"

"What?"

"The whores?" Realizing her voice sounded faint, distant,

she cleared her throat. "Were you going to touch them?"

"No. Hell, they should be so lucky. *I* should be so lucky. You ain't...*aren't*." He cursed beneath his breath. "*Aren't* exactly—"

For a second she stared, a cold, knowing chill gathering in her spine. "Helpful?"

"Sort of."

Tact wasn't something she associated with Flint. She wasn't helpful *at all*. She edged her gaze sideways. Of course she couldn't be anything other than impersonal. Only seeing him like this, the slow burning fuse sizzling deep inside him, she saw she'd overdone it, hadn't she?

"I just respectfully look is all."

"James..."

"And they're nice to me."

"I—I can be nice to you. If that is what you want."

"They like me. Hell, I don't know why. But they do."

"I—"

"Don't you say you do too. We both know that's a lie."

It was. But only in that she didn't just like him. Who was she kidding? And she never had just liked him.

She wished she could reach her hands up to cup his face. This close, what she read in there didn't only invite it; what she read in it broke her heart.

"Which is why I can't do this anymore." He set the book down.

She should have seen this coming. She *had* seen this coming. Only it was easier to keep staring the other way because of the things it meant giving away.

"Yes, you can. Because I can change. I know I can. I can stop—I can stop *this*. I just—"

"This is me you're talking to." He hardened his mouth. "So just quit it. You've never been anything less than sore at me for dumping you on that quay. I get it."

"You don't."

"And making you choose me instead of Malmesbury. Or one of these other damned jackasses. I get that too. I got it at the time."

"That is not so." She gulped. Tell him. She was going to have to tell him.

"I been getting it since. Twice. Three times a day. No matter what I do. Which is why I'm not hanging about to get it anymore."

"No, Flint."

He frowned, looking at her for a long moment. "How do you know I can even make you this baby anyway? You could be wasting your time, for all you know. Far as I know I never made a baby in my whole life. And I've done it plenty."

She bent her head. There was no *if* about this. What stood between them was a secret she could no longer keep.

"You already did."

He must have stepped closer. Or maybe she did, because she felt his chin brush her head and his breath sharp against her.

"You did with me. I never had a miscarriage with Thomas. I was never pregnant by Thomas."

"Fury…"

"You have a daughter. And I couldn't—I wouldn't get rid of her." She knew if she told him everything she could not put the rules back. But what surged through her right now, these were consequences she would deal with after. And it was no surrender of her principles, but a slap in Storm's face as much as her own, if he walked out.

Although the thought that he would was far away when she felt his hands catch the sides of her face. He raised her head to look at him. She had never seen such a look on his face before. Sick, fit to kick himself. Bewildered. But, above all else, tender. And the way his heart beat beneath her hands as she placed them on his chest was enough to convince her she had done the right thing telling him.

"You mean, when I left you, you knew you were—"

"By about two months. Storm Fontanelli."

"Storm?"

"She was born in one."

"And you *knew*?"

"Please, that doesn't matter now. What matters…all that matters if you won't stay and do this for me is you do it for her. I need that money. To keep her. It's all I'm asking. I can't…I won't let her have the upbringing I had. It's the reason I've done everything."

"But—"

"Kiss me." Begging had never been her intent. But in that second she edged her arms around his neck. Heat. Fire. Flame. What she had denied herself several days ago was all she wanted to feel. Tastes so sweet and hot, she knew she was within her rights experiencing the pleasure his mouth gave her. So much as she remembered, the need for more of him was excruciating.

His body, hard through the layers of clothes, made every bone in her own flame and then dissolve. Had his fingers not spread across her face, she'd have fallen.

If she went further now, like this, then she threw away forever the chance of keeping control of this situation. She needn't pretend to insanity, or curiosity, when she'd made rules because she knew, not just every inch of this man's body, but what these inches were likely to do to her.

"What are you saying, Fury?"

It was strange, to hear him ask when she'd kissed him. But the fact her fingers found his shirt and tugged it from his waistband was answer enough. It was enough she gave him, enough she did this. He couldn't want more.

"No, listen, I need to know." His fingers worked over her cheeks. "I left you like that. How did you manage?"

"There's such a thing as corsets."

"You met Thomas then?"

"Protectors aren't for virgins."

Being Flint, no doubt he imagined the carnal logistics of this. But all she could see was the dark stubble on his jaw and the fire in his eyes, as she untangled him from his shirt and tossed it on the floor.

"I landed him at a price. He believed I was someone else. You have to help us, Flint."

"Help you?"

"You have to give me this baby. Believe me, there's no other way. If there were I'd have taken it. Did Thomas ever think Storm was his? Did I try to pass her off as his? There was no way I could do that. I went away. I took what money I'd left from the sale of Celia's jewels, the few you left me with."

"Hell, I thought you'd stolen them…right?"

It wasn't right. But his skin, his skin was beneath her hands. His sculpted chest, warm and golden. His neck. His face. His hair. Like old times. Only the brush of his lips felt different somehow. Softer. And more *respectful* somehow. Although there was no mistaking the hard press of his body said he wanted his pleasure.

"I thought I was going to have to find another protector once she was born. But Thomas thought I had been pregnant to him and that was why I left, to deal with matters discreetly."

"Get rid of her, you mean? Why didn't you? Why, when I left you?"

There was only one answer to that. But it would leave her with nothing to give it. She had always loved him. If she had a last night to be spent on earth it would be with him. That was the extent and depth of her passion. It was why she could never have aborted Storm, why she stood here now. But it wasn't the depth of his.

Still she quivered, as his head bent. Maybe it was what she'd told him. Maybe it was just that she was finally going to let him do this properly, but his mouth had an astonishing fierceness about it, as well as a sweetness she'd never experienced with him before, for all that he took control as if he were going to devour her.

She wanted to tear off her gown but her feet left the floor. Instead she wrapped her arms and her legs around him and let him carry her to the bed.

She sank onto the pillows, gasping to feel him work her stockings down off her legs in a second. All the time the touch of his hands was so much like honey on her skin, she marveled at his male perfection. He never faltered. He never fumbled. He knew how to undress a woman and make her feel wanted. To fill her with such desire, heat flooded her veins.

Her own fingers shook; she could barely find the fastening on his breeches. A few tugs and she dragged them over his narrow hips. The feel of his hard, golden skin made her wild with wanting.

She pressed her lips to his face, to his chest, his heart pounding beneath them, barely able to wait as his fingers started on the lacing of her corset. The scent, the feel, the impassioned look of him sent such cascades of pleasure through her, as if all those times in the last week hadn't existed. This, his breathing and his gaze upon her, was all that did.

He slid her chemise over her head. The breeze from the harbor cooled her heated skin, which boiled at the thought she was finally naked. He slid his hands down her arms, as if he wanted to touch every inch of her.

What spiraled out of control in her center was already so heated, she hardly needed him to.

"Please." She moaned, tangling her fingers in his hair as he bent to kiss her breast. "I can't...I can't bear this. You have to... We can do all this later, I swear. I promise." Her voice shook. "I just want you."

He creased his lips. Tilting her head back, so he could fill her mouth with his tongue, he drove into her, taking her beyond frustration to a place so full of pleasure, she gasped in relief.

She wasn't even at the edge. That place she used to think she would die on, it was so exquisite.

No sooner had she done so, than he did it again. Heat exploded and it was what she wanted. To feel every inch of him like this, pleasing her, so she couldn't stand any more. So her body rippled and she gasped, as sweet pleasure pulsed, hot and wild, through her. And she believed she stood at heaven's gate, where she had ascended to.

It should always be this way. Always.

For a second she lay, feeling the stupidest of stray details filtering into her consciousness. The shouts of laborers working on the quay. The wind blowing through the open shutters. But most of all feeling him come to completion. Feeling it all the way to her toes so her whole body was liquid warm.

She curved her lips inanely. It had always been like this between them. No wonder she'd been afraid when experiencing him, what she just had was everything and nothing she'd tried to prevent. She'd not only plummeted from the tightrope stretching the gorge, but been obliterated in the firestorm sweeping it.

What was one more set of pins beneath her nails though? An awful lot better than seeing the man lose faith in himself. Than seeing him walk away from her.

What she did, she did. Life was composed of moments. Why shouldn't she have had this one? The time would come for her to put this back. Tomorrow or the next day.

Especially now the mattress shuddered as he collapsed on his back in that way he always did when sated.

She curved her lips further. Actually, it wasn't half bad. She had a lot to thank those two whores for. To think today could have been like any other.

"Fury."

She didn't raise her head. Truth be told, she loved the way his voice came from deep inside him. At least she loved it when his arm didn't edge beneath her shoulders like this.

"Yes?"

Except there couldn't be any harm in it. It wasn't as if he were the kind to want a cuddle or anything like that. He wasn't the embracing sort. After the way things had been he probably wanted her to press her lips to his chest or something. Why not? Her toes still tingled with the remnants of the pleasure he'd given her. And his chest was a work of art, his skin warm beneath her lips.

"About...about Storm. I just don't understand why you never told me. Didn't you think I had a right to know?"

She lifted her head. He was so beautiful, late afternoon sun and shadows playing across his face, she was glad her heart was already broken. And there was nothing to lose further by kissing his lips. Or letting him squeeze her closer.

In terms of what existed in her heart for Flint, he was dangerous. But only if she let him be. In some respects Flint was the safest man to be with, now she'd removed the barricades. Because he didn't want her, she thought, edging her lips free. And if he looked at her as if he did, it was because she'd ceased breaking his balls. But desire her? Oh, dear God, no.

Everything had spiraled out of control because of these rules. She realized that now. She probably had realized it then. Now he understood her reason for having them, even a man proud as Flint would behave. Give her his seed. Leave when the time came. Ask no questions. If there was one thing Flint had an astonishing head for, it was business.

If she didn't have Storm it would be different. She'd be back in that place she had been seven years ago. But Storm's future was at stake. Fury was the only one who could guarantee it.

And Flint wasn't exactly father material. Just look at him. It made him even safer.

"No, you didn't have a right and I couldn't let you know." She set her head on his chest. "In case you hadn't noticed it was a bit difficult since you were sailing your boat out the harbor at the time."

"You still could have told me. Where is she?"

What was this? Even his voice sounded troubled. And what the hell did he think he was doing teasing tangles from her hair? Flint never teased tangles. He caused plenty.

"She's in England."

He wasn't disappointed, was he, that Storm wasn't here in Genoa? How could she be? Next to the fact Fury wasn't Celia, Storm was her best-kept secret.

"Susan's sister has her. There are governesses and teachers who I pay for. But I want her to go to school properly."

He stilled his hand. "You meaning for young ladies?"

"I want her to have the very best. I know that's something you understand. Schools, Europe, clothes. All the things I've not been able to give her, because so far I've had to hide her away. And I've had to siphon money everywhere I could, using it for that and one or two other things."

Like blackmail.

"Were it ever to come out I had her or that I wasn't Lady Celia, I'd have been finished. I realized that the moment I married Thomas. Probably the day Susan rescued me from that quay and took me to her brother's lodging house. It was her idea in a way."

"What's Storm like?"

She bit her lip. "Why do you want to know?"

"Why do you think? So I can feel like a worthless piece of shit, leaving you and her on that quay."

She jerked up her chin. She could of course deny it; his grin was certainly cocky enough. But she wasn't quick enough.

She passed her tongue around her lips. She had to get control of this, didn't she, so things would revert to what they both knew of the situation? His seed, his freedom. Because this wasn't like keeping him away from her body, or staying away from his, with a few scribbles on a piece of paper. The contract hadn't been invented that would solve this. "What would you have done with a baby?"

He tightened his fingers in her hair. "Well, I—"

"My bet is you'd have made it take its first tiny steps along the plank."

She sat up. Had she honestly thought at the time Flint had left her, her life could get no worse? She was wrong. She didn't understand what he was thinking. Or what she'd read in his eyes. But she knew she must find her stockings, her chemise, get out of here now, before it was too late.

Reaching down she tugged on a stocking. "And what's more, you'd have keelhauled it for dribbling down its chin or yours."

He fidgeted on the bed. "You could have given me the—"

"Marooned it on some island for dirtying its napkins, or peeing on you, or just doing all the hundred and one other things babies do."

"How do you know?"

"I just do." She pulled her chemise over her head. "As for whom Storm is like, well, she's got your eyes and your attitude." Fury kept her gaze fixed on him. "But the rest is quite all right."

It was the cheapest poke she could take. But it had to be

done.

It didn't matter that the feel of him inside her had been even more delicious than she remembered. That it had felt right, perfect, as if they should always be joined that way. That the hoarse cry he'd given when he gave himself up to her, made her soul, never mind her body, convulse.

It didn't matter what existed in the very fiber and chambers of her heart for him.

Flint was not a man who would ever love her back. He was only a man she would want. She would only hurt herself again to believe otherwise.

The door shut behind Fury, and Flint sighed. He wasn't angry. Even if she was wrong about some of the things she'd said. He wouldn't have marooned a baby on an island for peeing on him. He'd have keelhauled it for that. She was still right.

A baby and all the baby things, like peeing and dribbling and dumping a load in a napkin—he'd have torn his hair. And crying, now. Crying. He'd sooner cut off his ears than listen to crying.

And babies seldom came alone. No. Babies were strange apparitions that way. Advance guards. For entire battalions. Armies of little brother babies and sister babies that came uninvited. Just marched right in. Each, a separate entity, requiring the kit of a field marshal. And the elastic pockets to pay for it too.

The falderals he'd seen processing in Fury's wake along Fishside Wharf might not have been hers at all. They were probably baby falderals. Which was another thing.

The space they took up, it would have been a miracle on a par with the five loaves and fishes had there been room for him on the *Calypso*, even after he'd just heaved Celie's trunk off it, if he let Fury and that baby on board.

Heaven-sent gifts? Whatever ignoramus thought that up didn't know the right word for millstones.

Or maybe he did? The world would grind to a halt if a man realized that was his reward for screwing.

Flint conceded all that. He even conceded there was a method in her pointing his thousand and one deficiencies out to him. So why was conceding it and accepting it two different things? Especially the amount of pride this last year had eroded.

He just should have known that having her want him once wouldn't be enough.

Chapter Ten

Flint arrived at the villa at nine the following morning in the carriage he had insisted on, just as he had insisted on keeping the room at Frau Berthe's. Even as he paid the driver, he spotted the reason he'd insisted on keeping that distance, spreading a white cloth over a large garden table, and thanked God for his foresight.

Only she could wear a scarlet dress at this time of the morning and get away with it too.

Maybe not just she. Women of his acquaintance could and did. But here was someone he didn't think of as that. Someone for whom the kick of arousal was instant.

Instant? It was worse.

For a second, as he dallied through the trees, he wished he could retreat. Turn right around and run. She was so damn beautiful. He just prayed, as a twig snapped beneath his boot and she glanced up and saw him there, she didn't see his signs of confusion. Because it was starting to mount in an unmanly way about this. And the flame of her there in the scarlet dress made it worse.

"Flint." She edged her hands down her gown. "I didn't know you were here."

He canted his jaw. "Well, you know the bad doubloon,

sweetheart." He forced a smile. Just. Actually she smelled delicious. As for her hair, pinned at the nape of her neck, he had the strongest urge to loosen that. "Always about somewhere."

She had attempted yesterday to reinstate businesslike barriers. It was just difficult when an image of her writhing beneath him in the throes of ecstasy swamped his mind for him to do the same. He swore he could even hear her moans.

"What's all this?"

She pushed a stray tendril of hair back from her forehead. His palms sweated in that second.

"I was going to eat here in the garden. The villa is so stuffy this morning. But we can go indoors, if you want. It's not a problem."

Now, here it was. The conundrum. Why he felt so discomfited, sweat lay along his palms. If he didn't do this, then it meant Storm would never have the things *she* wanted for her. The things she hadn't had herself. Never mind the things, what he'd sussed yesterday of this whole sorry situation, Storm would have nothing. Not even a roof over her head. Or a sock to call her own.

What kind of father was he to let that be? He already knew the answer to that.

He'd go indoors. They'd have sex. Just like yesterday. What he was here for, right? What he wanted? Right? More than anything, to satisfy the unbearable itch in his balls. For her. In that dress, then preferably, without it. Her honeyed skin and those pretty eyes and her pliant body, all there for his touch. And this incredible sexual current that always seemed to exist between them.

She would get pregnant because they had had sex...wrong.

Because then, she would walk out his life. And he would never make love to her again. He would never do anything with her again.

"Whatever you're offering, sounds good to me."

Fury hoped so. She wasn't prepared for this encounter. However, the grin and the close way he stepped reassured her. What steamed between them tortured her. But she'd far rather it was torture than what she had to do yesterday because she'd never thought to see the day she might have to seduce James Flint Blackmoore.

And just for a second there, the discomfited way he'd lowered his gaze and tried to step back into the bushes forced her to wonder if the lure of the ocean was so potent, he couldn't wait to escape.

He crooked his mouth into a lazy grin. "I'll take coffee. Or whatever."

She tried to keep her own discomfort hidden. Close like this, as if there wasn't any distance between them, she couldn't prevent the answering smile that came to her lips. He was wicked when he looked at her like that. As if he knew exactly what the *whatever* was going to be. Well he did know, didn't he, which was why the tiny hint of sensual tenderness she also glimpsed beguiled her so.

She could barely pour the coffee straight with what steamed in her veins, though, and that concerned her. It would be better to go indoors and take what she could of him, while he was like this, as opposed to having to seduce him.

But if she felt unable to pour a cup of coffee straight right now, how was she going to do more?

Breakfast, particularly breakfast out here, made them like a couple. What unwelcome things might she glimpse if they sat down in such congenial settings? More talk about Storm? Susan might join them and that would be worse, to see him sitting in the basketwork chair, smiling, white teeth flashing in that

incredible way, his long legs bent so you could barely keep your
hands off, further building her anticipation.

It was still the lesser of two evils.

"I'll leave it up to you to choose."

Nice of him.

"Coffee, then since I've poured myself a cup." She strolled to
the end of the table. "You always liked it black from what I
remember."

He held up his fingers. "With just a hint of cinnamon."

"And demerara sugar." She tilted the steaming silver pot.
Like the business with the floor, Susan would be furious at the
slopping mess on the white cloth.

"A pinch of that too."

"But no milk."

"You remember."

Grasping the tongs, she was very aware of him studying her.
Weighing her up against the white cloth. She didn't like it. His
words were accompanied by a disarming grin. She supposed she
hadn't seen how much like a sailcloth it was.

Well, it was like a sailcloth till she blobbed coffee on it. And
splattered a whole sugar lump into his cup when what she'd
meant was to pinch a grain the way he liked it.

She saw him tighten his mouth. Then she heard his long,
exasperated exhale of breath. She tightened her hand on the
tongs as he strode toward her.

After yesterday, she shouldn't be astonished to find him
wanting to kiss her. But out here like this, a full open-mouthed
devouring, as if he could not wait?

"What are you doing?"

"What do you think?" He eased back. "Then we can have
breakfast, sweetheart. Won't that be nice?"

She looked at him. Appalled. What if Susan came outside?
Or worse? What if Malmesbury arrived and saw Flint running

his hand down her leg like this, trying to reach the hem of her gown? To edge her buttocks onto the table, so he could get between her legs?

But it was one way, she supposed, if she couldn't put the rules back. A way that avoided yesterday's mishap.

* * *

Fury sat down at her gilt-framed mirror. It was early evening and she wanted to restore some semblance of order to her tangled hair.

Flint in the copper bathtub wasn't what her eyes should dwell on right now. All the same they did.

"Oh, for goodness sake." She threw the brush down. "Will you please just…" She reached for the jar of cream. "Do something about that."

He lifted his head, his gaze colliding with hers, as the jar splashed into the tub.

"Hell," he protested. "What the blazes are you doing that for?"

"What do you think?"

He glanced at her for a second, feigning ignorance.

"Your back."

He reached down into the water and fished up the jar. "So this is your solution?" He drew his brows down. "Cu —"

She jumped to her feet. "That's what it is, so it should be suitable for you then." She felt her skin redden. "Now you may do as you choose with it."

"Then I will." He plunked the jar down on the tiled floor. His eyes shone with that little feasting spark, his lips set in that sardonic little smile he liked to keep, she had started to think absurdly, for her alone.

"You'll get blood poisoning. From that cut," she added, before he could say anything so offensive she was forced to tell him to leave. "It's not my affair. Just don't do it before I conceive the heir. Because I don't want to have to explain to Storm why her father couldn't take the help, the perfectly good and sensible help that—"

Oh God. What was she doing? Sweeping forward? Bending down and grasping the jar? No wonder he froze.

"All right. Sit forward."

"I'd sooner have the scratch."

He slid and ducked his head under the water. Of course. This morning in the garden had been everything she remembered of Flint. No lingering looks. No endearments. Only straight, *thank you ma'am* sex, which even with Flint sizzled still so hot and sweet it bound her to him more. So she shouldn't rise to this bait.

He didn't like the cream, fine. It hadn't actually been used for what he thought. Susan had bought it for her in the market, the first time Thomas couldn't. And he blacked her eye.

But Flint sticking his head under the water reminded her of every slight she'd suffered on the *Calypso*. As if, for all she had sex with him and had his child, she wasn't fit to spit, at a distance, on his boots.

She knew, she understood, he didn't love her. Yesterday was an aberration. Must he be so cruel though, when she stood this close to the edge? All she'd wanted to do was examine his back. He was obviously suffering. It was something she understood.

"No. Believe me, you wouldn't."

Water cascaded from his face. "We agreed no touching." He shook his hair out of his eyes.

"You think I want to? Even with a pair of fire tongs, given what probably made that scratch?"

"Aren't you getting hell of a fussy about yourself there."

"I am not fussy about myself. We must just hope the Beaumont heir doesn't take after its cowardly father."

"Fine." He tilted his jaw in that cold, glaring way. "But I'm telling you now, it's a scratch."

Fury almost swallowed the soap. Dear God, Flint, the great and mighty wasn't going to comply was he? She acknowledged the effort it took was probably greater and mightier. Flint's pride being greatest and mightiest of all.

"Well, if it's a scratch you wouldn't keep" — he sat forward and she strove to keep her voice steady — "wincing."

"All right. So it's a mess. You satisfied now why I don't want you touching it?"

He lied, of course, about sparing her fingers. But that fact was marred by what crisscrossed his back. Silver wheals, which had no doubt been red and seeping like the one marring his shoulder blades. She edged her gaze downward. No wonder he winced. It looked to her as if as fast as one sore had healed another had been inflicted.

Her throat dried. This was a business transaction. This morning, despite everything, he'd taken control. It was to his credit he had. She should do the same. But the slight trembling in his body undermined her.

Before he could stop her, or she could stop herself, she placed a hand on his shoulder. "Don't move."

"That'll be difficult. Don't we have another session to go?" He offered a lazy smile.

She ignored it. "Not now, we don't. Tilt forward. I'm going to clean it properly, as someone should have done weeks ago. Pass me the sponge." Clearing her throat, she held out her hand. "Now."

Flint sat stone still. If he gave up that sponge, he gave up his self-control.

Like hell he did. He was a very self-controlled man. Water. Lotion. Rude to refuse but he'd reinstated the rules earlier, keeping his thoughts focused on what was important. No questions asked sex. No questions asked sex wasn't as easy as he'd have liked. It wasn't so hard either. He'd had a lot of it in his day. So he was in a position to know. Sitting down to breakfast after had been nice. This, he was less sure about.

He suspected that was why he trembled a little.

Reaching over, he offered the sponge. "There you go."

"Turn."

He didn't take this kind of treatment from women as a rule. But it was only water, wasn't it?

"No, Flint. I mean this."

All the time when growing up he hadn't had anyone he could remember wanting to mend anything for him. Just whatever drunk Ma turned tricks for to survive, wanting to break him, as well as Ma herself, letting him know how sorry she was she'd ever let him be born. Especially the way his daddy had walked out.

He bent his head, his hair fanning his face.

"So, Flint? Lady Celia."

He jerked, and it had nothing to do with the sponge pressed to his skin. What was she mentioning her for?

"You never told me how you knew her."

Wasn't this just— He shrugged. Anything to break the dripping silence.

"Because you never said what she was doing in your daddy's inn."

He braced for the face-full he was sure to get. What she did next made his heart bang like a hammer. She ignored him, in favor of dipping the sponge in the water and squeezing it out on his back.

His trembling increased, his eyes focusing harder on the tub rim. Tiny rivulets trickled over his skin. Their coolness made him aware of just how hot his blood burned.

She went again, this time edging the sponge against his skin. Standing up would look churlish. The beatings she'd had from that damned Thomas. And she'd kept Storm. The thought was one he shouldn't think now. But coolness iced his back.

Hell. It was only water, wasn't it?

"You know this probably needed a stitch?"

"Probably. But there wasn't much point when Malmesbury was just going to lay it open again."

She shifted her knees on the floor. "I asked you a question."

He didn't want to answer, but the room fell very still. Just the drip of water. And this stroking made him feel he was drowning. Made him feel that he couldn't see through the mist and fog.

"Celie had a passage on the *Calypso* from Martinique. She was related to the governor. I was doing some work for him. That's how I got to know her. All right?"

She stilled her hand, and he realized how much he craved it not to, and at the same time he thanked Christ it had. What sweated on his forehead, it was like she peeled bits from him.

He needed to get out of here. He didn't just guess her mouth had dropped open. He edged his gaze and caught it. The silence was disconcerting. It had nothing to do with the fact he never let her do this on the *Calypso*. Or that he'd blurted these words. Gritted them rudely.

If he didn't edge his gaze back...

If she didn't lower hers...

She put down the sponge.

"I guess you're an expert...at this." Recollecting himself, he made a stab at normality. After all, when he thought about this morning and the necessity of putting things back, it wouldn't do to let her think he was the awkward one. "With things Thomas did."

She shrugged. "No, Susan's actually the expert. Not me. I

don't know where I'd be without her, the things she's done for me."

He'd be happier if she didn't sigh and ponder.

"This — this cream isn't... Susan got it for me. She bought it after Thomas started getting impossible. It will cool it. Now I've done this much, I think you should let me finish."

What should it matter, if she went away and he never did anything with her again? Nothing really. So why did unease grab his gut? When he was a man of iron control?

"All right."

A man should know — he should know when he was beaten. And as this morning had proved, he wasn't.

"Yes, of course."

Although he did wish she wouldn't hesitate and it didn't take an eternity to unscrew the jar lid.

"It won't take a moment."

A further eternity to set the lid on the floor. Christ only knew how long before she dipped her fingers in. So each second's delay, before his yearning flesh felt her fingers begin working their magic, prolonged his agony.

Down she went and down, smoothing, kneading, rubbing. Gentle. Never hard. She bent so close, her cool breath brushed his skin.

What did it matter, if she went away and he never did anything with her again?

He turned his chin. *Everything*, he thought, staring at her pretty red mouth. Nailing her this morning hadn't done any damned good. Not with the strength of the currents here.

He just wasn't going to fall for her, or anything. Was he? How could he?

He already had.

"I shouldn't have said it, right? About the cream. It's just me. You're actually very nice there."

"What?"

No doubt an insult would be preferable. And no doubt if he now made love to her, as he was going to do, properly, not like this morning, he couldn't reconstruct this.

But she shouldn't have touched him, because he didn't care about the consequences.

Chapter Eleven

"**M**adam?"

Dear God, must Susan trouble her now, when her head throbbed? And her stomach... Bending over, Fury retched into the ceramic chamber pot. Despite the fact she'd already emptied her stomach in the same way not ten minutes ago, the retching was uncontrollable.

"Madam, don't you think you should see a physician?"

"What for?" She dabbed her mouth with the back of her hand. Her stomach heaved again before she could stop it. "Empty that, for me, will you? If you can't, I'll do it. It's just—" Straightening, she tried to gain control of her shaking knees. "It's just this won't stop."

"Fury!"

She broke off as Flint's voice sailed up from the garden. The last thing she needed. Mustering herself, she set the pot aside on the bed and staggered to the open shutters.

"In a minute. I'm not dressed."

Her stomach gave another heave. She released the curtain drape.

"Madam, I don't understand why, when it's so obvious what this is, you don't tell him."

"Is?" Fury didn't understand why she didn't tell him either.

Well, she did. She just preferred not to.

"Because it might be anything." The room swam in waves around her. "The fish I ate last night for supper. I must be sure first. Nothing can be left to chance."

"And yesterday?" Susan's eyebrows rose. "And the day before?"

There was one thing and one thing only that was responsible for this, and it wasn't any fish eaten for supper. Or breakfast either.

"Last time I was fit as a fiddle. I wasn't sick once." Fury grimaced as she walked across the floor. It was why she hadn't noticed for so long she was late. "Maybe it's not. I can't send him away on a whim."

She eased down at the dressing table. Of course, she knew. She was late. It was time to go home to England. The heir was conceived.

So she hadn't understood three days ago, when nausea first struck, why she felt so awful. Not about the nausea, although, of course, the nausea was bad enough.

She couldn't possibly feel that way, when something was so right, that it was wrong. Yet she hadn't told Flint.

This was a business transaction. The last two weeks since she'd told him about Storm, she'd undertaken a walk on a very different tightrope. A rapturous journey across some dazzling peaks and wanton valleys of pleasure.

It had never been less than safely undertaken. Because in her heart she knew that was all it was and thanked God her children had the same father and she would always keep that bit of him. So this did not make sense.

"All pregnancies are different, madam. The thing to go by —"

"Yes, yes." Fury reached for the perfume bottle and spilt a little on her warm wrists to cool them. The heady fragrance made her stomach heave. It was her favorite too. She would need to find another and hope he didn't notice the reason. The color of the walls was quite offensive too. But she could not afford to paint them.

"Madam, it's not like it's something you can hide. Not like the last time anyway." Susan gestured at the chamber pot. "You've just been lucky he hasn't caught you being sick."

"He's not living here, is he?"

"And you're going to go on pawning…what? This place is getting bare."

Fury sighed. Another thing. But when she weighed that against having Flint beneath her nose, in her bed, living back here at the villa, she understood the logic of it. What burned in her might have raged out of control otherwise.

"Of course I'm not, Susan. I just don't like the way Malmesbury treated him. I'm sure he doesn't want to go back to that."

As if. Flint would take off the moment he found out. The hurt that thought caused her wasn't something she wished to consider here.

"Malmesbury has ships, madam. Maybe he'd allow James to work for him on board one, seeing as he's a seagoing man. You still have your book, remember."

"But, of course." Why did Susan have to have a helpful answer for everything? Fury set the perfume bottle back down and reached instead in the drawer for her lily of the valley cologne.

James, the seagoing man, and Malmesbury. That would last all of two minutes.

"Madam, he is Storm's father, isn't he? Only you said that day, that day on the dock, Captain Fl—"

Fury dragged her chin up. She didn't want to be reminded of that. "What on earth makes you think that, Susan?"

"Intuition. You know him too well."

"Do I?" She supposed she did. She had never thought about it like that. "Let me assure you that doesn't mean I like him. Just because he...he—"

"Gives you ecstasy?"

So, Susan had heard.

"—can be read like a book, does not mean I know him. On the contrary, it just makes him readable."

"Just think." Susan chuckled. "Both your children will have the same father. Lady Margaret will be delighted."

"Children?" Flint's voice cut in, and not from the garden.

Fury almost dropped the perfume bottle. How long had he stood there? How much had he heard? And with Susan clutching the chamber pot. Fury rose so swiftly she felt she was at sea and the choppy waves threatened to throw her as she advanced across the floor. He swam into her vision, but she set her lips in a curve.

"James." She always called him that in front of Susan. The pretense was ludicrous or Susan wouldn't smirk, as she closed the door behind her, thankfully taking the chamber pot with her.

"You didn't come down, so I came up."

"I was going to in a minute. I was just washing and dressing."

She took his hand. They had sometimes taken breakfast on the table in the garden. They had once done other things too, she recalled with a flush.

She wanted to offer him more than her hand. But she realized, with a little shiver, that speaking of coming up, she had vomited. The taste and smell would be on her breath. She edged her tongue forth. On her lips too.

"Dressing?" He curved his lips into a faint smile. Desire was, of course, the normal state for him to exist in, making it helpful to have chosen him. Only there were times she realized, as he leaned toward her, she wished she hadn't."Yes." She turned

205 of Lady Fury

away. "So I could come down to breakfast."

"What's this? More rules?"

"What? Me dressing for breakfast?" She reached down for her shoe. "No, there is no rush surely? We have all day."

That much was true, although she didn't know how she'd manage through the whole one, the state she was in. The floor didn't just come up to meet her as she bent, it swam. She thought she would be sick on it.

"But you're not dressed. So…"

True. He took a step closer and she straightened. He was going to kiss her. He hovered over her, and he probably stood close enough to see the tremors that racked her frame.

Time to tell him, wasn't it? And release him from the necessity of having to make love to a woman he despised. After all, hadn't she felt his hesitation at times?

Felt? She had witnessed it that day at Frau Berthe's.

This was something he did for Storm. No matter what he'd said about Fury being nice in certain places, it was folly to believe he meant it with any more sincerity than he thought a whore was also nice in those same places.

He should know.

She scarcely needed another day on the tightrope. Certainly not in her present condition.

But even after all he had done, perhaps because of it, some foolish part of her wasn't quite ready to gaze at a horizon upon which dust didn't even linger.

"Of course, Flint, if you want, we can go to bed now. I just— need to clean my teeth first."

"Hmm." Wrinkling his nose, he drew a breath. "Lily of the valley."

"Yes. The jasmine was finished."

Turning on her heel, she hurried to the washstand. *What the hell was going on here?* That was what he was asking himself, wasn't it? It was probably not too dissimilar to her own thoughts. What the hell was he breathing her scent for?

He might even be doing mental calculations. Standing there in the bright band of sunlight that shafted through the open shutters, he probably was.

Across the room, his gaze met hers and narrowed, as if he knew she watched him. For a moment she stared across the top of the screen, and then she lowered her gaze again.

All she wanted was the heir. But the strange thing about life was that *all* was never enough. Now she just wanted to keep this a little longer.

"When you're ready, then, sweetheart."

She wasn't, but he had ambled to the bed. Amiably. Which if he was doing mental calculations, he wouldn't. So she wasn't going to say. She rinsed her mouth and stepped from behind the screen.

The irony was his mother would probably have told him some cure for this God-awful sickness, but she couldn't very well ask him. Still, it was a triumph to walk across the floor, when she felt her legs had been replaced with stumps.

"Well, I am ready." She climbed onto the bed. "Then afterwards I can lie here, while you go and do whatever."

"Breakfast. Unless you want me to stay here with you this morning?"

The way her stomach heaved had nothing to do with that notion. The thought of food perhaps. But he reached for her and she grinned.

"Of course you can. But aren't you hungry?"

"Absolutely." He ran his hands up her bare arms. "Don't you want breakfast this morning though? See, if you do, I can wait till you've eaten."

Why the blazes did he keep talking about food? As if he knew she couldn't put a thing past her teeth.

"Later."

"If you say so."

His hands eased inside her wrap. He pulled her hard against him, kissing her. The pressure was less than usual. In fact there was almost something sensuous in the feel of his lips today. Sensuous too about the way he edged the robe off her shoulders, leaving them exposed.

Feeling the mattress sway beneath her knees, she trembled. He drew her closer, so although she felt dizzy, the hard points of her nipples brushed his shirt. Then he removed that. The jostling intensified her nausea. If only she could lie down. She would in a minute and then this would all be all right. But for now… She swallowed.

In addition to her discomfort the sun blinded her as it shone across the bed. She should never have opened the shutters this morning but she had done so in the hope of feeling better. Then she had retched long and hard over the balcony. The thought made her feel worse than she already did.

She only prayed Flint hadn't been in the garden at the time.

Actually she didn't. She prayed for this to be over soon. Was there even a point to doing this when her head pounded? She should stop this now. But his eyes held hers with that hot gaze. The one that, under other circumstances, made heat streak over her whole body. Except now, what broke out…

She swallowed. The thought of returning to the stuffy atmosphere of Ravenhurst, of never seeing him, never feeling his mouth, his hands, on her body again, made her throat clench. That was a dull, gray life of propriety and duty, which would claim her soon enough. A secured future. One for which she longed. But one that could never include moments like this. She must enjoy the moment.

She found the fastenings of his breeches. All the same it would do no harm to hurry things along a little.

"You're eager this morning."

A word might be her undoing, especially with what hit the backs of her teeth. She sighed. Gliding sideways she cast herself onto the mattress. The room spun, but she fixed her eyes on the ceiling. Now she was lying down she might feel better. After all, her troubles started this morning when she had gotten up. So, if she just lay down from now on, would he even notice?

"I am a little. It's how you make me."

His jaw dropped open. As if she lied through her teeth. She was going to do something else through her teeth in a moment, if he did not hurry up.

"Is that so?" He edged her wrap apart so his fingers touched her naked waist. "It's just you've never said so before."

"I'm sorry about that. But you know we agreed, you know how much we need to do this for Storm. So…"

He bent forward to claim her mouth and she groaned.

"But, I fear the fish I had last night for supper just isn't— isn't agreeing with me very well."

"You want me to stop?"

She was glad she was lying down. Him? Stop? Although he hadn't really started. He wasn't good at mastering his frustration that way once he did start though. In fact, she couldn't think that he ever had in the old days.

"No, I want you to give me…I want you to give me this baby. It's regrettable when I don't feel well, but it is a sacrifice I must make. And I shall be all right in a minute. I just didn't want for you to kiss me, when I—I—"

In a bid to avert what was coming she turned her face to the arm he had stretched out beside her. Despite the fact he edged a finger inside her now, what was coming wasn't what she hoped and enjoyed.

"I'm going to be—going to be—" She hesitated on the word *sick*. It was obvious, by the distressing noises that came from her throat, what she was going to be. Yet she swallowed hard, turned her head and considered — the ceiling was even more beautiful than usual, wasn't it? The frolicking nymphs and that embossed…whatever it was called, that thing of Cupid. And Flint gazing down at her, puzzled longing stamped on his handsome face.

"Fury?"

"A moment, please."

Alarm shot through her although she strove to sound stalwart. He was going to ask. She didn't know if she could bear it. But she couldn't stop this.

"If I could just sit up."

"Of course. Hell." He pulled back. "You look pale. Are you all right?"

His eyes, a cool, gleaming blue, assessed her. Apprehensive rather than knowing. Had they been knowing she doubted she could now go on with this.

"Can I get you anything?"

"Some air." It was very necessary. Flint never got anyone anything. Unless the anyone in question was himself.

Sitting up she felt better. At least she felt less likely to retch. More able to explain. She sucked in a calming breath.

"That fish, that fish last night, just wasn't… Do you know, Susan wasn't very well either?" Susan would forgive Fury this lie. Another to add to the multitude. "She was up all night. I had to — I had to look after her."

"You don't say."

His scrutinizing response didn't fool her. He knew. Or he'd have said something cutting. He was set to go, and she was set to resemble a prized idiot. Imagine, not knowing what was wrong with her. Or worse. A desperate woman, trying to keep hold of a man with lies. A wanton. She just wished to hell she hadn't lied.

"She only got better a few hours ago. I thought — I thought I'd have to send for the physician."

So why did she keep doing it?

He must know. If there was one man who wasn't stupid about this matter it was him. Her throat dried. She lowered her eyelashes rather than meet his scrutiny.

"At least, I almost had to send for him."

"I guess that makes three."

She blinked miserably. It did, didn't it? Her, him, and the baby. He drew back. Here it was. She had never felt more stupid. Giving him this amount of balm for his masculine ego. At least she could go home to England and forget.

"You know, Fury, I was up half the night?"

"You were?" She fought to keep her voice from rising a whole octave. "I mean...you were?"

"Felt like I was anyway. I gave up in the end trying to get some sleep. Hell, you know, there was me thinking you were trying to poison me."

Her eyes widened. The damn cheek was not something she would take issue with here. Not when there were too many others. Was it possible she was mistaken? Susan was mistaken?

No. That would also mean the food was off the day before as well.

"Isn't that the sort of thing you do, sweetheart?"

She tightened her jaw. She wasn't so grateful she had to suffer his insults. "Perhaps we haven't discussed this. But *when* this is over, I intend — "

"When? You mean it's not?"

Uncertainty flickered. When he must know why did he ask? But if she told him the truth now, she'd look even stupider.

She strove to sound assertive. "No. Of course, I will tell you when I am pregnant. Obviously there is no question of you returning to Malmesbury's service, if that's your worry. You've just said yourself, that fish. That horrible fish." She turned her head.

The little twist to his mouth, the uncertainty of it, and the furrow between his brows were things she honestly didn't recognize.

"Fish was off, sweetheart. You should lie down. Rest. We can get to this later. What's one less session? We have all day, don't we? Now, I'm going to get myself some breakfast."

Breakfast? And he had been ill half the night?

She lowered her gaze. The one thing that would make any sense here, didn't. He couldn't possibly care for her. Even if he did, and she no longer said he didn't, it could only be the tiniest fraction of what she felt for him.

Why fool herself about that?

Because then she'd have to believe that maybe he was suitable to guarantee all their futures, when she knew damn fine he wasn't.

* * *

Her lies didn't fool Flint. She was paler than usual. Hell of a so. And her eyes weren't green. They were forty shades of yellow.

The fish? His backside. He'd seldom heard such — when it came to describing such things, *fish swill* seemed about right. Politer than horseshit.

He tiptoed across the room and drew the shutters.

Never mind seldom hearing such rubbish, he'd seldom talked it either.

Blame it on the fact he was adrift. *Pregnant.* It wasn't as if he could congratulate her.

Not when he wasn't meant to know.

Why didn't she want him to know?

Frowning, he snapped the curtains shut. Before he ever set

foot in this house, he could have answered the question about what she was playing at confidently. The way the dockside hussies queued for him. But she'd cured him of that notion, hadn't she? What if all that kind forgiveness about Storm was an act? And really she planned on getting him lifted. Banged up in jail.

"I'm going downstairs now. I'll be back." He hesitated. It was hard to believe though, the open way she'd been with him these last few weeks. "You need anything, or you don't feel so well, just holler. You hear me?"

Pregnant. Never mind her. It wasn't even as if he could congratulate himself. Storm's future was guaranteed. Halleluiah. *For her.* He wasn't a lousy father. No. He was the man who had been asked to do something quite novel.

So now the moment arrived, the one he dreaded, but knew was coming, what had he done? Told a pack of lies about being ill as her. He wasn't pregnant. And his boat had just sailed into view, fully rigged on the horizon. Was he mad?

Staying he risked even more — of himself. Years ago, when he'd felt threatened in that vague way by her, he'd taken steps to ensure his future. But this close he could see the soft rise and fall of her breasts. He supposed it had been easier then. He had been different, master of his world. She had been different, at his command. This partnership was different. More challenging. More equal. More enjoyable.

He supposed he just didn't want it to end. He'd no idea what the future held. Who did? But he thought about what his bed might. It was going to be empty, without her. She seemed right in it somehow. She seemed right for him. And a dockside whore didn't compare.

So he didn't see why if she wanted to pretend for the few weeks they had left, he shouldn't either. He would have his boat soon enough. And what better thing to make him feel like a proper man again than making love to the woman who carried his seed?

* * *

"Madam?"

Not again. Fury dragged a pillow over her head to obliterate the sound and groaned. Then she threw back the sheet and retched. Every muscle in her stomach ached. A horrible, empty ache because she was barely able to eat.

Other parts of her ached too. But that was a very pleasant ache. Eight weeks had passed, and how long she was meant to keep Flint thinking she still needed to conceive, she'd no idea. Being pregnant must do things to a woman's body. She hadn't realized she would feel so ravenous. For him.

"What?" She croaked. Couldn't Susan see how ill she was?

"Madam!" Susan grasped her wrist and shook her. "I wouldn't disturb you, but you have visitors."

"Oh, God, not Flint at this time in the morning. Can't he wait?"

"No. This is Malmesbury. And Lady Margaret."

Fury all but shot from the bed. Had her stomach felt queasy before, it heaved like an ocean now.

"Lady Margaret? But Lady Margaret never leaves England. She never—"

"Well, she's here now. And she wants to see Thomas."

Fury thought she was going to faint. Thomas? He lay at the bottom of the ocean.

"I told her you were indisposed."

"I am."

"But she was most insistent."

Whether she was or not, Fury would have to face her. It didn't matter what secrets her book held, she did not want Lady Margaret speaking to Malmesbury. What if it came up in the conversation that Thomas was visiting his father? Lady Margaret would be most surprised. The old duke had been dead as a post for two years. She must do something.

"Pass me that gown."

"But it's scarlet." Susan stared at the heap on the floor in dismay.

"I don't care if it's aubergine with green spots. It will have to do." Fury held out her hand. Malmesbury would want Flint back. And she had promised Flint otherwise. She could not let him think she'd double-crossed him.

She dragged the silver hairbrush through her hair in quick jerks, all the while aware her hands shook as if a fever lay all along her veins. Then she tossed some cool water on her face. It didn't help. She still felt horribly jarred, and her stomach twisted in knots.

She could not be caught out. Not now. Not when the end lay in sight. But Lady Margaret abhorred her. And Lady Margaret was capable of anything. Would it not be simpler to run? Just take what she could and flee?

"Go downstairs. Do what you can to offer them refreshments. Eavesdrop. I need to know if anything is said."

"Yes, madam."

"I don't need to tell you what about. And if he should appear, warn Flint."

It would just take him ambling in without a cravat, flashing those lazy blue eyes of his, for Fury to be drummed out of here. Lady Margaret's eyes were needle sharp. It would be just her luck for this child to come out as his very spit. Then how would Fury pass *that* off as a family resemblance? Uncle Montague? Or Victor?

Worse, what if he just appeared like he had that day in the garden and kissed her? With Lady Margaret present, he'd have to kiss her too. It was unthinkable.

Dragging the dress over her head, she fastened it as briskly as having ten thumbs instead of two allowed. But how awful to have to do this when her head pounded and blinding starbursts filled her eyes.

As for that slimy poke, as Flint called him, it was a close run thing as to who she wished to see less, him or Lady Margaret. How could he be here at the same time as her? Fury thought she'd dealt with him weeks ago. Obviously not.

She met her own troubled gaze in the glass. Did they hang women in Genoa for fraud, deception, and shoving their foot into their husband's chest, causing him to fall down the stairs by accident? Then having him dumped at sea? Probably.

She clamped her lips shut. At all costs if she was to protect Flint, she couldn't afford to let the poke know she was pregnant. Her stomach's behavior wasn't something she could count on controlling. She must somehow dispose of him fast as possible. Also she was rather pale, wasn't she? She pinched her cheeks. She was thin too though. It was in her favor.

Crossing the floor, her heart thudded and her palms sweated. Not for the first time she wished she'd never embarked on this. How she descended the stairs she had no idea.

The downstairs hallway stood empty, but even as she approached the sitting room she could hear voices. Lady Margaret—it was her all right—was holding forth on the vile heat of the nasty Italians. She must have meant the climate, since the men were not likely to ogle her. Why come here if she could not bear it?

While Malmesbury, what little Malmesbury could squeeze into the tirade anyway, offered fawning agreement. He was not a man to do so. Ever. It could only mean one thing. He knew all about Thomas. Most importantly, he knew where Thomas was at that precise moment. He was probably going to blackmail her for that book.

For a second Fury wanted to turn and run. But where would she go without a legitimate penny to her name and, now, two children to support?

She supposed one thought, and one thought only, now made her straighten her shoulders and grip the handle.

She had been foolish to drag on the association with Flint. After all, what was she going to do? Sit here till she grew as big as a house side and the villa was depleted? He wouldn't stay around her then. He liked his women trim.

Maybe the dowager toad's presence was not a bad thing, if it now brought her to her senses and forced a facing of that fact.

"Mama!" Throwing open the doors, Fury forced a wan smile.

Lady Margaret ceased in mid tirade to cast her eye upon her.

"Susan has just informed me you were here. And you, Lionel."

It was the way to address them, wasn't it? As if she had nothing to hide. And after all, now the cellar stood empty, it would be a hard job proving it.

"And so she should have." Lady Margaret spoke evenly, bitterly. "At ten o'clock in the day and you not even stirred. Pray tell me, are these disgusting habits Italian?"

Lady Margaret was not one to show her enthusiasm, for Fury in particular. She was hot, she was bothered, and her ruched bonnet was not the thing to wear in this heat. On either side of the ribbon her cheeks drooped so fantastically, Fury marveled she could speak. Although she was not the least surprised it was rudely.

"Things are very different here from in England, Mama."

"Frankly I don't care what they are. When in England one should do as in England. And when in Italy, one should do as in England too."

"Which is why I am so astonished to see you here, Lionel." It would help matters greatly in terms of what she should play here if she just ignored Lady Margaret and proceeded to glean some inkling of what exactly they were doing here together. Or whether they were here together at all. Perhaps it was simple chance, an unlucky throw of the dice, which had somehow caused them to career into one another. "Did you somehow meet Mama here in Genoa? Are you already acquainted?"

"I met her by chance when she disembarked from one of my ships looking for Thomas."

Did she imagine it, or had the room become stuffier all of a sudden?

"Is he back yet from visiting his father?"

Lady Margaret started up in shock. "His father?"

Lady Margaret swiveled her head. It spun so fast, Fury made a gesture of denial even as she expected it to grace the tiled floor, followed by herself. She seemed to stand there forever feeling their eyes feasting upon her. Although, in reality, no more than five seconds passed, during which time she quashed her desperate need to escape. Not to mention the dark contorted images that rose of herself dangling at the end of a rope.

"His Grace has been dead these twenty-three months."

And didn't Fury know every blasted moment of it?

"How can Thomas be visiting him?"

Oh. It was over, wasn't it? Unless she could think of something, something to save herself from what was coming next.

"Indeed he could not, Mama." She licked her lips, which were not unaccountably dry all of a sudden. "Certainly not, His Grace. I am sorry you have that impression."

Lady Margaret's eyes narrowed as Fury stumbled on. Malmesbury's too. Which was why she wished that silly little smile wouldn't play around his mouth.

"His holy father in Rome is who Thomas has been visiting."

"His what?" Lady Margaret gaped, her mouth open.

Truth to tell, Fury was utterly surprised herself.

"Thomas is a Protestant. A pillar of the church. And a Freemason. Why on earth would he be visiting the Pope?"

A Freemason? Fury barely swallowed her shock. To think there were things she had not known about Thomas. But why shouldn't he have been visiting the Pope? What else was she meant to say here?

"Thomas went on a pilgrimage, Mama, concerning matters, it is a little too delicate to discuss here."

"I think you had better discuss them."

"Indeed." Fury cast Malmesbury a sideways glance. "But these are matters which, alas, I cannot before a gentleman."

"Before a—"

"Please, Mama."

So long as she got Malmesbury to leave, she believed she could do this. Lady Margaret was all sorts of awful, and were she to know her son lay at the bottom of the bay, she would be that and more. But she was still a woman. A woman who wanted a grandchild.

"I see."

"Lionel, you will leave us? Lady Margaret is of a delicate constitution." Another lie. Lady Margaret had the constitution of a rhinoceros mated with a hippo. But if Malmesbury didn't go she would lose this. "There are things her ears would blush to hear, concerning the necessity of Thomas undertaking the journey to Rome."

She just needed to be careful not to hint she was pregnant. Then he would be back here demanding Flint. Hopefully the carrot she dangled was enough though. She prayed so because her head ached, and it was all she could do to stand here, the way her stomach churned.

"I will ring for Susan."

Fury approached the little brass hand bell, rusted with disuse, and jangled it. Susan would be around somewhere, and then they would begin. As for Malmesbury, well, saying His Lordship was just leaving, was certainly the way to deal with him. When Susan arrived to escort him out, she shot Fury a look of pure admiration.

Fury waited till the door had closed again, then, suppressing a shudder, sat forward. "It's like this, Mama, those conditions you set us were difficult to meet."

Fury hesitated. It was all very well knowing the focus Lady Margaret's presence brought to the sorry situation she was in. It was equally fine knowing she was pregnant. The question here was what to say about Thomas's demise. Should he be still visiting his father in Rome? Or…what was she going to say?

"And Thomas—Thomas felt it best to—" She folded her hands together. "In truth, he believed he had led a sinful life marrying me."

"I'm not surprised. You know my feelings on the matter."

"A sinful life in many regards, and that was why God visited on him that brain tumor. So he went…" Fury felt her palms prickle. "I have news. The pilgrimage Thomas left on has in fact been blessed, whatever you may think of his change of heart and faith. Even before he left it must have been. I am two months pregnant—*James?*" Her voice shot up to a shriek.

Flint strode in from the garden. Strode, not ambled, in that way that generally precluded a *getting to it.*

"James?" Lady Margaret's expression was different from most women's in that her brows slammed down, not up, as if she confronted a viper.

Fury's heart scudded across several beats. If the mixture of hunger and fury in his eyes was anything to go by, he didn't intend being sociable.

Her lungs tightened. She could feel each breath sharpen

there in her throat, as if something too large clogged it. For just an instant she felt as if she were drowning in some great depth, as if the ocean rose around her and she was no more than a tiny cork being tossed around. But at least his attention diverted. He hadn't grabbed her and kissed her.

"C-captain Ames." Fury attempted to rise.

What was he doing here? What had he heard? Whatever it was, it was sufficient for him to prowl the room, with a panther's grace. Tall, sleek, and silent. The sunlight shone on his unsmiling face, and his gaze scrutinized the floor.

Thank goodness it did. If he had leveled it on her, she'd collapse. Because there was only one thing that could make him look like that.

"You…you scared me."

"Captain? Who?" Lady Margaret demanded.

Somehow, Fury tore her eyes from his seething presence and raised her chin. "Lady Margaret, this is—"

"I'm afraid it's no good." He growled, in that low drawl of his. "We can't keep what's been going on to ourselves. We need to tell Lady Margaret everything."

"Everything?"

Fury was going to faint. But she shot to her feet in a ruffle of red silk. At a minimum she should have told him she was pregnant, instead of having it seem she only wanted to extract something from him, and that he was of so little consequence, now she had, there wasn't even the need to say so. But was he mad? Did he want her to hang?

"Captain Ames, I am afraid I don't know what you mean." Even as she stepped forward she felt her legs shake. Her throat clogged further, and perhaps that was why the room swayed, because her lungs were starved. Now, when she most needed to be strong, for her voice to sound confident and bold, it shrunk. She quivered. Her hands went cold. Pride alone commandeered her tongue. After what he had done to her seven years ago, she should have remembered he wasn't safe to be with. "There is nothing to tell. You know that."

"There is." He approached her. "And Lady Margaret here has a right to know, seeing as it concerns her son."

Whether she was going to faint or not, she was going to pretend to do it anyway. What other choice did she have? Especially when she caught a glimpse of Flint's eyes and knew it was over between them. The room spun in sickly waves around her.

She shut her eyes, bracing for the cold smack of the floor tiles against her knees, for the moment when her body jarred. Then she let herself go, sagging downward. Except the hard smack never came.

Instead, someone caught her.

"Get the maid." Flint didn't care if he yelled at Lady Margaret. So long as he didn't do something stupid, like calling Susan by name. He wanted her here now, so he didn't demonstrate his knowledge of the route to the bedroom.

"The maid?"

"She'll be about somewhere. Hurry."

He gathered Fury up and held her against his chest. It was the first time he'd ever done so and he wished he hadn't. She felt so light it surprised him. She made his heart hammer. And he didn't want his heart to hammer. Or feel what thrummed in that second. Or her to fit against him like a glove for that matter.

For two pins, if he didn't get her up the stairs, he'd carry her out this house.

Even if he knew her well enough to know she was probably pretending.

"I need to get Her Ladyship upstairs but I don't know where the bedroom is."

"The bedroom?" Lady Margaret shot to her feet. "But that is…that is completely unheard—"

"I don't much care what it is. Her Ladyship's condition's delicate. And what she's hiding from you is the fact His Grace is missing. Now, unless you want to be responsible for Her Ladyship losing this baby or you have another successor to the dynasty, she needs a physician."

"Thomas is—Thomas is—"

He didn't abhor the idea he might scare her. Lady Margaret needed more than scaring. So if she dropped to the floor, the way Fury almost had, it wasn't his concern.

Fury, for perhaps the first time ever, was his immediate concern. Which was why, while it relieved him to see Lady Margaret get off her big backside, he left her and strode into the hall.

Fury might be pretending. She might not. But she might lose this baby and for the first time Flint didn't think he could face it.

Chapter Twelve

"It's all right, you can open your eyes now."

Fury gritted her teeth, not only to hear Flint speak but to find the neck of her dress undone.

Still, she would have been more incensed to see him grin when she edged her eyes open, adjusting them to the shuttered darkness of the bedroom.

He leaned over her, regarding her with easy intimacy. A gentle amusement, which was the complete opposite of the way he'd carried her up the stairs. But there was the faintest look of apprehension too.

She recalled the strong, tight way he'd held her against the hard wall of muscle in his chest. He had been worried. Maybe just for the briefest instant. Only now, of course, the crisis ended, he wasn't the type for fuss. Merely the type to enjoy opening her dress.

She took a deep breath. "Where is she?"

"Lady Margaret?"

Who else? Fury had a horrible feeling this wasn't over.

He drew back. "She's lying down in the Blue Chamber. She's got the smelling salts and Susan. She'll be fine." He eased himself down onto the edge of the bed.

"What did you say to her?"

"What do you think? I told her that her precious son was lost at sea."

"You didn't!" Fury did her best to keep her voice lowered, even though the Blue Chamber stood at the other end of the landing. The prescience that this only made things worse intensified. As if Thomas's ghost had risen up to haunt her for pushing him on that staircase and keeping him in a box. "How could you?"

He frowned. "Because you didn't leave me a whole lot of choice with that little story you told about his holiness, the Pope."

"What was I supposed to say? That Thomas is lying dead at the bottom of the bay, because you put him there, after I kicked him down the stairs and kept him in a box in the cellar for several days?"

He canted his jaw. "Well, how about a thank-you for getting you out the hole you were in?"

"It wasn't a hole. I just didn't know he was a Freemason. They keep these things secret."

"And you didn't seem to know he was a Protestant either. Is there anything you do know?"

They were going to quarrel. It was not the place with Lady Margaret along the corridor. Maybe Flint had left Susan with her. But no doubt Lady Margaret had disposed of her and had her ear to the wall. Then there was Malmesbury. The thought of Malmesbury made Fury sick to the pit of her stomach.

"Flint, I am grateful. It's just *her*. Lady Margaret. You have no idea how much she hates me."

"Isn't that funny? She was soon guzzling out my hand."

Of all the nasty, recalcitrant, self-seeking *toads*. She supposed she should just be grateful. Even Lady Margaret wasn't immune to this man. But when Fury thought of all she had suffered at that woman's hands, and Thomas too, because of her silly dictate…

"Of course, you like to imagine."

It was just the thought of Flint encountering that lack of immunity with other women. Women far younger and more beautiful than Lady Margaret. He was going to now. There was no question of it. Despair engulfed her.

It wasn't wrong he was so handsome, so beautiful. It wasn't wrong she had succumbed to him as all other women did. It was terrible.

Sighing deeply, he turned his face to the side. "Look, I did it for you."

"Me?" Oh, that was rich.

"Hell. It's not exactly like it's a lie, you stop and think about it for a moment. It's probably quite smart. Smartest thing either of us could come up with in the circumstances. 'Specially if his body ever washes up."

Fury felt sicker. As if the whole thing had suddenly come home to her. And she could see Flint was right. It was just she'd had no idea, when he had stridden through the sitting room shutters, this was what he intended.

She should have. Flint was an astonishing man to have around in a crisis. It just—well, she wasn't going to have him around. Not after this.

"Go on." She touched a hand to her temples where a headache gnawed.

"She accepts he left Massa along the coast some time ago in a skiff, but never arrived here."

"A skiff?"

He eased his long legs out. "Could have been hired anywhere. And you hired me to find him."

"I hired you?"

"As Captain Ames. All right, it doesn't solve Malmesbury, if he finds out Ames and I are one and the same man. So, you better pray he doesn't. But it's the best I could think of at short notice."

It was. But she couldn't stay here now anyway. She'd realized that before she opened the sitting room doors. It was just ironic it should take Lady Margaret's presence to bring her to her senses and show her the sheer idiocy of her situation.

"You've been waiting for news. Confirmation, which I've just brought you. Now, of course, you're lying down. As is she. Maybe she's pretty well devastated about Thomas, but she's not exactly displeased about the fact the fish wasn't off."

A delicate way of putting it. Fury felt the color seep into her face in hot waves.

Even his handling of this, his behavior down the stairs was something she couldn't fault. There had been no talk of rat's tits, as in he couldn't give one. Or unseemliness about her condition, as in how she got into it.

She only wished to her bones, there had. She loved him so much. And she was only one more woman to him.

"I was going to tell you. But I just found out myself," she lied.

He tilted his chin, the faintest smile carving his cheekbones. Whatever he was going to say, she couldn't afford to hear it.

"I had my suspicions." She adjusted the neck of her dress. "You will appreciate, now you have met Lady Margaret and seen for yourself what she's like, I needed to be sure before I went home to England. She would throw me out otherwise. Cut me off without a penny. But then, this morning, just before you arrived..."

"Really?"

He stood. Maybe it was the fact that Malmesbury had called, but she could see how this might look to him.

But that was false. She would never have betrayed him. They'd been so close. Tears pricked her eyes. The funny thing was, he hadn't seemed to notice she was pregnant. How was that? He knew this was a business transaction.

She sat up. "Listen, you need to go. I don't have much but there's money there at the back of that drawer in the dressing table. It's my passage back to England."

"You don't need it?"

Of course he'd ask. Because he didn't know about the things she'd pawned for this God-awful passion. But it wasn't her place to take issue, despite the alacrity with which he prowled to the drawer and yanked it open on various things. That damned book included, she realized, remembering she'd forgotten to lock the drawer yesterday.

Still, he was hungry after all, for what he wanted. And he hadn't been bad to her. Not this time. And when she thought about that welt on his back, she knew it was dangerous for him in Genoa now. She didn't want Malmesbury anywhere near him.

"I won't need money now Lady Margaret is here." Her throat clogged. How ridiculous, when she had always known how this would end. And it was with him raking in a drawer like this, for her last penny. And it was on her to reclaim Signor Santa-Rosa's candlesticks and other sundry items, including the dining room silver, from the pawnshop too. "I'm sure I can prevail on her to pay what needs to be paid. Anyway, I don't know I can travel on a ship right now, so it won't be needed. Take it to get away from here. Down to Massa, or wherever. Malmesbury has merchant ships. So you mustn't leave from here. You need to go somewhere else."

Even as Flint reached into the drawer to enclose the purse she'd stuffed at the back of it, he paused. It wasn't just the sight of the book that made him fear to leave her here at Malmesbury's mercy. He could feel each word she said sharp in his breast, sitting there just hard enough, so that if he moved they pricked him.

His mind told him it was ridiculous. This was his chance to be free of her. Finally. To get out of here and get back to his old life. But his deepest self said that life would be nothing without her.

He couldn't understand it. How could he even contemplate walking out the door? He tried conjuring every conceivable joy, every conceivable memory of that life: The dockside whores, the clink of gold, the laughter of his crew. Because he couldn't understand it either, how the hell she could win over that. He supposed she always had. He just hadn't wanted to see it.

He lowered his gaze, catching sight of himself in the glass. And even worse, seeing her, beneath that damned pale-faced hanging of Messalina. Something in him stilled.

"You know, sweetheart, it's been nice."

"I know. But—"

If she didn't mind him leaving and all she wanted was the heir, then why had she pretended? When she could have ended it? It must be, no matter how she'd cut him and treated him with contempt, the same reason why she'd kept Storm.

He exhaled sharply.

What was more, she was pregnant with his child. He wasn't sure about the kind of father he might make, but he wanted to find out.

"Fury, come with me."

She regarded him with an intense gaze. Above her Messalina's face was a white oval and every bit as shocked as he suspected his own must look.

"We could head to Massa now. Or wherever."

"We? Slip away, you mean?"

Obviously. There was no other way to do it. She could not very well parade out of here, or him either. A ceremonial procession before Lady Margaret.

"Exactly. You're catching on fast."

All right, she was pregnant but he'd soon find a way of looking after her.

She sat back. "Oh, that's fine for you."

"We can get Storm."

"Storm?"

"All right, I know it's a shock to you, but these last weeks…"

These last *damned* weeks. They had skewered everything. And that was why she bolted upright. How could she be so damned foolish as to let herself believe they wouldn't though?

"Well, you're not going to sit there denying they weren't nice."

"Yes." It came out strangled, and she opened her mouth again but closed it, no sound coming out.

What was there to decide about after all?

"There you go. So—"

"But I don't think that's such a good idea. Have you gone stark raving mad?"

Wasn't it dandy that was what she thought? He had to have, hadn't he, to suggest this? But he had some money in Jamaica. Not enough to offer her this, but even so, it was a start, better than nothing.

"Why do you think that?"

She couldn't say, could she? He waited. He waited for what seemed an eternity, his hand frozen around that damned purse he'd taken out the drawer. All right, he admitted it, until she had told him of Storm, he'd been nothing but difficult. Blackmailing, lying, cajoling. The exact same as her though. But his offer wasn't uttered on a whim. It wasn't offered because of Storm.

It was offered for her to agree to it. She was going to agree, wasn't she?

"You're kidding," he said, when she didn't answer.

She bent her head, obviously trying to think. He stood there, waiting to hear the result of these ministrations and did not leap over there to haul the words out of her mouth as he so wanted to.

"You're not."

"Flint…"

If she did this, ran off with him, then she'd lose everything she'd worked for. Dreamt of and suffered for. She could never put it back. Was that why her hands fisted on the damask cover?

"It's not that. England is my home. I thought you knew that, and I have made it plain. Once the child was conceived—"

"You're afraid. That's it, isn't it?"

Damn that uncertain smile she fixed on her face. She fluttered on as if he hadn't offered what he just had.

"Since you press me, I will tell you. No, it is not that. These are the things I want, have always wanted, for Storm and this baby."

"And there's things I don't?"

"If you are going to think of yourself—"

"For the baby."

The way he breathed the words made her widen her eyes and her jaw tremble. Until now, until she'd hit him with these stupid rules, passion had been a variant he only claimed in bed. Not in his personal life. And she had been confident she could talk him around. After all, she was the pregnant one. So, it wasn't as though he could very well take the baby back.

"The matter is settled, if that's the case. The only way to give Storm and this baby those things is to let it take up its rightful place in society."

"Rightful? Ain't that dandy?"

She pushed the cover aside and rose from the bed. "In time, yes." She plumped the pillow. "It will be very dandy indeed. What is more, you agreed to it being dandy weeks ago. So I honestly don't know what you're taking issue with now. Just think. This baby, your baby, will have the very best. It may even be a duke, if it is a boy. I've hurt your feelings, not telling you first, for which I apologize."

"You think I can't give it these things?"

Her busy hands stilled, holding the pillow against her stomach. "Do you really want me to answer that?"

"You *are* afraid."

"Oh, really? And you're completely insane. So, what this baby will turn out like—"

"What's insane about it? You take what money you have and we go. All we need is passage out of here. I can do the rest."

"Here's the thing." She flung the pillow back on the bed. "I don't have any money because you took it all."

He hadn't taken a damned thing. "How come?"

"How about the callaloo? Then there was the fried chicken. And let's not mention the rum. But that was only part of the trouble, because then you had to have the berth at Frau Berthe's. The one that just had to be paid up front. Two months. Oh, and not being content with that, it couldn't be empty. Because then there were the whores."

Maybe it was only to a piercing whisper, maybe she didn't mean it, but her voice rose, her skirt rustling as she swept about the room, picking up this, fiddling with that.

"I told you I only ever looked at them respectfully."

"Your respectful looks have cost me a fortune." She snapped a trinket box shut. "So even if I did want to come with you, I couldn't. Not now. Everything is in hock. And it's not mine to hock. I'm quite sure they have penalties for that here the same as in England. Do you want our baby born in prison?"

"Prison?" Right enough. There did seem to be fewer items for her to fiddle with than before. "You're the one who didn't admit you were pregnant."

"Well, I am now. So I don't."

"Jesus, you think I'd allow that?" He stopped short of taking hold of her and shaking some sense into her. "That's why I'm not just asking you to come with me, I'm begging."

"Oh, for the love of God, let's be honest here."

"What? About how that would be?"

"You forget. I know exactly how that would be. I know from past experience."

He might have known it would be that. And he *was* begging. He, who had never done such a thing in his whole life. Not when his mother's lovers beat him, not when he had been kept for days without food or water in that rat-infested cell in Jamaica, wounded and in chains.

"Seven years, Fury."

"And seven seconds is as long as you'd want me when I get to seven months pregnant, if it's even that long." He made a move toward her, but she held up her hand. "Do you think I've not seen? That I don't know? Oh, not just you particularly. It's a fault of your species."

"Fury—"

"The length is irrelevant when logic says we must part. There is no future. Not for us together. And if you stay, now you've gone and told Lady Margaret about Thomas, there may not even be one for us apart. Malmesbury is going to pounce. I will use my book, of course. But even that has its limits. You have to go."

For a second her eyes blazed, then, when he didn't respond, she turned and strolled across the floor in the direction of the bed. Of all the invitations he'd had from her, this wasn't one.

When she could have the money at stake in a dukedom, why would she have him?

He just hadn't thought. Actually, he didn't know what he thought. Only that he couldn't go on standing there, trying to get his heart to cool. His brain too.

She paused. Now came, if not the actual dismissal, the complaint about the fact he still stood there. His eyes skimmed her back. Wasn't she even going to turn and face him? She stiffened her shoulders and eased up her head.

"But if you should ever get to England, I'll be at Ravenhurst. It's in Hampshire."

As he strode to the door, the thought nagged: Did she mean him to go there?

He closed the door. On the landing he stood for a moment, collecting his thoughts. Yet he could hardly do it for what jangled in his brain. He went down the stairs and out through the sitting room doors into the garden, his feet taking him there while every other bit of him jangled in a state of angry shock.

In a corner of his mind, he believed this would get better in a day or two. It would, wouldn't it? Only that seemed a lifetime away.

Later, wandering the streets, he went over what she'd said about England. If she didn't want him here, she wasn't likely to want him in England. So the hope that gave him vanished like a spark in cold air. Because he had hurt her before. Hurt her, or not—and he knew it wasn't not—he'd changed from then. He saw it. Knew it. Breathed it. Why wouldn't she? He no longer believed she hated him *that* much. Not the way she'd been these last weeks.

The only clear focused thought he possessed, beyond anger, beyond pride, was that her departure loomed, and in this impossible situation he'd created for himself, he didn't have the least idea what he could do about it.

But he knew he had to do something. She'd no idea what she'd started in him. And he wasn't going to rest until he proved it to her.

* * *

Fury muffled a shriek as a hand covered her mouth. Then she muffled another as she tried to rise from the bed and her forehead collided with hard bone in the shadowed darkness.

"Ouch! Jesus," a male voice said. "Keep still, will you?"

"Flint? Oh my God."

"Shh."

"What are you doing here?"

"I came to say goodbye to the mother of my child, sweetheart." His soft, warm breath brushed her lips. "You didn't think that was it earlier, did you?"

She groaned deep in her throat, striving in vain to move away. By God, this man could not take a hint, could he? She looked at his chiseled features in the band of silver moonlight fanning through the open shutters. It didn't seem possible that he was here. At two in the morning, a hundred miles from where he was meant to be. Where she'd hoped he'd be by now.

She might have known he'd be back. Larger than life. And twice as dangerous, with Lady Margaret a stone's throw away along the corridor and Malmesbury just waiting to pounce. True, if ever a man could take care of himself, Flint could. But the vicious way Malmesbury had beaten him and the way he regarded Flint as his property made her blood shudder. A woman with very little left to fear and yet she did, because if Malmesbury was to somehow do anything to Flint, she'd have to do something to him and she doubted it would be anything pleasant.

"Lady Margaret is in the house. She's—"

He kissed her mouth, smiling against her lips. "You want me to go check?"

"No. I don't want you to go check." She tried to push him off. "I want you to go. Now. Before—"

"Hell, I just want a cuddle is all."

A cuddle? That would be a first. The man was notorious. It

was ridiculous to think so, when her pillow lay soaked with tears. She wished he didn't command so much of her thoughts.

She did not want to have to explain it to Susan in the morning what had run from her eyes the entire time she'd lain here, thinking of that stupid offer he'd made her.

"Bed's lonely without you. Anyway, you were looking poorly earlier."

"Bed? I was never in your bed…" But then she recalled that day she had been. The extraordinary heat of that moment of giving and taking. But she crushed it. When so much stood within her sights, when only the thought of Storm had kept her strong in the face of his offer earlier, it was absurd to think of such things. One day, perhaps. Not now. Now she had enough to deal with. "How did you get in here?"

He grinned. "Now, sweetheart, that would be telling."

"No, it wouldn't be. Did you climb up to my window?"

"Shove over and I'll tell you."

The little flickering grin. The boundless energy. This was more like him. She was glad to see it. This morning had been so unlike him, it tore her heart, what bits she had left to tear, because some of it had died long ago. It must have or she'd have accepted his offer. She had longed with every fiber of her being to hear it, and he'd been so impressive standing there. She didn't think she'd ever seen him look like that.

But there was no denying his body heat beckoned and this morning she'd found herself in trouble, precisely because she had thought so. No denying either this morning had been a pack of lies she thanked God she had not listened to.

"Come on. You think I'm going to take advantage of a pregnant woman?"

Much was the word he missed. Then if Lady Margaret found him here, hell would also be beckoning. She shifted against the bed.

"You —"

"Especially one who's got my baby in there."

Something about the words added a frisson of alarm. And excitement. As did the knowledge that she did have his baby. A cuddle was only a cuddle. Even if she was not quite fool enough to pretend that was all that might happen, this morning had ended badly. She did have his seed. And his seed guaranteed her and Storm's future. And he had learned a little bit about boundaries, hadn't he?

"I mean, it wasn't like I knew before that you did. Or I'd have refrained."

What a beguiling liar. "All right. But, I warn you —"

"Shh. You want Lady Margaret to hear?"

He flung the covers back and spread his long limbs out beside her. Like hell she'd warn him. Since he was sublimely ignorant of the meaning of the word.

But now he knew she was pregnant, she felt obliged to. To let him believe he still had rights, when he didn't, would be a mistake. It would make her look very bad indeed. No better than a dockside hussy.

What was more, he had known before. He must have.

His hand flattened on her stomach, as if he wanted to cup the precise spot his seed lay planted. A mistake she was unfortunately willing to make. A layer of cool cotton separated his fingertips from her flesh. Yet she could feel their heated touch as if it didn't exist.

"Flint, I just want your word that you're in this bed with me and this is all it's going to be. A respectable cuddle."

Touch me, she wanted to say.

She desperately needed not to. Yet, to feel him there in the cool darkness — well, it had been cool, until he had lain down beside her — was a torture.

"Hell, I'm going in the morning." His low voice drawled

against her ear. "That's a genuine promise. It was all arranged this afternoon the moment I left here. Of course, I won't do anything you don't want. This is just goodbye."

Did he imagine that she didn't detect the faintest note of sheepishness in his behavior? Being Flint he wasn't going to apologize or make some crass remark about being swept off his feet by her charms this morning. Not if a team of wild horses dragged him up, down, and around the harbor front, before propelling him into the water.

No doubt he had burned slowly, in that way he always burned. Then left here and kicked a wall or something. Before returning to actuality and seeing the total idiocy of his plan.

If only she could say that knowing she was right about that, about him, didn't make her want him more. Want him so her heart began to pound.

But it didn't.

And she had done everything to put that longing away. Everything wasn't enough when he lay as close as this, cool moonlight chiseling his face. His eyes looked unfathomable, an older, more *achy* Flint. The scent of his skin poured over her.

It was absurd, when they had said goodbye this afternoon, to let herself be drawn in by a look, a kiss. She should turn the other way. But his arms enveloped her.

She wanted this last night with him. He had come to himself. There was no danger. And he would never come to England. She only wished he might.

It would be too dull and bland for him. The weather too cold. The people, certainly the ones she knew, too colorless. Anyway, how would she entertain him there, except on an occasional basis? With what she was, what he was? No. There was no future.

She raised her chin. Of course he didn't want to cuddle any more than she did. She wanted pleasure now and she meant to have it. She kissed his mouth and his tongue answered hers in an exploratory sweep. She had no idea how he managed out of his coat and boots, she was too wild with wanting, except he must have, because they were gone by the time she felt his lips on her throat. He slid the fabric of her robe apart and pressed his mouth to her shoulder, her breast, his lips trailing fire down her body, a singing pleasure she never wanted to stop. A singing pleasure she knew she should fight.

But she had always thought if she had a last night to spend on earth it would be with him, and really, this was it. The hot velvet throb of him was too delicious. But it wasn't just that, it was knowing as she ran her hands down his body, searching for the fastenings on his breeches, that this went beyond lust, it went beyond emotional pain.

It went to the realms of being something she would always treasure. And that, as his mouth moved over her body, finding the spot where she wanted him most, made it very, very special, in a way it had perhaps never been before.

* * *

Flint pocketed the book and went on his way, leaving Fury sprawled on the bed as the first hints of dawn streaked the sky. It had been tricky when she woke up like that. He'd just hoped she hadn't noticed what sat in his back pocket.

Now it was safe in his coat's inner one, he could afford to wipe a little of the sweat from his brow. Then he slipped over the balcony and jumped to the ground, landing with a soft thud.

He slipped across the lawn like the seasoned privateer he was and edged out the side gate to the little side street, where Malmesbury's coach waited.

* * *

Fury shut the drawer and walked across the floor. Then she

returned and yanked it open.

The last four days had been hectic. A whirlwind in fact. But in all the mad preparation—the to-ing and fro-ing to the pawnshop, which Lady Margaret had been expectedly sticky about (*How could* my *son possibly clear off for Rome without settling with his creditors?*), the procuring of seats on a coach to Turin because she was unable with the repeated bouts of morning sickness to travel by sea, and the packing up of what she owned—she had still been certain of one thing. The book was in the drawer.

What was more, it could not have left without her knowledge.

"Susan, have you seen my book?"

"Your book, madam?" Susan squinted at her across the top of a pile of freshly laundered chemises.

"My book. You know the one. The one I don't want Lady Margaret to see."

"Isn't it there, where you usually keep it?"

Fury prayed for calmness. The book represented years of dirty-little-secret gathering. Everything in fact that gave her leverage. And the drawer was empty except for a few hairpins, some scraps of paper, and the key for some cabinet or other. How could it be empty? *Look again*, the voice in her head whispered.

"You mean you haven't packed it?"

"Madam, I wouldn't touch it. Not with some of the stuff in that."

That was just it. Not just leverage. But safety. No matter what she felt about the dubiety of what she did, that book was vital. It was vital now to her very survival. Not just a barkeeper's daughter from Jamaica, masquerading in society as something she wasn't. A barkeeper's daughter from Jamaica, with a child in her womb that had been conceived under highly unusual circumstances.

Of all the years she had feared discovery, surely this moment was the worst.

"But I assure you, Lady Margaret's not been in here." Susan set the chemises down on the bed and crossed the floor to look for herself. "I've kept tabs on her."

Panic rose and swamped. "Then who?"

"Now, just think a moment, madam, if maybe you took it out yourself and maybe, just maybe, misplaced it, as can happen, even with something so valuable as that book is to you."

"No."

"And especially the house as it is just now. Everything topsy-turvy."

"I assure you, no matter how topsy-turvy. I have been a little busy. A little preoccupied. But that book and all the letters and things that were in it, the things I've paid for, isn't something I'd let vanish from my sight."

"All right then. Just think when you were last in that drawer."

"Last in that—" Fury did think about when last someone was in that drawer. Or rather, who. She shut her eyes and tried to banish the thought from her mind. It was stupid of her.

"Flint was the last one in there."

"Well, there you go then, madam," Susan spoke in that way she always did. As if there were no difference between the house falling down or winning a hundred lire. "Problem solved."

"But Flint didn't have it. I was there—"

But the thought thudded, as loudly as her heart: He didn't have it *then*. Was it coincidence he returned here that night, took his pleasure, and then departed? With her book?

In the glass she saw herself whiten, the color seeping down from her face as if someone had pulled a plug on it and washed it all away. In fact, as if it were hemorrhaging.

The room and all its contents seemed to shrink. Even Susan's fussing sounded far away. She had kept the recollection of that night pressed like a flower in the leaves of her memory. And he, just like before, had…had…

She thought she would fall, what surged through her body was so devastating. Like a roaring tide.

"Madam, are you all right?"

She barely managed to speak. "Fine."

"It's just…you don't look it."

"Yes."

"Madam…" Susan moved toward her.

"No! I don't want to sit down." She clawed a breath into her tortured lungs. What was she doing, when Susan had been so kind, had rescued her that day on the wharf, after she had sat there for hours? She had even taken Fury to her brother's inn. "I'm so sorry. I shouldn't speak to you like that. I just—"

Susan's cool hand clasped Fury's arm. "Madam, listen to me. That book will turn up, I'm sure."

Like the bad doubloon?

She straightened, the terrified pounding in her heart blocking out everything else. Even the consideration of how bad this must be for the baby.

"Perhaps."

But she knew pigs would encircle the Lanterna first. On beautiful gilded wings.

She need make no mistake.

She would never forgive Flint for this.

Chapter Thirteen

Fury stared at the rain gleaming down the uneven glass of the café window, obscuring almost all of the bustling harbor front. Not that Fury felt able to take in much of her surroundings. It had taken Lady Margaret less than a minute to recommence berating her. The instant they sat down in fact. Something about a delay finding a porter.

"Of course, it is all my fault, Mama."

After all, they had traveled for over five months across France. Most things were.

A wonder though Lady Margaret hadn't just boarded the bags herself, the rest of the *Julie-Anne*'s supplies too, then piloted the vessel across the sea to Dover, fanning it there with her large black ostrich feather fan. It would have been nothing to a woman of her sterling capabilities.

"Did I say that?"

"A first, then," Fury murmured to herself, smoothing a tendril of damp hair back from her forehead.

"You said something?"

"No, dearest, Mama. Certainly not of interest."

Ignoring Susan's flicker of amusement, she raised the coffee cup to her lips. She longed to lie down. Perhaps even fall asleep before the ship set sail. After the nightmare of the last five months, the thought of getting on a boat made the gorge rise in her stomach. She would be sick again, she knew it. As she had for almost every day of the past seven months. Like its father, this baby caused nothing but trouble. Still, they were here now at Calais. Soon she would be at Ravenhurst.

"It is just taking so long." Lady Margaret set up an indignant gust from her fan. "We do not need another delay. We should have been home weeks ago."

"My fault too, I am sure."

"I am sure some women cannot help being burdens."

Fury shuddered, feeling the tiny kick of life inside her. Maybe it was because she was past this now, but Fury did not care what she said to Lady Margaret. After what Flint had done to her over five months ago, was it any wonder?

She didn't want this baby. There were times when she hated it. It was not the baby's fault. It was hers for almost believing him. Where she would be now, had she been stupid enough to run off with him, was the least of it. His use of her that last night, to get that book, had emptied her soul.

She hoped he rotted in hell with it. As for what grew inside her—a means to an end, wasn't it? To think she had worried about Flint. Never once that night had she thought he had come to hurt her.

Fury set the coffee cup down. "I tell you what, Mama, I will go and sort this out."

"In your condition?"

Fury rose to her feet. She could not face another glowing report on when Lady Margaret had been pregnant with Thomas. How robust she had been and what a shoddy weakling Fury was by comparison. Lying about in bed, dying, half the day. Her head in some basin, bucket, sink, or other. For months now. If she heard that she would do something silly, like tell the woman this wasn't a first pregnancy.

And all she had suffered with that one had been a broken heart.

"I don't see why not. It's not catching, is it?"

"But that man who examined our papers was adamant we wait here, until he sent for us. You cannot wander a dock, like some...some *common creature* — "

Fury knew she meant hussy and suppressed a bitter smile. If only she knew. The docks she had wandered on and why.

" — bringing the Beaumont name into great disrepute."

That too.

"Already, I have found your behavior with that Captain Ames to be exceedingly questionable."

"Only exceeding, Mama? I would have thought — "

"He carried you up the stairs." Lady Margaret fanned herself harder, as if something in the memory made her hot enough to faint. "Fortunately that was in Genoa."

"That's normal there. May I remind you, since it seems you have forgotten, I was indisposed and Susan was present? I am sure she would have seen if there had been anything unseemly going on."

How strange. Even the recollection that Flint had opened the neck of her gown raised no flicker of heat with her.

"That is as it may be. I insist you stay here and raise no more gossip about yourself."

"In my condition I think it's most unlikely I would be taken as a whore. At least, I doubt any man would want to pay for me."

Susan sprung to her feet, smothering her amusement. "I'll come with you, madam. The one who examined our papers was more interested in dealing with the *Palerna*. He's probably forgotten all about unimportant people like us."

"I don't see how." Lady Margaret fingered her throat, indignant.

"Anything's possible, Your Ladyship. Madam's right. You wouldn't like the *Julie-Anne* sailing off and us stuck here another fortnight or something?"

"True."

"Old boot," Susan whispered the moment the café door clanged shut behind them. "Who does she think she is, talking to you like that?"

"My mother-in-law." Fury stepped into the cobbled, rain-slicked street.

"I vow I could swing for the old toad myself. Doesn't she understand how ill you've been?"

"She is grateful. Probably for that too." Fury smiled wanly. "But there is an heir or heiress."

"You watch she don't take that off you and do you out the money. There's never any saying with an old cow like that."

"There's never any saying with anyone. Now let us find that man."

They ducked beneath an archway into a narrow passageway. The stench, despite the rain, of rotting fish guts and sea brine overpowered her. Although the exit stood only a few yards away, Fury delved in her reticule for her handkerchief. "My God, I must have left it in the cafe."

"Madam, I'm sure I have one."

"No. It's—"

Fury didn't finish. A figure stepped from behind the soaking barrels. She was still drinking in his extraordinary menace when, with a suddenness that defied her, he clamped something across Susan's mouth.

A handkerchief? Fury's thoughts slowed in bemusement. Why did he have the very thing she didn't? Had he somehow taken it from her to place it over Susan's mouth, behind which she made wild, protesting sounds? And—oh good Lord—what was that across her own?

She tried to jerk her head around to see who held her. But she had walked too fast and lost her breath. So the one she gasped was deeper than she had meant to take. The white muffling handkerchief was her last clear, conscious thought as the acrid smell sank into her throat, then down into her lungs.

* * *

A voice pierced Fury's consciousness.

"Madam! Madam! Please, God, wake up. Please. Please. We need, we need to—"

What they needed to do was lost in the maelstrom rising about her. Actually, the maelstrom didn't just rise about her. It heaved. She had never felt sicker in her life. As if she swayed over mid-ocean. Except even in mid-ocean she had never felt as though she were sick and drowning. With an effort she pried an eye open. Then she pried the other.

"My God, Susan." Seeing the familiar, if somewhat blurred figure, Fury tried to rise. "What are you—let me lie down again. I'm going to be—"

"Oh, madam, thank God."

That she was sick? Fury thought not.

"I wouldn't trouble you."

Please God, would Susan stop shaking her like this?

"But, madam, you have to wake up. We've been kidnapped."

"Kidnapped?" Fury sat up, striking her head on a wooden beam. It did nothing for what was in it. Her head that was, although she suspected the beam also suffered.

"Oh, God, madam. We're on a boat."

"A boat? How can we be on a boat?" Her voice sounded muzzy. Her tongue felt as if it didn't belong to her. She tried sticking it out of her mouth to make sure. It tasted so disgusting she pulled it back. No one should breathe that.

"Listen, madam."

"Hmm?" Battling the awful ache in her forehead, Fury stared. The floor did seem to be swaying. Although the way she'd hit her head, anything would. That beam, the narrow bed, even the smell, what she could discern of it through her clogged throat, were all familiar.

But a boat? How had they come to be on a boat? She didn't remember, and the way the room swam and swayed didn't aid her ability to fill the gaps.

"Lady Margaret?"

"*Lady Margaret*?" Susan shook her harder. It was not a question Fury should ask, obviously. The venom it engendered. "Never mind that old frog. She's probably the one who's done this. Oh, madam, please tell me you remember. That alleyway? And what happened in it?"

It would be nothing exciting in her condition. "The alleyway?"

"Oh, madam, please tell me the baby's all right."

"The baby?"

Baby? Was she having a baby?

Fury's hand edged to her stomach. Sure enough there was a bump. A solid one, and it appeared to be attached to herself. It also appeared to move. At least, something unfurled beneath her skin.

She *was* pregnant. How revolting. Especially in her current state.

"Oh my God." She pushed the woolen blanket aside.

"Oh, madam. You remember." Tears ran down Susan's cheeks. "And we will get out of here."

Out of where? They had been at Calais. And now? That handkerchief had been doused in something. Again she stuck her tongue out. Something so horribly mind-numbing, she struggled to fight her way back from it.

"Of course we will." Although she hadn't the last idea how.

"You don't know how scared I've been. Wondering who would kidnap us."

"Who would? It doesn't make sense. None of it. We can't have been kidnapped."

Of course, she was a little ashamed that her first thought was for that and not the baby. But the baby was all right, wasn't it? A damn sight better than herself right now. She lowered her feet to the creaking wooden floor. And that was as much as she was prepared to give it, the damned trouble it had been and who its disgusting thief of a father was.

"Then why is the door locked, madam?"

"Locked? Don't be silly. Jammed maybe. But locked?"

"Why is everything swaying?"

So it was, Fury realized, feeling as if her right leg had been chopped short at the knee with the way the floor tilted up to meet it. Locked? Even the way Susan spoke sounded as if she gurgled. For a second Fury thought she'd misheard. Locked was too horrible to contemplate. Why would the door be locked?

"I'm sure it's a mistake. Lady Margaret wouldn't do this to us."

"Why wouldn't she if she knows about Thomas?"

"Because she'd have done it already."

"What if she means to have us thrown over the side? Or—"

"Now you're being silly. Get out the way. Lady Margaret would do no such thing, no matter how much she hates me."

It was a consideration of course. But one Fury refused to accept, although the door…was locked. From the outside. She drew back as if it had bitten her.

"You see. Madam, what if it's white slavery?"

"White, what?"

"You read about these things all the time."

Fury grasped the door handle and shook it. Not in her book.

you didn't. Although she wondered at her maid's choice of literature. She'd never have marked Susan down for such salacious nonsense. Yet, she supposed it made an interesting change from Susan reading her book's secrets. And of course now her book was gone it would give Susan something.

"Open the door." She hammered on the panel. "Do you hear me? Right this instant."

"Madam, is that wise?" Susan tried to pull her hand away. "You'll only bring them in here. And then—"

"Then let them come. And welcome." Fury shouted at the top of her lungs. She was not going to be intimidated by this. Hadn't she been all over the Caribbean? Parts of it anyway. "Because I've things to say to them, whoever they are. Keeping us locked up like this."

Besides if she did not find her way up on deck she would be sick. And even if she did, she would be sick. It—how could she think of what she carried as otherwise, given who its father was—was awake. She just couldn't bear to be sick here in this wormhole of a place. It would make it very unpleasant for both of them. She wiped a hand across her mouth.

"Madam, look. The handle. It's moving."

"Open the door." Fury resumed hammering. "Help me, Susan."

Susan froze. "Madam. I'm not sure this is such a good idea—"

"For God's sake, will you stop worrying? A maid and a pregnant woman. Just ask yourself, will you? Who is going to want to kidnap either of us?"

It was true, wasn't it? And it was madness to think otherwise. Unless Lady Margaret hated her so damned much, she planned to sail her some place. Some awful place, until perhaps she gave birth. Susan had wanted her to be careful about that.

But then the door creaked open, bit by bit, forcing Fury to step back. She did so with a prescience of doom that yet only increased her impatience to know the answer.

Then the one man in the world who would want to kidnap a maid and a pregnant woman stood framed by the dim light beyond, satisfying her curiosity.

"Fury, Susan." Flint strolled into the cabin. Dockside whores, for his perusal. Both of them. "Sorry for the inconvenience."

Fury parted her lips. The desire to strike him overwhelmed her so, she clenched her fists. But the waves slapping against the ship's sides seemed to rise higher all of a sudden. And that wasn't all that rose up. She tried covering her mouth but—

"I just don't know how you dare face me." She wished the contents of her stomach were not spattered down his shirtfront. Except he had drugged her with some foul-tasting concoction, so there was no hope of that wish being granted.

It was just Flint always became derogatory about things like that. How could she have given him the advantage when she needed to face him on an equal footing?

He raked his gaze downward over her. Of course, he would first admire his handiwork. Before admiring hers.

She clasped her cloak shut. It was nothing to her that she was seven and a half months pregnant, except it made her feel even dirtier. More slovenly, if that was possible, given what she'd just done.

"I was wondering that myself." He yanked the shirt out of his breeches and over his head.

Fury's eyes widened. What was this? Some kind of awful duel, where he now displayed his sculpted chest for her stomach's next heave? And then, removed more?

"But I worked up the courage." He balled and tossed the soiled garment out into the passageway.

"Here, madam." Susan shoved the chamber pot toward her.

"Thank you. No."

She was not facing him across that. She had her pride. Her dignity. If necessary this would be a fight to the death. He need make no mistake. With what had taken up residence in her heart these last months, she would not settle for less.

The ship pitched and she grasped the bowl.

It was better than grasping him. Particularly as he had no shirt on.

"I don't know how you have the gall to face Susan either." She spoke with as much dispassion as she could muster, given she clutched a large white chamber pot in one hand and wiped her knuckles across her mouth with the other. "Kidnapping is a capital offense."

"It might be were your shape a little different."

"What?"

Her heart hammered. How dare he? And how dare he kidnap her? For Lady Margaret? For what? Who?

"But right now — " The monster had the nerve to shoot out his arm and she watched, horrified, as he snapped his fingers at someone out in the passageway. A flash of red was tossed into the room, and he caught it with ease.

The reason he had dared kidnap her dawned, although how he could do so in her state fell beyond her comprehension.

From the start she'd known that beneath the casual, lazy manner lurked a ruthless specimen capable of satisfying his every need. But this?

She straightened her spine, feeling herself stare at the rich vermillion dress in his hands, as if her eyes would swallow it. A weaker woman might have started screaming. She knew they would. But Fury clung to self-possession, although the blood ran from her face.

"Here, I want you to put that on." He flung the dress at her.

"There's jewels in the box there." He jerked his head at the rickety wooden table. "Come to my cabin when you're done."

"When I'm done?" Fury shrieked as the dress flumped against her chest.

He could not possibly be serious, wanting her to dress up and look pretty for him, as he had before. Dear God, she was pregnant. Yet the dress's message was unmistakable. It was soft flowing French silk and indescribably beautiful. A piece of shining frippery, costing God alone knew what. Her color too. Although whether it was her size was another matter.

And he commanded her to his cabin, did he? Thinking what exactly? He could have his ruthless way with her? And she'd fall at his feet, as she had once before?

Coldness swept her, rising from the pit of her stomach. Taking a deep breath to master her furious reaction, she raised her chin higher. Then she dumped the dress on the cabin floor.

"Fine then. I'm ready now."

"Madam, *no*."

Of course Susan would try planting her stout body in the way. But the pistol hadn't been invented that Fury couldn't and wouldn't shoot herself in the foot with. One only had to consider the way her eyes were primed on Flint and the fact the dress lay on the cabin floor.

"I'm not afraid of him." Fury held her spine straight and head high. "He touches me and it will be rape."

Rape? In her present state? Was she serious?

In spite of all the desire for her Flint had experienced since her departure, all the torment, thirst, and hunger, *that* wasn't top of his list. Not right now anyway.

"Yes. You will testify on my behalf, should I return to this cabin in anything less than the state I leave it in, Susan. Take note."

That was a tall order. Given the state she already was. Obviously she didn't understand that was why he'd given her the dress, or she wouldn't have tossed it on the floor. To think he had suffered more than one sleepless night wondering if it was her size.

"You want to take an inventory check on that, sweetheart?"

"What?"

"Well, you've got a dab of sickness there." While it wasn't safe to put out his hand, Flint risked it anyway. He even risked his fingers brushing her breast. "And a big splurge there. I'd like to count the creases on that cloak, but, sweetheart, I don't want to get too close."

Maybe it was that her eyes looked like a viper's. Maybe it was her desire to strike him. Maybe it was her disheveled state. Whatever it was, Flint resisted the urge to grasp her. God knows why he wanted to. But he did. She looked like an outraged kitten standing there. Sweet and endearing. His heart gave a tiny flip.

It didn't matter that gut instinct whispered that cats had claws. Even now he knew he must wait his time. Wasn't the dress on the floor, instead of on her person? Of course, he knew she wasn't the old Fury. And it was going to take more than a dress to get his way out of this.

Even so, he'd hoped she might have expressed a little more interest in such a generous gift.

"Then just you remember it." She handed the chamber pot to Susan. "Now. Your cabin, I believe you said."

* * *

It disgusted her. Yet what other choice did she have but to hear him out? She'd smacked into yet another brick wall. A moment where she'd then been too stunned and too sick — too a lot of things — to appreciate one vital fact.

The dress didn't make sense. None whatsoever.

Flint's women were chosen with care. For their pretty faces and trim figures. He wasn't attracted to whales. He hadn't kidnapped her for that. No. And she'd be a damn fool to think it. To let the past govern her. A damn fool to let anger govern her, too, when every wave, every pitch, every roll of the boat took her further from the dreams of her future.

It was the only reason she swept along the passageway behind him, her faltering heels clicking on the wooden boards.

A single gold hoop glinted in his ear. The English Channel was hardly the place to resume his glittering career. So perhaps she should assume that having flogged off her book to the highest bidder, he now meant to extort money to head back to Jamaica. And that was why he invited her to his cabin.

Although the dress still didn't make sense.

It was difficult of course with his meanness, his lowness, when she carried his child, to be calm, collected — enough to consider his thinking in giving her the dress. Maybe he just wanted her to look pretty while they parleyed. Maybe he thought just because she wanted the Beaumont inheritance sufficiently to enter into a business transaction, a frock would sway her into overlooking the fact he'd kidnapped her.

Until this moment she had quite hated this baby. Now that she saw he gave less than two hoots about it, she pitied it. Imagine having a blackmailing skunk in one's family tree.

He stopped at a door and stared down at her with unwavering intensity. An intensity that made her glad this time her heart wasn't just covered in frost, but frozen solid. "You'd be a whole lot better to go back and put on that dress. Freshen yourself up that little bit, before you come in here."

"Here's the thing, Flint. I'm not going to. And you can't make me. Not anymore."

"All right. Don't say I didn't warn you." He opened the door.

Chapter Fourteen

It had been seven years since Fury had been in a cabin like this with him, she realized as the door opened on the brightly lit room. And in that time everything had changed. It was why she was astonished by what raked her. The humiliation that scorched all the way from the tips of her toes, to the roots of her hair at the sight of what greeted her. Two women, garishly dressed, sat at his dinner table, as if they belonged there.

That he should still have the power to do this to her. And worse, since her first thought was to admit he was right. She should have gone back to the cabin and tidied herself up.

For a moment she hesitated. To do so now though, would be to admit she was wrong, when he was no more than a snake, unworthy of such an act of capitulation.

Anyway, why the blazes should she capitulate, simply because her cloak and gown had vomit stains, her hair had loosened from its tortuous array of pins, and she smelled?

She sniffed surreptitiously. She smelled *bad*. But that wasn't the point. *These women*. She strove not to blink. Or show she was in any way affected or outraged by this latest piece of effrontery.

He wanted money. He could have it. She was uncertain how, because she was uncertain how she was going to explain why he wanted it to Lady Margaret. And already Lady Margaret had accused her of running up all sorts of debts. But surely she would find a way.

"Do you want to sit down?"

She didn't. But her eyes scanned the gleaming table.

Choosing the place to sit was an exercise in restraint and decorum. It would have been much easier were she under an illusion about what these women were and what they were doing here. And if she was able to eat some of what sat on the table in shining silver dishes.

But she wasn't. She trembled, trying not to let her eyes brim. The father of her child, the father of the Beaumont heir, Storm's father, was a philandering, thieving, kidnapping, blackmailing… While he had never had a father himself, *bastard* was not the word that came to mind. Neither was skunk.

"I'm glad you've decided to sit down."

Was he? She stared impassively at her fork. It would be very nice to jab it in his face. His eye preferably. But she smelled, she was pregnant, and she sat here in vomit-stained clothes. He was minus his shirt. She would not make herself look worse. Not before two trolloping whores.

"This here's Louise-Ann, and this is Marigold."

She jerked her chin up. *Marigold?* She was sure, whatever her name was, she had seen Marigold before. That day Fury had looked like a beekeeper.

"I believe you two might have met before." He opened the cupboard.

Please don't tell her Marigold had been with him since Genoa, sharing his bed. Please don't tell her Louise-Ann had too. She swallowed. To have been replaced, not just by one woman, but two, was no odds to her.

Indeed, it only confirmed what she already knew of the man. That he was physically incapable of keeping his breeches buttoned. Any woman believing otherwise was destined for a life of misery. She was glad it wasn't her. Glad she had not been stupid enough to run off with him.

Pride commandeered her tongue. "Charmed, I'm sure."

"Oh, Marigold and Louise-Ann won't be joining us."

"Oh, but Flintee, you promised."

Flintee? Yes this was her.

"You said we could, eef we were very good. And we 'ave been. We 'ave been saints."

Saints? Of what? The trolloping whores?

"Sorry, girls." He tugged a fresh shirt over his head. "Not this time."

"I don't see why not." Fury stared idly at her fork. "Stealing is also a capital offence. I wouldn't worry about having a few whores present."

"That's the thing. There's those who might say that about you, truth got out."

Blackmail? No, she would not rise to it. Not when it confirmed her expectations. Besides her reputation, while not lily-white, stood unblemished.

"But, ladies—"

Ladies? Disinterested, she raised her chin. He always called them that. But the manners, the tidy way he bowed. Had he been taking lessons? How to impress a whore?

"As ever, it's been a pleasure."

"Nooh, Flintee. Z'at 'as been ours."

This was taking it a little far, wasn't it? Kissing each of their hands in turn. But then why should he worry about catching something when the chances were he was probably riddled?

"Could we get on with this? After all, you told me to come here. Unless of course, it was to spectate?"

She didn't care that they all regarded her in horror. The women anyway. As if this was no way to speak to Flintee. As if they would like to claw her eyes out. It wouldn't be a first. Not when she thought of some of the places she'd hauled him out of. Of course he'd said he never cheated. And that counted for something?

He ushered them out, closing the door on their languid protests.

"You don't think very highly of me, do you?" His fathomless blue gaze moved over her.

"Let me consider the reasons for that. We have all night, don't we?" With difficulty she kept her voice level. She had been angry before, the first time she had faced him in Genoa. Look where it had gotten her.

Passion had still been in her heart then. Whereas now her heart was empty. Dry and broken as a shattered husk.

"I hope so. But that depends on you."

Oh really? "Let's start with the misappropriation—"

"*Palerna*'s not mine exactly, but I didn't steal it."

"I'm not talking about the boat."

His gaze didn't falter as he ambled across the floor and came to stand beside her, the lantern light glinting on the gold in his ear and casting a sheen over his corn-colored hair, as if it couldn't help but touch him.

A weaker woman might have let her gaze cling. But that had been her mistake before.

She could pretend, of course. She remembered enough of the letters and other items she'd painstakingly gathered to put on a show. Only it would be a hollow one, in danger of having the curtain snapped down on it at any time. That was the fear that now shackled her, because of him.

"I suppose that depends on what you mean by stealing. See, the law might say what you've got of mine there makes this eeksie-peeksie."

"I beg your pardon?"

She had never heard such an expression. For that matter it might have been pirate lingo. But she could guess its meaning.

He sat down in the chair opposite, easing his long legs beneath the table. "So I suggest, we do a deal."

A deal? Of course. Now came the list of terms. Sure to be as long as the yardarm. But disgust tightened her throat. Why was he talking about what she had of his, when his seed, for the book, had never been the exchange? It was a new level of low to try and bypass his crimes. Fortunately her heart was already dead. Or she might have felt the dagger this drove into it.

"So you don't deny it then?" She let a knowing smile curve her lip. "That you took my book?"

"Appropriated is a better term."

"Theft, whether you steal or you appropriate, is still theft."

He narrowed his eyes. "Maybe if you'd listened to me, I wouldn't have had to."

"I see. So it's all my fault you're a thief?"

"Let's just say, it was in aid of a good cause."

He reached for the crystal decanter in the center of the table, and she tilted her chin.

"And what about bringing me here? Was that also in aid of a good cause? Stuffing handkerchiefs over the noses of expectant mothers and their maids is one, I must confess, I have never heard of. Although, of course I don't know the names of each and every charitable cause in existence."

He stilled his hand in a way she'd seen before, if seldom. The betraying drop of claret staining the white cloth had nothing to do with the roll of the ship. Only right here, right now, why would it trouble him that he'd drugged her?

"If I'd asked the men to hold a knife to Lady Margaret's throat, you think you'd have just come along?" He sighed. "Hell, you'd have told them to cut it."

That was only partly so. Although even partly, in his eyes...

"How dare you think I care so little for my mother-in-law."

"Oh, you care about her, in that she's got money." He filled the two glasses, although she didn't miss the way his eyes sharpened on her face as he did. "You care about a lot of things that way."

"Goodness. Just hark at the pot calling the kettle various shades of black."

"That's why you wouldn't come with me when I asked you."

"You think so?"

Dear God, it couldn't be what this was about?

He was proud. She knew that. And she suspected that, like her, his childhood had fitted him in that mold. But would he go to these lengths because she'd refused him? If he had, there was only one explanation. He'd gone mad.

"I think I explained all that. But in case you didn't hear, let me try again. I do love money. It's the most important thing a woman can have when she's been left as I was in a strange country. A child on the way. No visible means of support. No family. No friends. No casual acquaintances even. And then years later bled dry."

His eyes didn't even flicker. "You've made a good job of naming all my sins."

"Not all of them. You're mistaken if you think that's the only reason I didn't come with you. No. The money is one thing. The charming ladies you asked me in here to meet are the main reason I never came with you." She smiled again. Let him see she'd had enough of this? Not yet. "Now you know, I vow you'd be as well giving me your terms."

"I apologize for kidnapping you."

"Not just me. Susan too."

"The men got confused."

"Confused?" She had never heard the likes. Or felt more

temporarily incensed. "You mean they can't tell the difference between a pregnant woman and one old enough to be her mother?"

"I mean they were rushed." He shifted, knitting his brows. "And you're not exactly one to come quietly."

A lie, of course. That justified nothing.

"Anyway, I digress."

She regarded the way he got to his feet, in bemusement. What he rummaged for, in the battered wooden chest he dragged from beneath the bed, increased her shock and her surprise. An elegant, lace cravat hung forlornly from his arm, as if it knew she'd be affronted by it.

She strove not to shift. She knew she had trouble biting her tongue but surely he didn't mean to tie her up? Or even worse, gag her? After all, he had kidnapped her. She shouldn't be surprised.

"It's what you want isn't it?" He tugged it around his neck. "Me to start behaving like a gentleman."

She lowered her gaze to the trellised soup bowl. *Him?* She was imagining this. A fault of whatever had doused that handkerchief. Dear Lord, maybe for that matter, she also had imagined Louise-Ann and Marigold? And these fine dishes here?

"Whatever it takes, sweetheart."

"What it takes..." She paused and ran her tongue over her lips, which were suddenly dry. A cravat? Why on earth was he wearing a cravat? "What it takes is for you to give me your terms and let us go."

How could it be otherwise? For over five months now she had felt nothing. Neither happy, nor sad. She had sworn never to forgive him.

"Ah?" He worked the knot with his fingers. "Isn't going to happen. Why do you think I've brought you here?"

"I confess I don't know." Somehow she kept her voice cool, although his words were hardly encouraging. "To show me you have whores and that you can tie a cravat?"

"I brought you—I brought them to show you I can be the kind of man you want."

She almost laughed out loud, the cool way he said it. "And what is that? A man who steals, drugs, and kidnaps?"

"The kind who doesn't go near women like that, sweetheart. No matter the temptation."

"Go near them?" Now she did laugh. Please don't tell her he had kidnapped her to show her that. Yet his stare burned. "Flint, you had them in here."

"Obviously I did. But I never did anything with them."

"Right."

"Hell, that's what you want to know, isn't it? Shape you are right now, and when you get further down the line, I can be trusted to contain my urges. Because, you think I don't know I've hurt you?"

God, it would be nice to think he could. But the shape she was in? Only Flint could make so uncomplimentary and basic a remark. Only Flint could let his eyes flicker over her while he did too. As if there was nothing wrong with what he said and she should be flattered.

"I'm sorry? And you want to be a *gentleman?*"

"Louise-Ann just wants to get to England."

"Oh? So she's working her passage?"

If Louise-Ann wanted to go to England, wouldn't it be better to smile nicely and find out when and where? To befriend these women if necessary. To play along with whatever devious little scheme he'd hatched?

After all, extricating herself, Susan, and her unborn baby intact from this situation, with the least amount of damage to her reputation, mattered the most to her. If Lady Margaret got wind of the fact Fury sailed on a pirated vessel with Captain Flint, who was one and the same as the Captain Ames who had helped her in the matter of her missing husband, she'd be cut off without a single penny.

But the talk about hurting her was too unnerving. Curse him. And curse herself. When she was unsure of just what scheme he was hatching, she barely needed talk like that. A sneaking suspicion came to her.

"Whose boat is this?"

"It's Malmesbury's, all right?"

After all Flint had said, the notion repulsed her. Yet, why wasn't she surprised?

"Maybe if you'd come with me when I asked, I wouldn't have felt the need to."

Well, this was a time for confessions.

"You took my book and you gave it to Malmesbury?" She managed, just, to keep her voice level. Her breath squeezed so tightly in her ribcage, she swore it shrank. "Is that what you did? Plotted my ruin with him? Because there is nowhere I can safely go and survive this. Nowhere. My children either."

"I didn't plot your ruin."

"From the start was it?"

"How the hell can you think I'd do that?"

"How the hell? Oh, quite easily."

"Haven't I got enough kept back here to protect you?"

"I'm very glad you think so."

Clearly feeling he'd sorted this to her satisfaction, he sat down opposite. "Anyway, you give me the damned chance I'm asking here, you won't need that book."

"You? That would take years." Rage clouded her mind. She wished it didn't. Yet, was it any wonder?

Nothing had changed. Perhaps not even herself. When she saw the things she fought here, when she knew the sheer necessity of keeping her heart armor-plated, yet she still had the capacity to hear, even if just by the dullest flicker, his words about hurting her, how could she say that she had?

But real love—oh, there was more to that, between a man and a woman, than him wearing a cravat and containing himself around whores.

Once she might not have thought so. But now, what burdened her had made her wiser. This kind of machination was exactly what she wanted to be free of. Because love was not what she heard mentioned.

Had she not suggested England to him, if he had been interested? Not stealing her book, kidnapping, and imprisoning her. She let a small smile play about her lips.

"Let me tell you something, James. Whatever deal you think you can make here. You can't."

"Why's that?"

He was confident of his ground, wasn't he? Surprising, for a man who hadn't always seemed confident in Genoa.

Although the boat swayed, she stood. As did he. He loomed taller than her. Still it felt better facing him standing up.

"I know for all these years you thought I killed Celia. But I didn't." She held up a hand to silence him. "I took water up to her room that morning. She lay dead. As simple as that. Some kind of seizure. I saw it was my chance. My chance to get away from everything. From my father's inn. And everything that went on there. From his drinking. And his whoring. From the washing and the cooking. And all the other tasks he had me do for the women who didn't just use his rooms as a convenient place to stay in. Because I never wanted to become one of those women."

Now she spoke of it, the first time ever, this chapter that belonged in a closed book, it felt very strange.

"You have no idea how I wanted to get to England and have

a new life. But you got in the way of that. I didn't mind. It was my own fault. You see, I fell in love with you. But then Storm came, so the new life…" The last thing she desired was to descend into self-pity. "The new life was difficult. I met Thomas. To start with he wasn't unkind. But I didn't think I could be happy with him. Because I think there was always you, even though I had put you from my mind. Even though, I know now, it would never have worked, the girl I was then, when I met you first."

"Fury, listen."

"No, you listen." She jerked up her chin to look at him. "You have no idea what I endured those last months with Thomas. The beatings. The humiliations. The accident on the staircase, for which I blame myself."

"I do. I saw it. The bruises. Why the hell do you think I stayed when I was all set on leaving?"

It was vital that just for once she tried to concentrate on her desires. Her proper desires. Not the fact he'd stepped closer and his hands, warm as they always were, clasped her arms.

Now, as never before, not even that night when he'd stepped from the shadow of her candle flame, had she been more aware how little she could afford to muddle this. He held her from her dreams. She, whose life at eighteen, he'd already ruined.

"It was all to have what was rightfully his. Rightfully mine. No more. There's Storm, after all. And now I finally have this chance to do that, to have the things I stole, ran away, and took a dead woman's identity for, do you think I'm going to stand here and allow you spoil it for me again?"

He was going to kiss her. Perhaps he wanted to disguise the blow to his pride, his face had flushed with fury. And she admitted, against her will, the impassioned way he looked, breathed, the way his hands cupped her face, the thought was not unpleasant. Except Flint settled everything this way. If she descended to it, the next step, pregnant or not, she knew all too well.

She swallowed, her throat dry. "We had a contract. A deal."

"This here's another deal."

He bent his head. His lips struck against hers, passionate and open-mouthed, his fingers holding her face in a powerful grip. The feel sucked all the breath from her body and she felt something buried deep inside her, beneath the covering of frost, start to thaw.

For a moment she reacted instinctively, to the heat flooding from his body into hers and racing through all her pores. Not because she wanted to, but because she had no other choice. The feel of his hands, the taste of his mouth was yet something she knew she must withstand. Or lose everything. Including her dignity before him. So she must, she wouldn't allow herself to abandon all rational thought and surrender mindlessly to him, as she had before. She would fight this. No matter how the room seemed to sway and every awareness was of him.

She waited till he pulled back, for the moment when he looked into her eyes. What she saw in his made her more aware than ever of her need to remember two words: *Book. Kidnap.*

She drew in a slow, shaky breath to quell her hammering heart. "I'm sorry, but you need to know exactly what you're up against here. If you think you can change my mind that won't do it." A stupid thing to say that would only encourage him to do more. "No."

He didn't flinch, although she knew she'd cut him. This new Flint's reactions were surlier than the old one's. She swore she could breathe his displeasure. But then he stood close.

"A few days. No more. To prove to you I've changed and I can be the things you want is all I'm asking here."

"A few days? But a second ago you said—"

He tilted his jaw and narrowed his eyes, emotion flashing in the crystal depths. "I meant it's not going to happen tonight, you and Susan walking free from here. But that's it. That's the deal."

Impossible. It couldn't be. Not even the mighty Flint could be that confident, could he?

Unease flickered. Of course, it was no trouble to agree to this. Good God no. Her desire for other things was formidable. Versus what he had done to her, all the things he'd done, it was indomitable. So, why did she feel the teeny tiny faint *clang* of a warning bell within? As if she might not be safe entering into this. Might not emerge unscathed at the other side.

It was just her pride that made her rebel wasn't it? And nothing to do with his swagger. Because his swagger was something she should and would delight in pricking, baiting, and deflating.

A few days were but a few days. She had so much to sustain her.

"And if I don't agree?"

He curved his lips upward. "You're not in any position. Here alone on this boat with me."

"Is that right? What are you going to do? Rape a pregnant woman?"

Actually he'd never thought a pregnant woman could be so appetizing. Of course, she was *his* pregnant woman. And he should have told her he loved her. But how could he when she stared as though he were something she'd found under her shoe?

"No, sweetheart." His gaze drifted down the bulge below the elegant line of her breasts. He didn't know if he'd felt more strongly about anything in his whole life than he did about that little bump. About her. "But I will keep you here."

"What do you mean keep me here?"

"What I said. See, I don't have a whole lot of time here. In fact, you might say this is a hell of risk I've taken. Even down to bribing the harbormaster. This is Malmesbury's ship, but this isn't his crew."

"I'd never have guessed. I don't suppose you're sailing in the agreed waters either?"

"Malmesbury's bound to know I've pirated this boat by now. A capital offense."

She stared, with predatory avidity from beneath her eyelashes, and he could as good as hear her mind whirring about how she could use all this to her advantage. He lowered his eyelids.

The thing was, *she couldn't.*

When he'd hatched this plan he hadn't expected her to take five months to reach Calais. He'd been ready to head for England and Ravenhurst when he got wind of the fact that *finally* she was here.

He'd reckoned a week, maybe two, a little consuming of humble pie, a little seduction, and once she saw the fine clothes and jewels he could give her—once she got over her initial surprise about what a changed man he was—she'd be his.

But now, his eyes sweeping her face, he knew he hadn't imagined her throwing the dress on the floor and vomiting on his shirt. And while seven and a half months wasn't nine, no matter how much he did the arithmetic, seven from nine was still two.

Now, he felt against the clock. What if she dropped that bulge here? His palms sweated for all that a smile touched the ends of his mouth and he released her. When his hunger for her amounted to starvation, why the hell didn't she feel the same?

"So then—"

"So, then you don't agree to this small thing I'm asking, I'm going to keep you here."

"You're what?"

Beguile—he must beguile her a little, the way she did him, for her eyes to flicker like that at the thought of being kept here. Yet was he really going to do that? Was she really beguiled, the way she now tightened her jaw?

"Till when?"

He swallowed. If he said this, he probably ruined his chances further, but he'd never imagined her not wanting him because of the things she wanted more. He hadn't imagined that story she told touching him. So he was tempted to let her go. Anyway, she was bound to know he didn't mean what he threatened.

"Till you either give me the baby or you give me Storm."

In so far as it was possible for a face to whiten when it was already an unattractive shade of green, hers did so now. "Are you mad? Storm?"

"She's the one being left out of this, isn't she? This fine new life you see for yourself and this new baby here."

Where feet and mouths were concerned, he knew he'd just stuck his size nines in his. But what never failed to surprise him was how one could start seeing things one had been blind to before.

She twisted her mouth into a sneer. "Because you were there the day she was born, holding my hand, welcoming her into the world, right?"

With difficulty he kept his voice neutral. "No, I wasn't. Like you were that girl, I was that man. You're right. What would I have done with a baby?"

"Which means you've a nerve to speak when I want the best for her. School. Europe. Marriage."

"And that's why you hide her away?"

"Hide her away? I don't—"

"And you won't tell me where she is, so I can see her?" That too, was a sudden grievance. A blindness illuminated by light.

"Because you want these things for her?"

"You left us, remember?"

She moved forward to the door. He wasn't going to let her end the interview. It was his misfortune to have made that mistake in Genoa. It had cost him dearly. He wasn't going to do it here.

"I'm back now. The choice is up to you. A few days is what I'm asking."

The tiny hesitation, while she stood with her gaze edged sideways, burned him. He'd said something he didn't mean but found he was seeing things as he'd never done before. Feeling things he'd never felt too.

For as long as it took, he'd keep her. Until she gave him what he wanted. She needn't bother treating this as a gauntlet to be picked up and worked to her advantage. As though she could play for time while she did something else altogether. Turning this cabin upside down for what was left of that book for example. He knew her too well for that.

"Why — why certainly."

He stepped toward her, and she cleared her throat.

"But even you must see the start is not auspicious. You will allow me to return to the other cabin while I think about this?"

"Of course, I will. You have till tomorrow night."

"Night?"

"Night."

He opened the door and gestured for her to go before him.

Chapter Fifteen

Fury stood in the oil-lit companionway, her hand raised, ready to knock on Flint's door. Susan's shocked words from last night popped into her splitting head. She shut her eyes tight, willing everything Susan had said away. Already her hands shook and head pounded enough that she wanted to tell Benito to take her back to her cabin. She didn't need Susan's damned words beating at her senses. As if Fury were somehow responsible for Flint's raging insanity. And now their hopes of getting off this boat were nonexistent.

Flint's appalling ultimatum yanked her back to the present and she knocked on the door.

"Come in."

She opened her eyes and fisted the fabric of her corded cream day dress, which Susan had scrubbed the stains off last night while Fury had lain curled beneath the rough blanket.

The red silk would be too clear a signal of her compliance. She wasn't compliant. Her blood boiled more than she thought humanly possible. But she was also vulnerable. More vulnerable than she'd been in her entire life, which was why she hadn't refused his offer to think things over.

But if those whores were present...

Gritting her teeth, she opened the door. "Flint."

After all, it was best to meet him with her head held high, her best foot set forward. Even if her neck felt as if it had been snapped along with her ankle and her head ached.

She was here to find out exactly what he wanted. It could not possibly be her.

And even if it was, that wasn't a request she would grant.

Flint turned from the washstand and she rebuked herself for allowing her eyes to roam over his immaculate body to his face. Damn, but the black coat became him. Except for sometimes wearing a black tricorne, she'd only ever seen him in scruffy brown. Blue, beige, or gray, or any other color. And those were all a compliment to his blue eyes. But black…

She quashed the horde of storming sensations: Breast. Heart. Veins. The voice in her that whispered he couldn't ever be a gentleman, but would any woman want him to be, looking like that.

Last night he had given her an ultimatum. Tonight she came here with one of her own. And not just that. The remains of her book must be here somewhere. If she could but get her hands on it, she would be in a better bargaining position. Malmesbury might have everything she had on him, but she hadn't solely collected information on that viperous maggot. She had collected it on everyone she came into contact with.

"You're not wearing the dress."

The way his cool gaze licked her was awful. The impossible wasn't attainable. She hated that he made her consider it was. And right on cue, he tilted and hardened his jaw. As ever. This was one occasion she'd rather walk the plank.

"It didn't fit," she lied. "I don't know how you think it could have. Or that I would be so trashy as to wear it, even if it did. Let's dispense with this nonsense about the frock, shall we? How about you tell me what you want? Exactly what you want."

"Hmmm."

She also hated that he always located the double entendre in everything.

Turning his back, he resumed fiddling with his cuffs. "The first is you sit down. Unless, of course you're here to tell me you've considered my offer and you intend refusing it."

"I think it's obvious I intend refusing it, because I don't regard you locking me in that room last night while I made my mind up to your satisfaction as conducive to acceptance."

"I told you my conditions."

Dear God, was that cologne he was slapping on his cheeks?

"They've not changed far as I know." He finished with the cologne.

"Then I shall sit down. Obviously there are things to discuss. If it's all right with you, and you're quite finished preening yourself, that is?"

He gestured at the feast laid out on the table in the center of the cabin. She gathered her skirts and approached it.

"Wait." He crossed the room and drew out a chair. "Let me get that for you."

Suppose, for the sake of argument, he did mean it. Suppose she went along with this charade for the few days. Suppose she didn't find him changed. Suppose she, in fact, told him where to put himself, as indeed, was more than likely right now. Was he just going to set her down in Dover, or Bristol, given what he had threatened about the baby and Storm? Probably not.

She took a seat and mustered a dignified pose. This present baby she had, at times, hated. She was not going to pretend. But if she lost that, she lost everything. Hopes. Dreams. Future.

If this was a choice…

If? Of course it was.

"That cologne is quite gentlemanly. I like it. And the table —
"

"You want some soup?" He snatched the lid from the tureen

and dunked the ladle, before she could finish. A few pale green drops spattered the tablecloth.

Soft white damask, she thought, resisting the urge to finger it. Probably stolen. Like everything else here. Not that she should complain about that though. Not right now anyway.

"The soup tureen is very beautiful. So intricate. Sterling silver." She reached out a hand to the dishes sitting before her. "And the bowls. The bowls are quite—"

"You want to eat this? Or you want to admire it?" Not especially gentlemanly. Nor was the way he loomed over her. But then, there was never any fooling him.

If he thought she feigned amenability, if in fact, he *was* serious, and this wasn't some crack-brained scheme, she'd suffer God knows what consequences.

"I can't eat it. Not the way the ship keeps pitching." She placed a hand over her bowl. "I don't think you understand. Or you think perhaps I'm lying. Which is why this game you're playing, this game you want me to play, is a waste of time. I'm in no state of mind right now, to be dragged in here—"

He shot his eyebrows up. Then they slammed together. "Dragged? Are you saying Benito dragged—"

"You know what I mean." He needn't make it seem as if he would protect her. Although when he had, that day he'd carried her up the stairs… She quashed the recollection. "Commanded here then, to see if you're a changed man or not. All I know is a changed man wouldn't keep me here against my will. He wouldn't threaten me with choosing between my children."

A muscle twitched in his jaw. "Our children."

"Whosever children they are. That's how I see it anyway. They'd put me ashore and conduct matters properly from there."

"Come to Ravenhurst, you mean?"

"I gave you the offer. I thought that maybe, I hoped that

maybe — "

"You hoped wrong."

"But isn't that what you're trying to be a gentleman for?"

"Not that I know of."

"That's how I see it."

The appeal to whatever soft spot he didn't possess was clumsy. Had she felt better, she would have done better. Or never done it at all. After all what was the point? Especially when she'd made her choice, even before she stepped in here. All this just confirmed the necessity of guaranteeing her future. By whatever means. If that meant sacrifice, then she would sacrifice.

She shivered a little. Then she straightened her spine and faced him with what she prayed was a neutral expression. After all, she'd decided on this.

"Here's the deal I'm going to make. I want to give you Storm."

Flint stared at her there, her lashes swept down to hide the glint in her eyes, although he knew damned fine that she stared at him, in addition to feeling he was going to burst with every beat of his heart. Wasn't she the very one who had begged him, and begged him, to get her pregnant, for Storm's sake?

Unless something had changed. Before he let his thoughts drift to what that might be, before he started thinking what a prized bitch she was, before anything, he needed to remember he had misjudged her once before. Look where it had gotten him.

All right, he had been seven years younger then. Did he want to be seven years older before he realized he'd done it again? And why?

"Storm?"

"Why do you sound so surprised? Of course, if you don't

want—"

"Who says that?"

She colored. Of course she would. Because like hell he would let her think he wasn't amenable to her little suggestion when she so clearly didn't mean it.

"If you don't want to know her whereabouts, that is. I mean, I-I'll let you meet her."

"Now, why would you do that? So we can all play happy family together."

Still, he couldn't deny the tidal wave of despair that engulfed him. Christ, consider this damned carrot she dangled. At him. *Him.* Who was nothing like the damned donkey she imagined. It was anything rather than accept him, wasn't it?

"Us? Of course, if you can't see me asking myself, if you can't ask yourself, what kind of mother keeps a child from its father? Especially a father she should meet? Who desires to meet her?"

He paused, looming closer. What was one more nail in his coffin if he pulled her out that chair she sat in, distant as the polar stars, toying with the soupspoon? The one he'd plundered a Spanish vessel for. Especially when he wanted her so much. Screwed some sense into her, like he used to. It would be difficult, when she was so heavily pregnant, to be less than the slow burning man no one could needle though.

"I don't know. Maybe one I'm looking at right now who thinks I'm stupid enough to fall for it?"

"The thing is, I'm the kind of mother who wants the best for her children."

She could have fooled him but he bit his tongue.

"And a pirate vessel—"

"Privateer."

"Let's not quibble about words. Because a ship like this is hardly the place to raise a child. You know that and I know that.

However, you can meet her, see if you like her, and then…then we discuss it. Because you pretending to be a gentleman, or a changed man, is silly. I'm not the only one who needs to make a choice here." She set down the spoon. "You do too."

* * *

"And then what, madam?" Susan tugged her cloak shut.

It was the calmest midday in four. As it always did, unless the water was millpond flat, a breeze blew though. This one peppered with sleet.

Fury dragged her gaze away from the tall, rangy figure half way up the foremast shouting orders at the men below.

What didn't matter?

Hadn't Susan been listening to a single word she'd been saying? Unless Fury was very much mistaken, the mast was snapped in half, held in position by ropes and rigging, or Flint would climb further.

Although she allowed that Susan might not understand the significance of that, being unaccustomed to ships of this size, Fury couldn't believe she wanted to rake over the bones of what had happened several nights ago. Or maybe she could.

"Then the boat pitched and he had to go on deck," she lied. "But as I said to you, I was confident he could get us through that storm, just as I'm now confident I can get us both out of this. Why keep asking?"

"Because I don't understand why he locked you back up, madam. That storm didn't strike till four nights later."

Why did people always think the worst of her? How could Susan believe it her fault that he'd reverted to type again? Her own maid, for goodness sake.

"Because he just did. Haven't we been over this again and again?"

She was not going to admit how Flint had marched her from

his cabin to hers in a furious temper, pushed her in and bolted the door, as if he found her ultimatum utterly repellent. Flint, the slow fuse, burning fit to explode. Of course, she might have known the notion of asking him to choose would put her in some very stormy waters.

He hadn't given her an answer though. Seeing his head turn her way, she smiled and raised a hand. It would not do for him to think her unamenable. Or Susan either. Not if that mast was broken.

Susan clutched her shawl to her throat with her other hand. "Madam, it's foolhardy. I vow and swear, in your condition—"

And how dare Susan think her plan more foolish than foolproof. Why, her plan was perfect. The coastline lay in sight. Provided that mast *was* broken.

"A fat lot you, or anyone else here, cares about that." She spoke through her teeth. "Thinking we should just sit this out. Oh, I can see you think he's a very fine man and all that. But let me tell you, he gets this ship back under way, he'll drag us both to Jamaica or some other God-awful hellhole and I will be ruined. I am probably ruined anyway. Do you know how many days it's been since he kidnapped us? It's been three alone since that storm struck."

"Madam, you know how much I've always cared. I'm the one who found you that day on the quay, after you'd sat there—"

For a whole day in the freezing cold of a land she'd never been in. She didn't want to be reminded of that. "To get us out of here, I said some things to him. All right?" Oh God. She was beginning to sound like him.

"I still think—"

"Maybe I shouldn't have said them. Any of them. I accept that. But, not only will it not come to that because he won't choose seeing Storm over captaining this tub, that mast is broken, I'm sure of it. This is our chance."

"Madam, you can't, whether or not you think that's the English coast over there."

"Think? I don't think, I know. Of course, if you had made some headway talking to those whores, over there..." She let her gaze drift for a few short, pointed seconds across the deck. "Who he was probably with for those four days before the storm struck."

"Is it any surprise I never, madam, being as this is the first day I've been let out because of you?"

Susan's scoffing and reproving tone rankled. How dare she blame Fury for this? Next Susan would be suggesting she should just accept the whores, accept *everything*.

"Because you won't appeal to his...whatever it is he's got for you." Susan sighed. "But it's something."

"May I remind you of my condition." Fury snapped her gaze back, from the whores, from him. Did galloping idiocy run in Susan's family? If so she must move Storm. She did not want the child raised by fools. "So that's hardly likely. Anyway, if you think for one minute I'm staying here and taking him anywhere near Storm, I'd sooner cut my throat. That was just an offer. A suggestion when he —" *Saw the paper thinness of what she offered?* She shrugged and glanced out at the swelling waves.

It was true though. The choice had never been about Storm and this child. The choice was between letting him have the few days or not. She had determined *not*.

Only, on reflection, it troubled her that the need to protect herself was paramount. It shouldn't be. Why couldn't she have sailed into that cabin and said, *of course Flint, you have a week?* Knowing it would be no trouble. That it was, spoke of a lack of dignity on her part. A lack of backbone. A lack. Period.

"Well, madam, it just seems a lot more sensible somehow."

"*What?*"

"Than you trying to get off this ship. Would it kill you just to let him at least see her? Just once? You know there's other ways of leading a pig to slaughter. What if he has changed?"

"Yes. And maybe that same pig will ride a fine black horse up and down the broken mast there. Now here he comes. Be quiet."

She tugged her cloak around her. Flint had dropped the last few feet to the deck and now that he'd straightened, his gaze fixed on her. She wanted to think it was because he liked the look of her. She doubted it, the way he knitted his brows.

"Madam..."

"Shh, Susan. He gets wind of anything and I swear it's over between us. I am getting off this boat if it kills me."

Of course, it couldn't be over, unless she did really move Storm, but there was no harm saying so. She kept a close eye on Flint as he muttered something to one of his men in passing. Ships had their own rhythms. Already she felt she'd fallen back into place here. Except of course, for the awful sickness. She tilted her chin. Would he amble toward her like this if the mast was broken though?

Yes. He might.

"Fury."

It was the first time she'd seen him since he had locked her up. But she didn't want to examine the marks of sleeplessness that stood out beneath his eyes. Or the four-day's growth of stubble on his handsome jaw. The uncombed nature of his hair either. Besides the liberties he took, in terms of the way he ambled toward her and the false way he grinned, were enough to suffer. She hadn't missed his glower a second ago.

"Is there something wrong with the mast?" No point beating about the bush.

She refrained from making her scan of the nearby shore too obvious. Although he should know, his frown didn't fool her.

If Flint, the patcher of various holed hulls and shattered

THE UNRAVELING OF LADY FURY 281

decks, was hard-pressed to bandage that mast up, why not add to his consternation?

"Nothing Nathan there can't fix."

"Oh, I see." Ignoring Susan's disapproving frown, she let her gaze filter across the deck. Then back to his face. She smiled. "Absolutely nothing to worry about then. And of course, a good supply of timber from the beach over there. I suppose we'll be underway in no time."

If he was at a true loss, there was no sign. That look was pure Flint. Lazy. Conniving. Deceptive.

"If you'd like to step into the cabin, there's something I want to give you first."

In her condition?

She tried not to shoot a stunned glance at Susan, but the shiver the words sent down her spine, her glance had darted before she could stop it. Also, he loomed in a way she could only describe as sexually menacing.

"No, James. The sooner you recognize I'm not the old Fury who once stepped into cabins with you at the drop of your breeches, the better. Unless you've made your mind up about what we discussed, in which case the only thing you can give me is an answer, I am staying right here."

He might have been captain, but she was no ordinary prisoner. If he needed a moment to take that in, unfreeze his gaze a little, fine.

"Is that what you think?"

"Indeed." In case he didn't understand, she made herself sound even primmer.

But with the way his eyes blazed, and the second it took to tamp down his outrage, she felt obliged to backtrack.

"What I mean is Susan and I will return immediately to our cabin." Give up the first piece of freedom in days? Was she mad? Ignoring the way Susan's jaw dropped, she continued. "Won't we, Susan?" On this she intended to stand firm. Maybe he had thought she'd be more amenable. He had saved them, she supposed. The storm had been violent. "I understand, of course, you have been preoccupied, but you can speak to me there, when you've made your mind up about what we discussed. Whether you can give up privateering or not to be a proper father to Storm and this baby."

Holding her cloak shut she stepped past him. At least, she attempted to. But he blocked her way, his ice-cold gaze freezing her.

"That there's a real pity. See, I was going to give you these papers. You know the ones you keep harking you want back. But seeing as you don't, I'll just put them ashore for safe-keeping with Louise-Ann."

Louise-Ann? She couldn't allow such a thing. Dear God. What was left of Malmesbury's secrets in the hands of some Dutch slut? Being sold to the highest bidder? No ifs, no buts about this. She wanted that book. So desperately, he was welcome to read her like one.

"There is no need to be so hasty, Flint."

"Quite so hasty? Or just quite so? Cabin door's open when you're ready to negotiate."

"Negotiate?" In his cabin, when she knew exactly what he thought and she knew exactly how this would look? How could she?

"Negotiate. The choice is yours."

* * *

Fury settled her gaze on what Flint placed before her on the table. Her book. With the heart, the guts ripped from it. Not just a great deal of what she'd recorded, but the proof of it all too. Notes, statements. Malmesbury must have a quite a lot on all those she had kept tabs on.

Lucky him.

But it would be an act of unprecedented folly to say *Is this all?* and scratch Flint's eyes. She hadn't swept in here to do that.

No. She had swept in here to discover what he had. And then decide what she did about it.

A ruthless, chiseling bastard like Flint, lounging opposite in the chair there, would hardly give everything away. For nothing.

With the shore so close and the mast broken, she was under no illusions he now wanted to end up empty-handed. He never had. If she'd been fool enough to fall for his pretty talk, she'd be in an even prettier mess now.

She thought of the tiny moments here that had almost betrayed her and her throat tightened. No. There were only two things this unsavory transaction could involve. Sex, as it always had. And money.

She swallowed. If he asked for money, then he didn't mean to ruin her. While sex, in her present state—well, then he did. Or maybe he just wanted to see her humiliated because she'd refused to run away with him in Genoa? Here didn't count, because she saw now how clearly it had all been a game. He was never not going to get to this point.

"So?" Of course she could refuse. She should have refused before. But if she refused, she would not get that book, would she? Or the few bills and statements he had kept. "It happens that you do indeed have some small things of worth—and believe me, they are small, the contents of the book itself were worth a fortune. What do you want?"

"What do I want?" For a long moment his stare sat, unwavering, upon her, a tiny muscle twitching in his jaw in the gathering silence.

"What do you want for this?"

He tilted his jaw. "That depends."

Of course it did. On who was more desperate. "On what?"

"On just how much what's here is worth to you."

She smiled. Why not? He'd taken her book, but she could read him like one. Money. Well, of course. She and Susan would be on dry land by supper time. Maybe even within the hour, without her having to descend to the tiresome necessity of escaping over the side.

She steepled her fingers. "Who says they are worth anything? But let's say for the sake of argument they are *to you* or you'd not have put them on the table. What do you want for them?"

"What you want to give me for them, sweetheart."

This was getting tiresome. Why did he look at her like that? As if she made a pretty display of herself sitting there, unable to hide the fact she'd come in here for one thing and one thing only. And it wasn't sex with him.

"My book? Which you stole." Which, the sight of on the table was almost too much to bear. "Tuppence-halfpenny, I should think. Except I don't have tuppence halfpenny."

"Is it always money with you?"

"Me?" Her palm slickened as she flattened it on the table. Surely he didn't expect her to haggle like a common whore? A woman of her standing? But, if it wasn't money, when money she could give him, when anything else, even if her heart had gone cold and it meant nothing—anything else was ridiculous.

Yet, money was her first thought as if she couldn't quite get by the fact he didn't love her. And still, some tiny foolish part of herself needed protecting from the wish that he did.

"Isn't this an even finer case of pots and kettles. The mast is broken. You think I don't know how this is over for you now land's in sight? So why don't you just tell me how much and let's be done with this? That way you'll at least get something."

"What do I want?"

He rose up from the table and her gaze darted sideways

over the scuffed leather boots not just infiltrating her vision, but standing right beside her chair. He leaned over, his arms caging her.

She could hardly believe it. Perhaps all this and the broken mast were just too much for him to bear. The interval between him last commanding a ship and now was long. Perhaps he was no longer capable of going nights without sleep and washing down grog with hefty doses of seawater, while keeping a woman in his cabin for pleasure.

Her heart hammered, although she strove not to let it betray her. "Yes." She stared at his knuckles shining white on the tabletop. "What do you want?"

He grunted at the back of his throat, his fingers digging harder into the tabletop. Flint the slow burner, angrier with each second that passed. Although she still wanted to cling to the notion that until he gave her his demands, she was in no position to decide how best to meet them. She was a little unsure what position she was in. If he pulled her out this chair. If he kissed her.

"Nothing." He sighed.

Fury jerked her chin up. Surely she misheard? *Nothing* was not the sort of word he uttered. It was not the sort of thing he'd told her to come here for. Why, she'd been fully prepared for sex.

"There's no need to look so surprised."

Of course, this was her book and he had stolen it. But now he had given it back, she should feel relief that he didn't want her. Shouldn't she? Not faint disappointment.

"You just thought the worst of me, didn't you? Because you can't help yourself."

If she didn't close her mouth, he'd know she was lying. "Well I—I—"

But the feeling was fierce, fiercer than it should have been, that he oozed disappointment. His mouth, set in a line, and the pinpricks of luminosity in his eyes weren't him somehow. It made his face shuttered so she couldn't read it. Worse, she couldn't tell whether that disappointment centered entirely on himself. It couldn't be that it sickened him to have feelings for her, despite her recalcitrance.

"You thought I brought you here for some immoral purpose. Correct? Like I used to all those years ago."

"The thought didn't cross my mind." Much.

"That's a change."

He straightened. Somewhat to her relief, she was forced to say. She understood, to a point, he was ruthless. One did not expect the mercifulness of a saint in a man who'd once offered her the choice between getting in his bed and walking the plank.

But the emotion that gripped him went deeper than that. The flicker in his eyes. The knitting of his brow.

"You usually have a dramatic imagination about me that way."

Which was why she couldn't prevent her gaze from stealing back to the table. Why would he do this? Give her the book? Unless he could get more for her.

"Go. Take everything. I want you to."

Was he serious? Silly to let this bother her, but if there was another agenda, why did she feel it wasn't quite *right* somehow to do what he said? What if he had changed? And what if she believed that and it was a mistake?

She reached out a hand and snatched up the book. The loose papers too. Opportunities like this did not come along every day.

"At least it will stop you rifling my cabin for them."

Her? The rest of the ship certainly. But his cabin? If she was left in it alone perhaps. "M-me? I don't know how you can say such a thing."

"Easy. That amount of temptation under your nose, you know you couldn't resist. 'Specially as this is where you'll be staying till the boat's repaired."

She froze, her eyes first darting sideways. She hoped perhaps she'd misheard. Surely, giving her the book and the letters meant... Actually she wasn't sure what it meant. "And why will I be doing that?"

"Why do you think?"

Ruin, of course. What else could it be, the lazy way his gaze searched her face. She would not, could not let him. She sprang for the door, any thought about him keeping her here for her own personal safety vanishing when she collided instead with him.

"How dare you?" She grasped the book tighter and swiped it at his chest as if it were a fan. Then she thudded it for good measure off his jaw. "If that is why you've given me these, you can keep them."

And yet, was it quite the thing to do, hitting him with a pile of paper, especially when the book spine split down the middle and the leaves landed on the floor? The cologne bottle or the sextant would be more effective. Only she couldn't reach either. Biting him was no better because he took hold of her wrists in a powerful grip and yanked her back even as she fought to get her hands on something heavier. She could barely move, although, of course she tried.

"In the unlikely event you calm down—" His drawl only incensed her further.

"And what about you?"

"Think of the baby. The heir to the Beaumont dukedom. What's more important to you than anything. Now, you might see me giving you that book and these papers has nothing to do with you staying here. But you know my feelings on a tidy cabin."

"I'm not picking them up again. Although I do applaud your conscientiousness in giving them to me."

"And you know my feelings on escape. You, and just maybe Susan, although I'm less sure about her. You think I didn't see the way the two of you were talking on that deck? You think I don't know what you're planning?"

God, this was madness. That twinge in her stomach alarmed her. Never mind anything else, the Beaumont heir could not be delivered in the hold of a pirate vessel. Only she felt her breath shorten and rage course through her veins.

"That's why you gave me these? So I would come in here? You nasty, low-down son of a bitch's dog. A bitch's whore. A—a—"

But how on earth could she now escape if she didn't lull him into a false sense of security? Was she mad? How could she lull him, ranting like this? And trying to hit him. Already she saw in the ice-cool of his manner, the searching stare, even the new low depth to his voice, that this was not a man to whom she could appeal.

"No. But I brought you in here because I'm keeping you and Susan apart."

As abruptly as if he'd tossed a bucket of icy water on her, she froze. "Until when?"

"Till the mast's mended or the baby's born, whichever is first. Now, do you mind if I get some sleep? I've not had any for three days."

* * *

She put on a brave show, Flint gave her credit for that, although he'd never seen her face so white. Later though, after he kicked his boots off and sprawled out on the bed, he was aware of a voice in his head pointing out to him this had somehow taken a turn for the worse.

He could scarcely remember being more brutal. Except perhaps the day with the trunk. But he just happened to desire her to the deepest depths of his veins. So much so it wasn't a trouble to stay away from other women, despite the fact he'd been celibate since he left her bed and it didn't look like he was getting any soon. Even if Marigold had not belonged to his first mate, he'd been ruined for that.

And the damned mast snapping, so near the shore. If he could get in the water and tow the damned boat back out to sea himself, he would. Because he knew damned fine what rat's piss all this talk of choices was. She'd do anything to get off this boat and away from him.

He'd said it now. And he didn't take it back. *The Beaumont heir.* That was his damned baby she had there.

If he couldn't keep her, he'd damn well keep it.

Chapter Sixteen

It was not that Fury wasn't used to desperate situations. It was that the water was so cold, far worse than anything she expected, like being stuck with ice shards. Hundreds of them. All at the same time. No wonder she gasped. If she didn't move though, she would freeze.

All she had to do was strike out for the shore there, being careful to make as little noise as possible. Flint might have slept the sleep of the dead for the last five hours, but she'd left the cabin window open behind her.

Fury bobbed her way through the lapping waves, the sticks, and seaweed that covered the surface of the water. She might have taken the jolly boat, which had been lowered to take Louise-Ann ashore earlier, but even she had baulked at that. Four men were required to row it.

Swimming was the one useful thing Flint had taught her. He had thought it might save her life some time. He didn't know how right he was. Of course, the water he had taught her in had been much warmer. As indeed had been his behavior toward her on those occasions. They had swum and dived in some wonderful places. She had no wish to think of them now but her teeth chattered so badly with cold, she had to remember something warm.

A pity she'd had to wait till dusk. It gave her the advantage of darkness, however, the water would have been warmer earlier and the shore, which had looked so close, would not seem so far away, as though someone kept tugging it away from her on a string.

Naturally, as she discovered, the second she grasped the jolly's rope and swung from the cabin window into the water, the only advantage in being pregnant was someone might take her for a whale.

After Flint's threats, what other choice did she have though? She'd not done all this to let him take the baby. Her dreams. Storm's future. What was wrong with him? And not just that. The taut, burning way he had looked. Eyes of icy steel. Yet eyes that had seemed to want to breathe her, to breathe her soul, while he stood over her at the door. It frightened her. Not as much as one fact though. She wasn't having a baby on a boat.

She wasn't having it in the water either. She smothered a shriek as a cold claw grasped the base of her spine. A very strange place to have swimmer's cramp though, wasn't it?

She came into the shallows and she staggered to her feet, gritting her teeth to prevent any shrieks escaping her. Already, the amount of water cascading from her gown, as if someone had tossed several bucketfuls over her, and her feet slapping through the shingle made enough noise to wake the dead. She had still to find her way off the beach.

Well, she would. Susan was on board the *Palerna*. This might be Fury's only chance to free her. Only it would have been more helpful if she'd managed to bring shoes. The shingle cut her hands and knees. As for that cramp crippling the base of her spine — that was unexpected.

She gulped and crawled into the sand dunes, landing with a thud on her palms and nose. Not now. It was too early. Why, she was barely eight months. And besides, all her labor pains with

Storm had been in her stomach.

No. She just had to rest for a bit. Difficult and all as it was, with the breath tearing in her lungs and her teeth chattering with cold. And knowing one terrible fact. An eight months baby would not survive. And, oh God, neither would she, out here in the open. Clutching her stomach, as if to hold herself together, she edged up against a dune. She took several short, ragged breaths to compose herself.

It may be she didn't want this child, but she couldn't let all this be for nothing. That would be too laughable for words. She wasn't going to laugh. She was going to sit here very quietly for a little while. Then get on her way to that scattering of cottages further along the shore she had glimpsed earlier.

* * *

"*Madam!*"

Fury heard the cry, faint at first above the wind tearing at her hair, and thought she imagined it. Then she heard it again. Stronger this time. Closer too.

"Madam!"

Susan. She had escaped and was searching for her.

"Susan!" Dragging herself onto her knees she croaked, "Susan!" She must have huddled for hours in the dunes, trying to find shelter from the whipping wind, after managing to crawl a little way further. But if Susan was here, then they'd be able to make their way onto the path. Reach the cottages. By morning this would all be over. A distant nightmare.

"Madam? My God."

Fury saw the light before she saw Susan. A huge ship's lantern flaming into her vision.

"Oh, Susan, I can't tell you how glad I am to see you." They may have quarreled earlier over Flint, but she owed everything to her.

"For God's sake, my lovey. Are you —"

Susan edged the lantern down on the sand. Before she could finish, Fury clung to her. It was so good to see her, and she was warm in a way Fury wasn't right now.

"No. I'm all right. At least I think I'm all right. But these pains. I just keep having these —" She was so ashamed to think she could screech like this, she closed her mouth to muffle the sound. The last thing she needed was to be in labor. If she muffled the sound, surely it would go away? "In my back. Cramp from swimming. It'll go in a minute. Yes. Then we can head up the path and get away from here. There's cottages up there at the top of the path. Someone will surely help us."

Fury didn't care for the way Susan's gaze froze as she swept the hair back from Fury's face.

"What do you mean pains? How many?"

"Not so many. Just... It's gone now. There. Thank goodness, eh?"

"Madam, I'm going for help." Susan got back up to her feet.

"No, Susan. I'm coming with you."

And yet, was it such a bad idea? She stayed here and Susan fetched help. So long as that help... A terrifying thought thudded.

"Susan, how did you get here? Did you escape too? Did you manage to swim?" Another wave of pain took her but she gritted her teeth.

"Captain Flint brought me. He's looking for you. So's half the *Palerna*."

"Half the — Susan... No, you can't... This...this is our chance." She shot to her feet. "Our only chance. You have no idea the things he's said to me. You need to go to one of the cottages and raise the alarm. There are smugglers. Or privateers. Or whatever. And you get help. But you do not tell him you have found me. He wants the baby. He told me. Threatened me.

It was what he called me to his cabin for."

Why did Susan stare like that? As if Fury had gone mad? Of course the magnitude of Flint's present insanity was hard to understand.

"And I am afraid, maybe he means to ransom me, Susan. Can you imagine?"

Why did Susan bite her lip?

"Yes. For money. So, you mustn't...*you mustn't.*" She clawed in several puffs of air. "Face Lady Margaret and tell her the Beaumont heir has been stolen by him? I can't do it. It would mean giving him Storm. And I can't do that either. Douse the light. The light, Susan. And go—go. Hurry."

Oh, God, Susan would, wouldn't she? Fury sank down again, clutching her stomach. They had been friends for so long.

Susan would never betray her to Flint.

Never.

Fury jerked her head up. So what the hell did Susan think she was doing leading him over the head of the sand dune? No. Definitely she was, exhorting, *this way, this way.* A horrific proposition. And definitely it was him. Not a hallucination. Or nightmare of the screaming wind. But James Flint Blackmoore. His lips compressed. His eyes like ice-slits. Sand spraying up to his knees as he skidded down to the bottom of the dune and thrust his lantern at the man just behind him.

"Here."

Clutching her stomach, Fury staggered to her feet.

"Madam. No wait—"

Susan need have no fear of it. To be dragged back to the *Palerna?* Locked in chains till she gave Flint one child or the other? No. If it was possible for a man to be controlled yet livid, Flint was it. But while it was a waste of energy, Fury still failed to desist from struggling as he grabbed hold of her wrist.

"Nice to see you too, sweetheart. Do you have any idea how

long I've been walking up and down this damned beach looking for you?"

She didn't. She was too busy trying to stay upright and stop the groan from issuing from her frozen lips. The awful one she neither wanted him to see or hear. That would be to say this was happening. It wasn't.

"No. I mean... I don't care that you were."

Certainly, it wasn't happening in front of him. The matter was of too much delicacy. Why, when she had had Storm, she couldn't have cared less where she had dropped her, so long as she dropped her. Women got to that stage. She had not reached it yet. Nor anywhere near it.

"No?" He glared. "Don't stop now. Get to that scream you're longing to give."

"I'm not... I..."

Her apprehension returned in full force as another spasm fisted her spine. This time as if it might snap it in two. Although she wanted to pretend it was nothing, she both tensed and sagged, her lips parting in a silent scream. As they did he caught her. Or maybe she caught him. Whoever caught who, she breathed the fresh, cold smell of his coat, and felt him tremble. And what seemed unwise a second ago, seemed right now, because she knew she would have fallen down otherwise.

"All right. I've got you."

"A false alarm." She gasped to feel him lower her onto her knees. "That's all. Is it any wonder? After what you did?"

"You can berate me for that after. Susan..."

He jerked his head at Susan and Fury shrieked to feel his hand edge down her gown, as if he were trying to untangle her skirt from around her knees. Or worse. She gulped. She didn't want him touching her. Susan either. Especially when she wasn't having this baby. Anyway, how would he know, just because his mother had been a midwife? Fortunately seawater had welded her skirt to her legs.

"All right, you want to play coy. I'm going to try and get you to the houses back there."

The houses were good. The houses still offered the chance of escape. Except she feared she might not reach them.

"You think you can put an arm round my neck?"

Another agonizing bolt shot through her. "No—oh God, Flint, I can't." She screeched, releasing him. "Please. I just…need a minute…"

This—this was bad, wasn't it? She had wanted this baby *because of money*. And then she hadn't *because of him*. But if she lost it, if she lost it now…she would, wouldn't she? The thought made her moan.

She knelt there, on the soft sand, the waves frothing several yards away, and a second became a minute as his gaze slid over her, as if in calculation. Then it became an hour. At least it seemed an hour passed before he peeled off his coat. In reality, it probably lasted no more than a moment.

"Here." He tucked the coat around her. He had to kneel closer to do it. So close she almost leaned against him.

Sweet relief flooded her. Somehow he was going to get her up the cliff path to the houses. Then this might stop.

He turned and called over his shoulder. "Nathan."

"Aye, Cap'n."

"Comb the beach. Get a fire going."

"Aye, Cap'n. On it."

"Flint, no. I can manage. I can get to the houses. Please." She clutched his wrist.

"And get someone up to the houses."

"No, Flint. I can walk… It's only over there."

"All right, sweetheart. Listen to me." He dragged her face up, so she squinted at him in the lantern light. "Listen."

"No. Not here. I can't have it out here. No."

A beach. A darkened, windswept beach was not the place for her to produce the Beaumont heir. She scanned his face in the hope of seeing so. But another spasm left her breathless. Were he not holding her against him, she'd have collapsed.

"It's early, all right?"

"No. I can't..."

"Look, Fury, when a baby's on its way, even you can't tell it to turn around and go back in again. And there's no point blaming you and there's no point blaming me. We got that fire going yet?" He yelled over his shoulder.

"Doing our best, Cap'n."

"Susan will help you. Now, isn't that so, Susan?"

"Absolutely, madam." Susan dropped down beside her. "I will do anything. I'm right here."

Fury bit her lip. Heaven help her, she was lost. Didn't Flint know? Susan didn't have a bloody clue. Even if the baby wasn't going to survive anyway.

"She can't. She can't do it." A terrifying prescience filled Fury. She tried to move, only she couldn't. "Please... Next you'll be telling me there's nothing to this."

Perhaps it was because he'd been angry. Perhaps it was because she was scared. Perhaps it was just his close proximity. But everything seemed to retreat. All she saw were his eyes intent on her and his lips curved in a faint smile.

"Well, there ain't. It's just a little hard pushing, that's all."

Actually, it was more than that. Her stomach tightened. It was bad enough he was here at all. Bad enough that she was being forced to deliver a baby in a sand dune, with the wind whipping about her ears. She, who enjoyed a certain dignity and control, was not going to do it in front of him, who was already behaving in ways not expected of a man, especially not a man like him. It didn't matter that she found his shoulder comforting to lean her forehead on.

Help must come soon, so he could go away and do the things men did at moments like this. Pacing the floor. Getting blind drunk. Collapsing in a heap. He would, of course. Because the most overwhelming desire to push overtook her. It was negated by the cramp clamping the base of her spine.

She cast a horrified glance sideways. "I'll do it. With Susan. If you'd just get help."

She clamped her lips shut before another howl escaped her. He traced the pad of his thumb over her mouth, the touch sending a tiny ripple of calmness through her blood, so the pain, just for that second, died away.

"It isn't going to happen. I'm not leaving you. Not this time."

"Yes, you are. You can't... I'm not doing this with you here..."

"There's nothing that happens here that's going to put me off. I love you, Fury."

She froze. The things he had done did not seem as if he did. Only, she was forced to admit, terror inspired her to think so. So that, even now, she feared to lose what glistened in her eyes. She had covered herself in frost, so every part of her grew cold and would not feel, because of that single part that longed to hear that word, yet had never known the hope, or expectation, that it would. When she'd loved him. Loved him so much.

"But...earlier. Earlier..."

Maybe it was the curve of his lips. Maybe it was the look in his eyes, as he leaned a little closer. But his lips brushed hers. If only for that instant. Something opened like a tiny flower inside her. Dazed and shaking, she stared at him.

"I was cranky, was all. But I swear to you, you get through this, the Beaumont heir gets through this, I won't ever be cranky again."

Pain surged up and overwhelmed her. He wrapped his arms

around her and held her so close, she heard the terrified hammer of his heart in his chest.

"Ma always set store by kneeling. All right?"

She nodded. What other choice did she have? She felt crippled. And he was so strong to hold onto.

"She also set store by screaming as much as you want to."

"But did she set store by men being present?"

"If they knew their stuff. Just hang onto me. Till help gets here. I won't look, if it makes you feel any better."

He couldn't know. It wasn't possible. But she did hang on. The man at her side reeked of practicality and strength. Although far from expected, and his actual physical presence here far from wanted, it comforted her to know she could rely on him. That Susan could too. Because Fury had never seen such conflicting fear and determination on the face of any woman.

And help, as the next wave of pain demonstrated, even if it ever arrived, wasn't going to come in time.

* * *

"It's all right. Come on, sweetheart. You can do this."

Could she? A cacophony of shouts erupted, and lights rode down the cliff face. Help was here. At last. But he feared it might be too late. And if it was, he would have killed her. Those stupid words he had spoken this afternoon. Not clever. Not nice. Not anything but the fault of his damned stupid worthless pride.

Love, as he'd come to understand it, didn't have room for things like that.

"Another push, madam, that's it." Susan's voice rang shrill. "It's here!"

But Fury had grown so weak and so cold in his arms, Flint feared she'd nothing left to give. She was even past screaming now, and she was bleeding.

"You hear that, sweetheart?" He buried his mouth in her

hair. "Help's here too."

"F-f-fortuitous."

"We'll have you off this beach in no time." He spoke with a courage he did not feel. He felt another limp spasm grip her body. Inside his mind he did one thing he never did and another he did lots of. Prayed and swore.

If she got through this, he'd never be proud again.

If she got through this, he'd give her everything she wanted.

And that was when he heard something he knew everyone gathered on this beach wanted most to hear. A baby's cry.

* * *

Gray light fingered the ceiling. Fury stared at it for several seconds. Then closed her eyes. She'd thought she understood need. Had experienced it as a driving force in her life. But she began to understand her own ignorance, when the needs were so simple. Cotton sheets. A fresh nightdress. No rolling waves.

When she thought about that nightmare of screaming midwifery, of Flint holding her to the end, tears scalded her. It was such a thing to give thanks for. He amazed her. Even now she remembered his voice piercing what had remained of her consciousness. The terrible grimness of his face. She was glad those in the party who arrived at the beach had been kind to him. Her last conscious thought was that he deserved it.

She would have died without him. So would Fortune.

Who would ever have thought Flint could take care of a baby? Her lips twitched. All right, brandy soaked rags were not ideal, for heaven's sake. And, as she'd suspected, he wasn't any good at some of the other things. It required Susan to wash and change.

But love was not about perfection. It was an all-compassing thing that found adjustment. That forgave. That looked and saw and knew. And without which there was nothing.

She loved him.

Of being stretchered off the beach in a homespun blanket, she remembered little. Of the first few nights and days spent here, she remembered little, except perhaps what she did remember of him, and she remembered for a reason.

Not at all a sensible thing, to find perfection in so small a place as this room, in this cottage. But there. Because they were a family. Or they would be, when she sent for Storm. Love gave. Love received. She did not doubt for one second he could not return hers. Not now.

And when she heard his footsteps cross the floor and she imagined him lifting their baby daughter from the cradle, she smiled, knowing one thing. She could not live without him. She had before. And it had killed her.

She flicked her eyes open. But what she saw there, bending over the cradle, wasn't from her dreams.

It was from her worst nightmare.

"Lady Margaret."

Fury's heart pounded. She had no idea how long she sprawled there, her head foolishly raised, while a tumult sounded in her ears and her sense of being in paradise, a paradise that was false, dripped away. Although to be fair, probably no more than a few minutes passed. Shock held her immobile.

When awareness returned, she realized she hadn't even asked herself what Lady Margaret was doing here. Or how she even knew Fury was here.

It could not be simple chance. Stupidly the thought flashed: had she been on the *Palerna* too?

But that didn't seem any more likely than the notion Lady Margaret had search parties scouring the countryside looking for her. So? Disquiet stirred.

"You are surprised to see me, perhaps?" Lady Margaret

bristled. She always did.

Fury just wished Lady Margaret would not bristle in here, standing like a giant shadow across her. Blocking out the sun from her world here. Her very nice world here.

She struggled to sit up. Lady Margaret was not a person to face lying down. She was, truth to tell, not a person to face at all. But Fury's bones were like paper.

She felt a guilty pang, praying that Flint didn't amble in here. When he had done so very much for her and she owed him her life, it was wrong. If he did, she was at least lying down.

But it was quite enough Lady Margaret was present. Already, in some queer way Fury could not quantify, she felt at a disadvantage.

"I wasn't expecting—" Because she wasn't and she hated being caught unprepared. What was more, now she thought about it, Lady Margaret made no mention of Fury's disappearance.

"That is perfectly obvious, or you would be dressed to greet me, instead of lazing in your bed, resorting to your filthy Italian habits."

As ever when she looked at Fury, Lady Margaret's eyes grew cold. Now the Beaumont heir, heiress rather, something else Fury probably couldn't do right, lay in the cradle, there was no reason for them to be otherwise.

"However, as I am here to see my grandchild, not you, you may do as you choose. A little baby girl I believe?"

"Yes, Mama." Fury spoke dutifully through her teeth, although it killed her. "Fortune."

"A hideous name. Chosen by yourself, no doubt. Well, we will change it. The proper name for a girl in our family is Regina. Although, of course, there is nothing wrong with, and you would be doing me a great courtesy, to call her...*Margaret*."

Fury flinched. Yes it would. But why on earth should she?

Even now, as she bent her ample bosom over the cradle, Fury knew the woman wished anyone, anything, the cat even, was the mother, rather than Fury.

"I like Fortune."

"You would, because vulgarly you have had the Beaumont one in your sights since first you met Thomas. There now." Lady Margaret cooed into the cradle. "Such a darling little face. I will say you've done well, Fury. I can see she takes after her father."

Yes. Well. Fury refused to rise to Lady Margaret's vile insinuation about herself because...if only Lady Margaret knew.

Of course, to say so...

Fury lay down. She had not thought, had she, about this moment. About the Beaumonts. The fortune and the inheritance. Not because the last person in the world she expected to see here today was Lady Margaret, although she was. But because in her ill, confused state, this world was perfect, containing everything she had ever wanted.

"Please tell me Grandmama's little darling was not born here, in this hovel."

It *was* perfect. "No. Actually, Fortune was born on the beach."

"The...*what?*"

Again the thought flashed. Didn't Lady Margaret know anything of this? Where did she think Fury had been for quite a few weeks now?

"Ben and Kate have been good enough to let us stay."

"You mean these dreadful fisher people didn't arrange for you to go somewhere else?"

Fury swallowed, feeling very uncomfortable all of a sudden. However Lady Margaret had gotten here, whoever had told her, she was here to take Fury home. If she went, she need be under no illusions about what she went to. Because the hatred would never stop.

And Flint…

If she went with Flint she sacrificed Storm's chances. Not her own. But did she want the hollowness of Lady Margaret's world for Storm? How could she tell Flint she didn't love him or take Fortune away when she always had and he was so damned proud of his daughter?

She thought about him here, in this very room. Pacing the floor. Feeding them both brandy. She thought about him on that beach. The strength of his body. The tenderness of his hands.

It wasn't really a choice, was it?

Flint loved her. He had seen her at her worst and he loved her. She had broken his pride with her fear and he loved her. He was so very proud. And she understood that and why he had said those awful, awful things. The ones that had nearly cost her Fortune. An act she forgave him for because she was as much to blame, not seeing how she was breaking him. Not just with her fear, but her damned obsessive need to have the things she believed he'd cost her.

So long as she had love, nothing else mattered.

She closed her eyes. When Lady Margaret went berserk, it was better to lie still.

"An inn or a country house. A vicarage even."

"Actually, Lady Margaret, you're right."

"I am never less than that. It astonishes me you have taken all this time to realize it."

"Fortune—Fortune does resemble her father."

"And so she should. In every regard."

"Alas, but that father is not Thomas."

"What do you mean?"

The explosion of shock was probably worse than Fury had feared. Lady Margaret clattered into a chair, which in turn clattered into the wall.

It was probably unwise to have spoken, when she could

defend neither herself, nor Fortune, against what would probably ensue when Lady Margaret clattered back out the chair again. This rashness was certainly something she needed help governing. But so long as she could call for Susan, it should be all right.

"Not Thomas?" Lady Margaret snarled. She snarled so Fury wondered if she should call for Susan now. "Explain yourself, Fury."

But that might be to inflame things further, when the possibility still existed that Lady Margaret might leave quietly.

"I thought I had. And I know this is hard for you both to hear and understand. But in case you don't understand, Thomas, in all the years we were together, couldn't have children. He tried. Oh, God, yes." Thinking of those times dried Fury's throat. Even now she could remember how he'd used his fists when he'd failed. But she couldn't tell Lady Margaret that. Not with Thomas lying at the bottom of an Italian bay, having supposedly perished on a visit to his holy father. "But is Fortune his? I'm afraid not."

"Not his?" Had Fury wrapped up some dog dirt and tried to pass it off as the Beaumont heir, Lady Margaret could not have sounded more affronted. Fury braced, waiting for the moment Lady Margaret crossed the room and attacked her with her reticule.

"Oh, you should be…you should be very afraid," Lady Margaret growled.

"Before you start screeching about what a disgusting whore I am, I tried. I tried for years to get you to like me. But you didn't. The deception would not have been necessary had you done so. Even if it was just a little. But there." Fury closed her eyes tighter to mask what filled them. She would not cry before this woman. "We won't speak of it."

"But we will speak of it, you thieving whore. You mean, you

were prepared to—"

"I wasn't just prepared. I did it. I slept with another man to father my child."

"How dare you?"

"It was up to me, so I did. But am I prepared to go further and lie to you, for that child to inherit the Beaumont fortune, and so I—I can have what I am entitled to as Thomas's widow? No. No, I'm not. Because unlike you, with your cold heart and your cold house, I now know there *are* other things worth having. My daughters are worth having. *Both* of them."

"You mean—"

"Yes. The reason I knew the fault wasn't mine."

Did it matter she had said that? Probably. Lady Margaret contorted her mouth. She breathed like a bull about to charge. Fury would have thought the woman might be glad to know she was being proved right.

She rolled over and faced the wall. "Their father is worth having. So please go away and leave us all alone."

"Their father? And who pray, is that? Some…some gutter-rat you—"

"I believe you met him as Captain Ames in Genoa. But his proper name—"

"Captain Ames?" Lady Margaret could barely contain herself. Fury had expected a little ire. A little slavering. But this, this was crowing. "Captain Ames? Do you mean the man whose boat you somehow took by mistake at Calais? The one who sent for me to fetch you home? The one I met on his way out of here, for good by the looks of him?"

How Fury kept her cool… Perhaps she was too tired, too weak to do anything else. But she closed her eyes tighter to hide what didn't just prick them now but what flooded in a horrible drowning pool. At least it answered some of her questions, didn't it?

Even after Lady Margaret slammed out, nearly removing the door from its hinges, she lay for a long time trying to consider her next move. Because she knew, no matter what Lady Margaret said, there must, there had to be one.

Chapter Seventeen

The crowded taproom of the wharf-side tavern seemed to mock Flint as he strolled across the floor and set his hat down on the scratched surface of the bar. A good crowd stood round the fire. Older men, fisher folks mainly, but no faces he recognized. It suited his purpose. The last thing he felt was amiable, and people here had been kind.

He'd had some tough times in his life. When his ma started taking up with men on account of his no-good daddy walking out on her years before. When he lost the *Calypso* and stood at that slave auction, grinning temptingly, in the hope some old buffer matron might buy him. When he got flayed by Malmesbury because he wasn't accustomed to spitting on shoe buckles.

But writing that letter to Lady Margaret, then getting Benito to take it to Ravenhurst, was the hardest thing Flint had ever done in his whole, entire life.

His daughter. His *daughters*. Plural. His. Just as Fury was his woman. And he'd given them up.

He eased onto a scuffed stool. "Rum."

Without a thought about having to captain the *Palerna* later, he tossed the glassful down his throat. Then he dug in his coat pocket and flung a handful of coins down on the surface of the bar. "Leave the bottle."

Had it been simply that Fury wanted so much more than he could ever give her, he wouldn't have let her go like this. No. Glowering at a tempting-looking whore, who edged onto the bar stool next to him, he tossed back another glassful.

It wasn't that though, was it? The reason he'd written that letter. His pride, his damnable, useless pride had nearly killed her. When the hell was he going to learn about his pride?

On the beach he'd thought maybe he could. But this last fortnight, being with her, being with Fortune, what he held in his heart for them — and hell, he still hadn't met Storm — terrified him. It was so intense, he feared ever hurting them again.

He'd nearly lost Fury. She still lay in bed weak as anything. Kate and the other women thought it was a miracle she survived. Anyway, he'd sworn that night what he would do if that miracle occurred. It wasn't just Fury who survived. He plain couldn't get over that.

"Pardon me, sir, but ain't you the one stayin' with Ben and Kate?"

He lowered his gaze. The woman had placed her hand on his arm. At his blank stare, she withdrew it.

"It's just a man gets lonely when their missus be indisposed."

Well, maybe some did.

"I ain't lonely, sister." Much.

Fury would have gone. Gone to Ravenhurst. To the wonderful life she wanted for herself and her children. *Their* children, he reminded himself, downing another glassful of rum. So it would be no odds to go with this woman. He wasn't going to though.

Love. All about sacrifice, wasn't it?

He just hadn't understood until this moment, what that word really meant. Sacrifice. Love, now. Love would have been to tell her. In Genoa. On the *Palerna*. Love, now, love didn't worry about mile-high pride. Love put itself out there. And it hoped. He did love her. Maybe he always had. Maybe that's why he hadn't wanted to know the truth of Celie all those years ago.

Of course Fury wanted a better life for herself. More than anything. Why shouldn't she have it? The things he'd done to her. Leaving her on that quay. Now that, when he thought about his ma and how she'd have been happy to be rid of him, that was something.

But it hadn't even occurred to him then, despite the careless way he'd taken his fill of Fury, she might be pregnant. And naturally that did things to a woman.

It would be nice to have seen Storm. To think maybe he could see Fortune. When he thought of the things he'd done, it sure would be an awful lot simpler for Fury if he didn't show up again.

He sank another glassful. The woman next to him persisted. No doubt waiting till he had drunk enough not to care what he was doing, although he wanted to tell her what she proposed was still cheating when a missus, whether she was still that or not, was as indisposed as Fury. He eased off the stool, pocketed the bottle, and headed for the door.

Skulking deep in his coat, he paused and glanced up the alley. Rain fell in torrents. Great. Now in addition to being soaked, he'd be soaking. The lousy English weather. Not that it mattered. Nothing mattered. Except getting back on that damned boat of his. Nathan had said the day before that the repairs were done. He'd inspected them with half a heart. Fury and the baby had still worried him.

Truth be told though, he'd never felt less like anything in his damn life. Imagine that, when boats and sailing had been everything to him.

But as for whatever that damnable whore from the bar thought she was doing, trotting along at his side...

"Look darlin', not that I want to be rude but I think I told you in there I ain't interested — *Fury?*"

Where the hell had she come from? She hadn't been in the tavern, that was for sure. Before he could think what the hell she wanted, she reached up, grabbed his face, and kissed him.

She'd taken him by surprise, so for a second his mouth reacted instinctively, even while his head jerked back and he tried to pull away.

Fury's awareness of her own physical weakness and what it had cost her coming here was acute, however. While she felt herself sag, she determined not to let him go. Her hands clasped the sides of his head, ready to pull him back against her should he try again. Not that he did. He was enjoying the kiss a little too much for that. And she suspected it was the type of kiss he would enjoy. Hot. Open-mouthed. Passionate. A kiss that didn't give him an opportunity to think, because she knew thinking would be dangerous.

"Lady Margaret liked the heiress then." He gasped, his eyes wide.

Of course, Flint would not be Flint unless he thought well of himself.

"Oh, she loved her."

"Loved? Sweetheart, that's — "

Before he could finish whatever it was he started to say, she dragged his mouth back toward hers.

"There will be kissing."

To do so here, in an alley, hungry and demanding, with no thought of the rain coming down or the passersby, as if she were as much a common whore as the woman she'd seen trying to pick him up inside the tavern, only added to her passion. She had never done anything like it before because Flint didn't require tempting. He always led in these situations. But it didn't matter.

If she lost him now, she would die. She couldn't control what flowed through her pores, filling every part of her. The knowledge that they belonged together and she could not let him part them, no matter what he thought he had done, strengthened her determination not to be that woman on the quay ever again, in a different way. A way that did not involve her hurting herself or him.

On this cold, gray afternoon, with the rain drizzling on her head, she was relieved when he swung her around and shoved her against the dank, brick wall, his mouth responding now, as only Flint's could.

It felt too good to stop and she surrendered, wondering where her restraint had gone. Every bone in her body seemed to dissolve. He kissed her, devoured her. And she wrapped her arms round his neck to draw him closer still. She loved the scent of his skin, the hard heat of his body, the knowledge of how much he wanted her, even the scent of rum on his breath. She couldn't imagine stopping ever.

But there were dangers, insidious dangers, if she did not push this to its conclusion. He had left her, contacted Lady Margaret, after all. For all he drank so deeply of her mouth, this kiss, that could just as easily be his farewell. Whether he wanted her or not.

"Whoa. Wait a minute, sweetheart." He pulled himself free as if she had bitten him. "Lady Margaret liked her. So, just how come you're here? Where's Fortune? You ain't given—"

One thing she didn't think was that he was stupid. Except at times when he deliberately wanted to be, emotionally. How else to explain the way he'd just kissed her and now stood like this.

"Why am I here?" Frustrated, she wanted to hit her fists off his chest. He had to act like this now, when she most wanted to be daring and bold? The kind who could reach for the sky and make it hers, instead of some foolish, angry wreck. "Why did you send for Lady Margaret without telling me? Why did you damn well walk out on us, after telling me you loved me? Because that's what you've done. That's what you've done to us."

"Because — because my pride damned nearly killed you."

His gritted undertone quivered through her and she understood. He might have kidnapped her, he might have taken her book, he might have done a thousand times worse than that, but at this moment, it didn't matter, and she must make him see. Because he hadn't said he didn't love her or that he'd done this to convince himself he didn't.

"You think I'm going to let that happen again?" He stepped right back now, setting her away from him. Dismissing her. His eyes sat like slits in his head. "I'm not going to let it happen again."

"Too damn right you're not." She felt her boldness flow back into her, as if the words were a charm that freed her from her awful anger and paralyzing frustration. "Now rule two."

Ignoring him, she moved forward. To do this she needed to. So close, while she felt so weak, she almost leaned against him. He tensed and so did she, as she edged a hand into his coat and plucked at his shirt.

He crinkled his brow. He looked bewildered. Astonished. Heavens, she was a little astonished herself. To think only a few short hours ago she'd been lying in bed scarcely fit to move a muscle. And now she didn't just move a muscle, she worked his shirt from his breeches.

"You won't be fully dressed at all times. I desire to look at your body before, during, and after, in all shapes and all forms." Bending her head she pressed her lips to his chest, tasting him.

His skin was warm and his heart beat beneath her lips. "I desire to kiss it."

"Fury, what the hell?" He bent his head as if he couldn't believe what he saw. "Will you stop this?"

She let her fingers roam over his back, until they reached the waistband of his breeches. She considered the decorum of continuing with this in so public a place, when she herself couldn't begin, let alone continue. But she did it anyway, exploring him with complete abandon.

"Rule three. I will touch you in any place, intimate and otherwise."

"Fury —"

"Maybe touching is as much as is possible right now and will only be for a week or two —"

He dragged her hand away, as if he had remembered that. Then he caught her face. "Will you listen to me?"

"No, I can't."

"Don't you understand? I made myself a vow that night on the beach. So you shouldn't be here."

"A vow?"

Alarm prickled, adding to her disquiet. A vow was horribly tricky. She knew herself just how tricky. Had she not vowed things regarding him? She had broken them, of course. It did not mean he would do the same. Already she felt the way he stroked her face was ominous. Flint, the possessor of no heart whatsoever, did not do things like that.

Of a sudden she felt like fragile porcelain. She seemed to stand there forever in the dirty street, feeling the heart leave her body. The soul too. So she felt like a hollow, crushable shell, from which the life had gone.

If ever there was a moment when she knew she could not live without him, this was it. But then, when she thought about it, that night on the beach *was* her last. And she had spent it with him, though maybe not as she had imagined. The old Fury had gone. Disappeared with the floating tide. And hadn't she herself nearly died?

"What did you swear? Tell me." She could hardly bear to hear.

"I swore if I didn't lose you I had to let you go, no matter what you want. And I didn't lose you."

"But you did everything to keep me."

"That wasn't an option. I couldn't lose you both that way."

Both. She reached her fingers up to his lips to silence him. "And so did I once make a vow and want these things. All of them. The money. The security. What I thought I was entitled to. But now I've learned vows can be broken when they're right but wrong. You're the one who taught me."

"I taught you?" He probably didn't think he'd taught her anything.

She squeezed her eyes shut to mask what pricked them. "This is wrong. It's so wrong."

"Sweetheart." No doubt his eyes searched her face. His fingers certainly did. "Look at you. You shouldn't be here. Why the hell did you do this? It's so stupid of you. I'm going to find a coach. Get you home."

"No. Because now, I've vowed that when it comes to rule five, I've decided there should just be this. Talking." She took a breath and reached her hand to catch his wrist. "Lots of it. And I should tell you, I still love you. I love you, Flint. I always have. Maybe from that very first minute. Yes. Now I think about it, maybe even from then. Because even then I know you captured my heart. And I know it's not suitable and I know it's not wise. But there it is."

She opened her eyes. He seemed to stare forever, as he had that last day at the cabin door, his beautiful eyes holding such deep emotion, the thought thudded inside her: It wasn't just the old Fury who'd gone. This was a different Flint. A melding of the old and new that made him even more loveable in her eyes, if that was possible.

"I just had some issues to overcome to find that out."

"You still love me?"

"Oh, you must know that. And if you go…if you go now…" His throat moved as he swallowed. "But you never—"

"Said? I should have. I should have lots of times. But I thought it had died. I thought you killed it." She couldn't help that she cried a little. She thought perhaps they were tears of joy. She hoped they were, because it seemed to her he'd moved a little toward her, or he wouldn't look like this. He wouldn't wrap his arms around her like this.

"Even after all the things I've done? Took your book and tried to make you choose? Left you on that damned quay?"

"Let's not pretend when I saw you again I didn't do things too. I did everything to keep you away, because I was terrified you'd bring me pleasure and that would be a betrayal of that moment. And then I thought I had to keep you there because I was terrified of what you could do to me."

"Me?"

"You. Only now I know I was wrong not to go with you in Genoa. Not to see. But now, well, now that's why Lady Margaret may love Fortune, but she doesn't want us producing another Beaumont heir. I trust I am making myself clear. I don't want you to remove yourself. I don't want you ever to do that again."

Standing on her tiptoes, she pressed her mouth to his. Although she'd noticed the taste of rum, it hadn't seemed quite so strong before. He'd been drinking heavily. And she was only glad she had been able to find him, although she would have never stopped looking.

"You went and told her?"

She nodded. "I did."

"You're damned crazy. Why did you do that? What have I got to offer you?"

"Everything. I don't care where we go. I don't care what we do. I actually think if Lady Margaret goes away and thinks about this, I may be a wanted woman."

A wicked smile lit his face. She knew exactly what he was thinking, even if it didn't match what she was.

"So what's rule twelve?"

"It can't any of it be in front of our children or Susan. Two of whom are waiting down at the shore. And the third we are going to fetch. I'm going to set it all down. Now, make your mark."

"My mark?"

Someone jostled Flint as they passed and he lowered his head. He didn't say a word and neither did she, though she knew when his mouth met hers where they were going and what he intended. The future, she realized happily.

With him at her side. There was nothing else she wanted.

~ About the Author ~

Shehanne Moore writes gritty, witty, historical romance, set wherever takes her fancy. What hasn't she worked at while pursuing her dream of becoming a published author? Shehanne still lives in Scotland, with her husband Mr Shey. She has two daughters. When not writing intriguing historical romance, where goals and desires of sassy, unconventional heroines and ruthless men, mean worlds collide, she plays the odd musical instrument and loves what in any other country, would not be defined, as hill-walking.

Discover more Shehanne More here

http://shehannemoore.wordpress.com/
http://twitter.com/ShehanneMoore
http://shehannemooreweeblycom.weebly.com/
http://furiousunravelings.wordpress.com/
http://www.facebook.com/pages/Kilting-the-Book/1400031303553598

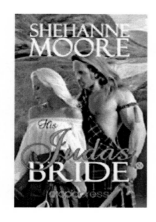

His Judas Bride
Shehanne Moore

To love, honor, and betray...

To get back her son, she will stop at nothing...
For five years Kara McGurkie has preferred
to forget she's a woman. So it's no problem
for her to swear to love and honor, to help
destroy a clan, when it means getting back
the son she lost. But when dire circumstances force her to seduce
her fiancé's brother on the eve of the wedding, will the dark
secrets she holds and her greatest desire be enough to save her
from his powerful allure?

To save his people, neither will he...
Callm McDunnagh, the Black Wolf of Lochalpin, ruthlessly
guards heart and glen from dangerous intruders. But from the
moment he first sees Kara he knows he must possess her, even
though surrendering to his passion may prove the most
dangerous risk of all.

She has nothing left to fear except love itself...
Now only Kara can decide what passion can save or destroy,
and who will finally learn the truth of the words... *Till death do
us part.*

Available now in digital. Coming soon to print.

~ Available Now from Etopia Press ~

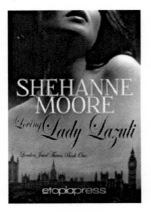

Loving Lady Lazuli
London Jewel Thieves Book One
Shehanne Moore

Only one man in England can identify her. Unfortunately he's living next door.

Ten years ago sixteen-year-old Sapphire, the greatest jewel thief England has ever known, ruined Lord Devorlane Hawley's life. Now that Sapphire's dead and buried, all that respectable widow Cassidy Armstrong wants is the opportunity to keep her good name, and prove she is not that disreputable girl. Especially when it means so much to her handsome new neighbor, Devorlane Hawley.

Hawley believes he knows precisely who his new neighbor is, and he's been waiting ten years to exact his revenge. All he needs is a bit of evidence, which has proved quite impossible to procure. But the lovely widow might just have something else he desires, some other way to sate his vengeance. Deciding a direct approach might be in order, he asks Sapphire to choose her fate—take him as her lover, or take her chances at the end of a rope...

Available now in digital. Coming soon to print.

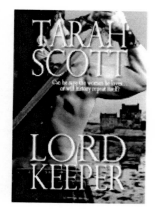

Lightning Source UK Ltd.
Milton Keynes UK
UKOW03f0740060514

231166UK00001B/10/P